Strictly Business

Strictly Business

Francesca Clementis

PIATKUS

All the characters in this book are fictitious and any resemblance to real persons, living or dead, is entirely coincidental.

First published in Great Britain in 2002 by
Judy Piatkus (Publishers) Ltd of
5 Windmill Street, London W1T 2JA
email: info@piatkus.co.uk

The moral right of the author has been asserted

A catalogue record for this book is available from the British Library

ISBN 0 7499 0604 9

Typeset in Times by Palimpsest Book Production Limited,
Polmont, Stirlingshire

Printed and bound in Great Britain by
MPG Books Ltd, Bodmin, Cornwall

For Carol McEvoy and over thirty years of friendship. And for Gill Bernie and Jenny Roman, over twenty years apiece. Must seem like a life sentence to you. But your friendships have been a life-saver to me. Thanks.

Chapter 1

When Kate Harris left her last job, her colleagues bought her a doormat as a leaving present. It was a joke, of course. And not a cheap one. They had found a company that wove her name and a cruel caricature into the mat.

An expensive joke. How appropriate, Kate thought wryly. Just like me. Seventy thousand pounds a year and incapable of asking a secretary to type a letter. Seventy thousand pounds a year and most of my working day spent dealing with administration and office bureaucracy that I'm too pathetic to delegate to my staff. Seventy thousand pounds a year and, after two costly years, I will be remembered solely as the one group director who made coffee. For everyone; all the time. They even moved the coffee machine into my office.

No wonder I consistently underachieve when so much time is spent trying to make people like me.

And no wonder I always burn out so quickly. I have to work evenings, weekends, whatever it takes, just to get through the daily workload – I'm hampered by my hopeless lack of leadership.

Kate smiled relentlessly through the farewell speeches that mocked her. She laughed politely as all the stories were rehashed: the one about the time ten of them went to that expensive restaurant for lunch and left her with the bill; and that occasion when she was giving a key presentation to a client in Rome and they'd switched

1

her slides with pictures of the team's photocopied back-sides; and last Christmas when they told her that the venue of the office party had been changed and she turned up at a lap dancing club, where a rugby club were having their Christmas do. She'd laughed then too, of course.

The stories continued until Kate could stand them no longer. She'd also run out of money, since it had been assumed that she would buy all the drinks, all night, for everyone and their friends and partners. And everyone else in the bar who recognised the portrait on the doormat and immediately grasped the implications for a free night out.

Kate hated the lot of them, or rather she didn't exactly hate them but felt that she should. She wasn't good at hating or anything negative like that. She had never shaken off the legacy of her upbringing, which had instilled the need to be good and kind and loving. Every time she came home from school, claiming to hate someone (usually for just reason, having been kicked, whispered about, or not picked for the rounders team until she was the last one left), her parents insisted on inviting the object of hatred round for tea. The theory was that Kate would find some common ground with the other child that would transform her previous hostility into a glorious pink haze of admiration and respect. They might even become friends.

It could have worked if Kate's mother had been able to cook anything other than boil-in-the-bag cod in parsley sauce with tinned potatoes and marrowfat peas. In other words, no chips. Once the unfortunate guest had been presented with this feast, Kate's future was doomed. It was bad enough being labelled as rubbish-at-games, but add to this a-mum-who-doesn't-cook-chips-for-guests

2

and she soared to number one position in the girl-you'd-least-want-to-go-to-tea-with chart. And all because she'd used the hate-word.

Such an experience sows seeds of deep-rooted, pernicious weeds that a person spends a lifetime fighting despite the certain knowledge that all resistance is futile. She became physiologically and psychologically incapable of letting the badness out.

Yet the torment didn't stop even when the niceness began. Now she was being punished for her inability to fight back, defend herself or just make herself feel better by lashing out occasionally. The injustice of this was a sting, burying its poison deep under her skin looking for a home where it could fester. She was not a serial killer or an internet stalker or even one of those appalling women who phone in the middle of *EastEnders* and read monotonously from a script, asking if you would like stonecladding or a Victorian conservatory. She was a nice person, that was all. She couldn't help it. And this was her reward: to be immortalised in a doormat.

She examined the picture more closely. Do I really look like that? she wondered. For while it was a caricature and exaggerated the lines of her bone structure, it was the caricature of a beautiful woman. Kate never regarded herself as beautiful or even particularly attractive. She knew that there was nothing wrong with her face but she had learned that it didn't turn heads or widen eyes or encourage wolf whistles.

She was classically pretty with long, dark hair tucked artlessly behind her ears, clear healthy skin, smiley wholesome features. In 1950s small-town America, she would have been very desirable. But in today's London where beauty was apparently most appreciated when contrived rather than natural, she was in every way a throwback.

3

The sad truth about Kate was that she belonged to another time and another place. Perhaps even another planet. For there appears to be no age in our history where a tendency to be virtuous is rewarded with anything apart from a film of your life story starring Julie Andrews or Ingrid Bergman in the title role. A consumptive death helped, always a good dramatic challenge for an actress perceived as lightweight.

And that's a tough fact to face in the third millennium, where looking consumptive has become redefined as something to die for rather than from.

Management consultancy may seem a strange choice of career for someone so ill at ease in the contemporary workplace. But Kate even had noble motives for this. Her father's small business had gone bust through poor management practices, i.e. through extending credit to everyone with a sob story, a war wound or simply a nice smile. His subsequent bankruptcy had devastated the family.

Consequently, Kate had always recognised the human ramifications of any struggling business, however impersonal the corporate infrastructure might appear. She liked saving companies, particularly family-owned companies. And she was terrific at her job, working tirelessly, coming up with creative solutions to brick-wall problems.

Clients respected her because they sensed her total personal dedication to their cause. Her colleagues envied her professional style and success rate which led to her being given the most prestigious projects. Spotting Kate's weakness in handling her own staff, they took pleasure in undermining her at every opportunity. Although this didn't affect her results, it made her daily working life miserable and drilled craters into her already crumbly ego.

'Excuse me, do you mind if I smoke?'

Kate looked around. The train carriage was empty except for herself and a timid-looking man, nervously fingering a cigarette. Kate glanced at the 'No Smoking' signs stuck to every window. She accepted that the question was rhetorical, a concession to social courtesy that a more self-assured man would have ignored. She glanced down at her doormat, wrapped securely in a black bin liner salvaged from a skip outside the wine bar. That explained it. He hadn't realised that she was someone who didn't merit social courtesies.

Maybe it was the fifth glass of wine or the bristles of the doormat, sticking through the bin liner and irritating her hand. Maybe it was the dry throat and tickly cough, legacy of four hours in a smoky atmosphere, or the memory of her leaving party. It was still in full swing when she slipped away, unnoticed and unmissed. They'll miss me when they run out of drinks, Kate grumbled to herself. She was in a foul mood and a headache was poking annoyingly at the backs of her eyes, demanding attention.

Whatever the reason, she spoke before pouring her words through her nice-girl filter. Her automatic pilot seemed to be temporarily out of order. This was a first. She didn't even smile and Kate always smiled at strangers ('Spread a little happiness,' her parents would chirp as they inched ever closer to their goal of becoming the Vera Lynn and Harry Secombe of South London.)

'Yes, I do mind. I bloody do. I mind a lot, as a matter of fact.'

Kate glanced up, looking for the hidden loudspeaker through which this strangely familiar voice was echoing. She saw nothing except some cryptic graffiti about Arsenal fans and and a rainbow-coloured advert promising cheap phone calls to Sierra Leone. No phantom voice.

5

Oh, she thought flatly, it's me. I said that. The man's expression confirmed her suspicion that she had indeed spoken, but it was not an expression she could immediately identify, at least not when aimed in her direction. Surely not, she argued sensibly with herself. It couldn't be, could it? Could it possibly be true that this man, this big grown-up man with no obvious signs of drug or alcohol abuse or genetic in-breeding, could be intimidated . . . by her? By Kate Harris?

And yet . . . and yet . . . he was putting the cigarette back in the packet, the packet back in his pocket. He was ever so slightly shrinking back into his seat. Defeated. Only a seasoned victim like Kate would have spotted such a subtle acknowledgement of failure.

The creaks and shudders of the antiquated train were suddenly overwhelmingly loud as they filled the silent carriage. Kate sat motionless, waiting for the man to come to his senses, to realise that he had deferred to someone more used to being ignored (on a good day) or ridiculed (on a bad).

Still the cigarette remained unlit. The man remained bowed. Kate remained Supreme Champion (unbeaten, unbowed) of the 21.25 Victoria to Epsom Downs Would-be Smoker vs Teensy-bit-belligerent Commuter with a Tickly Cough Knockout.

She wasn't sure how to react. Well, actually she knew exactly how. All her instincts were on their knees begging her to recant. Run over to the poor man, they were screaming, yank that cigarette from his jacket, place it tenderly between his lips and light it yourself in an act of contrition. Plead for mercy, apologise until your raw throat can apologise no longer. Think of your poor parents, how disappointed they'd be in you.

But there was a new voice in town, a brave, confident,

adult proclaimer, urging her to sit still. You see, it was saying, you can do it! You're not invisible. You can be seen and heard. You have bearing. You are someone who is listened to.

Yeah, right, Kate thought. When I'm so exhausted, so worn down, that all my civilising faculties have lost the will to function.

Her muscles twitched as the conflict played out inside her. And then, at Carshalton Beeches, the man stood up and tossed a mumbled 'sorry' at her before getting off the train.

Kate was stunned. He apologised to *me*. It's supposed to be the other way round, it's always the other way round. As the train pulled away, Kate watched the stranger shuffle towards the exit on his way to – what? To a life where he played a role of less significance than hers? Could it be possible?

YES! shouted the new assertive voice from within, punching the air invisibly as if stirred up by a life coach at a motivational seminar in California.

Her other, nice, voices were being drowned out. They were shaking their collective heads and uttering ominous warnings. Be true to yourself, they were chanting, smile though your heart is aching, happy talk keep talking happy talk.

Oh shut up, Kate thought irritably. And she switched the saccharine saboteurs off.

It was that easy. That was the lesson she learned. She could switch off one person and become the *other* person, whenever she wanted. Maybe everybody else had already learned the same lesson, she realised. How to play different roles for different situations. What was wrong with that? Perhaps all of the mean, vindictive bullies she had ever worked with were sweetie pies outside the office. Perhaps

7

they spent their Saturday nights distributing soup to the homeless, or helping toads cross motorways, or arranging flowers in church.

I could do that, Kate thought. I could pretend to be tough at work and still be myself when it really matters, with my friends, with my family.

She sat up a little taller, her back a little straighter, as she looked out at the dark anonymous suburbs shooting by. The city was behind her. She didn't look back. She wasn't going to do that any more.

On Monday she started a new job. That gave her the weekend to rehearse her new persona. Surely it couldn't be that difficult, she reasoned. I did all right just now without any preparation.

Sadly Kate was lacking one vital element at this critical juncture in her life-changing plan: a friend to tell her not to be so stupid. To point out that her hard talking had not just disarmed a deranged gunman holding a child hostage. The man had probably been too tired, on a Friday night, to argue with her, so it was no great ordeal for him to wait ten minutes before lighting up. None of the above justified embarking upon a massive pretence that she could not possibly sustain under the pressures of a new job.

And even if Kate heard these same objections whispering from somewhere within her own sensible, rational self, she wasn't listening. What good has listening to myself done in the past? she argued.

She tried to make out her reflection in the filthy carriage windows, anxious to see if she looked different. But it was so hard to tell. It could have been any face smeared across the opaque backdrop of dubious stains and angry etchings.

It didn't matter. Her appearance would be the easiest

8

aspect to change; she would enjoy the challenge. As the train approached Banstead, she struggled to the door carrying the detritus of two years' nest-building in her recent job. Never again, she muttered to herself, as she tucked the yucca under her arm to make hand-room for the framed photos, paintings by her nieces and nephews, cuddly toys and pointless executive playthings, given to her by well-meaning relatives, that she felt obliged to put on display. And the doormat.

It began to rain, an event that Kate took personally on this momentous day. Her arms were too full to be able to put up an umbrella, so she just had to keep her head down and hope that it would be a passing shower, or that a taxi would be parked right outside the station. Or that a bus would come along.

As the thunder and lightning tore across the sky, and the rain whipped against her face in vertical sheets, Kate ploughed on miserably. Of course there hadn't been a taxi, or a bus. Or even a maniacal minicab driver in a balaclava with whom she would have been prepared to take her chances on this wretched night.

Never again, Kate declared to herself. I won't be rained on again like this, with a yucca and paintings and a doormat and the rest. It will all be different next time. I will be different.

After a lifetime of settling for the cameo roles of perfect daughter, most compliant colleague, most passive girlfriend, dinner-party guest who never took the last chocolate, she was going to reinvent herself. In the new scenario, she was going to be a star.

She didn't notice the giggling couple rushing past, wrapped up in the romance of the storm. Like children, they were jumping in puddles, splashing each other, then shrieking in mock protest.

9

Kate passed them just as they leapt together into a huge expanse of water that was flooding the gutter. As Kate was splattered with a vast muddy spray, the couple looked horrified.

'We're *so* sorry!' they both cried.

Without hesitation Kate smiled, with a sunniness reminiscent of Doris Day. 'No, *I'm* sorry, it was my fault, I wasn't looking where I was going.'

It was the English thing to say and the couple accepted the apology as being insane but utterly proper, coming from this smiley person.

It was also the Kate-thing to say, the old Kate-thing, which depressed her. Oh dear, she said to herself, this is going to be harder than I thought.

Chapter 2

'So tell me again, what look exactly are you going for?'

Justine trailed behind Kate, watching her friend pulling hangers from rails, with no obvious rationale.

'The I'm-not-a-woman-to-be-messed-with look. The I-don't-make-coffee look.' Kate stood in front of a mirror holding up a jet-black fitted dress with a tightly fitting jacket. 'What do you think about this?'

Justine raised her eyebrows. 'I think it's more the best-dressed-guest-at-a-Mafia-godfather's-funeral look.'

'Yes, very funny, just not very helpful.' Kate shoved the suit back on the rack.

Justine shrugged. 'Sorry, Kate, but you know what I think about this idea.'

Kate turned to face her. 'It's all right for you, you're a midwife, you don't have to deal with office politics.'

Justine laughed. 'Kate, like you, I have colleagues, I have managers and I have clients. It's just that my colleagues are nurses and doctors, my managers are hospital and practice administrators and my clients are pregnant women. But guess what, I have to *deal* with them all.'

Kate reluctantly conceded the point. 'Yes, but I bet everyone likes you.'

'How long have you known me, Kate?' Justine snorted. She didn't wait for an answer. 'Twenty years, that's how long. And you admit yourself that you didn't like me when you first met me.'

Kate couldn't argue with that. They'd met at sixth form college. Kate had been dreading the new start. It took her a long time to make friends, and she'd been happy at her private school. But her parents couldn't afford the fees any more so she was forced to move on.

Justine's presence quickly dominated the common room even though she was new too. Kate envied her and feared her at the same time. She longed to be so at ease with people but she feared the sort of attention that such confidence would inevitably bring.

Since she and Justine were doing exactly the same A-levels, the gradual birth of a friendship was inevitable. And by associating with this dynamo, Kate began to accept that she would be thrust into the centre of college life whether she wanted it or not.

Slowly she became used to Justine's loudness. She understood that it stemmed from the same insecurity that made Kate so quiet.

Justine went on. 'I talk too much, too loudly, too fast. My own husband tells me that daily and he loves me to death, so don't pretend it's not true. I frequently say the wrong thing at the wrong time and seem to offend everyone I meet.'

Kate smiled. 'It's what everyone loves about you.'

Justine tilted her face to one side in amusement. 'None of your boyfriends have liked me . . .'

'Well, apart from them,' Kate agreed.

'And your parents and your brothers and most of the people you introduce me to and most of my patients' husbands and . . .'

Kate held up her hands in protest. 'OK, OK, I take your point.'

Justine softened her tone. 'The real difference between us is that I don't care whether all the people I meet like me. I don't need it. And you do. And the crazy thing is, if you stopped trying so hard to make people like you, you'd find that they liked you anyway. You're much nicer than me!'

It was Kate's turn to smile now. 'I'm just not brave enough to take that risk.'

'Rubbish!' Justine said. 'You must have been popular at your last job.'

Kate closed her eyes as she recalled the experiences of the last two years which were all encapsulated in the leaving party. 'I've just got one word to say to you, Justine – doormat.'

Justine lowered her eyes quickly so that Kate would not see her suppressing a giggle. It didn't work.

'It's not funny, Justine!'

'Actually, it is a bit funny. And, if you think about it, quite flattering.'

'Tell me one flattering thing about being given a doormat,' Kate asked incredulously.

Justine considered this carefully. 'Well, it must have cost a fortune to get that done. And since you only gave four weeks' notice, they must have gone to a lot of trouble to have it made so quickly. It's a real work of art. They must have thought a lot of you, otherwise it would have just been a bunch of flowers from the garage and a coffee-table monstrosity about Renaissance art from a discount bookshop.'

'Of course they thought a lot of me – I was a complete pushover, every employee's dream boss!' Kate shouted. The other customers looked round. Kate was still surprised at the sound of her own raised voice. In the eighteen hours since her confrontation with the smoker

13

on the train (which had taken on the impact of *Death Wish* in the telling to an amused Justine), Kate had found herself raising her voice more often to test its impact. The impact so far had been: her mother crying on the phone, the man in the newsagent handing her a free Twix as compensation for giving her the wrong change and a boy racer in his turbocharged silver BMW demonstrating a new hand gesture.

In each case the impact was dampened slightly by Kate's automatic and effusive apology. Damn, she thought, I've got to stop saying sorry all the time.

'I'm so sorry,' she said without thinking as a clumsy sales assistant poked her in the eye with a clothes hanger.

This was going to require more than a new frock.

Somewhere else, not very far away, one of her future colleagues was displaying ominous symptoms of the same compulsion to apologise. If Kate had known this, she could have called him up, bonded with him; they could have made coffee for each other . . .

'Sorry,' Andrew said, for the tenth time that day.

'I wish you'd stop apologising!' Rebecca snapped, also for the tenth time. 'You've done nothing but snap at me, sulk about the place, then say you're sorry, for the past month.'

'You're right, sorry,' Andrew replied.

Rebecca shook her head, sighed and went back to her magazine.

'Shall I make coffee?' Andrew asked.

'OK,' Rebecca answered, without looking up.

Andrew walked into the kitchen, grateful to have an excuse to get out of the room. He knew he was irritating

Rebecca but he couldn't help himself. And he knew he had to pull himself together if he didn't want to drive her away, for he was well aware that his hold on Rebecca was tenuous, fragile, woven delicately from a physical attraction like all of his relationships.

He would have been surprised to learn that his absolute belief in his good looks was evidence of his absolute lack of self-esteem. Because, in Andrew's opinion, that was all there was; there was nothing else to him beyond his regular face, his thick black hair that showed no sign of thinning and his thirty-two-inch waist that hadn't expanded since 1982. He never bothered to explore, develop or project any other elements of his personality because he thought they might let him down.

Ironically, it was this modesty rather than his face that all his girlfriends found most attractive (although his face was a bonus): the hesitant way in which he expressed opinions; his cautious attempts to comment intelligently on current affairs or mainstream film plots. No woman ever pointed this out to him, wisely understanding that he might simply incorporate the newly appreciated strength into his slim portfolio of vanity.

The day was not going well and Andrew wanted to avoid alienating Rebecca so early in their relationship. But he was finding it hard to control his despair.

A month earlier, he'd been passed over for a promotion that he'd felt sure was his and, two days before the new director joined the firm, a mush of strange feelings were stewing in his head. Now they were starting to froth over.

It was the inability to make sense of his feelings that was causing him the most confusion. For the first time he could recall, he was experiencing failure and he didn't possess the vocabulary to express his misery. His life story was a film of thirty-eight years' length, entitled *Born Lucky*. Except the script had suddenly been changed without anyone asking him, director, producer and star, if this was acceptable.

When he'd been called in to the MD's office, he had his smile ready, the one he believed communicated an unassuming modesty, the suggestion of surprise that little ol' Andrew should have won the prize once more.

'So I suppose you've got to give me the bad news?' he said cheerfully to Ben Clarkson, quietly confident that he was about to receive good news.

'I'm afraid so,' Ben said.

Andrew stopped smiling. Those were the wrong words, he thought. There was an awkward silence while Ben waited for Andrew to feed him the next line. It was how they communicated, banter which was strictly controlled according to prearranged rules. Andrew was usually the straight man, as seemed appropriate to his junior position. Ben delivered the punchlines which they both laughed at. This demarcation of roles suited them both. It provided each with a baseline of security from which they could dabble in other friendships and relationships and *to* which they could retreat when the other relationships failed, which they generally did.

But now Andrew was lost. He was not skilled at improvisation or any kind of spontaneity. He only entered situations where the probable outcome was covered by one of the responses in his limited repertoire. It eliminated most of the obstacles from daily living. That was his aim, to avoid obstacles, so that he would never have to confront the choice of whether to refuse, go over or around them.

Andrew had found the person he wanted to be when he was a teenager and he had not veered from that person

16

in the twenty years since. He was utterly consistent, predictable, reliable. All of his life choices were carefully made to suit his fear of change, his inability to deal with any threats to his obsessively protected status quo. One day, when he finally got round to the self-analysis that most of us go through when we're sixteen, he'd discover that it was this commitment to risk-avoidance that had determined his easy path through life.

He would never have applied for this promotion if Ben hadn't practically promised him that the job would be his.

Ben cleared his throat, realising that Andrew wasn't going to play the game. He'd naively hoped that their friendship would make this easier but it was actually making it a lot harder.

'The thing is, Andrew, the decision was out of my hands. The others decided we needed someone from outside, someone with different skills, new contacts who could help us to expand the business. And they'd heard about a woman who—'

Andrew jumped up. 'A woman! You're joking! Tell me you haven't hired a woman, that I'm not going to be working for a woman?' If he'd had a sword, he would probably have impaled himself upon it, such was the need to convey his full dramatic response to this, the worst possible news.

Ben shrank back slightly, not recognising this Andrew. He too depended on the continuity of their friendship, but for different reasons. Unlike Andrew, he had no other order in his life. He had no plans, no vertical progression to his career, no sense of self that he could refer to when making decisions and choices. He simply made himself up as he went along.

When he'd met Andrew on an assertiveness training

course eight years earlier, they were thrown together by being the only men among twenty-eight women. They felt like visitors in a strange land as, all around them, women bonded, cried, talked about their feelings and their thighs, ate everything put in front of them and bombarded the two men with random selections of meaningful looks, ranging from hostile to flirtatious.

After a week, Ben and Andrew had told each other everything there was to know about themselves. Of course, everything from a male perspective was different to a woman's idea of everything. They didn't, for example, pull out pictures of godchildren, or lend each other hand cream or talk about life. But they exchanged CVs conversationally, competing gently over degrees of impoverished childhood, O and A level results, sporting achievements, professional attainments, value of flat, eccentricity of mothers, that sort of thing.

They had one critical experience in common, however, that was to establish terms of reference in the years to come. They had both been sent on this course by a woman and, seeing that the course was predominantly aimed at women, they each perceived the act as sadistic. With the sample size of two, they came to the statistically meaningless (but very satisfying) conclusion that giving a woman power was inevitably to unleash a plague of Old Testament proportions.

They eventually left their respective employment and, two years later, Ben was in the position to offer Andrew a job. It was always understood that, as Ben rose in the organisation, he would pull Andrew up behind him. Ben understood that Andrew would never put himself forward for promotion, his lack of ambition being the only weakness in Andrew's otherwise formidable set of business skills.

18

'I knew you'd be upset, Andrew, but it's not as bad as it sounds.'

Andrew exhaled noisily in an attempt to steady his breathing. 'Frankly, it couldn't sound much worse.'

'I was outvoted on this appointment. But I'm the one Kate Harris will have to answer to.'

'I don't see how that helps me,' Andrew said dubiously. 'She'll still be senior to me. I'll still have to answer to her.'

'In the beginning, yes,' Ben countered. 'But we're a completely different set-up to her last company. She will be judged on her team's results, not just her own. I made it clear after her interview that I didn't think she had strong management skills. Once the rest of the board see how weak she is, they'll soon lose faith in her.'

'But if she's as good as you say she is . . . ?' Andrew interrupted.

Ben shrugged. 'She's only as good as her team. And you are on her team.' He paused. 'If you see what I mean.'

Andrew saw exactly what he meant and wished he didn't. He couldn't decide what was the least preferable option: to work for a woman or to become embroiled in a Machiavellian plot to undermine her.

Actually the most attractive option was to resign and become a deckchair attendant at Eastbourne.

Rebecca was pretending to read a book when Andrew came back with the coffee. She acknowledged the cup with a mumbled 'Thanks.' Andrew sat down near her and sighed loudly a few times, waiting for Rebecca to ask him what was wrong.

It was precisely because Rebecca knew what was wrong that she didn't ask him. 'I think I'll pop to the gym,' he said finally. He added one last sigh, just in case she hadn't heard the others.

'OK,' Rebecca said absently, turning the page of the book she wasn't reading. Only when Andrew had left did she put the book down in relief.

It's my own fault, she thought. Everybody said it was a mistake to get involved with a close colleague but I didn't listen.

It had been fine for the first couple of months. Of course it had been fine. That's why she'd chosen Andrew, because she knew exactly what she was getting. Working closely with him, travelling with him, spending countless nights in foreign hotels in inhospitable countries.

She'd recently come out of yet another relationship with yet another man who'd let her down. She'd taken it badly, worse than ever before. She'd done everything she could to make it work, to such an extent that she'd been belittling herself before the man could do it to her.

What was worse, she realised that she'd tried so hard to be the sort of woman that men, this one in particular, respected that she'd ended up forgetting the sort of person she'd been when she started.

Trying Too Hard, the curse of the modern woman, she thought grimly. But no more. She recognised in Andrew a complete absence of antagonism that others saw as weakness but she interpreted as self-possession. He didn't challenge anybody because he didn't need to. He never even thought about trying to change other people because he considered the possibility of changing himself so unnecessary.

And gradually Rebecca came to unwind in his company. She permitted herself to speak openly, marvelling at the way he accepted her words without using them as weapons back against her.

20

She couldn't quite remember whose idea it had been for her to move in with him, but so far the arrangement had worked well. Until the news.

'What's happened?' she'd asked, alarmed at his expression as he walked out of Ben's office.

'I didn't get it,' he said shortly.

He didn't need to expand on this. She knew that he'd been fully expecting to be given his promotion today. She also understood his inability to articulate his disappointment. Years of making herself sensitive to the feelings of others had left her with a real gift for intuiting the true centre of an individual's problems. For Andrew, the unexpectedness of the decision would be hurting him, rather than the decision itself. And then he made the announcement that was to cause the real fallout.

'It's gone to a woman.' Just like that. No need for thespian swoons or grand hand gestures. Rebecca immediately grasped the implications of the statement. This was a conversation she'd had on many occasions, both with Andrew and with her female friends and colleagues. The one thing they'd all agreed on was that a woman boss was a trickier proposition than a man.

'I can't believe you're saying that,' Andrew had said, the first time the subject had arisen.

'Why, because I'm a woman?' Rebecca had asked, amused.

Andrew decided to tread cautiously here. These were dangerous waters in which many a wise man had drowned before him. 'I just thought all you . . . all women tended to stick together, that's all.'

'We do on important matters.'

Andrew didn't ask her to elaborate. Whatever Rebecca's definition of important matters entailed, he just knew it would make him laugh, which would not be well received. Now I come to think about it, he told himself proudly, I know more about women than I realised. This gave him the courage to press on.

'But surely a woman being given responsibility is a good thing? You've often complained that being a woman has held you back.'

Rebecca looked at him in despair. He didn't get it. And why should he when most women are themselves baffled by the mixed reaction they often experience when they learn they are going to work for a woman?

Margaret Thatcher notwithstanding, the concept of women in power is still a relatively new phenomenon. Of course, women have always been in power in the home; they've just become less concerned about pandering to men's egos by playing down the fact.

To some, authority comes naturally. There are women who, from childhood, elicit deference with their quietly confident bearing. To them, a management appointment is little more than another jacket in a different colour. They already have the language, the style and the expectations of being respected.

But to others, it is a new role, one that has to be approached like any other dramatic persona. And if you're not a natural actress, you run the permanent risk of being laughed off the stage.

But Rebecca couldn't explain all or any of this to Andrew without confessing some of her own prejudices towards women bosses. One very particular prejudice in this case, which he must never find out.

'Of course I think it's a good thing,' she said, 'in principle.'

Andrew took the 'in principle' to be a sign-off to this particular discussion at the time. He happily signed off on any conversation that showed the slightest sign of turning into a debate.

But now the subject had stopped being theoretical and had become a great big fat reality for them both. She'd been forced to go through the same dialogue every day since.

'It's not so bad for you. I've already lost to this woman in the only fight that mattered.' Andrew's voice was beginning to sound ominously like a whine.

Rebecca harnessed her patience to try and reassure him. Here I go again, she thought, having to reassure a man.

'Yes, but she doesn't know that. Besides, I'll be working for her too. And I thought I was going to be working for you, so I've had to make readjustments as well.'

Andrew relented. 'Sorry.' This was the beginning of the sorries. 'It would have been great, wouldn't it?'

'Hmm,' Rebecca replied, deliberately vague in her tone. She kissed him, both to make him feel better and stop herself from saying what she'd been thinking. Because she couldn't decide what was the worst option: to work for another woman or to work for her boyfriend.

Actually the most attractive option was to resign and become an usherette at the Streatham Odeon.

Ben Clarkson had been counting the days. Two more to go, he thought. He didn't have Rebecca on whom he could vent his conflicting emotions about Kate's imminent arrival, yet Rebecca was occupying his thoughts because he was the man who had unwittingly pushed her into Andrew's life by treating her so badly.

It was the first secret he'd kept from Andrew since they'd known each other. As he'd never had a friend, as such, he wasn't sure about the rules, but he was absolutely certain that Andrew would have been shocked about his affair with Rebecca.

Andrew was a man who moved and thought and lived in straight lines. He never looked sideways or backwards, regarding that as a wasted gesture. Ben had watched his friend enviously as he pared down the complexities of life to a set of minimalist principles, absorbing the unavoidable and eliminating the superfluous.

Andrew would disapprove of any affair on Ben's part. It was nothing to do with Rebecca. Andrew had not seemed to be interested in her until a few months ago. Her break-up with Ben had left her bruised and it hadn't helped that she couldn't talk to anyone at work about it. In fact, Ben had initially been quite relieved when she and Andrew got together. He knew that Rebecca would never mention the affair, especially not to Andrew.

But he'd been concerned about how she'd react to the appointment of Kate Harris. He and Rebecca had fought bitterly when she was overlooked for promotion herself in another department during their affair. Ben had convinced her that a woman would never be made a group director in this company, not with the current board. And while this incensed Rebecca, she accepted it, deciding to get as much experience as she could before moving on.

It wasn't exactly a lie, Ben liked to kid himself, more of a prevarication. The fact was that Rebecca would never be promoted beyond her current position in this company because she wasn't good enough. If he hadn't been besotted with her, he would have told her so, but he guessed that it would be the romantic kiss of death to insult her professional ability so he glossed over the truth with a hastily concocted lie.

And now a woman had been hired. He kept waiting for Rebecca to knock on his office door to vent her frustrations on him. So far, she'd settled for malevolent glances whenever he walked by. He hoped that this was as bad as it was going to get.

But on Monday, Kate would arrive and he was terrified that her appearance would spur Rebecca to take revenge on him. Specifically, he was terrified that she would hurt him in the most vicious way possible by telling Andrew.

Ben was married and Andrew felt that cheating on one's wife was inexcusable, largely because it was messy but also because it caused pain. More to the point, Andrew would be extremely unhappy about Ben's involvement with Rebecca because Ben was married to his sister.

Chapter 3

It was six o'clock on Monday morning but, to Kate, it was Saturday night and she was John Travolta, getting ready to set the world on fire. She even had the soundtrack playing to set the mood. So what if this is mad, she told herself, I live alone; what is the point in living alone if you can't behave ridiculously occasionally? Before today, her idea of ridiculous behaviour had been to eat cold spaghetti bolognese for breakfast and wear Rudolph the red-nosed reindeer slippers.

But today was her premiere, her opening night. Curtain up on her glittering first performance as the New Kate. She found herself gyrating her hips to the Bee Gees beat, as she sucked her stomach in and did up the buttons on the narrow skirt and the tight jacket. Tight anythings were not usually her style. She had been mocked all her life for her dress code that could be summed up in her two fashion constants: the cardigan and sensible shoes.

Why does everyone find it so funny? she often wondered. Who would willingly choose to have blistered aching feet? Who would go cold all day rather than slip on a classic M & S cardie that can take you from the office to an evening function without ever looking out of place? By not looking out of place, Kate meant that she was perpetually invisible.

Any story that had an element of invisibility had attracted her as a child. This was probably because, in her childhood, the only alternative to invisibility was being picked on, laughed at and made to eat everybody's parsnips in school dinners. She practised magic spells, positive thinking, wish fulfilment, anything that might promise the impossible. Only when she reached adulthood and started choosing her own clothes did her wish come true.

She could walk into any room and be completely unnoticed. It allowed her breathing space to acclimatise herself to a new and scary situation before she eventually had to speak to strangers.

And it seemed to make sense to carry the strategy into her working life. Fortunately, the nature of Kate's work allowed her to dress pretty much as she chose while she was in the office. When she went out to meet clients, of course, she had to adhere to the rules. She had a suit for such occasions, tailored but floral, which conveyed professionalism with a welcome undertone of individuality. She coordinated it with blouses, brightly coloured confections with bohemian flounces. It was a little crazy, unconventional, but she just about got away with it, a tribute to her professional reputation rather than evidence of slipping standards in executive wardrobes.

Now she knew that the invisibility was a myth. She wasn't unseen, she was consciously ignored by onlookers who took one swift look at her and decided she wasn't worth closer attention.

Let them ignore this lipstick, she challenged her reflection as she applied a ferocious red to her lips that gave substance to her whole face.

Let them ignore this hair, she dared the brush sweeping through her sleek, perfectly straight bob.

Let them ignore these shoes, she winced, squeezing her feet out of their beslippered luxury into razor-pointed stilettos.

She examined the final result curiously. And while they're not ignoring all these spectacular facets to me, she thought nervously, they'll have no time left to notice the look of utter, paralysing fear in my eyes. I can't do this. I can't do this.

'You're *actually* going to do this,' Justine had said, marvelling at the transformation.

She'd popped in to see Kate after a gruelling night shift assisting a difficult birth. When she'd rung the doorbell, she'd been greeted by the sound of clickety-clacks stumbling towards her, punctuated by words she'd never heard her friend say before.

After some muttered curses, Kate had answered the door. Justine stared at her. For one second she thought she'd come to the wrong house, even though she'd been with Kate when she chose the clothes and had her hair cut. But the final picture was so much more than the sum of the various parts.

Even in her flustered state, Kate was magnificent.

'You look like Bette Davis or Barbara Stanwyck or one of those other Hollywood ice maidens,' Justine pronounced, still standing on the doorstep in shock.

'I can't do this,' Kate wailed, dragging Justine through the door and pulling her shoes off in despair.

'Of course you can,' Justine said. 'I wasn't completely convinced on Saturday but now I've seen the finished picture . . . *I'm* terrified of you and *I'm* your best friend. In fact, I'm too nervous to ask if there's any chance of a coffee in case you toss your glossy mane imperiously and hurl a glacial scowl my way.'

'Don't be ridiculous, Justine.'

'I'm not being ridiculous. I promise you, I would tell you if you hadn't pulled this off, but you have.'

28

Kate limped into the kitchen to make coffee.

'Why are you limping?' Justine asked.

'Those shoes were pinching my toes,' Kate shouted back.

Justine marched into the kitchen. 'Don't be so pathetic. I've just seen a woman spend fifteen hours in absolute agony and she didn't make as much fuss as you are about your bloody feet.'

Kate groaned. 'Pardon me for being pathetic. The thing is, I've never worn high heels, not ever, and I just don't think my feet can handle them. I couldn't even walk to the door without falling over. What chance have I got of getting to the station without breaking my ankle?'

Justine considered this reasonable objection. 'And even if you did, I suppose it would rather spoil the effect if you stagger into the office looking like a drunken hooker.'

'Thank you,' Kate said, not knowing quite what she was thankful for.

Justine was thinking. 'The trouble is, shoes are important, they complete an outfit, tie a look together. That suit and that hair and face coupled with a pair of your cushion-soft old-woman moccasins and you'll look like a rich bag lady.'

Kate narrowed her eyes. 'Have you come round here deliberately to sabotage my morning or will you be getting to the positive bit some time in the near future?'

Justine ignored the question and the sarcasm. They'd been friends long enough to have a mutual shorthand, a common language that permitted them to litter their conversations with irrelevancies that could be ignored, telegraphing the important bits in the knowledge that they wouldn't be missed or misinterpreted.

'Do you possess any footwear whatsoever that is not

designed for geriatrics on walking holidays?' Justine asked, not optimistic about the answer.

Kate thought about it. 'No. Unless . . .'

'What?' Justine asked eagerly.

'Do you remember when I was bridesmaid a few years back for my cousin?'

How could Justine forget? She'd had to accompany Kate on quite a few major drinking sessions to help her face up to the prospect of walking down the aisle in a giant cerise lampshade. This, on a woman who hated attention.

Kate continued. 'I still have the shoes. I remember you saying they were quite daring for me.'

Oh yes, Justine remembered the shoes. True, they had heels of a sort. But they were very, very pink.

Rebecca had sixty pairs of shoes in front of her in colours that could inspire an entire paint range, from Buttercup to Midnight via Urban Decay. But although the colours displayed a scary commitment to variety, the heels were uniformly deadly. High, pointed, a chiropodist's nightmare.

Rebecca knew them all intimately. They were her children, each pair with its own personality. Her choice of shoes played a critical role in each day's outcome. A bad choice could ruin the day.

And this one was bad before it started. The prospect of Kate Harris joining today cast a black cloud over Rebecca from the moment she woke up. There was only one way to make her feelings known to the woman. The blackest, shiniest, highest shoes she possessed: the Saturday Night Specials, kept separate from the others in a token of respect for their potency. She rushed off to the bedroom to find them.

*

Kate had rushed off to her bedroom to rummage around for the evidence of this heinous crime against good taste. She emerged holding the pair aloft like the FA Cup. They were even pinker than Justine recalled, a verdict she would have considered impossible if asked earlier.

Justine brushed past her and desperately turned out all the shoes on Kate's state-of-the-art shoe rack, with built-in airing and deodorising facilities. Kate clearly took her foot hygiene so seriously that Justine wondered if it warranted psychiatric investigation. But that was another drunken night's conversation.

'Kate, dare I ask why you possess twelve pairs of shoes which are all exactly the same?' she enquired, hoping that she was masking her incredulity.

Kate laughed. 'They're not all exactly the same. Well some are, those are shoes that I liked so much, I bought another couple of pairs when they were reduced in the sales so I could replace the others when they were worn out. The others look the same but have decorative features so I can ring the changes.'

Justine peered at them and, indeed, could just about discern some subtle differences in the uppers. Who am I to judge? she asked herself. I buy shoes that don't even fit me because I think they make my feet look petite. I buy shoes that I wear once then forget about. I even buy espadrilles every year, in the full knowledge that the hideous looped rope will tear the soles of my feet to pieces. Cheap but deadly. So who's the lunatic?

She said nothing but quickly concluded that there was nothing here that Kate could possibly wear with those clothes. She pointed defeatedly at the pink shoes. 'You may as well try them on and see how they look.'

Kate slipped her feet into them like Cinderella. She

stood up and twirled. 'What do you think?' she asked, with an enthusiasm which was tragic.

Justine swallowed. Carefully, now, she told herself. Kate is holding on to this new image by a fragile hair. With split ends creeping up the shaft. 'Black does go with everything,' she ventured at length. This was all there was to say.

Actually, they added a vulnerability to the immaculate presentation that began with Kate's hair and now ended at her ankles. They could prove a useful distraction. They would surely confound any attempts to pigeonhole Kate. Justine was surprised to find herself reassured by the flaw in the portrait of cold perfection that had opened the door. And she wisely guessed that Kate herself was finding comfort in this scrap of Kate-ness underpinning her new alien self.

'What are you thinking?' Kate asked Justine nervously.

Justine smiled. 'I was thinking about all the hundreds of times I tried to get you to change your image. And here you are.'

In fact, she'd been having the same discussion with Kate since she was eighteen:

'Why do you insist on wearing those long cardigans over those shapeless cheesecloth dresses? All the time? Wherever you're going?'

Kate patiently tried to explain. 'It's because I've found something that suits me so I'm sticking to it.'

'Sweetie, those clothes wouldn't suit anybody! They should only be worn by students who wish to convey their utter disdain for physical appearances. And in that case, they should be accessorised with some CND badges and a permanent expression of existential angst.'

Kate sighed. 'I like them because they cover up my chunky calves and my childbearing hips.'

Then would follow the hips-and-calves dialogue, a popular but tiresome element of many female friendships.

'Kate, how many more times do we have to go through this? You have fabulous legs, of course you do, you were a great swimmer. They're bound to be muscular and, guess what, women pay hundreds of pounds a year to join gyms to develop muscles like that.'

'Well, I hate them,' Kate said petulantly.

Justine ignored the interruption. 'And as for your hips, the only reason your hips are defined is because you have a tiny waist. Again, the legacy of all your swimming. And, guess what—'

'Yes, yes,' Kate would intervene, eyes closed at the familiar lecture. 'Women would kill to have my curves. So how come all the clothes are made for straight-up-straight-down boy-girls?'

Justine pursed her lips. She hated this conversation because she envied Kate her figure. Despite having had three children, she was one of those straight-up-straight-down boy-girls, and knew she wasn't going to change now. She'd resigned herself to . . . well, herself. She still favoured the gamine feathery crop that was fashionable for precisely three weeks in 1979. She still bought her clothes from children's ranges. She still looked fourteen.

All the hot passions of adolescence had passed her by as she attracted the boys who found her angles unthreatening. She was the girl that boys wanted as a friend. She was good at sport: good at spitting wet bits of tissue at the ceiling during maths and making them stick; good at knocking on doors and running away. The things that matter.

But what she really wanted was to be pretty and delicate and feminine. To be gazed at furtively from behind Latin textbooks. To have her name carved on to boys' toilet walls in conjunction with obscene propositions. She ate more and more, trying to develop some curves on her determinedly bony body, but the only thing she developed was oily skin.

Over the years she'd watched with bemusement as Kate squandered her assets, stubbornly covering up any treacherous curve that might threaten to whisper, 'LOOK AT ME!'

Of course, occasionally Kate's resolve had slipped. She'd take off her cardigan, forgetting she'd tucked her blouse into her skirt, or absent-mindedly fasten a tight belt around one of her sack dresses. Such reckless acts seemed to have a knock-on effect on her personality, enabling her to relax, to forget her constant terror that someone had probably fixed a sign on her back reading WALK ON ME – PLEASE.

And it was these lapses that had rescued Kate from a solitary existence. Having glimpsed the spark of life, the hint of attractive originality that Kate had allowed to escape, men had laboured to draw her out, to liberate her from her inferiority complex.

There had been subsequent relationships, emotional tugs-of war with a succession of weary men trying to rip off her cardigan (metaphorically speaking, of course). They usually fell in love with her, told her so, but she never believed them. So they always left her.

Justine would nurse her through each break-up with a superhuman patience that only alcohol could fuel.

'Why do they always leave me?' she would ask miserably, never waiting for Justine to answer. She knew what her friend would say and didn't want to hear it.

But while Justine ached for Kate and her self-imposed isolation, part of her stifled an irritation that someone with such fantastic raw material could make such a hash of a life that should be relatively easy.

Justine always knew that her material would never entitle her to multiple opportunities. She was grateful when Steve asked her to marry him. He was a doctor and she was a nurse. She used to console him after his heart got broken as, one by one, the girly nurses he pursued nibbled away at his self-esteem with their cruel rejections. It was inevitable that, one day, he looked at Justine and saw a new possibility, a strange and wonderful alternative to this crazy pursuit of love, a future free of combat, a life of amiable companionship, the blessed relief of a good, comfortable marriage.

And Justine was sure that she would never get a better offer, so she accepted.

Kate was staring at her with her arms folded, a mock-stern expression on her beautifully made-up face. She knocked on Justine's head. 'Hello? Is there anybody at home?'

'Sorry!' Justine said. 'You look great. Truly you do.'

Kate took one more look at her reflection, trying to familiarise herself with this stranger. She breathed in and out slowly. 'I can do this. I can do this,' she whispered. Justine kissed her affectionately and followed her out of the house, willing her to succeed in this ambitious deception, wishing she herself faced a challenge that scared her.

Because when Kate had asked her what she was think-ing, Justine lied. A thought had suddenly buried itself deep inside her like a fiery little meteor, one she would have to deal with later. Look at Kate, it had urged. She's changed herself, turned herself into someone different. I wonder if I could do that. And if I could, what would I turn myself into?

Rebecca examined her reflection in the ladies' cloakroom mirror. What have I turned into? she asked herself. I used to be a nice girl, that's how everyone would have described me. Now, within the course of six months, I've had an affair with a married man, then moved in with his best friend and I lie awake wishing horrible disfiguring illnesses on a woman I don't even know, just because she's got a job that I wanted.

She was touching up her make-up, a remedial course of action that was a critical part of her personality. Rebecca had learned as a teenager what Kate was just discovering at the age of thirty-six, that every person is a blank canvas. Girls learn early, some earlier than others, the advantage of being able to paint qualities on to their faces while men have to wait for age and experience to etch character on theirs.

When she was fourteen Rebecca went to her first disco, a school function. This was a big occasion for the small Suffolk village where she lived. Her school was five miles away and her two closest friends were spread out over adjoining villages. They tended to meet in each other's houses, playing Stevie Wonder albums and fantasising about love lives that they could only enjoy by proxy in the real-life photo stories in *Jackie*, the magazine of choice for all girls at that time. They would pore over articles about how to kiss, practising intently on the inside of their arms. They would argue ferociously over the advice given about problems on the Cathy and Claire page, jealous to the point of sickness that none of the problems had any relevance to their own lives.

They were all bright girls, all had won places at the top grammar school in the area. Academically their lives were on course, which left their minds free to dwell on more serious concerns such as: would any boy ever go out with a grammar-school girl?

Then, one week, *Jackie* had a free gift attached to its cover, a little clear plastic pot of glossy turquoise eyeshadow. The following Saturday, the three girls huddled together in Rebecca's bedroom, round the tiny dressing table mirror. The Smiths were singing 'Heaven Knows I'm Miserable Now', a record celebrating a relentlessly grim life-view that was strangely attractive to teenage girls with little to be miserable about.

As they sang along, humming over the parts where the lyrics were impossible to distinguish, they applied the lurid green powder with clumsy fingers. The result was alarming in retrospect but, at the time, they thought they looked gorgeous; the effort was rewarded when they all got asked to dance at the disco. More to the point they all got picked for the last dance, Spandau Ballet's True.

Although this was their first encounter with boys at all and therefore void of any points of comparison, it didn't diminish their unswerving belief that it was the magic powder that rendered them desirable. They would one day learn that boys of that age were quite indiscriminate in their choice of girls providing they weren't fat, a cruel fact of life that confronts most large girls at some point in youth. And also providing they wore the right clothes, another cruel fact of life learned by girls who were cursed either with bad dress sense or a mother who bought all their kids' clothes from the catalogue lady who called each week.

But Rebecca and her friends conformed marvellously. What a relief, Rebecca had thought, on discovering that all the girls were dressed identically in mid-calf-length jersey skirts and puff-sleeved blouses topped with short-sleeved acrylic tops. They all bopped from side to side on clumpy buckled patent leather shoes with thick high heels. And they all wore turquoise eyeshadow. Not only did Rebecca love the feeling of belonging to the crowd, but it was clear that the boys liked the uniformity too. It saved them having to risk losing face by making bad decisions asking the wrong girl to dance.

It was a lesson that Rebecca would carry with her throughout her evolution into adulthood, adapting her routine as her understanding of her features and how to enhance them became more sophisticated. She learned how to make her one face play many different roles. She could paint a professional face, a frivolous face, a come-to-bed face or the highly technical it-looks-as-if-I'm-not-wearing-any-make-up-but-I-am face.

She came to understand how the right face, a straightforward portrait, made the beholder relax instantly, how it was a relief to grasp the point of another person by reading the signs drawn unambiguously across eyes, cheeks and mouth.

She applied the same philosophy to her clothes including, of course, her shoes and even to the way she talked and the things she said. In Rebecca's opinion, to make your way through life, every encounter, personal, social or professional, should be regarded as an interview where you have to meet the requirements of each interviewer if you want to progress to the next stage in your personal development. Just as nobody would go into an interview unprepared, in the same way she prepared herself mentally at all times to be ready for a swift adaptation of herself into another self.

But now her faith in the strategy was wobbling. She

had been satisfied by Ben's assurance that the only reason she'd been overlooked for promotion was the outrageous sexism of Ben's fellow directors. Looking back, she realised how he had even turned this to his advantage.

'I've pleaded your case,' he'd insisted mournfully, 'but they're dinosaurs, the lot of them. Jobs for the boys, that sort of thing. I mean, to be brutally honest, that's why they voted me on to the board, because they assumed that I was one of them.'

This self-deprecation made him appear doubly attractive to a nice girl like Rebecca, who immediately forgot her own ambitions and concentrated on reassuring Ben that he had surely attained his high position on merit.

What a fool I was, she thought grimly. It never occurred to me that I was dealing with someone who knew how to play the game like me. Even worse, he outmanoeuvred me, he assessed my game plan, my strengths and weaknesses, and beat me.

Her hand was steady as she applied the glossy nude lipstick. Nothing ever made her hands shake. Blotting her lips on a tissue, she appraised her appearance objectively: thirty-one but could be anything from twenty-five to forty-five; attractive but not pretty and not beautiful; the sort of strong features that would never be either fashionable or unfashionable, and could therefore be manipulated into any face she wanted; hair swept back in a layered bob that required extended blow-drying to keep in shape.

It'll do, it's as good as it can be given the modest raw material, Rebecca concluded. She looked more closely, wondering if her eyes lacked intelligence, a deficiency she could not remedy cosmetically, if that were the case. Or could it be that I'm not as good at my job as I think I am? Bad thought. One she'd consider more carefully at a less stressful time.

She was going to watch Kate Harris very closely indeed. She wanted to know what this woman had that she didn't. Because once she'd identified the exact qualities that set Kate apart from and above her, she would capture them, add them to her repertoire and make them her own.

Andrew glanced briefly at the mirror, just to make sure that everything was as it had been the day before, that his eyebrows weren't meeting in the middle and his nose wasn't becoming old-man bulbous. He knew this was irrational but it helped set him up for the day to know that he hadn't changed overnight in some barely discernible way. Any number of things could happen to him over which he would have no control, so it was essential for him to retain a firm grip on those aspects within his domain.

Every one of his girlfriends had left him because of his obsessively controlling tendencies. But every person he had ever worked for had praised his meticulous attention to detail that made him an irreplaceable member of any team. So what was a man to do?

This was a rhetorical question. There wasn't a single thing he could do about it. He was the man he was for real, attributable reasons that he appreciated and therefore didn't fight. There were advantages and disadvantages to this. Up until now, they had been divided straight down the middle into professional success and personal failure. And the personal failures didn't matter to him.

But now it was all topsy-turvy. His career had come to a halt, which equated to a backward slide in a business where forward progress was the only state of motion recognised. At the same time, he had somehow acquired a woman completely out of his league and she had moved in with him. What was going on here?

Both of these events appeared to be out of his hands and he wanted to change that state of affairs as quickly as possible. The only problem was that Andrew didn't have any experience in changing states of affairs. He generally maintained such a rigid hold on the various strands of his life that there was never any need for intervention. He simply never let matters reach the point where they could cause him a problem. And the fate fairy had seemed happy to leave him alone in his sealed bubble.

But in the four weeks since he heard about Kate Harris, the fate fairy had been curiously active. Rebecca had been doing strange things with her make-up, a sign that he had quickly learned foretold trouble, or at least imminent change, and Ben had become evasive, especially in the office, which suggested some kind of politicking underway that Ben was keeping from him.

Encouraged by the constancy of his reflection, he made up his mind. 'Today's the day,' he announced to the mirror. 'I will go out and collect up all those wild cards, put them back in the box where they belong. I will not acknowledge that my life can be turned upside-down by outside influences. I have run my life by myself up to now. I am going to sort this all out my own way. I will trust my own instincts, make my own decisions, forge my own way.' With his skill for clichés, if all else failed, he could develop an alternative career writing lyrics for Eurovision song contest entries.

He was practically strutting as he left the men's cloakroom to meet Kate Harris for the first time. But while it was worthy to begin depending on his own instincts, it was a bad, bad decision.

41

Give Andrew factual problems, he could give you a dozen rational solutions. Throw in some human issues and he'd stop playing the game, take his ball and go and find another playground.

Since he'd never needed to use them, Andrew had the underdeveloped instincts of a five-year-old child. And this wasn't a twee suburban Montessori nursery where the biggest conflict he could cause was a tug-of-war over an abacus. A few reckless actions in *this* classroom could cause some real damage.

As he slammed the cloakroom door behind him in a rare show of defiance, a soap dispenser smashed on to the floor, causing the first spillage of the day.

He met Rebecca walking towards the office. It was only two hours since they'd been eating Weetabix in his flat. That had been strange. Even in retrospect it was odd.

He'd found himself watching her when he thought she wasn't looking.

'Why are you looking at me like that?' she'd asked, self-conscious under his scrutiny.

Embarrassed at being found out, he took a large mouthful of breakfast to buy himself a minute of composing time. Rebecca recognised the ploy. She knew all the ploys, seldom having taken a step in her adult life without there being a prearranged purpose. She was doubly alert, therefore, to his next words.

'Erm, have you done something to your face?' Andrew finally asked. Not a controversial question to anyone except Rebecca. Her hand went to her cheek protectively, unconsciously.

'Why do you ask?'

Andrew knew from her wary tone that he'd asked a bad question. And now she was making him explain himself. 'No reason. It's just that, well, your eyes look a bit different to how they looked in the night.'

Rebecca's face slowly reddened. Andrew thought she was going to shout at him or cry or throw her bowl at him.

'Yes,' she said quietly. 'I have.'

Andrew was aware that this was significant but he had no idea why. In his view, it was neither odd nor normal to be wearing make-up when getting out of bed. It was just the mechanics that interested him: precisely when Rebecca had got up to apply it? The 'why' would obviously be incomprehensible, so he wouldn't even go there.

'Oh,' he said feebly. 'I was just wondering, that's all,' he added, hoping that this would close the topic down. As a tactic, it was not a successful one.

'I suppose you think I'm crazy now, don't you?' Rebecca asked, her voice rising.

No, Andrew thought, I'm the crazy one for ever having asked the question in the first place. When will I ever learn that any comment on a woman's appearance, apart from a bland 'you look great', is always dangerous business?

Andrew had plenty of experience with women; he just never learned from any of it. It hadn't been necessary. As in every other aspect of his life, he hadn't needed to make any efforts to find love, it just happened easily. He was a charming, lovable man and women seemed to need little encouragement to be attracted to him. Of course, once they got to know him, they found him intensely annoying and quite impossible to live with. But this simply meant that they felt guilty about leaving him, since he was clearly so sweet and could not help his nature. So when they left him, it was always gently and amicably, and generally came at a time when he was finding them irritating as well, not fitting in with his compulsion to regulate his environment.

He'd never had a broken heart nor had he caused one, a remarkable achievement for a man in his thirties who had been as romantically active as he had. So when he made mistakes, as he was now doing with Rebecca, he didn't bother absorbing them into his consciousness, preferring to toss them out as anomalies, blips on an otherwise straight line ascending to success and prosperity.

Once more fate had intervened to rescue him. While he'd been pondering his weirdly wonderful existence, Rebecca had given up waiting for an answer.

'Well let me tell you, *I* think I'm crazy.'

What a relief, Andrew thought. 'Of course you're not,' he said, charitably but unconvincingly.

Rebecca ignored his comment. She was elsewhere, years back in her past. 'When I was fifteen, I went on a school trip to Germany. I was sharing a room with three other girls. The first night I took off my make-up with these little pads called Quickies.'

She waited for Andrew to make some sort of sound to indicate that he was listening. He was listening but didn't know what he was supposed to say. Am I supposed to know what Quickies are or were?

'Right, Quickies,' he offered cautiously.

Rebecca went on. Wow, I must have said the right thing, Andrew deduced. I should have trusted my own instincts years ago, I'm really good at this stuff.

'And when I came out of the bathroom, everybody gasped and then burst out laughing. You can imagine how I felt.' This time, she didn't wait for an acknowledgement. 'Anyway, someone said they didn't recognise me without my mascara, that my eyes had practically

44

disappeared.' Now she paused for Andrew to interject something appropriate.

He laughed. Well, he thought it was funny. He looked at Rebecca. She wasn't laughing.

'It wasn't funny,' she said.

'No, absolutely not,' Andrew agreed quickly.

'I've never forgotten that night. I went straight back into the bathroom and put my mascara back on. You see, I'm very fair-skinned so my eyelashes are light, anyway, you can imagine what they look like.'

Andrew said nothing. Absolutely nothing. The birth of wisdom is an awesome sight.

Rebecca was satisfied by his silence. 'And they'd got used to seeing me in mascara. I didn't wear much because it wasn't allowed in school, just one coat, enough to add a bit of colour, to define my eyes, you know?'

Andrew didn't know. Didn't have a clue. He nodded sympathetically.

'I'll never forget the shock on their faces. There are some things in one's life that are said, often something casual and trivial, a tiny judgement, that never go away. And this was one of mine. I knew right then that I would never allow anyone to see me without mascara on again.'

She's mad, Andrew realised.

Rebecca was on a roll. 'I mean, obviously I've had my eyelashes dyed now . . .'

Obviously.

'But as I've got older, I've needed to keep them topped up. During the night, they become a bit thin again so . . .'

'You get up and . . . top them up before I wake up and see you,' Andrew finished her sentence. He was alarmed at how normal it all sounded when he put it like that.

'Exactly!' Rebecca was relieved that he understood.

Andrew understood one thing: that Rebecca had two faces and he'd only seen one of them. He wondered if another whole person lurked unseen beneath the built-up eyelashes. He would have to find that out, using those new instincts he'd just uncovered.

Rebecca relaxed after this confession. They discussed the difficult day ahead. They'd made an agreement that they would go into the office together, meet the new woman with a united front, let her know what she was up against from the very start. But although they did indeed go in at the same moment, they weren't united any more. They were slightly out of sync, shifted off axis by new snippets of knowledge, changes in perspective, altered priorities.

They smiled at each other, touched each other's hand, exchanged silent messages of support before they went in.

It was to be one of the last displays of true solidarity they ever shared.

Chapter 4

Ben Clarkson heard Kate coming before he saw her. All of the offices and corridors were floored with polished wood. It was one of his ideas, to make everyone aware of the constant movement throughout the day, to be galvanised by the rising and falling click-clacks and shuffles and thuds as executives approached and moved on, promoting the flow of creative energy.

Initially the noise drove everyone crazy until the time arrived when they became deaf to the sound, immune to the pulse. Ben however was always listening, sensitive to variations in daily patterns, ready to step in and address lapses in motivation or commitment. It was his gift, one that would be completely useless if he were the sole survivor of a plane crash in a Borneo jungle, for example, but which served him well in a management consultancy where a buzzing dynamism was the expected soundtrack.

He looked briefly down at his desk then immediately looked away. Yep. Still a mess. Every few months he'd have a big tidy-up but he only felt comfortable when there was disorder around him. It reflected his character. Even being married to a neat tidy woman hadn't affected him. His wife could sew missing buttons on his shirts but only a miracle could turn him into a person who aligned the correct buttons with the correct buttonholes with a hundred per cent success rate.

But he'd done just fine so far without having to change.

It was eight forty-five. Those who were in the office were tapping away at keyboards, slurping coffee-of-the-week abominations, yawning, humming the easy-listening ballads or frighteningly sub-garage anthems they'd been exposed to on Saturday night. The rest were in the bathrooms, painting over the etched scars of excessive waking and not enough sleeping.

The footsteps approaching Ben's office were of a rhythm he didn't recognise. He was surprised that they weren't what he was expecting of Kate Harris. Neither nervous nor subdued, they sounded more like the tentative syncopated steps of a young girl trying on her mum's high heels. Definitely not a grown-up. He peered through a tiny hole on the elaborately carved door, hoping for a sneak preview of this woman who was causing trouble weeks before she even got here.

He couldn't remember her from the interview in which he took a backseat role. He was so sure that Andrew would be getting the job, he hadn't paid much attention to the other candidates. He had a vague recollection of an insipid, prettyish woman who only came to life when talking about her professional experience and ambitions.

As he crouched, he caught sight of his reflection in the avant-garde mirror. He didn't dwell on the image; he never did. Not because he wasn't vain, but because he was and hated the constant disappointment in his appearance. He was cursed with the sharp memory of being a beautiful child with choirboy curls, a scattering of golden freckles, angelic eyes and soft lips that all his aunties just loved kissing.

Then he hit adolescence and it all went wrong. He shot up, becoming too tall too quickly, an unwelcome event he responded to by developing a slight stoop. The curls unravelled, became greasy and unmanageable, determined to jump out from their fierce crop, no matter how short he had his hair cut. His freckles became a canvas on to which his acne could add splashes of scarlet. And his soft mouth remained soft, the lips big and doughy, lovely on a toddler, horrible on a teenager and even worse on a grown man.

He never recovered his boyhood potential. While the extremes of those years were eased, the haziest mirror in the kindest light confirmed his suspicion. He was not a handsome man.

This frank self-assessment happened early enough for him to accept it and carry on with his life in the knowledge that he would have to find his advantages elsewhere. This marked the beginning of his aimless ramble through life, acquiring strengths, notching up achievements, ticking off conquests, whenever the occasion presented itself.

The plan, such as it existed, was to exploit himself to the full, define himself comprehensively, then decide how he could best use this combination of qualities in a viable life plan.

Nearly forty, he still hadn't concluded his explorations. He was still rambling, succeeding effortlessly at a business into which he'd drifted after university, married to a woman because it seemed bad manners not to be, Jenny being Andrew's sister, and profoundly uninterested in everything apart from his wife at this time.

The appointment of a woman had unnerved him, particularly since he had been overruled by all the other interviewers. He felt as if he'd been shunted to a siding, out of touch with current thought. He hadn't dared voice his feelings about women in power in case he discovered he was alone in his sexism.

The threat, as yet unspoken, of his affair with Rebecca coming out inflamed his anxiety.

In recent weeks Kate Harris had become the focus for all his intangible unease. It was vital that her time here was short and ended in a hasty departure. He would play an active part in this. That should pacify Rebecca. And Andrew. And Jenny, who had barely spoken to him since he told her that her brother was not being given the promotion he'd been, well, foolishly promised by Ben.

He waited for his nemesis to knock on his door. So when she walked straight into his office, almost tripping over him, he was unprepared. This was not how he'd planned to meet her. He'd intended to be reclining slightly in his chair, jabbing fast and fluently on his Palm organiser with the dinky plastic stylus, smiling ironically at a private joke, becoming stern and menacing when he finally looked up at her. Instead, he looked like a peeping Tom, standing just inside the door in a slight crouch, his hair flopped over his forehead instead of swept back like a William Hurt that showed signs of evolving into a Bobby Charlton before too long.

He jumped up, ran a shaking hand through his hair and smiled at Kate Harris. Except this definitely wasn't the Kate Harris he'd interviewed six weeks earlier.

One swift glance was enough to warn him that the sweet lady had been reconstructed. Despite the girly shoes, this woman had redefined herself as a great big stomping pair of boots. He felt downtrodden already. He had intended to assert his authority with a few expertly delivered put-downs before setting his strategy of domination and conquest in motion.

It looked as if he would need to come up with a change of strategy very, very quickly. Kate extended her hand with a cool smile. Ben took it, returning the smile with a calm he didn't feel, hoping that Kate wouldn't notice the tremor.

Kate wouldn't have noticed if his hand had an extra thumb and was covered in fur. Her feet were killing her and her skirt had been scything through her waist from the moment she stopped holding her stomach in. This was a terrible idea, she now accepted, and she'd changed her mind about everything. But it was too late to back down. She'd look ridiculous if she reverted to her true nature while dressed like Cruella de Vil.

'Do you really think I look like Cruella de Vil?' she'd asked anxiously.

She was hoping that, by rehearsing these opening moments dozens of times with Justine, she would be able to get through the first few minutes on autopilot.

Justine groaned. 'You look fantastic, for the thousandth time, powerful, a life force, *not* a doormat.'

Kate scowled at her friend.

'Can we continue?' Justine asked, in mock frustration. 'Now, the critical thing to keep at the front of your mind is that you must always get the first and last word in during every encounter,' she counselled. 'It will immediately establish the balance of power in your favour.'

'How did you learn this sort of thing in your work?' Kate asked in wonder.

'A woman in labour needs to trust her midwife,' Justine pointed out. 'Mother is usually scared and needs to be reassured that she's put her faith in the right person. She's actually putting her life and the life of her baby in my hands. If she thinks I have any self-doubts, she will have every right to panic and ask for someone who knows what they're doing.'

Kate sighed. 'The crazy thing is, I do know what I'm

51

doing. I have no doubts about my ability. Why should I? I get results, I meet and exceed all my targets. It's all the rest I can't handle. All the office stuff.'

Justine considered this. 'Then you've got to learn how to act. Pretend to be assertive with your staff and colleagues. Play a part.'

'I can't do that,' Kate said.

'Of course you can,' Justine insisted. 'I'll teach you.'

And in the course of a Saturday afternoon, Justine taught Kate everything she'd ever learned from watching TV police series. It was where she'd learned all her own techniques. From Angie Dickinson's ludicrously named Pepper to Jane Tennison via all the female detectives in *NYPD Blue* who never sacrificed their glamour at the altar of commitment to law and order.

Justine strode around Kate's living room like Orson Welles. 'Now, do you remember how you told me that, on those rare occasions when you actually asked someone to do something, you always found yourself adding a "sorry" at the end of your request?'

Kate nodded in shame at the memory.

Justine continued. 'Now this can work in your favour. Think of it this way: whenever you need to give instructions to a secretary, for instance, then just imagine that every sentence you deliver ends not with the word "sorry", but "scumbag". Of course, you don't actually say "scumbag", that would be a tad too confrontational.'

Kate giggled. 'How am I supposed to do that with a straight face?'

Justine groaned. 'I'm not being literal, just trying to get you to put yourself into a certain frame of mind that others will respect, imbuing you with a definite authority. Now go. Get out there and win that Oscar!'

*

52

So when Kate looked at Ben Clarkson, who seemed to be growing in stature as his initial unease faded, she immediately began picturing him in her mind as a grubby unshaven drug dealer in a prison cell, shouting 'Pig!' and 'Dude!' and other vague words Kate remembered from *Starsky and Hutch*. Kate hadn't watched that much TV since the 1970s. Now she was a cool police superintendent, with the looks of Glenda Jackson in *A Touch of Class* and the haughtiness of Katharine Hepburn in *The African Queen*.

The sight of his desk distracted her. She was tempted to find a ruler in the mess and smack him over the knuckles with it. God! How can he work efficiently like that? she asked herself before returning to character.

She tossed her hair back until she remembered that her long wavy hair had been chopped off and her new severe cut was glued in place with industrial-strength hairspray. ('Don't stand or sit within two feet of a naked flame,' the hairdresser had intoned with the gravity of a four-minute warning.) Kate had nodded, too intimidated to ask what would happen if she should venture out in a storm when lightning threatened.

'I'd like to be shown my office then introduced to my team as soon as possible. Please,' she added with an imperious half-smile that just about redeemed her request from being rude. (Scumbag.)

Ben was startled by her abruptness. This bizarre performance, for that was how it appeared to him, was throwing him off-kilter. What was she playing at?

'Now, if it's not too much trouble,' Kate repeated firmly.

'Right, of course,' Ben said, still standing awkwardly by the door. 'Oh, er, welcome to Visions in Strategy!' He did a little tap-dancing shuffle to accompany the

53

welcome. Why did I do that? he asked himself angrily. This woman's making me crazy.

It was fortunate that Kate was so physically uncomfortable or she would have burst out laughing. Justine was right, she was forced to concede, people are thrown off-centre by a strong display of authority. This man bore no resemblance to the Ben Clarkson who'd interviewed her.

That man had been cool, collected and absolutely uninterested in her. She had been the one to be unnerved that day. His disassociation communicated one of two facts: he didn't like her or he didn't respect her. Since she sensed that she was performing well in the interview, she had to conclude that his antipathy towards her (promoted from apathy by her neurotic sensors that immediately assessed the degree of being liked by everyone she met) was strictly personal.

She'd been surprised to get the job and assumed that he held the least power in the panel of five who had interrogated her.

But now as he wavered in front of her, holding the door like an eager-to-please concierge, she knew that whatever distaste he'd felt for her then had been translated into a nervous acceptance of her as an equal. Whether he liked her or not was another issue that she'd examine when she came out of character later. Right now, all that mattered was to maintain this fragile momentum that was producing astonishing results.

'Thank you,' she said briefly, striding out into the large open-plan office and letting her eyes plot a slow, analytical course over the area like Marlene Dietrich imperiously trying to pick a young lover from a sea of eager Lotharios.

She was so wrapped up in her act that she hadn't noticed

everyone staring at her. She felt a treacherous blush creeping up her throat on its unstoppable campaign to plonk a red flag of victory on her tempting white cheeks.

Justine had prepared her for this to a certain extent. She'd applied some gunky green cream under Kate's foundation that was supposed to counteract redness. But it couldn't hide a blush completely. Kate had to act swiftly to halt the scarlet attack. Justine had a strategy for this as well.

How strange, Kate had thought, as Justine bounded around the room with endless techniques for reinventing oneself. Where did she learn all this stuff? Why did she need to learn it? Has she used any of these herself? Slowly, as Kate was transforming herself, she was reevaluating Justine, wondering if she'd put on some masks and costumes when Kate wasn't looking, whether she was the same person she'd always been. Another thought that needs to be worked through at a less fraught time, Kate decided.

'As soon as you feel yourself going red, you must immediately calm yourself down, slow down your heartbeat,' Justine had advised.

'How do I do that?' Kate had asked, without any doubt that Justine would have the answer.

'Imagine you're Ma in *The Waltons*,' Justine said. 'You've got 146 children and you're living in abject poverty in the middle of a depression. But you've got these inner resources that keep you serenely beautiful, radiating that beatific glow that keeps your ragamuffin brood on the straight and narrow, always in a clean frock with your hair in that bun thing that is never untidy until you let your tresses flow freely and sensuously for your John.'

Kate looked at her friend curiously. 'Do I know you?'

55

she asked, puzzled. 'This is like *Invasion of the Body Snatchers*. You look the same but, in essence, you are the mere husk of the Justine I've known all these years; the words are the words of a madwoman who has sat in front of a television set all her life, with the curtains drawn and a copy of *TV Times* stapled to her lap.'

Justine placed her hand on her hip. 'Do you want me to do this or not?'

Kate held up her hands in an expression of mock surrender. 'I'm Ma Walton,' she laughed. 'I can do that.'

'I'm Ma Walton, I'm Ma Walton,' she intoned silently as the eyes of a dozen keen, slick executives watched her standing before them. She suppressed all her instinctive desires to make them like her by smiling at each of them. She was too busy trying to remember the name of all the Walton children. 'John-Boy, Ellen, the little one with the long hair, the boy with the braces who was always falling off his bike in front of war deserters . . .'

It was working. The blush had stopped. And, unknown to her, it was having another effect. She was distancing herself from her audience, making herself appear remote, mysterious. If only they knew what was going through her mind they might not have been so intrigued, but Kate was quickly learning that reality took a poor second place to perception when it came to first impressions.

Ben was alarmed by the reverential hush that Kate was inspiring. 'Let me take you through,' he said hastily. He was about to rest his hand gently on her back to lead her, but something stopped him from risking such intimacy, however casual and harmless.

Kate felt his hand brush against her jacket then withdraw quickly. She smiled inwardly at his uncertainty. It was her first taste of power and she liked it. A lot.

Ben didn't like this at all. He needed to tip the balance of power back in his own favour. It was a small gesture, but he switched direction abruptly.

'I think I'll introduce you to the team first,' he announced coolly. He stepped carefully around her, his long gangly limbs extending in all directions like wobbly tentacles to avoid any inadvertent contact with this ice maiden. She followed him, suppressing her amusement at his discomfort but cursing him for the little victory.

As she walked through the office, her shoes came under the scrutiny of the besuited folk who had just been mesmerised by her appearance. Eyebrows twisted, perplexed by the pink, very pink, things on the feet of this impressive figure. They added an arcane topnote to a woman they thought they had typecast. She was now taking on the status of an enigma. Clever old Justine for predicting that the shoes would have an impact.

But that was the easy part, Kate cautioned herself. None of those people will be working with me directly. They can afford to be generous with their appraisal. The next step is the tricky one.

She was right to be wary. Ben was weaving in and out of desks, tossing out words of encouragement, personal comments that obviously pleased all the staff members. He's a smooth worker, Kate conceded.

Then he stopped and turned to face Kate, more composed now. This was his territory. Foreign territory for Kate, hostile ground. He knew what she was facing; she could only imagine it.

Three people were perched on the corners of their desks, laughing and joking. They must have known that Ben and Kate were standing there but they continued as if they were alone.

Kate was beginning to feel unsettled. This was a

pre-planned manoeuvre, she knew. So did Ben but he allowed it to continue for a few seconds longer than was courteous to Kate.

'Guys?' he said finally.

The three stopped mid-joke and turned to face Ben, carefully avoiding eye contact with Kate.

Ben silently congratulated them on their resolve. He hoped they would realise that the playing field had altered, a substitution had been made and an amendment to the gameplan was called for.

Rebecca understood this immediately. She took one look at Kate and identified a rival in the self-improvement stakes, not in Rebecca's own league, but a woman who was taking herself in hand. And it looks like it's for the first time, she thought.

It took Rebecca no more than a few seconds to evaluate Kate's efforts. The make-up was not skillfully applied. The eye-liner was not dead straight, the lip-liner not perfectly aligned to the shape of her lips, the blusher not symmetrical. And while the colours were fashionable and projected a businesslike image, they were not suited to the face underneath. Rebecca recognised another nice girl. Below the painted highlights sat features of un-compromising wholesomeness. No matter how hard Kate tried to depict herself as Joan Crawford, she would always be Debbie Reynolds.

And those shoes . . .

The shoes aside, (and Rebecca couldn't imagine what statement Kate was hoping to make with them apart from 'the bulb in the shoe cupboard has gone') the clothes were good but a little too uncompromising to Rebecca's skilled eye.

Rebecca herself always factored in a 'just in case' element to her clothes. Today she was going for the businesswoman approach, so she chose an expensive suit like Kate but the fabric was a feminine lilac check and the lines were soft instead of angular. This was 'just in case' she needed to project another dimension to her personality to achieve an unforeseen objective such as begging a favour from the lads in Production.

Kate, on the other hand, had gone for the one-dimensional *Dynasty* look from the 1980s. Can't see her asking for an extra blob of mayo with a flirtatious wink in the sandwich bar, Rebecca observed wryly.

'Kate Harris, Rebecca Ramsden, Andrew Darlington and Sally.'

Kate cringed as Ben committed the cardinal error of omitting the secretary's surname, as if she was not professionally entitled to two names. She would never be so insulting. Well, the old Kate wouldn't, she checked herself. She made a mental note never to use Sally's surname herself. She really was receiving a comprehensive education in how to belittle and patronise without trying.

She forced herself not to shake Sally's hand first, a policy she'd previously always stuck to in an attempt to ingratiate herself and convey her commitment to egalitarianism. If a cleaner happened to be passing, Kate would shake his or her hand first. She had never realised that, while it was a kind thought, it straightaway conveyed her overwhelming need to be liked by everyone, to be popular. Malevolent buds would pop open in her audience as a weakness revealed itself so early, just asking to be exploited.

She shook hands with the group in the order that they had been introduced. She even dimmed her smile minutely when she came to Sally, a tiny adjustment that was noticed and resented.

Sally was angry with Andrew, who had cruelly misled

her. He'd embellished Ben's description of Kate until in Sally's imagination she had taken on the look and feel of a Charles Dickens foundling, pale and pathetic. Andrew and Rebecca had every intention of involving Sally in the plan to undermine Kate, so it had seemed sensible to lay some foundations for a basic disrespect. But this person bore no resemblance to the spineless waif she'd been promised. This was someone who seemed to command, demand, respect. This was someone guaranteed to make Sally angry.

Actually Sally was angry full stop. She was twenty-six years old and had been angry for all of them; with her mother for not teaching her to be selfish, with her father for making her believe that her beautiful face would open every door – she quickly learned that the only doors opening for her were leading to bedrooms. She'd been angry with the education system for not inspiring her, thereby forcing her to leave school at sixteen without any decent qualifications. She'd been angry with all the employers who had hired her to perform meaningless tasks, appropriate to her lack of qualifications, and had refused to notice her intelligence and abilities buried beneath her determinedly petulant face. And, most of all, she was angry with Visions in Strategy, this company that had taken her on as a junior secretary, trained her, sent her on courses, put up with her moods and led her to believe that she was being primed for an executive position.

She could not see that it was a true miracle for her to have risen as far as she had. She was a good secretary but her appalling attitude towards just about everybody would always prevent her from progressing any further. The only reason she managed to fit into her present position was that Rebecca had formed a bond with her, identifying with Sally's suppressed rage at being unappreciated. Neither of them took responsibility for their own failings and each relished the discovery of a kindred soul to reflect and affirm their grievances and perceived injustices.

Theirs was a friendship of sorts, one that baffled everyone else in the company. Sally's lack of charm had managed to alienate her from all the other secretaries and her openly hostile behaviour had led to her being black-listed by all the other departments. Her attractive face brought her opportunities but her sharp tongue quickly shut them down before they developed.

That's not to say that people didn't make an effort. Sally was constantly being invited out after work, to the pub, clubs, the cinema. But she always turned the invitations down and never with any explanation or apology. This irritated the other secretaries, who decided that she obviously considered herself better than the rest of them. And when executives invited her to join them for evenings out, she declined as well. This labelled her as a bad team player.

Basically nobody else liked her, and nobody wanted her working for them except Rebecca. Because she understood her. She was just like Sally, except that Rebecca had the experience that comes with age as well as the intelligence to cover up her bitterness, soften the edges and present a more acceptable picture of herself. She had made it her goal to teach Sally her tricks and help her out of the self-inflicted black hole which was sucking her in.

The news that a woman had been appointed had sent Rebecca and Sally scurrying to the wine bar almost daily. During a drunken lunch a few weeks earlier, Rebecca had told Sally about her affair with Ben. Fortunately Sally was loyal to Rebecca and didn't even consider using this to further her own career. Besides, Sally didn't appear to have enough interest in broader office politics to bother formulating a devious strategy.

But the consequence of this was that Sally was the only person on whom Rebecca could vent her fury at Ben's lie.

Sally was equally furious. She'd been thrilled when Rebecca had told her Ben's reasoning behind Rebecca's failure to be promoted. She'd adopted it as yet another hook on which she could hang her career standstill. If no woman could be promoted in this company, then it was through no inadequacy of her own that she was still a secretary. And while she appreciated that Rebecca's outrage had stronger justification, she was happy to take some of the umbrage for herself.

'Cow,' she'd muttered more than once to Rebecca, who would nod ominously back. They'd convinced themselves that Kate obviously had some kind of hold over someone to get this job, particularly in the light of Andrew being overlooked, and his being the MD's friend. There was only one kind of hold that they could think of.

'Do you think she knows one of the directors?' Sally asked.

Rebecca shook her head. That had been her first question and Ben had denied it. But she had another thought.

'You don't think Ben hired her because . . . ?' Rebecca asked, running a finger nervously round the rim of her glass. She didn't need to finish the sentence. She and Sally were perfectly attuned.

Sally's head whipped up. 'Of course he did!' she whispered harshly. 'I mean, think about it.' She began to count off reasons on her fingers. 'It's not as if Ben hasn't cheated on his wife before.'

Rebecca swallowed awkwardly. Sally didn't notice her embarrassment. She wasn't that sort of friend. She continued counting on to her second finger. 'There's no way that Ben would let Andrew down unless it was for a really good reason.'

Rebecca nodded in agreement.

'And thirdly,' Sally went on, 'how else could a woman have been given that kind of job in such a misogynistic company?'

Rebecca hoped she hid her surprise that Sally knew such words. She hadn't yet been able to get to the bottom of the question of Sally's intelligence so she frequently underestimated her. She tried not to patronise Sally but the girl did herself no favours when it came to self-promotion.

Rebecca considered this, then shook her head. 'No that can't be it. After all, I slept with Ben and I didn't get promoted.'

Sally screwed up her nose at the objection before coming to a new conclusion. 'That's it!'

'What's it?' Rebecca asked, hoping against the odds that Sally was going to say something to make them both feel better.

'Don't you see? That was where you went wrong! Maybe if you *hadn't* slept with him, played a bit hard to get, maybe he might have done something to win you over.'

Rebecca wasn't convinced. 'You mean, he didn't promote me because he didn't have to?'

'Exactly!' Sally replied. 'And I bet this Kate Harris is smarter than that.'

'So what you're saying is that Ben fancies her and is giving her the job in the hope that something will develop?'

'Well, it makes sense, doesn't it?'

Now if two men were having this conversation, they would be hauled before a tribunal for even suggesting that a woman would be either hired or overlooked for sexual motives. But these were two women, each desperate to find reasons for their current sense of failure that didn't involve any acknowledgement of their own shortcomings or another woman's superiority.

'I suppose so,' Rebecca agreed reluctantly, not wanting to rile Sally by arguing with her.

Over the month leading to Kate's arrival, Sally tried hard to convince her co-conspirator that it was the only possible answer. But if Rebecca was truthful, she would have to admit that she thought this hypothesis was unlikely. She didn't think Ben was that calculating. Their own affair had been very unplanned.

Rebecca hated Ben right now. When he'd broken off their affair, he'd given the standard line about feeling guilty about betraying his wife, about wanting to make the marriage work. Then he'd become very emotional, saying something like: 'I won't bore you with the old standard clichés of: "It's not you, it's me," and "I still love you but I'm not *in* love with you," or "I don't deserve you." No, you mean more to me than that. So I'm going to be honest even though it doesn't make me look very good. I think we've drawn to a close. If I know it then, deep down, you probably know it too. So before things become nasty, while it's still good between us. I'm ending this.'

Then he'd kissed her hand, looked at her lovingly and left. The apparent sincerity of the parting had fortified Rebecca through the early bad days and nights. Yet, in retrospect, it all seemed rather staged.

Although she couldn't imagine him hiring a woman

for her looks, she relished any possible explanation that gave her additional reasons to despise him. Whereas Sally's resentment was professional, Rebecca's was most definitely personal. She was a woman scorned.

They hate me, Kate thought miserably. Every one of them hates me. And she was right.

What would Justine do in my position? she wondered. No, she corrected herself. That's the wrong question. What would Ma Walton do? She began transporting herself back to Walton Mountain, breathing in that fresh air, that aroma of grits cooking on the range. She found herself smiling sweetly. What exactly are grits? Kate suddenly wondered, just in time to realise that she was in completely the wrong character.

Oh my God! Not Ma Walton! That's for blushing occasions. That's the wrong programme. I'm supposed to be in *Cagney and Lacey* now!

She immediately switched her smile off.

'Andrew. Rebecca. Let's meet in my office in thirty minutes. Sc—' She just managed to stop herself from adding 'scumbag' to her announcement. She quickly turned to face Ben, who jumped at her movement.

'My office, please?' she said shortly, immediately recoiling from her own words. Damn! she muttered to herself. Too rude, not imperious enough. Get it right! She quietly added a second 'please', this one less forceful than the first.

Ben stood for a second, uncertain how to respond to this order and confused by the twists and turns in her tone. He had never been so flustered by a woman, or for that matter by a man. Every time he made a decision on how to deal with Kate, she threw him again.

What was all that about? he thought, as he'd watched

65

Kate's face assume a lovely, face-transforming smile, only to see her consciously turn her mouth down and revert to her icy self.

Rebecca hadn't noticed. She was too busy watching Ben's body chemistry with Kate, keen to disprove Sally's theory. There was no doubt that Ben was nervous in her company; and he was not a nervous man. He didn't seem to care enough about anything to get worked up about it.

Rebecca was so wrapped up in her antipathy for Ben that she didn't stop to consider that she herself, or rather the continual threat she presented to him, might be the reason for his discomfort.

She returned her appraisal to Kate. Something burned inside her. Not quite jealousy, because she no longer wanted Ben for herself although she'd been broken when he left her. But she had to acknowledge a dimension of physical envy in her resentment. If Kate had been unattractive, or even insipid, which was how Ben had described her after her interview, then she might have been able to tolerate her presence.

But this woman was stunning. She had the job Rebecca wanted, which probably meant that she had superior workplace skills, and she had easy looks as well. Even with poorly applied make-up, it was hard to botch up that kind of face. Plus, Ben seemed to be in awe of her. He had never respected Rebecca, she knew that now. No. She simply could not bear this.

Sally was more interested in Kate's contradictory behaviour, which she'd noticed immediately. She possessed an innate expertise for spotting a fake. As they used to say when she was a kid, 'It takes one to know one.' Sally smiled inwardly at her observation.

Ben cleared his throat and ran his hands through his

hair in a gesture of stress. 'Right then. Yes. Of course. Your office. This way.' He raised his arm, careful once more not to make contact with the woman who he was beginning to suspect might be an alien life form.

Kate walked in the direction he was pointing, dodging slightly to avoid Ben's outstretched arm. As he led her towards her office, Andrew turned to Rebecca.

'What did you make of her?' he asked.

Rebecca considered her answer carefully. Everything she said had to be tempered by the fact that Ben was Andrew's brother-in-law. She had to hide her true feelings on the matter.

'I think she's a bitch. Did you hear the way she spoke to us? As if we were lackeys.'

Andrew nodded in agreement. 'I really hate it when a woman comes in and acts all macho and bullish as if she has something to prove.'

'Maybe she does have something to prove,' Sally suggested.

Andrew ignored her. 'I mean, what's wrong with being nice? Or simply polite?'

'If she asks me to make her coffee, I'll tip it over her head,' Sally snapped.

Andrew looked at her. 'But I ask you to make me coffee and you've never seemed to mind.'

Sally shrugged. 'That's different. I don't mind *you* asking.'

'Why is it different?' Andrew asked, genuinely curious.

'It just is,' Sally replied irritably.

Rebecca didn't say anything. She'd never dared ask Sally to make her coffee, but she couldn't say with any clarity why that was. The whole issue made her uncomfortable. She decided to change the subject instead.

'Well, she wanted to let us know she was the boss from day one,' she said.

'She did that all right,' Sally muttered. 'Do you fancy meeting up for lunch, Rebecca?'

'Oh Sally, sorry, I can't today. Ben's told us we've got to go out with Kate, welcome her to the company, that sort of thing.' She held her breath, waiting for Sally's martyred reaction to this unwelcome reminder of the gulf between them in the office.

'Fine. I'll have a yoghurt or something,' Sally sighed, and flounced off. She really did flounce. It was one of those actions, normally reserved for amateur dramatics performances, which suited Sally's quiet but deadly temper perfectly.

'I don't know why you spend so much time with her,' Andrew said.

'If you don't go out to lunch with Ben most days, then I would never have to,' Rebecca snapped back. She turned her back on him, sat down and began bashing the keys on her computer.

Andrew watched her for a few seconds before doing the same.

Something's wrong, he thought. Maybe I can help make it right. Not fully, of course, I'd have to change myself to become the sort of man Rebecca wants me to be. But I can move things along at work, show her I can bring about change elsewhere. It was the new proactive, risk-taking Andrew thinking this. Sadly, he was hopelessly underqualified for such an undertaking and was about to cause even more damage before the week was over.

Chapter 5

Ben opened the door to the office with a dramatic gesture. Stop making dramatic gestures! Ben screamed inwardly. 'Here's your office,' he announced feebly.

'Thank you,' Kate said in reply. She looked around. It was perfectly clear and uncluttered. There were no plants. The huge glass-topped desk was empty apart from a sleek silver phone. The filing cabinets and cupboards had nothing on top of them, no photos, no useless executive toys, no tasteless ornaments presented cruelly by colleagues in the certainty that Kate would feel obliged to place them on display.

And no coffee maker. Kate allowed herself the smallest of smiles at this observation. Ben spotted this and leaped on it eagerly.

'I'm glad you're pleased with the office. I'll leave you to settle in.' He opened the top drawer of the filing cabinet. 'Andrew has organised the documents on the Saltech presentation that's coming up. You might like to have a quick glance through before lunch. Twelve forty-five OK?'

'Of course,' Kate answered coolly.

Ben hesitated, again confused at her abrupt changes of facial expression. 'Right, I'll be off then,' he said swiftly and left, shutting the door behind him as quietly as he could.

Kate collapsed into her chair and kicked off her shoes.

She scrambled about in her handbag for some painkillers to soothe the headache that had been building up since the moment she arrived in this place. That's when she missed the coffee-maker.

Damn, she thought. What do I do now?

Kate had never asked anyone to make her coffee. She didn't know how to do it. She opened a drawer and found a company phone list, then read through the whole list to find Sally, since she didn't know her surname. Next she placed her hand on the phone and pictured herself as Robert De Niro going through his method acting warm-up exercises before becoming a homicidal Vietnam veteran.

I am a strong woman, I am a strong woman, she said to herself, dialling Sally's extension.

'Sally Guinn,' she answered crisply.

Kate wanted to slam the phone down; she wanted to bring her own coffee-maker into the office and make it for everybody like before. Now she knew exactly why she had always done it before. It was easier, safer.

But she caught sight of her reflection in the polished surface of her desk. You're different now, it said.

'Could you bring me a coffee please, Sally?' The voice, with the perfect blend of authority and courtesy, barked out before she could stop it. Then she found herself saying something else. 'If there is a rota, then of course I will be happy to take my place.'

She hadn't rehearsed that part. It came from somewhere else. But it was absolutely the right thing to say, a smart thing, because it deflected Sally from her planned malevolent response.

'Oh, er, right. Well, there isn't a rota as such, not as such.'

Kate interrupted Sally before she persuaded herself into starting a rota. 'OK then. Thank you.'

She put the phone down and wiped her hand, which was hot and sweaty from holding the receiver so tightly. She slowed her breathing down, aware that such a stressed reaction was ridiculous. I did it, she told herself, feeling as if she'd abseiled down a simmering volcano.

She pulled out the files and placed them on the desk in front of her. She instantly relaxed. This was what she was good at; she had a gift for assimilating facts and organising them in creative chains, coming up with lateral solutions to linear problems.

By the time she'd finished reading the key documents, she realised she had five minutes to spare before Andrew and Rebecca arrived at her office. She decided to ring Justine and update her on the morning.

'Hello?' It was Justine's husband, Steve, and he didn't sound very cheerful. Perhaps he is just pretending to be a miseryguts for professional reasons like me, Kate thought charitably. Perhaps deep down he is a dazzling ray of sunshine.

'Hi, Steve, it's Kate. Are you not working this morning?'

'Yes, Kate, I'm conducting open-heart surgery as we speak,' Steve answered.

Kate flinched at the sarcasm, trying and failing not to take it personally. In this instance, though, she was right to take it personally.

'I hope you're satisfied,' Steve continued.

'What are you talking about?' Kate asked, her heartbeat quickening with the rising hostility she was hearing in Steve's voice. She couldn't bear anyone being aggressive towards her and couldn't think of a single reason why Steve would be behaving like this. She'd never said 'scumbag' to him as far as she could recall.

'Justine has had her hair cut,' Steve said coldly.

Kate was even more confused. She'd remembered Justine mentioning that she was off to the hairdresser after leaving her this morning.

'I don't understand,' she said weakly.

'She's had it *cut*. All cut off. And dyed blonde!'

Kate was stunned. Justine never had anything more than a trim, every month so that it would never look too different. Kate used to tease Justine about it. 'You go on about my dress sense being caught in a time warp but look at your hair!'

Justine would always become defensive. 'That's because there's nothing wrong with my hair. It suits me like this. Everybody says so.'

'Justine, it suited you when you were fourteen. You've changed a bit since then.'

'No I haven't,' Justine would snap. 'I look exactly the same. I even get asked my age in pubs if it's a bit dark. Admit it.'

Kate had to agree that Justine had stayed looking remarkably young despite having three children and a career which involved gruelling shift work. She also suspected that Justine was unhappy with this fact although they never discussed it.

'Maybe if you changed your hair, it might make you feel different. More different,' Kate added, gently teasing.

'I don't want to feel different.' That was how the subject always ended.

But now Justine had taken the big step. And it was obvious why Steve held her responsible for this drastic action.

'It was watching you go through that ridiculous charade that made her do it.' Steve was sounding sulky now. It was a relief to Kate after the rage; it suggested that he was calming down.

Before she could defend herself, she was interrupted by a sullen Sally plonking a mug of coffee down on her desk, spilling a drop, just a drop, but it made the point.

'Thank you,' she mouthed with a half-smile that she hoped didn't appear too grateful.

'I gave you milk and no sugar, since you didn't tell me what you wanted,' Sally said accusingly.

'Sorry,' Kate answered automatically, feeling a dreaded blush start its climb.

Fortunately, Sally was in mid-flounce out the door and didn't hear. Kate went back to her call.

'I'm sorry, Steve,' Kate said miserably, reverting so comfortably to her favourite word. And she meant it. Her own makeover had made her feel very uncomfortable and she certainly wouldn't recommend such a drastic transformation on her friend without good reason.

'How does she look?' she asked tentatively.

This served to crank Steve's mood back up to rage once more. 'She looks like . . . like . . . I don't know how to describe her, like a post-apocalyptic milkmaid!'

Kate giggled and regretted it straight away. 'Sorry, Steve. I didn't mean to laugh. But it will grow out. And she can dye it back to its original colour.'

This didn't pacify Steve. 'You don't get it, do you? She likes it. She's going to keep it like that. And now she's gone shopping to buy new clothes!'

Kate took all this in. 'Look, Steve, I can't talk right now. Tell Justine that I rang and I'll see her later.'

Steve exhaled to calm himself down. 'No point, she's working tonight. I'll tell her you called and that you want to see her. I'm relying on you to get her to pull herself together, to tell her that she looks ridiculous.'

73

'I'll tell her the truth and I'll decide that for myself when I see her,' Kate replied curtly.

Steve held the receiver away from his ear, not recognising the assertive tone to Kate's voice. He wasn't to know that Kate was doing the same thing, not recognising the assertive tone in her own voice.

'Right,' he said, uncertainly. ''Bye then.'

Kate put the phone down without saying goodbye. Even more surprising was that she did it without thinking, an act which would come back to her later and bother her. It wasn't like her to be ill-mannered, not like her at all. Scary after only a few hours in character. But for now she was more concerned about Justine. Concerned and intrigued. If Steve is right, and she is reinventing herself like me, she thought, then as *what* exactly?

Ben struggled to keep the conversation going over lunch. While he was not happy with Kate's existence, he found it difficult to be rude to her. And he was beginning to find her intriguing. He was seeing bits of himself in her: the uncertainty, the vagueness, lack of purpose. She was a mess of contradictions, even more so in the restaurant.

It was most noticeable when she was distracted. When she was talking, she began collecting and piling up all the plates and cutlery. She managed to stop herself from actually carrying them out to the kitchen. The waitress was astonished, unaccustomed to such helpful customers. Another waiter spilled a couple of green beans on the table when he was serving Kate and she automatically apologised effusively. More interestingly to Ben, she didn't seem to know that she was doing it.

Andrew didn't notice any of this. He was too intent on getting the measure of her professionally so that he could formulate a plan to wreck her hopefully shortlived career with Visions in Strategy.

Rebecca was more interested in the interaction between Ben and Kate. She could see that Ben was very focused on her, but she couldn't tell what it meant.

Kate was finding it difficult to maintain her new image so she kept her own speeches as short as possible.

'So Andrew, tell me about Saltech.'

Andrew raised his eyebrows. 'Everything you need to know is in my files. Haven't you read them yet?'

Kate felt the treacherous flush creeping up her face again. Ma Walton, Ma Walton, she chanted to herself. 'I have,' she said calmly, 'but I'd like to hear your opinion on the presentation, not just the bare facts.'

Andrew conceded the point. 'We have six weeks to make this presentation. Three other consultancies will be doing the same. If we win, then we – you, Rebecca and I, that is – will be handling the business. It would be the biggest account we've ever won.'

'You don't sound very enthusiastic about it,' Kate pointed out.

Andrew couldn't resist the challenge. 'That's because I've done all the work—' Rebecca kicked him under the table. 'I mean, Rebecca and I have done all the work, and it seems unfair that you should breeze in and take all the credit. And to be perfectly honest, we felt that we didn't need anybody else on board to help us.'

Kate felt sick. It was just like being back at school when the boy sitting behind her would tie her pigtails to the chair. When she stood up, the chair would be tied to her head. Andrew resented her. But, in a rare moment of insight, she recognised that she could make this man coffee every day for the rest of his life and he would still resent her. He even resented the *idea* of her at the moment. That made it easier not to let her resolve be broken.

'I'm sorry you feel like that,' she said, keeping her voice as even as she could. 'But I believe you applied for this job and were unsuccessful. So we have to assume it was decided that I would be most likely to complete the task and get a positive result.'

Her coolness appeared stranger since she was dabbing unconsciously with her napkin at a pesto sauce stain on the waiter's elbow. 'It's OK,' the waiter was whispering to Kate, 'it doesn't matter.' Kate was ignoring his plea. 'It was my fault, let me get it off,' she said, barely drawing breath from her little speech to Andrew.

Since the waiter had acquired the stain from another table, he knew he was in the hands of one of those crazed women that waiters occasionally encounter. He had to let her get the nurturing out of her system before she would let him go. He also guessed correctly that she would say she was sorry another two or three times before the meal was over.

Rebecca observed this interaction curiously. Kate appeared to have metamorphosed into a Dickensian serving wench, submissive and humble. Bizarre, Rebecca thought. The woman's not as cool as she likes to appear.

Andrew didn't notice anything. He was seething at Kate's put-down. He wisely kept quiet, partly because he didn't want to lay all his cards on the table and partly because he hadn't dealt them out yet. Andrew had never dealt the cards before. He'd always played with the cards given to him. It was a new role for him and, although he wasn't wearing pink shoes, he was just as uncomfortable in his new role as Kate.

Kate abruptly stopped tending the waiter's stain and

76

glared at him. Yep, he thought, absolutely crazy, completely irrational, I'm going to make some other sucker take over this table. They're welcome to the tip. He left, shaking his head.

There was an awkward lull which no one was willing to fill. Ben rose to the challenge. 'So tell us a bit about yourself, Kate? Are you married?'

Rebecca let out a guttural sound that she thought was rather expressive. The others looked at her curiously. She rubbed her nose with the napkin, trying to put the blame on an itchy nose. Kate felt that she was on more solid ground here. 'I'm not married, no. I don't let anything distract me from my career and I don't plan to. But I've got five brothers.'

The unconnected extra fact slipped out. She had drifted back to secondary school when the possession of five brothers was something to boast about. It took her a long time to find out that five brothers were only socially useful if they were older than you, not younger.

She was saying things for the sake of filling a conversational gap. She had always performed that function at parties, always been the perfect guest, even if it meant looking and sounding foolish. But this wasn't a party, and she was no longer that old compliant Kate.

She continued briskly. 'That tells you all you need to know about me. Let's get back to Saltech, shall we?'

'Don't you want to know about us?' Rebecca asked, in mock innocence.

Kate cringed inside. This was hopeless. She'd embarked upon a dramatic part without learning any lines. She hadn't a clue how to keep this facade up consistently. She vowed that she would get through the rest of the day as best she could then spend the whole evening rehearsing her performance.

'Of course I do. I just thought you might prefer to keep things professional until we all get to know each other a little better.'

'But how can we do this if we don't open up a bit? After all, you've told us about your five brothers and no husband.'

Kate examined Rebecca's face carefully but could see no malicious intent there. That was because Kate was lacking the necessary apparatus to find it.

Rebecca continued when no objections were raised. 'We should really start with Ben, since he's the boss. So come on, Ben, open up.'

Ben fired off a quick warning glance at Rebecca before the others looked to him.

'Not much to tell, really. I'm married—'

'Happily married, would you say?' Rebecca interrupted sweetly.

'Of course he is!' Andrew exclaimed. Kate jumped at this unexpected defence. 'Sorry!' Andrew said, softening his tone. 'It's just that Ben is married to my sister, Jenny. As Rebecca well knows,' he added, glaring at Rebecca. Ben looked down and said nothing.

Kate was starting to enjoy herself. Fantastic, she thought, tension that has nothing to do with me. I'll just sit back and let them take pot shots at each other.

'What about you, Andrew?' she asked. 'Apart from having a sister married to Ben, that is.'

'Well, I'm not married but, that is, well, it's no big secret, but . . .'

Rebecca gave up waiting for him to reach the point in this interminable sentence.

'What he's trying to say is that he and I live together.'

Kate was startled by this. For the first time, she saw her problems extended way beyond her personal image. She was an outsider who had been tossed into the middle of a tightly interwoven triangle. They all had personal as well as professional connections with deep roots. She was supposed to make a team of them. Although Ben would not be playing a particularly active part in the presentation, his position as MD meant that he would be involved at every stage and would be present on the day itself.

Ironically, it would have been simple for her to fit into the group if she'd been herself. They would have found her presence unthreatening and would probably have accepted her more quickly. That's what she thought.

But Kate couldn't know that they wouldn't have accepted her if she'd offered to handwash their clothes and bake them cakes every day. Andrew and Rebecca both wanted her job. Ben wanted Andrew and Rebecca to be happy. Kate, any Kate, wasn't wanted.

'We're going to have to build a team if we're to succeed,' she said firmly.

'We already are a team,' Andrew replied.

Kate faced him down. 'You *were* a team. Now you're a new team. And I'm the head of that team.'

Ben could see that both Rebecca and Andrew were thinking of saying something inflammatory. He intervened hastily.

'So why don't we all raise our glasses to the new team. And to Kate. To Kate!'

Andrew and Rebecca raised their glasses with forced smiles. 'To Kate.'

But Kate wasn't listening. She had seen something, or rather someone, out of the window.

'Would you excuse me a moment?' she asked, disappearing into the street before anyone could answer.

*

'Where's she off to in such a hurry?' Andrew asked, as Kate rushed outside.

'No idea,' Ben said. 'But it's a welcome break. You know, you two aren't making this situation any easier.'

'Why should we?' Rebecca asked. 'Andrew should have got that job and you know it.'

'I've explained to Andrew—' Ben began.

Rebecca didn't allow him to finish. 'Yes, yes, yes. And you've left it up to Andrew, and therefore to me, to sort this out.'

Ben leaned forward. 'The presentation is in six weeks. In four weeks, I have to meet the board and report on the status of the job. Now if, and that's a big if, Kate has not pulled this almost together by then, I will be in a strong position to recommend that her contract be terminated and Andrew take the project to completion. The four-week clause is in her contract,' he added.

Rebecca cheered up at this. 'That's not so bad then.'

'I'm not so sure,' Andrew said. 'I mean, we *do* want to win this account. Isn't it risky to mess about playing political games rather than concentrating on winning the business?'

Rebecca tutted. 'Oh Andrew, listen to yourself. You said it, we didn't need anyone else. We still don't. We can do this without her. So let's get rid of her.'

Andrew was still concerned. 'I still don't know. She seems pretty assured. And she's incredibly focused. We can't actually sabotage the work because that will reflect badly on us.'

Rebecca smiled. 'What we have to do is shift her focus so that she starts making mistakes.'

'How do we do that?' Andrew asked.

'You heard what she said. She's not married because she's too committed to her work.'

'And so?' Andrew said, still not sure where Rebecca was leading.

Rebecca sighed. 'And so, we find someone to distract her. A new boyfriend who'll take her out for lots of late nights, call her all through the day, turn up at the office unannounced and whisk her out for long lunches, that sort of thing.' She looked at Ben and Andrew.

'Don't look at me!' Andrew said in alarm. 'And don't look at Ben either, he's a married man!'

Yeah, right, Rebecca thought. She could comment on that. But that was not important now. 'I'm not thinking of you two, you idiots, but you must know someone between you.'

Ben looked dubious. 'We don't even know what sort of men she goes for.' He slapped himself on the head. 'What am I saying? This is madness!'

'Do you have any better ideas?' Rebecca asked. 'Or any ideas at all? Either of you?'

The two men shook their heads in shame.

'Right,' Rebecca said crisply. 'Now you're quite right that we don't know what sort of man she might like so you'll have to throw a party and invite all the men you know and we'll see which one she goes for.'

'What am I supposed to tell Jenny?' Ben asked. 'She'll hate this. She hates subterfuge and lies and manipulating people.'

'He's right,' Andrew agreed glumly. 'She's horribly straight.'

'Then you'd better work on her. And quickly. We need to do this by the weekend.'

Ben looked out into space. 'This is the worst idea I've ever heard.'

Rebecca lifted her glass. 'It's all we've got in the time given, so let's just go for it, shall we? To Kate?'

Ben and Andrew raised their glasses. 'To Kate,' they repeated, without much enthusiasm.

'Where the hell has she gone?' Ben asked, looking around.

Kate ran down the street, reluctant to shout out her friend's name, unable to accept that it could possibly be her. Finally she caught up and overtook the woman who she'd seen striding along outside the restaurant. She spun round to face her.

'My God, Justine. It's you! It is you, isn't it?'

Kate drank in every inch of Justine's being, frantically searching for anything familiar to reassure her that this person was her oldest friend. But on the surface, there was nothing. Justine had gone beyond the concept of makeover, as if she'd been taken apart and all the raw material tweaked and altered until it could no longer be put back together in the same way.

'What have you done?' Kate asked, barely able to breathe with the shock.

Justine touched her head. 'Hardly anything. Just a cut and colour. You were right. I do feel different with a new haircut. More grown-up. It's great, I should have done it years ago!'

'But, Justine, it's not just a haircut, is it?' And it wasn't. The 1970s wispy feather cut had been shorn into a ferociously blonde asymmetric bob, with bits sticking out at the top and sides which probably had a technical name but looked like bits sticking out.

'Don't you like it? Justine asked anxiously. 'Do you think it makes me look like mutton dressed as lamb?'

Kate was taken aback by the questions. It hadn't occurred to her to wonder whether she liked it or not. All she could take in was the incongruity of this high-fashion hairstyle on her friend's head. She stood back and looked at Justine appraisingly.

'Well, actually, I can't believe I'm saying it, but it looks terrific. *You* look terrific. You really do. Just . . . different.'

Justine hugged Kate. 'That's because I *am* different. You inspired me this weekend. Watching you reinvent yourself like that. And, in many ways, you and I are alike. Neither of us likes change, even though we nag each other about it all the time. But you changed yourself and it gave me the confidence to do the same.'

Kate pulled away gently. 'But there's a difference, Jus. I didn't change, not properly, I just bought a costume and some props and pretended. The way I look now, well that's the same as you putting on your nurse's uniform to go to work. This is my new uniform. Both of us knew that it was just an act. Deep down, I'm the same as I always was. Outside the office I'm the same as I was. I'm happy the way I've always been.'

Justine shrugged. 'That's your choice. But I'm not happy the way I am. The way I *was*,' she corrected herself.'

That's when Kate noticed the new clothes. Justine had always been a jeans girl. She always said that she dressed like a boy because she had a boy's body, and because Steve liked her that way.

'Your legs!' Kate shrieked.

Justine looked down in alarm. 'What about them?'

'You've got legs!' Kate exclaimed.

'Ha, ha, very funny,' Justine replied.

'Do you realise that, in the twenty years we've been friends, the only time I've seen you in a skirt or a dress is at school. And when you got married.'

'And my uniform, don't forget,' Justine added.

'But that doesn't count because you always wear those horrible thick tights with it.'

'Huh! This is the cardigan queen talking!' Justine exclaimed.

They smiled companionably. At the same time, they caught sight of the two of them in a shop window. 'Wow, look at us! Hot babes or what?' Justine asked.

They both burst out laughing, seeing themselves as the least likely hot babes they knew. But then they stopped. Each was uncertain of where to go from here.

'What are you doing here, Kate?' Justine asked.

'Oh no! I was so shocked to see you, I just ran out of the restaurant! Still, it was nice to be able to escape.'

'Not going too well, then?' Justine asked.

Kate grimaced. 'Couldn't be worse. None of them wanted me there in the first place. And now that I've exposed them to the debut of my Queen Bitch act, they don't like me either. Unwanted and unliked. Fabulous.'

Justine stroked Kate's shoulder. 'Stick with it. You've got nothing to lose, remember that. Think of how badly you've been treated at all the other places you've worked, how you've been walked over. Give this a try. It might be harder at the start but once they've accepted you as you are, they might form a grudging respect for you. You're still great at your job, that's why they hired you. Don't ever forget that.'

'Thanks, Justine.'

They kissed each goodbye affectionately and Kate turned back towards the restaurant. As she paced along, psyching herself up for the next scene in her performance, she thought about Justine and how she had taken her transformation one step further than Kate.

The phone conversation with Steve popped into her mind. 'No wonder he was so rattled,' Kate thought in

84

amusement. Steve regarded his marriage to Justine as a carefully balanced see-saw. It worked because each had established their place on their end of the plank. There was no space for shift or compromise; each had to hold on to all the things they had brought into the marriage. They could neither add to them nor let anything go.

Steve was supposed to stay a doctor even though he longed to open an antiques shop and Justine was supposed to stay a midwife even though she longed to be a writer. She was supposed to look after the kitchen and kids and he was supposed to look after the car and the finances. She was supposed to be grateful to him for marrying her and he was supposed to be faithful to her. He was not supposed to shave off his beard and she was not supposed to cut her hair.

Their three children teetered in the middle, holding the contraption steady, happily unaware that the see-saw would crash down the minute they stepped off.

No one could have guessed that Justine might get off the see-saw first. Kate shivered when she thought of the implications.

She walked back into the restaurant and was surprised by the three phoney smiles that greeted her. Surprised and very suspicious.

'Sorry about that,' she said. 'I just saw somebody that I . . . hadn't seen for a long time.'

Rebecca waved her hand dismissively. 'That's OK. Actually, while you were out, we had a think about what you were saying earlier.'

Kate looked worried. 'What was I saying earlier?' she asked cautiously.

'About how we should get to know each other and bond as a team.'

Kate was certain that she hadn't exactly said that. But Rebecca didn't give her the chance to object. 'So Ben decided it would be a good idea for us all to get together socially.'

They all looked at Ben, who hadn't been aware that he was to be set up as the fall guy. He smiled maniacally as they waited for him to expand on his 'good idea'.

'Yes, well, er, Jenny, my wife, and I were planning a party on Friday and we thought it would be nice if you could come along. Andrew and Rebecca are going to be there, obviously.'

Obviously, Kate thought ominously. What a joy this sounds. A whole room full of people who will neither want nor like me because they are all friends and family of people who neither want nor like me. Think of an excuse. Think! Think!

She didn't think quickly enough.

'That's great then!' Rebecca said cheerfully. She had plans for Friday. She would deliver an ultimatum to Ben. With his wife nearby, he would not be able to refuse.

'Great,' echoed Andrew sincerely, relieved that the responsibility had been handed over to Ben.

'Great,' Ben said with as much eagerness as he could muster, which was not a great deal.

Kate choked on the word. So she just nodded and smiled a tight, enigmatic smile.

'No,' Jenny said, dicing onions expertly. 'I'm not up to it. You know how tired I've been these last few weeks.'

'But you wouldn't have to do anything, sweetheart,' Ben said. 'We'd get caterers and bar staff and cleaners to clear everything up afterwards.'

'But, Ben, why does it have to be at such short notice?

86

I mean, Friday! We don't even know if anyone will be able to come.'

'Well actually, Andrew and I made a few calls, just to see who was around, that's all, and we could get quite a good crowd together.'

'But you don't normally entertain new members of staff here. Not like this. And I don't see why I should have to entertain her at all. You know how I feel about Andrew being passed over like that. After you practically promised him the job was his.'

Ben removed the knife from his wife's hand and tenderly turned her to face him.

'It's for Andrew that I'm doing this, Jenny. It's really important that he gets on with Kate Harris. There is no guarantee that Kate will be staying, as I explained to you, in which case Andrew could still get the promotion. Provided he keeps his head down.'

'He's still fuming, isn't he?' Jenny said.

Ben nodded. 'We just need to get him relaxed about Kate, accepting the situation for the time being, until we get the opportunity to make some changes.'

'I suppose if it's for Andrew . . .'

Ben hugged Jenny. 'I knew you'd understand.'

Jenny brightened up. 'There is one other good thing to come out of this.'

'What's that?' Ben asked.

'I'll finally get to meet Rebecca. I can't believe Andrew is living with someone and I haven't even met her yet!'

Ben closed his mouth tightly. 'I'm not sure how well that's all going. It might be sensible to give them a bit of a wide berth.'

Jenny picked up a wooden spoon and hit Ben playfully on the arm with it.

'Don't be so silly! This is the first serious girlfriend Andrew has had for, well, I don't know how long. Even if it doesn't last, I'd still like to get to know the girl. Besides, she works for you. I've met most of the people you work with. Just not Rebecca. Now, leave me alone with my onions!'

She kissed him affectionately and turned back to her task.

Ben was grateful that she didn't see the expression on his face. The panic. The dread. He had been so fraught with the stress of organising this party, an idea he thought was patently stupid, so anxious about how he would persuade Jenny to go along with it, that he'd completely forgotten Rebecca.

Ben had managed to keep Rebecca and Jenny apart so far. He'd hoped that the relationship with Andrew would fizzle out before a meeting became inevitable. Andrew's relationships tended to run a fairly predictable course. It had been looking promising recently. Rebecca had been getting snappy with Andrew, who had been taking the early steps on his habitual self-destructive path.

But there was no escaping Friday's confrontation. In other circumstances, this wouldn't be too much of a problem. Rebecca knew of Jenny's existence and, besides, the affair was over.

But there was one thing that Rebecca did not know, something she would discover as soon as she met Jenny.

During Ben and Rebecca's affair, he had spun the standard line about his marriage being a sham. He had maintained this line throughout the relationship, which he ended five months ago.

But Rebecca would immediately learn that Ben's wife

was pregnant, more than eight months pregnant. And if Rebecca was angry with Ben before Friday, then she might well spontaneously combust when she saw Jenny's enormous bump.

Chapter 6

Kate was slouched across her sofa when the doorbell rang. She groaned to herself and considered ignoring the caller. It couldn't be Justine; she was working, and nobody else she knew would make an unannounced visit. She'd made it clear to people over the years that she wasn't a fan of surprises, whether they were parties, visits or announcements.

She liked to be ready for all events. If she was expecting a visitor, she liked to tidy up, have the kettle boiling, wine in the fridge, snacks and cakes in the cupboard, all eventualities prepared for. She liked to have clean hair, clean clothes, a happy smile. She liked her house to be a haven of hospitality, just like her parents.

And with her face scrubbed clean, her shampooed hair in a towelling turban and wearing her favourite Tom and Jerry pyjamas, she was free to be herself again. She was her parents' daughter once more.

Whoever was ringing the bell was persistent. Kate reluctantly dragged herself up from the cushions and answered the door.

'Sweetie pie!'

'Pumpkin pie!'

'Mum. Dad. What's happened? Is it one of the boys?'

'Aren't you going to invite us in, Katie?'

'Sorry. Of course. Come in.'

Her parents kissed and hugged her fondly as they went into the house.

90

'Mum, you never come round without phoning first. Just tell me if something's wrong.'

'Don't be such a worry wart,' her mum said. 'Why should anything be wrong?'

'Just tell her, Edie,' her dad said irritably.

'Tell me what? Now I'm *really* worried.'

'It's nothing. Hardly anything. Your father and I are thinking of emigrating to New Zealand.'

If they'd announced that they'd been arrested for drug dealing in Marrakesh, Kate couldn't have been more stunned.

'I don't understand,' she said. 'Where does this come from? You've never even mentioned this before. And why New Zealand? It doesn't make any sense. Are either of you ill? Is there something you're not telling me?'

Her hair had come loose from its turban.

'Have you had all your beautiful hair cut off, darling?' her mum asked with some concern.

'Yes, but that doesn't matter now. Talk to me, both of you!'

Her dad coughed loudly. Kate spotted a look flash between her parents; it wasn't one she recognised.

'It's like this, honey,' he said, 'I've been offered a job out there.'

Kate sat down. 'What sort of job? You're supposed to be retiring in a couple of years' time.' After his business had gone bust, Kate's dad had taken on a clerical job in a small accountancy firm. Kate had always believed he died a little that first day and a little more every day since.

Edie decided to answer on her husband's behalf. 'We're going to sell the house here, use the money to renovate a little house just outside Wellington and put on shows. You found it on the internet, didn't you, Stan?'

Kate rested her head in her hands. 'Put on shows? What on earth are you talking about?'

Stan tutted tolerantly. 'What do you think we're talking about? Haven't we always said that we'd love to stage our own plays and musicals?'

Kate looked up in exasperation. 'No, Dad, you've always said how much you love all your amateur dramatics productions. You've never mentioned emigrating to the other side of the world so that you can become some kind of impresario!'

Her father shrugged. 'Why is it such a strange thing to do? I have financial experience and I have stage experience.'

Kate gasped. 'I can't believe you don't see the madness of the scheme. And can I ask how long have you been planning this?'

'A few years now,' Edie replied.

'About ten years,' Stan said at the same time. Then he corrected himself. 'I suppose the honest answer is that we've always been planning it. And now that Frankie is settled . . . well, we always said that we'd stay until none of you needed us any more.'

Kate should have said it then. That she still needed them, even though she was the eldest and the most successful. She still needed her mum and dad. But she let the moment pass.

'Oh, Mum,' she said instead, swallowing the lump that was rising in her throat. Now she was grateful of a lifetime's experience of suppressing her emotions. 'I'm really happy for you. For you both. Especially for you, Dad.'

She realised that this was his big dream, and assumed that it was her mum's too because she didn't say otherwise.

She squeezed her dad tightly, then her mum. But although her mum squeezed her tightly in return, Kate felt that she was holding back. She didn't have the chance to question this because Edie had pulled away and was examining her clothes, which were still piled up by the door where she'd stripped off the second she came through the door.

'Katie, are these all new?'

'Oh, er, yes, Mum. I thought it was a good idea to get some new stuff for the new job.'

Edie looked at her daughter shrewdly, then at the clothes more closely. 'But these are not your sort of thing at all. They're . . . different. Very different.' Now it was her turn to be worried. 'Is everything all right? With this job, I mean.'

'Of course it is, Mum,' Kate said reassuringly. 'I just decided it was time for a new image.'

'You mean Justine decided it was time for a new image. She's been on at you for years to change. I'm amazed that you've never realised that she just wants you to do what she's too scared to do herself.'

Kate was struck by her mother's perception in recognising something in Justine that Kate had only spotted today.

'Is that why you've never liked her, Mum, because she's always trying to change me?'

'No, it's because I worry that you'll end up like her, marrying a man purely because he asks you, working all hours, juggling a career with children, settling for whatever's handed to you, never reaching out for something better. You can do better. You *must* do better. Don't ever let her convince you that her life is as good as it gets. Because it's not.'

Kate smiled. 'Mum, you brought us all up marvellously. I wouldn't dream of marrying a man who didn't bear at least a passing resemblance to Cary Grant.'

'Just remember, Katie—'

'I know, Mum,' Kate interrupted gently, 'if I don't hear an orchestra playing, then it's not real.'

'I don't mean literally, of course, I'm not that batty,' Edie said. 'But, if it's real, then you should believe in the possibility of magic. That's all I'm saying. So. Tell me about this change of image that has nothing to do with Justine.'

Kate explained her plan to her parents as simply as she could, leaving out the bit about the doormat which she knew would upset them in its cruelty. 'You think it's crazy, don't you?' she said when she'd finished.

'It doesn't sound very nice,' Edie said doubtfully. 'And you're a nice girl, I don't know if you can be anything else. Besides, being nice is nothing to be ashamed of!'

'Dad?' Kate asked hopefully.

'It sounds a bit complicated,' Stan said. 'Wouldn't it be easier just to be yourself?'

Kate shook her head. 'If you knew what these people were like, you wouldn't say that. They are really mean. None of them want me there and I have a horrible feeling that they're going to try and drive me out.'

'Can they do that?' Edie asked.

'Oh yes,' Kate said, explaining the four-week clause in her contract. 'If they knew what I was really like, they would go straight in for the kill. My only hope is to fend them off for four weeks then, once they know they're stuck with me, with luck they should settle down and accept me. I have to stay on top the whole time, I must never lower my guard. That's why Justine and I went for the full effect, hair, clothes, make-up, the lot. It's got to be the performance of my life.'

Her parents looked at her in astonishment. 'Can you believe her, Stan?'

'I can't, Edie. I really can't.'

'*Now* what you are going on about?' Kate asked, exasperated.

Her mum spoke clearly and slowly as if addressing a foreigner or an idiot.

'Here you are, embarking on a dramatic performance, choosing costumes with a midwife, of all things, when on your own doorstep you have two people with a century of experience of cinema and theatre between them. There isn't a single situation that we won't have seen played out a hundred ways by the truly great performers of our generation.'

Kate lifted a finger to interrupt. 'But, Mum, I can't start spouting Lauren Bacall lines in twenty-first century Kensington. I'd sound like a fraud straightaway.'

Stan tutted and sighed. 'Give us a bit of credit, love. We're not suggesting you learn lines, just that you learn some attitudes, some poses, some mannerisms to get you into character. Then your own lines should come more easily. You'll be much more consistent in sustaining the role.'

Kate thought back to some of her more extravagant lapses from character today. She knew that she had only got away with her occasionally bizarre behaviour because this was her first day and her colleagues didn't yet have a handle on her. But she would have to be more careful from now on.

Her parents were right. Insane but right. She needed their help.

'So can we start tonight?' she asked.

'What on earth are you doing?' Rebecca asked Andrew as he struck ludicrous poses in front of the living-room mirror.

'I'm practising how I'm going to handle her tomorrow,' he said, not needing to say who the 'her' was. 'I don't know what games she was playing with us today, but she kept us on our toes. It's hard to deal with someone who's so unpredictable. So I want to have some moves and countermoves ready.'

Rebecca smiled at his solemn eyes and determined mouth as he went through some training warm-ups worthy of Sylvester Stallone in *Rocky*.

He continued to experiment with postures and stances. Aware that Rebecca was watching him, he moved on to exaggerated Charles Atlas positions, even attempting to raise and lower the individual muscles across his shoulders in time to the Genesis CD that was playing.

Rebecca began to laugh. 'I love you when you're like this, Andrew.'

Andrew twisted round in surprise. 'Did you say you loved me?'

Rebecca held up her hands in innocence. 'I said I loved you when you're like this. When you're being . . . I don't know, stupid, mad, foolish. I've never seen you let yourself go before.'

Andrew turned away, taken aback by this declaration. He knew she hadn't meant it; he wasn't a fool, he could tell that she was drifting away from him. But it unmasked a big hole in his life.

None of his girlfriends had ever said 'I love you' to him.

Girls had told Andrew they'd loved him but it had always been in forced response to a direct question, or as a polite riposte when he said he loved them. And since he never truly meant it himself, he couldn't take their own words at face value.

Andrew had defined love for himself when he was

fourteen. If it worked and it lasted for both of you then it was love. That was it. He hadn't put a time limit on the 'lasting' part but, since he'd never had a relationship that had lasted more than six months, he was confident that he hadn't missed out on his one big chance in this lifetime.

Rebecca was the first woman to say 'I love you' to him first. And even if it was a jokey reaction to his daft behaviour, he was still struck by the significance of this. He badly wanted the words to be true, not necessarily from Rebecca, but he wanted someone to love him. Now or soon.

But to let someone love him seemed a risky venture. He'd have to change, he was certain about that. And he'd have to open himself up to the possibility of real pain. He didn't know if he had it in him to take that sort of chance.

Rebecca was looking at him strangely. 'Are you OK?' she asked him.

He nodded, then realised that he was holding his breath. But he couldn't hold his abdominal muscles in any longer. As soon as Rebecca left the room, he let them out in relief. He laughed to himself. Finally he understood about the mascara.

Steve watched Justine get undressed. It was four am and she'd tried not to wake him as she came in from her night shift. But he'd only been sleeping lightly, unnerved by Justine's actions today. He pretended to be asleep, hoping to enjoy the subversive pleasure of watching someone who doesn't know they're being observed.

But there was no pleasure, just a creeping unease that his life was unravelling and he was scrambling around, trying to pull the long, twisted yarn back into its tightly wound coil.

Justine sat at her dressing table, examining her hair in the mirror. It was dark, which made it difficult for Steve to make out the details of her face, but he was convinced he saw the onset of a smile.

Justine was indeed smiling but not from any satisfaction. She was trying out her expressions with her new hair. She'd never looked at her face properly before. There hadn't been the need; she knew what she looked like, the same as she'd always looked. She'd put on the same make-up every day throughout her adult life: the same single coat of cheap brown mascara, just enough to stop her eyes from disappearing; the same pale blue eyeshadow that zipped in and out of fashion over the years; the same coral pink lipstick favoured by Jackie Kennedy, Princess Diana and assorted newsreaders and minor celebrities in between.

But the transformation of her hair encouraged her to inspect the raw material of her face as if it were a scientific exhibit. And while the features were much as she remembered them, it was her expressions that fascinated her.

She'd been surprised to discover that her thirty-six years of experience had endowed her with such a limited selection. She had a few smiles that ranged from mild amusement to quiet joy via a moderately happy grin, together with some angry and sulky frowns where her mouth contorted into jagged red slashes. They made her laugh.

But when she let her face relax, allowed it to go its own way, it settled into a slightly droopy statement of vague discontent. And as she watched her face move about in response to her own appraisal, she counted an alarming number of frowns: of disappointment, of frustration, of despair, of exhaustion, of regret, of sadness, of anger, of bitterness, of futility . . . and then she lost count.

She tried out some new smiles, since she certainly didn't need any more frowns. She tried one that appeared hopeful, one that was teasing, one that was carefree and one that was just overflowing with the awareness of potential, of promise, of purpose. She liked that one a lot. Yes, she thought, I'll make that one my own.

After a few more rehearsals, Justine could produce the smile on command. Satisfied with her day, she removed her make-up. She eased herself quietly and carefully into bed, anxious that she didn't disturb Steve. Then she fell straight asleep, with the slight remnants of her new smile still staining her face. Steve watched her for a long, long time until he too fell into a disturbed sleep.

'Are you OK? It's not the baby, is it?'

Ben jumped out of bed and rushed over to the window where Jenny was standing rubbing her stomach.

'Go back to bed,' she said tenderly. 'I'm fine. What's the time, anyway?'

Ben looked at the digital clock shining in the darkness. 'Four thirty-five,' he said, whispering, even though they were the only ones in the house. He put his arms round her, resting his hands on her bump.

'Wow!' he exclaimed as his hand was kicked three times. 'No wonder you're awake. And no wonder you're so tired every day if this is going on every night.'

'That's OK,' Jenny said. 'Only a few more weeks to go.'

Ben laughed. 'You're kidding! That's when it really begins. The night feeds, the teething, the crying.'

'If this is your way of cheering me up, then it's not working!' Jenny laughed.

'Shall I rub your back?' he offered. 'I need some practice for the labour.'

Jenny turned on him with a devilish smile. 'Trust me on something, if you try and rub my back when I'm in labour, I will divorce you. I want drugs, remember, DRUGS!'

Ben held on to Jenny tightly. 'This is what I've always wanted,' he said quietly. 'A proper family. Nothing else matters. Everything starts with this and revolves around it.'

Jenny knew how desperately her husband longed to be provided with some kind of solid security on which he could begin to build, to make plans. His parents had divorced when he was twelve and he'd never seen his father again. It had left him with a sense of in-completion, a feeling that he couldn't move forward until he'd gone back and repaired his past. Since that was looking unlikely, his next best option was to lay down new foundations.

Up until now, he'd been merely treading water, flailing about, snatching at any incidental success and fleeting happiness that was on offer. But it was all changing and he had every intention of changing to fit his new circumstances. These were circumstances of which Jenny was completely ignorant.

Firstly he had to deal with anything that might threaten his future, which was why it was absolutely vital that he sort out this work situation so that Rebecca was appeased and wouldn't cause any trouble with Jenny.

Rebecca. What a terrible mistake that was. He couldn't even remember why he'd got involved with her in the first place. It was another of his characteristically unplanned, spontaneous forays, like walking past this house when it wasn't even for sale, knocking on the door and making the owners an offer. Most of his off-the-cuff decisions led to fortuitous endings.

But not Rebecca. She was his first infidelity. Maybe that's why he did it. Because he never had before. Because he could, and there was no immediate reason not to.

But her continued existence in his circle posed a permanent threat to his marriage. At that point it struck him that there was only one solution to the problem of Rebecca. She had to go. That meant she needed to leave her job and leave Andrew. And he had to achieve these two objectives without her suspecting that he played any part in it. It was vital that they part on good terms. It would be tricky, but surely not impossible.

Nothing else mattered. He was going to have to plan this, which, since he was not a man who made plans, involved a conscious transformation. But he would do it. He had to. As of tomorrow, he was going to have to get tough and devious. Even though he was the least tough and devious person he knew.

Kate slept well once she'd finally gone to bed. Her parents had agreed to stay the night when they saw how late it had become. Also, they'd opened a bottle of wine and neither her mum nor her dad was fit to drive.

It was the first time they'd stayed in the same house for many years. When parents and children live reasonably close to each other, stopovers become redundant.

So Edie and Stan couldn't resist tiptoeing into their daughter's bedroom to watch her sleeping. They stood in the doorway for what seemed ages but was actually a couple of minutes.

Kate looked like a child again as she cuddled her pillow with one leg sprawled on top of the duvet.

'Are you thinking what I'm thinking, Stan?' Edie asked.

Stan nodded. 'She still needs you,' he said sadly.

'Us,' Edie corrected him gently. 'She needs us.' Stan didn't answer.

Chapter 7

'So where are we on Saltech?' Ben didn't knock before marching into Kate's office.

Kate was taken aback by his entrance, but she'd had a good night's sleep and she'd readied herself for confrontation today.

'I've read all the documentation and have begun making notes but, don't forget, I've only had one day.'

'And one night,' Ben added pointedly.

'And one night,' Kate agreed calmly, grateful to her parents for teaching her how to appear inscrutable, even while her insides were churning up under this deliberate assault.

'Think Grace Kelly,' her mum had advised. 'You are the Ice Queen, your face painted over immaculately so that no one can see when your expression changes.'

I am the Ice Queen, I am the Ice Queen, she repeated to herself, trying to shove out of her mind the previous image of herself as Farrah Fawcett in an elegant crouch pointing a shiny gun at a handsome villain. It was essential that she keep her images separate to avoid cross-contamination. Grace Kelly would never say 'scumbag', for example.

'However,' she went on with glacial calm, 'I reached a point where I didn't want to work in isolation from Andrew and Rebecca. And you, of course. I believe you emphasised the importance of us working as a team on this. So unless the team is moving into my house, then

103

there will inevitably be occasional hours of my waking life when I will not have any useful purpose to the company. If that's OK with you.'

Then she smiled her most appealing smile. 'It's one of the most valuable weapons you have, my love,' her mum had said. 'Use it to follow up your don't-mess-with-me speeches. It will completely disarm them. They'll reel around, punch-drunk from your sudden change of direction.'

And it worked just as her mum said it would.

Ben didn't know how to react. He'd been seething at her obviously pre-written little speech about working as a team, and was already mentally writing his own cutting counter-speech. But then she smiled and all at once, his resolve drained away. To say something cutting to her when she smiled like this would be like tripping Bambi up on the ice.

He didn't even need to be this offensive. He wasn't interested in ruining Kate's career any more. He still hoped she'd leave and make way for Andrew but that was a lower priority. He had changed tack and was now going to concentrate his machinations against Rebecca. However, he was getting into character as a tough and devious man and Kate seemed a good choice of person on whom to try his tough act. She didn't know him that well and wouldn't spot any inconsistencies.

He was right. Kate didn't see anything out of the ordinary in his performance. But that was because she was using all her faculties of discernment on her own. Ben could have walked into her office dressed like Father Christmas and she would simply have interpreted this as an opportunity for her to try out her elf character.

Oh yes, Kate thought. I'm going to be unstoppable.

Oh yes, Ben thought. You're good, very good, but I

need to win more than you do. My stakes are higher.' He left her office, preparing to go and polish up his new image before he tried it out on his other colleagues. Before he closed the door, he turned back to face Kate.

'You're still OK for Friday, aren't you? My wife is looking forward to meeting you.'

Kate looked surprised. She couldn't imagine why these people would want to socialise with her when they all disliked her. She suspected that they were playing some kind of game which she didn't, couldn't, understand. Is that what corporate life is like for all bitches? she asked herself. If it is, then it's back to Julie Andrews for me in my next job.

'Er, yes. I'm looking forward to it too,' she said with impressive sincerity.

'Good,' Ben said and walked out, or rather strutted, like John Wayne in *True Grit*.

If only they'd both come clean about their role-playing, they could have had shared rehearsals in the boardroom at lunchtime and not wasted so much valuable plotting time.

Ben bumped into Andrew as he left.

'Sorry,' Andrew said as he stepped neatly out of the way.

Ben beckoned Andrew into the corridor. 'Forget it. Listen, I've been thinking about Friday. Is it really plausible that Kate is going to meet some guy and then melt into a quivering lovestruck jelly the next day?'

Andrew shrugged. 'It's like Rebecca said. Have either of us got a better idea?'

Ben nodded. 'I just think we shouldn't leave it to chance.'

'What do you mean by that?' Andrew asked.

Ben hoped he was looking impassive, because he'd spent all night formulating this plan but he wanted it to sound like a casual suggestion.

'I was thinking, even if she did like one of the men we introduce her to, they might not move things along as quickly as we would like. I mean, after Friday, there's just three weeks to go before the board evaluate her progress.'

'So what are you suggesting?'

Ben took a handkerchief out of his pocket and pretended to blow his nose, then swept the hanky across his forehead to mop up the sweat that was threatening to pour. He was surprised at the physiological effects of deception. He couldn't recall this happening while he was lying to Jenny about Rebecca.

Perhaps that was because, in that instance, he hadn't planned the deception. It just happened, he reasoned with himself. So it wasn't my fault, he deduced cheerfully. That's all right then.

In this case, however, he was master of his destiny and everyone else's destiny as well: Rebecca's, Kate's and Andrew's. And ultimately Jenny's. Their baby's too, he added reluctantly, not even wanting to consider the possibility that Jenny might deprive him of their child if she found out about his affair.

'Are you feeling OK?' Andrew asked with some concern.

'Yes fine, fine,' Ben replied. 'Just a bit tired, that's all. Jenny's very restless at night right now, keeping us both awake.'

'Of course,' Andrew said. 'Still, not long to go, eh?'

'Right,' Ben agreed, anxious to get back to his plan. 'So, as I was saying, what we really need is for Kate to get together with a man who will sweep her off her feet

106

and guarantee that her mind is kept well and truly off her work. From the very beginning.'

Andrew shrugged. 'Sounds logical. But I don't know how you can guarantee that happening. Unless you hire some actor/escort sort of man to play the part.'

Ben shook his head. 'Too unreliable. No, I think the best person for the job would be someone with a strong motivation to get the job done.'

Andrew still didn't get it. And then he did.

'Hang on. You're not suggesting that I . . . you can't be serious! Surely—'

Ben held up his hands to silence Andrew. 'Just listen to me for one minute. We're not talking about a big deal here. And it's not exactly a lifetime commitment, either. All I'm suggesting is that you win her over at the party, then spend the next three weeks . . . distracting her.'

Andrew stood back against the wall with his hands behind his head. 'I can't believe what you're saying. You're asking me to set myself up as some kind of gigolo—'

'Don't exaggerate,' Ben interrupted. 'It would be a bit of playacting, that's all.'

'Well, if that's *all* it is, then why don't you do it?'

Ben raised his eyebrows. 'Because I'm married? Does that sound like a good reason? Whereas you're not.'

Andrew stared at his friend. 'Have you forgotten Rebecca? The woman I live with? The woman we both work with?'

'But, Andrew, you'll be doing this for Rebecca.'

'How do you make that out?' Andrew asked sceptically.

'If Kate goes, you will almost certainly get her job. That will allow Rebecca to apply for your old position. I know it's not such a big promotion, but it will put her in

107

the right spot from where she can move up. And she'll have someone working under her for the first time.'

'Yes, but that hardly . . .' Andrew interjected.

Ben continued. 'If you don't do this then, frankly, I don't know how we're going to be able to stop Kate from pulling this off. If that happens, you'll stay where you are and Rebecca will stay where she is. And you know how miserable she is stuck at that job grade.'

Andrew certainly did know. He thought that her frustration at her lack of progress was the reason for the escalation of her moods. It couldn't only be down to her irritation with him. He knew about women's irritation, he experienced it regularly. This was something more complex.

Ben could see that Andrew was wavering. He began to talk faster, with more urgency.

'Don't you see. It's the only way. You're doing this for you and for Rebecca.'

Andrew didn't bother explaining the declining status of his relationship with Rebecca. It wasn't relevant. He had his own self-interest, which was more than adequate justification for wanting to get rid of Kate.

Ben captured a glimpse of Andrew's ambivalence when he'd mentioned Rebecca's name. 'Is everything OK between you and Rebecca?' he asked hopefully.

'Of course it is, everything's perfect,' Andrew insisted, not wanting to discuss the matter with Ben, who tended to tease Andrew about his predictable relationship cycle.

Ben managed to stop himself from groaning at this. Perfect? But surely she must be reaching the stage of climbing the walls and begging to be let out. It was *that* time, after all. Unless she was happy to put up with Andrew's little ways. Maybe after her affair she'd felt the need for some security; perhaps even the ultimate security.

Ben shuddered. This grim prospect made it doubly important to get rid of Rebecca. The last thing he needed was for Andrew to make things permanent with her. She'd be a member of the family, for goodness' sake! He'd never be able to relax again. It would ruin everything.

'Then you'll want to do all you can to make her happy and I think you and I both know that Rebecca's happiness comes primarily from her career.'

Andrew agreed reluctantly. 'But what do I tell her? She's not going to be very happy about his, however unselfish my justifications.'

Ben sighed. 'That's up to you. But I think it will be best if you say nothing. I mean, it's only for three weeks. And it's not as if you have to *do* anything with Kate. Just take her out, flatter her, smother her with attention, you know. In fact, it will probably be better if you *don't* do anything with her. Keep her on edge, in anticipation. She won't be able to concentrate at all.'

'What makes you so sure that Kate will even be interested in me?' Andrew asked ingenuously.

Ben laughed. 'That's what I like about you. You're vain without ever becoming arrogant!'

'What is that supposed to mean?' Andrew asked, vaguely offended.

'Andrew, what woman has ever turned you down? Ever?'

Andrew thought about his. 'I suppose I've been lucky with girls. But that doesn't mean that Kate will be interested. I mean, you know me, I'm the sort of man that women leave once they get to know me. They start to find my domestic systems annoying, even though they make perfect sense if you want your home to run efficiently. Kate seems a smart woman, she probably knows what I'm like after our first meeting.'

Ben laughed. 'You're incredible! You've got less self-esteem than the average thirteen-year-old girl.'

'It's nothing to do with self-esteem. I know my limitations, that's all.'

'Trust me on this, Andrew, she'll be crazy about you.' Ben couldn't prevent the note of envy from tainting his words. He was the male equivalent of the girl with a great personality. Andrew was the one who didn't need a personality: he had a face. And although Ben's success, both personal and professional, was the greater, he could never shake off the irritating suspicion that Andrew's path through life was easier.

Andrew looked miserable. 'I think I preferred Rebecca's idea. Are you sure we can't go back to that one? I've invited eleven men. Kate's bound to like one of them.'

'You know as well as I do that this way is more certain.'

Andrew sighed. 'I suppose Rebecca will understand. After all, the idea was sort-of hers.'

'No!' Ben exclaimed, making them both jump. He coughed to conceal his nervousness. 'You can't tell Rebecca! She'll throw a tantrum, wanting to know what was wrong with her original idea. You know what she's like!'

Andrew knew exactly what Rebecca was like and was forced to agree that Ben's prediction was probably spot on. He was about to formulate the question which asked how Ben could know Rebecca so well, when Ben grabbed his arm companionably.

'Is it worth the hassle of getting Rebecca's back up? For the sake of a few weeks?'

Andrew grimaced. 'Rebecca's bound to guess that I'm up to something. I'm a lousy actor. She'll be furious.'

110

He didn't want Rebecca to be angry with him, even though she would soon be leaving him. It was one thing for Rebecca to depart out of frustration at his irritating ways. He could handle that. He always did; its inevitability was a comfort blanket. The great thing about not having relationships that lasted too long was that there was never time to cause each other the real pain which comes from knowing each other deeply.

The rows were superficial, the partings were easy. And if he was missing out on the rewards of a profound and knowing love, then he didn't know, because he'd never experienced it.

He didn't want things with Rebecca to be different. He didn't want accusations of betrayal and dishonesty. He didn't want her to despise him, or to be damaged by him. He didn't want anything to be different, because he could only deal with things that stayed the same as they'd always been.

Ben was finally starting to feel optimistic. 'That's fine. Look, I'll help out here. I'll make sure that Rebecca doesn't suspect anything. And you mustn't feel guilty. It's just a few meals and phone calls, that's all. It's hardly a betrayal. And in three weeks, it will be over.'

'All I'll say to you is that I'll give it a go, Ben. And we'd both better just pray that Rebecca doesn't find out.'

Ben watched him go into Kate's office. He had no intention of praying for that. He was relying on Rebecca finding out. He was relying on Rebecca leaving Andrew.

I am a tough and devious man, he reminded himself, as he tried to quell the sense of self-disgust rising in his throat like nausea.

Kate looked up at Andrew to see him smiling, which bothered her. It was the first friendly face she'd encountered since joining the company and the face was stuck on someone who yesterday had been openly hostile.

Her mum was right. A judiciously presented smile can be as dangerous as a barbed put-down. She had the good sense to say nothing until she learned a little more about Andrew's latest motivations. This is going to be exhausting, Kate thought. They're probably going to wear me down by changing their approach from day to day.

New Zealand must be lovely at this time of year, she sighed to herself.

'How's it all going?' Andrew asked, with a little too much boyish charm.

Now Kate was really suspicious. 'Fine. Thanks. Was there anything in particular you wanted?'

In fact, Andrew had intended to go into Kate's office and antagonise her, hoping to put her off her work. But he'd had to change his approach after his discussion with Ben. He was finding it tough to adapt so swiftly. Before he could answer, Rebecca appeared.

Damn, Andrew thought. He'd forgotten that he'd agreed this with Rebecca earlier. Rebecca was going to follow on after Andrew to give Kate the feeling of escalating tension, to make her nervous.

Rebecca was surprised to see Andrew still there. He was supposed to have gone in, given Kate the impression that she might have missed a critical point in the files then exit quickly, leaving Kate to start rifling through all the files again.

Then Rebecca was to do the same, this time sowing the seed of doubt that one of the graphs had a numerical error, leaving Kate to face an enormous maths problem to solve.

But Andrew was standing there grinning like a schoolboy

with a crush on a teacher. His smile dropped when Rebecca came in, but he didn't move.

Kate watched their reactions to each other and worked out that the two were not working in perfect harmony just now. Interesting, she thought, sitting back and waiting for one of them to say something.

Andrew looked impassively in front of him. Rebecca glared at the side of his face then cleared her throat before speaking.

'Erm, I'm sorry to bother you but I think you've been going through the Saltech files?'

Kate said nothing. 'Unless you're asked a direct question, then say nothing,' her mother had counselled.

Rebecca seethed when Kate didn't respond. 'Well, it's just that I think there might be a problem. When we were doing all the charts, one of them had a mistake in them.'

Kate still said nothing even though her instincts made her want to rush round and hug Rebecca, who was squirming.

'We were going to correct the mistake, Andrew and I that is, but then when they were getting your office ready, they bundled all the papers together and we don't know which one had the error.'

Kate bit down on her tongue hard to stop herself from speaking. Andrew was finding the silence, as well as Rebecca's embarrassment, excruciating, so he stepped in.

'That's right. That's what I was coming along to tell you as well. And, er, to offer my services.'

'For what?' Kate asked, intrigued at this new spirit of cooperation that yesterday's enemy was demonstrating.

Andrew kept his head facing rigidly forward so that he wouldn't have to face Rebecca's accusing expression that

113

was piercing hot holes in his cheeks. Traitor, he imagined her hissing silently.

Andrew's voice was faltering as he cranked the treachery up another notch. 'To go through the files with you, explain everything, find any errors, that sort of thing. It should bring you up to speed more quickly than you reading it all through yourself.'

Rebecca couldn't prevent a tiny gasp from slipping out. Andrew tried to send telepathic messages to her. I'm doing this for you, he was screaming inside, I'm doing this for you! It was somewhat dishonest, but better than nothing.

But Rebecca didn't tune in. Her telepathic skills were otherwise employed dispatching messages of her own to Andrew, post-watershed suggestions with anatomical and scatological references.

'I'll leave you to it, then,' she spat, flouncing out of the office, a highly satisfying act that she'd been learning from Sally. Andrew smiled apologetically.

'She's a bit . . . tired,' he suggested.

'Whatever,' Kate replied crisply. 'Well, let's get to it.'

Unfortunately for Andrew, Rebecca heard his last comment from the other side of the door. It provided the flame needed to ignite her fuel-soaked anger. She marched back to her desk. Sally had watched her approach and rushed over to find out what had happened.

'I can't believe what happened,' Rebecca muttered.

'What? Tell me!' Sally pulled up a chair and sat down next to Rebecca.

'Andrew is in there with that woman, cosying up to her, smiling at her!'

Sally's mouth dropped open. 'You're kidding! What's he playing at?'

114

That was what Rebecca was asking herself. 'I don't know. He's been behaving strangely all morning. But I didn't pay much attention. He's been annoying me a bit recently. And then this morning, we'd agreed that we were both going to wind Kate up, get her to waste a day or so on a wild goose chase around the files.'

'So what's he doing in there?' Sally asked, thoroughly enjoying somebody else's problems.

'Believe it or not, he's helping her sort it all out!' Rebecca replied. She sat for a while, unravelling paper clips and picking at loose threads in her tights.

'Are you sure that's all he's doing?' Sally asked.

Rebecca's head whipped up. 'What's that supposed to mean?'

Sally recoiled from the vehemence. 'Nothing. It's just a bit strange. One day, he's agreeing with you that she's a bitch and you must do whatever it takes to get rid of her, then the next day . . .'

Rebecca brooded on this. 'Do you think she's attractive?' she asked Sally.

Sally pursed her lips in thought. 'I suppose so. If you like hard-looking women.'

Rebecca considered this. 'Am I a hard-looking woman?' she asked softly.

Sally put her hands on her hips. 'You're joking! You're not a bit hard. You're gorgeous. Pretty and feminine.'

Rebecca laughed. 'I get the point. You're the most wonderful secretary and I'll make sure your appraisal says so!'

Sally stuck her tongue out playfully at Rebecca. 'Ignore what I said, there's no way that Andrew could prefer Kate to you.' Rebecca didn't hear her. 'Do you fancy lunch?' Sally asked.

Rebecca looked up and smiled gratefully. 'That will be

great. Or we could go out for a drink after work? Get really hammered. That would get right up Andrew's nose!'

Sally looked away. 'Er, no, lunch is better for me. I have to get home tonight.'

Rebecca shrugged then narrowed her eyes. 'Come to think of it, you never go out after work, not with anyone here.'

'That's because I'm an anti-social old bag,' Sally replied cheerfully.

'You never turn down a free lunch, though,' Rebecca pointed out.

Sally pretended not to hear this and returned to her desk.

Rebecca tried to get on with her work but found it difficult to concentrate; eventually she picked up her handbag and decamped to the ladies' cloakroom.

She stood in front of the mirror and ran her fingers over her beautifully made-up face. She'd seen the way Andrew had been looking at Kate and, while she didn't exactly understand what the look meant, it had forced her to look at Kate from a different standpoint.

Kate was a beautiful woman, but Rebecca couldn't tell if she was more or less beautiful than herself. She was just different. Andrew's attitude in Kate's office made Rebecca feel insecure.

She responded to this challenge the only way she knew how. She looked in her make-up bag then zipped it shut firmly. Yup, she said to herself. It's time for change.

Justine unzipped the sleek, black bag and tipped the contents on to her dressing table. The beauty consultant had spent two hours showing her how to apply the new colours herself. By the end of the session, Justine was confident that she would be able to replicate the look at home.

'That's not exactly the point,' the consultant said.

'What do you mean?' Justine asked.

The woman, whose face was painted until it no longer had any characteristics of her own, explained. 'I've shown you one combination of colours, that's all. But I've also pointed out how you can highlight your various features to achieve practically any kind of look. So experiment. You can be whoever you want to be.'

With that promise, Justine had invested almost £100 on palettes of lip, cheek and eye colour. Using her rudimentary maths skills, she calculated that they offered 300 different combinations.

Great, Justine thought. Now all I have to do is think of 300 women I want to be. And I'll start with—

'Good God! What have you done to yourself?'

Justine spun round to see Steve standing in the doorway, staring at her in horror.

'What do you think?' Justine asked, turning her face from side to side so that her husband could get the full effect.

'I think you look like a stripper who's put her make-up on without a mirror,' he said bluntly.

Justine bit her lip to stop herself from crying. Only Steve had ever made her cry in her adult life. He didn't mean to, he just knew her too well and was threatened by the realisation that she knew him too well. They were welded together whether they wanted to be or not, and, year by year, each went through phases of wishing to be unwelded. When that had happened, it had fortunately coincided with the other partner experiencing a fit of tenacity and strength. Like many couples, they'd learned that an acceptable marriage can be held together with the exceptional determination of just one partner.

Justine and Steve assumed this was a natural function

117

of marriage. They rode out the tough times and welcomed the occasional moments of happiness with surprise, never taking them for granted. But each of them knew that the other had settled for something inferior and steady rather than take a chance that something fabulous and fragile might come along.

This didn't make it a bad marriage, just one that was rife with potential for damaging each other. And neither wanted to do that. They sort of loved each other, generally liked each other and definitely cared for each other. But it was hard to be spontaneously kind all the time and easy to be cruel when one was tired or bored or frustrated.

So Steve said cruel things and Justine stored them up in a ball of festering resentment that she buried way down inside. She didn't blame him; she was equally cruel to him, but in a different way, hurting him with her indifference and her obvious disillusionment. She judged him silently but visibly and he knew that he was found wanting.

And the miracle of this complex, destructive web woven by two mismatched people is that nobody they knew had the slightest notion that they were anything other than a happily married couple.

But Justine's sudden change of image signalled a more significant danger to Steve. Actually, to Justine as well if she was being honest. It signified a desire to change, which is no bad thing in marriage except when, as in this case, it is a unilateral decision.

This was a new situation for them both and they didn't have the language to deal with it. Steve wanted to tell Justine to go back to the way she was, but he didn't know how to do it without sounding Victorian.

He swallowed and took a few deep breaths. 'I'm sorry,

118

Jus. I shouldn't have said that. You don't look like a stripper . . .'

Justine smiled. 'What about the rest of it?'

Steve pretended to think about it seriously. Then he smiled too. But they didn't approach each other.

'So what do you really think?' Justine asked bravely.

'You look different,' Steve said steadily. 'I wasn't prepared for it. It was a shock. Imagine if I came home with my hair permed and wearing a leather jacket and tight jeans.'

Justine giggled at the image this conjured up.

'Yes, you'd laugh,' Steve said. 'But then you'd worry. You'd start to remember all those articles you read in women's magazines about men in their forties and their mid-life crises. I bet you'd start examining my shirts for lipstick stains.'

Justine began to protest but Steve stopped her.

'I'm not accusing you of anything, honestly I'm not. But it's frightening for me to see you change yourself. I have to ask myself why you're doing it. It can't be for me, you know I'm happy with you the way you are, I mean, were.'

'Steve, I'm doing this for me, that's all, for me. I'm not looking for anyone else or anything else. I promise.'

She reached out her hand to Steve and he took it. He tentatively touched her hair then pulled his hand back quickly. 'What have you got in there?' he asked, wiping his hand on a hanky.

'Gel and hairspray,' Justine said. 'Oh, and volumiser and leave-in conditioner.'

Steve looked down at his hand as if it might start to dissolve. 'Now you've finally managed to convince me that you're not looking for another man. There's no way you could be expecting a man to run his fingers through that hair without offering him the facilities of a decontamination chamber afterwards.'

Justine scowled. Steve laughed. They both relaxed.

'I have to take it all off now anyway. I'm off to work.'

Steve nodded solemnly. 'Yes, it wouldn't do to scare your pregnant ladies.'

Justine looked at him affectionately. 'I love you when you're like this,' she said softly.

But Steve didn't hear her. He was too busy changing his clothes. And Justine didn't say it again.

'Sally, can I have a word?'

Sally slammed down the phone she'd just picked up. Ben looked alarmed.

'Sorry, I didn't mean to make you jump. Go ahead with your call, if you like.'

'That's OK,' Sally said briskly, 'it can wait. Now what can I do for you?'

'It's the other way round. I was wondering if you'd like to come to a party on Friday night at my house. It's to welcome Kate Harris to the company and make her feel part of the team.'

Sally said nothing but her expression communicated her feelings perfectly well. 'Sorry, I can't. I've got something else to do.'

Ben pulled up a chair and sat in front of Sally. 'Think carefully about this, Sally.'

'What do you mean?' Sally asked.

'We're a small team and you are part of it.'

Sally snorted. 'Yeah right, the dogsbody part, the coffee-making part, the typing-till-midnight-when-necessary part, the manning-the-phones-while-you-take-long-lunches part.'

'Yes, yes, I get the picture,' Ben interjected.

120

'The only reason I'm saying this is to save you the bother of the team speech. When all the other members of the team have moved on, I'll still be here, making coffee, typing till midnight etc. And all the dinners and parties in the world will not make a blind bit of difference to my status.'

'That's not true.' But Ben knew that it was true. He'd been trying to be decent by inviting Sally, by not excluding her. He regretted the gesture now. All he'd managed to do was antagonise her.

He chalked this up as one of his rare errors of judgement. Normally he got it right, almost entirely through chance, of course, but his success rate gave him an unjustified confidence in his people skills.

Ben was his father's son. When he looked in the mirror he saw his dad, Graham Clarkson, a physically unattractive man who had learned to compensate for his appearance by constructing a fearsomely attractive personality. He became a sexual predator, each conquest bolstering his fragile ego; until he met Ben's mother.

Isabel was too good for him, anyone could see that, and eventually she saw that too. But it took her many years to come to that conclusion. Graham was fundamentally a good person, who never intended to deceive or hurt anyone. But he was damaged by the awareness that he would always have to work twice as hard as the average man to overcome the negative first impressions that he would inevitably engender.

So his decisions were self-motivated even though, in his heart, he was an unselfish family man, devoted to his wife and only son. He couldn't help himself and his charm went a long way towards redeeming him in Isabel's eyes.

He breezed through life just looking for success,

whether it was personal or professional, each small victory giving him the impetus to propel himself towards the next. He had no goals, no long-term plans, only the daily need for self-affirmation.

Despite this lack of planning his career was hugely successful, his random dabblings in business occasionally placing him in advantageous positions at auspicious moments.

Ben watched this, desperate to learn the techniques that he too would need to acquire if he were to overcome his unfortunate physical inheritance. He became a drifter, a dabbler, a charmer and, like his father before him, he attained swift success.

But Graham's momentum finally faltered when his irrepressible charm became once more concentrated on women. And this was when his lack of planning skills finally let him down. His wife found out about all the affairs. At first she didn't divorce him. Instead she punished him by not divorcing him, by living with him in hurt silence, her love withdrawn permanently, a fixed look of disenchantment etched across her hurt face.

Then she divorced him, took her son to live on the opposite side of the country and never saw him again.

This, his one failure, was the one he could least endure. He was broken by the collapsed marriage, by the knowledge that he had failed and hurt Isabel and his son so badly.

He took early retirement and died at fifty-five, too tired to fight for himself any more.

Ben tried to learn from this as well as from those golden triumphant years. He made conscious efforts to look beyond himself at other people, to be kind, to discipline himself to think before he acted.

He swore too that he would be a better father.

But he found it too difficult and so he decided instead that he would just try not to repeat his father's bigger mistakes.

Then he had the affair with Rebecca. Now he was trying to manipulate lives around him to cover up that glaring error; he had a really bad feeling about where this was going to lead.

Even so, this invitation to Sally was a genuine one. He felt bad that she was excluded on so many occasions. He thought it would be nice to invite her, that it would make her feel good. Deep down, he hoped that each act of kindness might wipe out each of his less altruistic deeds. He'd started to hope for the existence of a cosmic justice, not knowing how else to redress the dangerous imbalance in his moral life.

But all he'd done was make Sally resentful.

Fortunately for Ben, none of Sally's antagonism was directed towards him. Somewhere in her flawed analysis of the situation, Sally had come to the conclusion that the catalyst for everybody's dissatisfaction at the moment was Kate. She couldn't understand why Andrew was suddenly being so nice to the woman, or why Rebecca had suddenly become more concerned about her make-up and was moody.

Well, *they* may not care about what this woman is doing to us all but I do, she thought. I liked things the way they were, just me and Rebecca and Andrew and Ben. Besides, there's something that doesn't quite add up about Kate Harris and I'm going to find out what.

Sally was in a good position to make this judgement. She knew about acting, about pretending to be one thing when she was actually someone different. She had her own secrets which she covered up expertly, but then, she'd been doing it for years. That's why she was so good at it.

And frankly, she'd spotted that Kate was an amateur within minutes of meeting her.

This was why she changed her mind about the party. 'Sure I'll come,' she said abruptly to Ben. She wasn't sure how she was going to fix it but she'd find a way of getting there.

Parties are dangerous places, she thought. It's an alien environment, drink is flowing, everyone is relaxing, lowering their guard. Yet this is when their guard should most definitely be up. Secrets can slip out and I reckon some big ones are scheduled for a fall.

Chapter 8

'So what are you going to wear to the party tomorrow?' Justine asked. She had to raise her voice to be heard over the unusually loud music. They hadn't been to this particular restaurant since it had changed hands.

Kate didn't answer immediately. She was transfixed by Justine. 'What have you done to your face?'

Justine unconsciously raised her hand to her cheek. 'Nothing. I mean, I went to see someone who showed me how to do my make-up, that's all.'

Kate examined Justine's unfamiliar features. 'It's amazing. I didn't realise you had such big eyes or cheekbones.'

Justine laughed. 'You sound like the wolf about to eat up Little Red Riding Hood! It's really easy when you know how. It's all about finding your cheekbones and aligning them with your mouth.' She spotted Kate unsuccessfully suppressing a laugh. 'I know, I know, I sound like a teenager, but I never did all this when I was younger. And it's really good fun. You should try it yourself.'

'Yeah, right! So what does Steve think of all this?' she asked, recalling his hysterical call.

Justine shrugged. 'He's gone a bit neurotic, thinks I'm fed up with him and looking for a new man!'

'And are you?' Kate asked lightly.

Justine spluttered. 'Don't be so silly!'

'But try and see it from Steve's point of view. What would you think if he started changing his image?'

'That's exactly what he said. Frankly it wouldn't bother me. If he wants to have his hair permed or start wearing kaftans, that's fine. As long as he doesn't get a tattoo, of course.'

They both burst out laughing at this. Tattoos were a regular topic of ridicule for them. Since they'd been at school and their staggeringly weedy physics teacher revealed the hint of a tattoo on the back of his neck, announcing I LOVE MY MUM in red, they'd been unable to take anyone with a tattoo seriously.

'Don't let's go there again,' Kate warned. They then went through all the tattoo stories from their past, giggling like schoolgirls. Kate was relieved that her friend hadn't really changed, any more than she had. She said this to Justine.

'That's what I've been trying to tell you! Go on, try it yourself!'

'You're kidding! Do you not think I've done enough? You saw me on Monday, I've never worn such red lipstick. And have you forgotten my clothes? People stared at me on the train, that's how outrageous I looked.'

'Kate, you idiot, hasn't it occurred to you that people were staring at you because you looked fantastic?'

Kate looked sceptical. 'That's very sweet of you. Comical, but sweet. I know my limitations. I know I don't need to wear a paper bag over my face but I also know that I'm not a head-turner.'

Justine slammed her hands down on the table in frustration. 'You really can be very thick sometimes. And I mean that in a caring, loving way, of course.' Kate flicked a drop of wine at her. Justine went on. 'The reason you've never turned heads in the past is nothing to do with your

126

face or even your figure and everything to do with how you present yourself.'

Kate sighed. 'Here we go again.'

'I'm only saying it again to make the point that it wasn't you that was being ignored, it was your cardigan and that hair.'

'Don't start,' Kate warned.

'I'm sorry, but when I saw you walking in, I wanted to scream. Since I'm absolutely certain that you didn't wear those clothes to work, you must have gone home and changed in record time.'

Kate squirmed with self-consciousness as she felt Justine's eyes pouring scorn over her outfit. Actually calling it an outfit was a compliment unworthy of the mismatch.

She was wearing a floor-length cheesecloth skirt in a sombre black floral pattern. This was topped with a long black cardigan which managed to conceal all of Kate's fabulous figure and was adorned only by the dramatic frills of a gypsy blouse peeking from the cardigan's sleeves and collar.

If this had been 1850 and Kate had been in mourning for a much-loved husband who'd died a long, painful death, then her choice of attire would have been perfect. Unfortunately, for a night out with a friend in a restaurant that screamed 'FUN!' from its dazzling chrome-and-white interior, it was a hopeless miscalculation.

But this was Kate's favourite outfit, the one in which she felt most comfortable. And although Justine insisted that Kate dressed like this to make herself invisible, Kate truly thought she looked attractive. It was the 1960s folk singer look, very Marianne Faithfull, feminine, ethereal, interesting. Since she didn't feel any of those things, but would quite like to, it seemed a perfect way of redefining herself.

The problem was that this was the twenty-first century. Marianne Faithfull was appearing in sitcoms, for God's sake! Bob Dylan was playing golf. They'd moved on – everyone had moved on. So when people saw Kate dressed like this, they didn't get it. They looked her at and thought: 'Who died?'

But Kate didn't know this. Justine tried to tell her but she didn't believe her. Besides, she didn't have an alternative; she hadn't found any other statement she preferred to make with her image. Fashion passed her by, too transient for her to absorb. Kate wasn't a transient sort of person, she was a long-haul woman in every respect. She didn't even bother going out with a man if she didn't see a strong possibility of a long relationship.

Kate and Justine sat in a stubborn silence, each refusing to yield to the other in this familiar stand-off.

Justine weakened first. 'Go on then, say it!'

Kate sighed. 'What?'

Justine flung her arms up impatiently. 'You know what, the line about the men who said they loved the way you looked.'

'Well they *did*!' Kate reacted churlishly. 'I mean, you're always saying I've never changed my style, but why should I? I've done just fine the way I am!'

'Really?' Justine asked. 'Would this be a reference to all the beautiful, meaningful relationships you've enjoyed throughout your adult life?'

Her sarcasm earned her a peanut lobbed skilfully at her nose by Kate. Justine continued, unswayed by the assault.

'Let me see . . . . Of course there was the perfect Jamie. He loved you the way you were until he learned that your clothes were not an expression of a unique personality but a thirty-year-old security blanket trapping you in a self-imposed time warp.'

'He lived with me for four years!' Kate objected.

'Of course he did,' Justine replied. 'You enslaved him with your obsessive nurturing tendencies. You did more for him than his mother! Not only did you do all his washing and cooking, not only did you do everything around the house, you got up early at weekends to bake bread for his breakfast, you put home-made biscuits in his briefcase, you polished his shoes . . .'

'But I don't mind doing things like that, I'm good at them.'

Justine ignored Kate's interruption. 'You ironed his socks, for pity's sake!'

'He liked the feel of creases against the uppers of his shoes,' Kate said weakly.

Justine hit herself on the head. 'Listen to yourself! Never mind the doormat your old workmates bought you, your old boyfriends could have clubbed together and carpeted your house wall-to-wall with your passiveness.'

'That's unfair,' Kate whispered, fully aware of how fair it was. 'Besides, none of that takes away the fact that men have found me attractive. Like this.'

Justine grabbed her friend's hand impulsively. 'But what kind of men?' she asked.

Kate knew the answer to that. Men who were not as preoccupied with physical appearances as their peers, men who recognised her nonconformity and surmised that she represented the potential for a different kind of relationship.

The ones who expected something flamboyant and extravagant left before she'd even slipped off one of her sensible shoes. The others sank gratefully into her welcoming servitude and stayed until they overdosed on Kate's sugar.

Kate knew this and preferred not to dwell on it. With difficulty, she switched her attention back to her present situation. Clothes, it always seemed to come down to clothes.

Her uncomfortable experiences of the last few days dressed like Joan Collins only confirmed her suspicions that it was much safer sticking to the one persona, even if it was the same one established in her teens, a period notorious for appalling taste and judgement.

But sitting here tonight, she felt slightly out of sorts with herself. It was the hair: the one aspect of herself that she wasn't able to reverse. When she'd looked in the mirror after dressing, she'd frowned. The picture was flawed, or rather it was different. Both meant the same to Kate. From the neck down, she was exactly as she'd always been. Kate was instantly calmed with the reassuring sameness of the reflection.

Yet the head, the face, they were all wrong. The sleek bob made her look too smart, too worldly, too . . . grown-up. She tensed her neck and shoulder muscles, separating the two parts of her body. Nothing she could do about it now. Even Kate recognised that buying a wig in her original hairstyle was an eccentricity too far.

She was saved from Justine launching on her tiresomely familiar critical assault by the approach of two men to their table.

'Excuse me, we were wondering if we could buy you a drink?'

Justine and Kate both automatically looked behind them to see who these men might be talking to. It couldn't be them. They weren't the approachable type. They'd learned this in their early twenties and quickly come to terms with it. In fact, it was a welcome release from the expectation of attracting attention. Justine was relieved because she was married and Kate because she hated attention.

There was nobody behind them; the men were talking to them, or rather to Justine. It was Kate who made this observation. Justine was oblivious to the fact, not yet used to her new look, still perceiving herself as the woman she'd been for the past twenty years.

Kate watched with amusement as a pink shadow crept up Justine's face. Justine had just worked it out. She turned to face Kate in panic. Neither of them were equipped to deal with this situation smoothly. The two men, clearly regretting their choice of women, were already looking around anxiously for an escape.

That's when Kate looked around for the first time herself. She couldn't believe they hadn't noticed it already. Every table was occupied by groups of men or women. No couples. No mixed groups.

Oh no, Kate thought. It's Singles Night.

She wondered how she could communicate this telepathically to Justine but it wasn't necessary. Justine had lost her air of panic and was smiling calmly at their visitors.

'That would be great. Thanks.'

Kate tried frantically to catch Justine's eye to dissuade her from this reckless move. But Justine was either too preoccupied or deliberately ignoring her. Before Kate could think of any other diversionary tactic, the men had pulled up two chairs and sat down.

'I'm Max and this is Callum.'

'I'm Justine and this is Kate.'

They all shook hands, or rather, Kate shook hands and the others complied awkwardly. Oh dear, Kate thought

131

flatly. Obviously not the done thing on Singles Night. Probably should have licked my lips provocatively and teased their trouser legs with my outstretched foot. So shoot me.

Justine, seemingly more at ease with this encounter, had become animated and welcoming. Not like Justine at all, Kate thought. Within seconds, the men's body language made their intentions transparent. Max had very slightly adjusted his seat so that he was facing Justine while Callum had similarly turned towards Kate.

Kate found herself rating the two men to see who had come off best in the deal. Like being back at the grammar school disco, she told herself wryly. There wasn't much in it. Both men were tall and dark-haired. Neither had a hump or pock-marked skin. She supposed that Max would be considered the better-looking of the two, with his hair styled immaculately close to his scalp, his confident smile that was perilously close to a smirk and the jutting chin that was covered in either designer stubble or his dinner.

Callum on the other hand did not look as if he wanted to be here. You and me both, mate, Kate agreed silently. He had a nice face, that was the easiest way to describe Callum. Kinks were escaping rebelliously from his otherwise straight hair, his babyish blue eyes held a permanent frown of anticipation and his mouth looked as if it wanted to smile but dared not. He was struggling to find something to say, since he had accurately read Kate's expression of non-compliance.

'So Kate, do you come here often?' He immediately cringed at his cliché and Kate laughed. That was the sort of thing she would come out with. Callum looked at her in surprise, then he smiled too. They both relaxed. A little.

While Max ordered a bottle of wine, Kate noticed Justine fiddling with something under the table. When she pulled her hands back up, Kate saw what her friend had been doing and she felt her stomach contract with tension at the implications.

Justine had taken her wedding ring off.

Ben stood by his office window, looking out over the London skyline, twisting his wedding ring nervously. He always worked as late as possible at the office when Jenny was away. He was lost in the house without her. He would be lost anywhere without her. He'd ambled round the building looking for someone who'd come for a drink with him. He didn't want to sound desperate, even though he was desperate, and consequently he ended up sounding offhand. Even his stalwart companion, Andrew, had left on time. He was rushing home to cook a special meal for Rebecca, hoping to soften her up before he embarked upon his reluctant pursuit of Kate.

Rebecca was alone in her office, jabbing at her computer keys as if they were mosquitoes.

'Working late?' Ben asked, stating the obvious.

Rebecca didn't bother looking up. 'Obergruppenführer Kate Harris and her faithful lieutenant Andrew found a few anomalies in the Saltech files that I've got to sort out. And if I don't do it tonight, I'll have to put up with her clipped little reminders all day tomorrow. She's like something out of *Prisoner: Cell Block H*.' This would have amused Kate, it being one of the few TV programmes from which she hadn't stolen a character to use in her act.

Ben heard the note of displeasure in her voice when she spat out Andrew's name and relaxed inwardly. Perhaps they would have a massive row tonight and Rebecca

133

would refuse to come to the party tomorrow. That would make things easier.

'I don't suppose you fancy a quick drink, do you?'

Rebecca looked up in astonishment. 'You are joking, aren't you?'

Ben was surprised at her reaction. 'I'm not suggesting we rent a hotel room for an hour. Just that we have a drink. Jenny's away for the night . . .' He didn't need to say any more. Rebecca could fill in the rest. She knew all about his fear of being alone – it was what had pushed her into his life in the first place.

But she was dazzled by his detachment from the accepted standards that dictated most normal people's interaction with others. She could not see how he could possibly find it reasonable to think that she would even want to talk to him socially, let alone have a drink with him. He was a married man who had seduced her and dumped her when he got bored of their affair. He was the best friend of her lover who also just happened to be his brother-in-law. And he'd hired a woman over them, the biggest sin of all right now.

She was tired and her mind was full of muddled thoughts, about Andrew and Ben and Kate and this job. So she resisted the temptation to set about concocting the perfect acid riposte.

Instead she turned back to her computer and shook her head slowly. Ben shrugged his shoulders, unhurt by the rebuff, and went back to his office.

It wasn't just solitude that Ben didn't do well. It was also silence, and inactivity. Even now as he stood still, he was tapping his foot, clenching and unclenching various muscles, thinking a dozen unconnected thoughts. Eventually he decided to go for a drink by himself. He was a sociable man and was bound to find someone to talk to.

134

Jenny had phoned from her mother's house. She'd been to visit her today and had felt too tired to drive back so she decided to stay the night there and come home in the morning. She needed a good night's sleep to get her strength up before the party tomorrow night. It was something she had done occasionally even before she became pregnant; on such an occasion Ben had made the mistake of asking Rebecca out for a quick drink.

When he looked back, it all seemed so innocent. He hadn't intended for it to become a full-blown affair. He hadn't intended for anything to happen at all. That was how he forgave himself all his mistakes because none of them had been planned. Nothing in his life was planned and he hadn't made that many mistakes so, all in all, he thought his life proved a worthy argument in favour of spontaneity.

But the baby changed everything. Jenny had her own strategy for dealing with Ben. She was organised and she was strong so she took over the elements of his life that required some organisation and dealt stoically with the fallout from some of his rasher choices. But he didn't think she'd deal with an affair quite so stoically.

Not after her experience with her parents.

Jenny watched her mother playing unconsciously with her wedding ring. She found herself doing the same and stopped herself, disturbed by any sign that she might be turning into her mother.

'You know what day it is today?' her mum said, sighing.

Jenny closed her eyes and counted to ten to control her impatience. 'Yes, Mum. It would have been your wedding anniversary.'

Barbara Darlington tutted in exasperation. 'Not "would

have been", it *is* my wedding anniversary. This is the anniversary of the day I got married. Just because my husband chooses to ignore our marriage doesn't mean it didn't happen.'

Jenny knew better than to reason with her. They had gone over the same argument on a regular basis. It went nowhere and always became personal, each trading intensely bruising blows, each unintentionally causing the other more pain than the original divorce had all those years earlier.

'Whatever,' Jenny said levelly, stroking her stomach and wishing a different life for her child.

Barbara straightened her back officiously. 'There's no need to take that tone. I know what you're thinking.' Jenny refused to be goaded and said nothing. This only served to rile her mother even more. 'You can sit there all smug if you like, you wait until you've got a child, see how attentive Ben is then. Your father and I were right as rain in the beginning.'

Here we go again, Jenny thought. Everything was wonderful, idyllic until I came along.

This wasn't the classic story of the unwanted child spoiling the perfect relationship. Jenny was not unwanted, she was wanted too much and for too long. After Andrew had been born, it had taken a further ten years of frustrated effort on her parents' part before Jenny was conceived. By then their expectations were so high that Jenny could not possibly fulfil them.

It had been different with Andrew. He had been born within a year of their marriage but he made little impact on them. Barbara continued with her career as a barrister and effectively handed Andrew over to an au pair to bring up. This was not common in the 1960s and it was only later that Barbara questioned her own judgement.

136

Leo, her husband, was a solicitor and they both had a full social life along with plenty of money. But as the second child they longed for did not arrive, their needs changed. They found themselves panicking that Andrew might be their only child and they had missed most of his childhood. They promised that things would be different if they were blessed with another child. Especially if it was a girl.

After Jenny's birth, the marriage ceased as mother and father invested all of themselves into parenthood. They had no love or time left for each other, which was fine while they both felt the same. But once Jenny went to school and needed their daily attentions less, they began looking to each other once more to fill in the gaps. When Barbara's husband looked to her, though, he found her wanting. They'd forgotten how to be married, how to be people defined in their own right, rather than simply Andrew and Jenny's mum and dad.

For Barbara, it wasn't so important that their marriage was less than satisfying after all these years; the fact that they were still married and had their children was all that mattered. And it was her lack of concern for the deteriorating relationship that finally led to Leo leaving her.

He'd tried, really tried, to keep things going, to return their marriage to its former state, but Barbara wasn't interested. She'd rekindled her career as a barrister after a long break and had less time than ever for Leo. He booked weekends away that she always had to cancel at the last minute. There were broken dinner dates, forgotten anniversaries and the absolute withdrawal of all but the most perfunctory affection.

Leo met someone else and left Barbara on their wedding anniversary, a date that each had forgotten but which struck them both separately later.

Andrew was seventeen at the time and was away at boarding school. He got over the shock relatively quickly. Jenny was seven and adapted as well as could be expected to her father's departure. It was her mother's bitterness that she found harder to accept. Leo remarried and had three more children in swift succession leaving Barbara to face the conclusion that their difficulties in conceiving had most likely been down to her. This was one insult too many.

As Barbara brought Jenny up, she found herself unconsciously injecting the girl with her own acrimony. She failed, largely due to Jenny's growing sense of comprehension for her father's action and partly due to Leo's mellow gentleness that provided the necessary counterpoint to the bitter tunes her mother sang.

Despite her mother's efforts, Jenny did not grow up hating men or distrusting them. She loved and trusted her father. But she did have strong feelings about what constituted a good marriage. And when she married Ben, she laid them out plainly.

'Neither of us must ever do anything that jeopardises this marriage without working through all our problems until we reach the point when the problems can't be resolved. We must always put our marriage first and, if we should be lucky enough to have children, then we must make a deliberate effort to nurture our marriage at the same time.'

Ben agreed with it all. He knew the full story of her parents' split and understood her real need to avoid repeating their history. Besides, it all made sense. He had his own fractured family history to draw upon. He had no intention of ever jeopardising their marriage, no matter what happened.

Then he forgot his intention.

Barbara was mid-drone when Jenny pulled herself to her feet, not easy when she was in a low, sagging armchair and her centre of gravity appeared to have dropped to her knees. She picked up her bag and went to the cupboard where the coats were kept.

'What are you doing?' her mother asked her.

'I'm going home,' Jenny replied wearily. 'I'm tired and I'm not in the mood to spend half the night listening to you go on about Dad and how he ruined your life and how all men ruin women's lives.'

'Don't be so stupid. You're not going anywhere tonight. You're exhausted. You'll have an accident.'

Jenny contorted her bulky body to put on her coat. 'Mum, if I feel too tired, I'll pull over and sleep in a lay-by. That will be preferable to subjecting myself to your hysterical ranting for the thousandth time in my life.'

'But I'm only speaking the truth,' Barbara said, folding her arms in a classic defensive gesture.

Jenny turned to face her. 'Mum, the truth is that you are an attractive woman who had an amazing career as a successful barrister until you retired. You brought up a daughter, mainly by yourself, who turned out to be happy, well-adjusted and also a successful barrister. You've had more proposals in the last twenty years than I can even remember. You are alone now through your own choice. You are not a victim and I refuse to listen to you insisting you are for one more minute. So enjoy your wallowing because I'm going home. I'm not playing this game any more.'

With that, she kissed her shocked mother on her cheek and left, closing the door gently behind her.

Barbara waited until she heard Jenny's car pull away, still hoping that she would change her mind and come back in. She sat down to compose herself, still wound up after being interrupted mid-tirade. Then, unable to contain her anger any more, she picked up the phone, preparing to leave an accusing message on Ben and Jenny's answering machine.

But the line was engaged.

Rebecca put the phone down, feeling a lot better. It was so much easier to say how she felt when Ben wasn't actually in front of her. She'd got it all out of her system and felt energised.

He's got a surprise in store when he gets home, she thought happily.

Chapter 9

Kate almost jumped back when she walked into Ben's house. It was an ocean of men peppered with the occasional woman. Two to be precise: Jenny and Sally. Kate brought the total number of women up to three.

Ben walked over to take her coat and greet her with a polite kiss.

'Glad you could make it, Kate. Come on through and let me introduce you to a few people.'

Men, you mean a few *men*, Kate corrected him silently. She followed Ben into the cavernous open-plan living area, conscious of her short skirt in this testosterone-foggy atmosphere. The men didn't even bother trying to hide their appreciation of Kate's long legs.

How did I ever allow myself to buy this skirt? she asked herself crossly.

It was Justine who'd made her go out and buy yet more clothes.

'You can't just turn up there in the suit you wore to work,' Justine had said on the phone this morning.

'Don't change the subject,' Kate had warned her. 'I'm not going to let you off this phone until you tell me everything that happened. And I mean everything.'

There had been a long silence. Kate assumed that Justine was trying to decide what or how much to tell her. She stuck to her now-favourite strategy of staying silent and waiting until the other person cracked first.

Once more it worked.

'Nothing happened,' Justine blurted out.

'Nothing?' Kate said sceptically.

'Almost nothing,' Justine said weakly.

Kate closed her eyes. It was as she'd feared. From the moment she'd seen Justine's bare finger, she'd known where the evening was going to end. But she hoped she knew Justine well enough to believe that it hadn't been planned.

She didn't know why she was so surprised. Justine's transformation had been so dramatic and obvious that anyone could have seen she was not the same person she had been before.

Changing a hairstyle is one thing. It is a given that most women will experiment with their hair at key points in their lives, sometimes at random points. For a while it will change them slightly, give them more or less confidence, and they will either settle into the new style or slowly grow it out, reverting to the safer, more familiar look.

But Justine was different. She had resolutely *not* experimented with her hair or any other aspect of her appearance. For her, there was no gentle yo-yo effect in her life. She stood on a solid, steady platform, never looking backwards or sidewards or even forwards, letting life happen to her as she clung to the security of her own consistency. Whatever happened to her, she would face it with all the weapons that had protected her since adolescence. It was a conscious and logical decision in her eyes, since she had managed to avoid any major unhappiness or emotional upset in this way.

But now she was flinging off her armour, all of it, and donning a suit of flimsier substance. Her hair, her make-up, even her clothes, she'd changed them all. How could she possibly stay the same? And she wasn't standing still any more, she was walking fast, building up to a running pace, grabbing greedily at all the life that she had shunned up until now. Her momentum was gaining and she could not be stopped, not by reason, not by distraction, not by a friend's concern. Justine would not stop running until she fell over.

The removal of her wedding ring was like a starting pistol, launching her on a race she could not possibly win. Even if she experienced a sense of victory for just participating, her ultimate loss was inevitable. It had to be; she had no idea what the rules of the game were. And as a married woman with three children she would not be the only casualty on this obstacle course.

'Don't say it, Kate,' Justine pleaded softly.

'Oh, Jus. If you and Steve are having problems, this isn't the way to solve them.'

Justine laughed sadly. 'But we're not having problems. This is nothing to do with him. It's me. If I can just experience a bit of living, find out what my life could have been like if I hadn't opted out so early, then I'm sure I'll be able to accept my future with . . . contentment.'

'God, Justine, you make your marriage sound like a death sentence.'

'Well, if you think about it, Kate, it is a life sentence.'

Kate didn't want the details of what happened. It was enough to know that *something* had. Justine sensed that her friend was dropping the interrogation and eagerly returned to her original point.

'You'll have to buy something new,' she said.

'When am I supposed to do that?' Kate asked incredulously.

'You take a lunch break, don't you?' Justine pointed out.

143

'Can you come with me?' Kate asked. 'You know how useless I am.'

'Sorry, I can't.' She didn't add: 'Because I'm working.' Kate didn't ask what she was doing. She didn't want to know. She'd known Steve for so long that, although she would never call him a friend, she felt uncomfortable being complicit in his betrayal.

'You'll be fine,' Justine assured her. 'Now you've got your style sorted out for the office, you just need to continue the theme into the evening. Go back to Harvey Nicks where we found the suits. They'll be bound to have something similar.'

Kate had no confidence about choosing something appropriate and had a nagging fear that, without firm guidance, her nervous hand would reach unstoppably for an expensive variation on the cardigan-and-baggy-skirt theme. Particularly since the theme had served her quite well the night before.

Once the wine had arrived and both she and Callum had drunk the first glass too quickly, they began to enjoy themselves. Kate was concentrating her main attention on Justine. Max had moved closer to her. They were laughing with too much animation and Justine had suddenly become touchy-feely, a quality that she had always despised in others before now.

That was probably why Kate felt so relaxed with Callum: she had no nerves left to worry about him. Then he said something that caused her to focus on him more fully.

'Sorry?' she said. 'What did you say?'

'Just that you look nice.'

Kate sat back in amazement. Callum thought that she was joking.

'Yeah, I'll bet you think I'm just saying that, you must hear it so much.'

Kate looked at him more closely, searching his face for signs of insanity that she might have missed on first glance. Nope. He definitely appeared sane. Even more remarkable, he appeared normal.

While Kate had been told she looked nice before, it had generally been by people that even she would define as strange. Or old. Or her mother. Or vicars. Never by men of both her generation *and* her mindset. No, that was not true, she reminded herself. There had been men who'd appeared both normal and interested in her. But experience always eventually taught her that they were fundamentally flawed, lacking the tiniest seed of decency.

Callum seemed, really seemed . . . OK. Demented optimism? she wondered, cautiously.

'Are you mocking me?' she asked seriously.

Callum was offended. 'Of course I'm not. Why should I be?'

Kate poured herself another glass of wine, finishing the bottle and not caring whether this was socially acceptable or not. She took a deep breath, needing to concentrate on being honest after yet another day of painful insincerity.

'Because I don't look like anyone else here. And I've learned that sameness matters to most men.'

Callum smiled. 'I hate sameness. Actually I hadn't paid much attention to all the other women here. Precisely because they *do* all look the same. It was only when Max dragged me over that I even noticed you.' Then he flinched again at his own lack of tact.

Kate laughed. 'So how come you look like all the other men here then, if you admire difference so strongly?'

145

Callum looked down at his clothes. 'There's not so much scope for men. I'm not the type that would wear stripy trousers and comedy smocks. I just wear what is easy and makes me feel comfortable. Isn't that what you do?'

Kate had to agree.

Callum continued, 'It's just that my choice is a little more conventional than yours.'

'I envy you,' Kate said without thinking.

'You shouldn't. You look is perfect. Individual, feminine. Frankly it's a welcome relief from all the hard-faced women I work with.'

Kate felt uncomfortable. 'What exactly do you do?' she asked.

'I'm a money broker. And you think the women here look the same? You should see my office. It's as if a group of perfectly attractive, intelligent, individual women have willingly stepped on to a conveyor belt, only to come out the other end as a unit of clones.'

Kate intervened reluctantly. 'That's a bit unfair. I mean, they're just wearing a uniform, that's all. It's no different to men wearing suits.'

Callum disagreed. 'It's not just a matter of clothes. These women put on a whole lot more than a suit. They change their facial expressions, so they appear tough. They eradicate every soft edge, anything that might be interpreted as weakness, as if they can become men simply by wearing a tailored jacket.'

'You're not being totally fair. The clothes they are wearing are still feminine. They wear skirts, they wear make-up. If that's not feminine, I don't know what is.'

Why am I arguing like this? she asked herself. I agree with him.

Callum conceded the point, probably because he didn't

want to argue. 'You might be right. But I still think it's sad that women can't be who they want to be in work. Men may all wear the same uniform, their suit, but they're not afraid to be their own person.'

Kate had stopped enjoying herself and Callum had noticed. 'Sorry,' he said hastily. 'I'm sounding like a sexist pig. Let's change the subject.'

But they never quite regained their initial ease with each other and Kate was happy when Justine announced that she needed to go because she had an early shift in the morning.

The goodbyes were awkward, largely because Max and Justine had plainly agreed that they would be leaving together. Kate glared at Justine before making a dash for the exit, after a mumbled goodbye to Callum, who looked mortified.

'I'm really sorry if I upset you,' he said as she turned to leave.

'Of course you didn't,' Kate said unconvincingly. Then she'd left.

Kate shuddered as she replayed the whole evening, but she also experienced the odd prod of regret. It had started out so promisingly. She'd seemed to connect with Callum for a few minutes. Oh well, she sighed.

The morning went by quickly. There was a lot to do now that Rebecca had sorted out all the glitches in the files. They had to start pulling the presentation together. It was to be an expensive multimedia event and needed a lot of preparation. Gone were the days when you photocopied typed sheets on to acetates, Kate thought sadly. All this presentation needed was some original music commissioned from Elton John and its Hollywood credentials would be complete.

Kate was delegating as if it were an Olympic event. Each morning she picked out the critical creative tasks and appropriated them for herself, dividing the rest between Andrew and Rebecca.

Their reactions were strangely diverse.

'Andrew, I need you to go through all the charts and input the latest figures, then pass them on to Rebecca who can incorporate them into the commentary. I'll get on with the analysis and proposals for future development.'

She waited for an explosion. Her brain simply couldn't compute the fact that all she was asking of Andrew and Rebecca was to fulfil their job description, that Kate herself had been taken on at huge expense to concentrate her skills on such analysis. Her experiences during her first week of practising the art of delegation had caused her to reflect on all her previous jobs.

In her former incarnation, she would have done all this herself. She might even have given the creative job to one of her juniors, to pander to their high expectations, even though she would have no intention of using their work. Mad, she told herself now. Quite potty. And what had the others been doing all day while she was doing the entire team's work?

Plotting ways to torment her, apparently.

Although it still didn't feel natural to be giving orders, she was beginning to understand the point of the hierarchy. Now all she had to do was find a style of management that she could adopt without exhausting her limited dramatic skills.

She was still using the 'scumbag' method which stopped her from adding a pleading 'please' or 'sorry for asking' or 'no, I should never have asked, give it back and I'll do it myself, and by the way, can I get you a coffee?' to each request. She kept her sentences sparse, consequently sounding ruder than she would have liked. But she didn't know how to find a middle road. Maybe it will come with time, she told herself optimistically.

Andrew had been surprisingly cheerful with his allocated task. In fact Kate wondered if he'd taken some kind of drug since Monday. Unless *this* was the real Andrew and the sullen, aggressive, resentful creature she'd met on that first occasion was an alien projection, beamed in from a parallel universe. Maybe he'd been premenstrual or whatever the male equivalent was.

Certainly he was being consistently cooperative and pleasant. A little too pleasant, in fact. He made her so much coffee that she wondered if he was the company doormat. She didn't consider the possibility that he might have a crush on her, which any other woman would have immediately suspected, because she'd never before attracted enough attention in the workplace to inspire crushes. And she didn't suspect any kind of devious plan, because she'd never been important enough to anyone to warrant such labyrinthine plotting. She'd always been easy to beat. Humiliation was the quickest way to defeat her.

If they didn't know that now, then surely time would teach them, she reminded herself glumly.

Rebecca had more than compensated for Andrew's Pollyanna submission. She had let out a Marlene Dietrich sigh and waited for Kate to react.

Kate was finding Rebecca's hostility very irritating now that she no longer took it personally. To her own surprise, Kate had undergone a transformation in more than just her outward appearance. Once liberated from the energy-consuming obligation to make everybody like her, she had the time and spare emotional faculties to take a real look at her colleagues.

She'd startled herself by learning that she could be intuitive. She quickly identified Rebecca as a woman who was frustrated with her career and was transferring the blame for this on to the most convenient scapegoat, in this case Kate.

This was a major breakthrough in Kate's development. Some people, lots of people, go through their entire lives taking everything personally. It's nothing to do with lack of self-esteem and a lot to do with seeing oneself falsely as the centre of the universe, both in one's own eyes and the eyes of everyone else.

Kate started to be a winner when she stopped allowing other people's cruelty to do any more than graze her ego, rather than smash a bloody great hole that would never completely heal over.

So the theatrical sigh didn't even tickle Kate, who graced Rebecca with a level stare.

'Is there a problem, Rebecca?' she asked.

Rebecca glanced furiously at Andrew, willing him silently to back her up. He was refusing to meet her look.

'It's just . . .' Rebecca fumbled.

Kate interrupted her smoothly. 'I've given you an important job to do. Is there anyone else you think I should give it to? Sally, perhaps?'

Kate knew that this suggestion would alarm Rebecca. Although Rebecca considered Sally a friend, it was a friendship based on each respecting the other's status. So Rebecca always paid for lunch and Sally always did Rebecca's typing first. Neither considered the other an equal, each ironically considering herself superior to the other.

The idea of Sally being promoted away from secretarial tasks was unthinkable to Rebecca. She'd worked hard to protect the mystique of executive work as opposed to clerical. If Sally were ever allowed to discover the truth, that there is little difference and that anyone with an average brain could do the work of most senior professionals, Rebecca's whole self-image would be diminished.

But she couldn't say anything else. Not that she needed to, since Kate had recognised this fragility in Rebecca's ego within the first couple of days of meeting her.

Rebecca resorted to the flounce out of the office once more. Damn, she said to herself, I must find another move. Flouncing is inherently ridiculous in a Chanel suit.

After she'd left, Kate caught Andrew's eye and they both broke down in laughter. It was unforced on both sides and neither knew how to move on from the moment, both uncomfortable with spontaneity in this contrived situation.

Kate cleared her throat to buy some time. Andrew decided to seize the initiative, since his mission was more clearcut and had some pressing time constraints.

'Look, I don't suppose you're free at lunchtime, are you?' he asked suddenly.

Kate was taken aback by the unexpected offer. While there was nothing untoward about two colleagues going out for an informal lunch, she was aware of Andrew's relationship with the prickly Rebecca and she was concerned that she might be building yet another wall of division through the small group.

In any case, she had a truthful excuse. 'Sorry, I'd love to but I have to go shopping. I need to buy something to wear to Ben's party tonight.'

Damn, she screamed at herself. She'd been disarmed by their shared laughter and it had caused her to lower her guard. Whatever air of mystery and respect she had attempted to construct about herself would crumble and

151

disintegrate if she carried on with girly declarations like that.

Andrew leaped on her personal revelation. 'That's OK. I could come with you,' he said without thinking.

This time they were both alarmed. Andrew couldn't believe he'd said it. He didn't know this woman, and, even if he had, he would never have offered to go shopping for a party frock with her. He wasn't that crazy.

Get a grip on yourself, he ordered himself firmly. She's going to sense my desperation and despise me, like all my girlfriends do eventually. And it would be a disaster if we got to that stage without going through the honeymoon period where she thinks I'm Mr Wonderful. I've got to move fast, but not so fast that she misses me completely.

Luckily for him, Kate was too concerned with planning her own response to be bothered with analysing Andrew's motivations.

Surely this can't be right, she asked herself. But she had no one to ask. Maybe top women executives take male junior executives shopping with them as a matter of course. How would I know? I've never had the time to go shopping at lunchtimes, either with men or women. Is it appropriate or inappropriate?

She had to make a quick decision. There was no time to phone Justine. Her head was throbbing with the stress of considering the offer. A lot depended on her answer. If she said the wrong thing, she could be blowing her cover and showing herself up as the naive little ingenue she had worked so hard and so successfully to cover up with masks.

In the end, there was one factor that helped her decide what to say. She couldn't think of one acceptable reason to say 'no'.

She wanted to scream, 'I don't want you to come!

This is going to be bad enough anyway. I'm a mess with clothes. Now I'll even have to keep my act up in Harvey Nichols. Go away! Leave me alone. Let me have an hour of solitude where I can let myself go.'

'That would be great,' she said calmly, now knowing why all those officers in *The Bill* kept bottles of whisky in their desk drawers.

Jenny walked around Harvey Nichols in a stupor. She was looking at clothes in her original size ten. The assistants were ignoring her, clearly identifying her as a mad pregnant woman who might just collapse on their floor and give birth if they showed her any encouragement or the slightest acknowledgement.

She had only some vague irrational idea of what she was doing. She was yearning for her pre-baby figure, before the baby had even been born, reminding herself of the person she'd been before she became pregnant, trying to see herself through Ben's eyes, both then and now, imagining how the change in her body and status affected the way he felt for her. And she was looking for distraction; shopping for clothes had always been a reliable distraction.

She couldn't stay in the house, she hadn't even been able to sleep in their bed. When Ben came home and found her sleeping on the sofa, he put it down to back problems. In fact she was only pretending to sleep. Sleep was impossible after hearing Rebecca's message on the answering machine. And when Ben woke up and found her dressed, immaculately made up and ready to go out, he put it down to an attack of 'nesting'.

'You're off to buy baby things again, I'll bet. I've read about it in all the books,' he said affectionately, trying to put his arms round her.

She wriggled away from him. 'Don't,' she said, 'I'm tired and uncomfortable.' He smiled, so tolerant that she wanted to slap him. She wanted to slap him for other reasons too. But she couldn't think about that at the moment. She was determined not to do or say anything rash. She was days away from giving birth to her first child. There was so much at stake that she had to stay calm, although she felt close to hysteria.

So it was Harvey Nicks with its young, opulent smells and air of affluence and achievement. It was her shop, she felt right when she was there. Yet it wasn't the same today. She'd been wandering round other stores in Knightsbridge before coming here. Nesting, as Ben had predicted, but for less traditional reasons.

She wanted to remind herself of what was happening to her, the big thing, that is. She wanted to feel and buy tangible objects to connect herself to the baby and connect the baby to the home, Ben's and her home. She knew it was vital that she didn't separate herself from Ben on impulse. She had to make her decisions carefully and slowly.

She paid for all the clothes and nursery equipment on her own credit card, unconsciously ignoring the couple's joint card. It seemed right. Then when there were no more material possessions that a newborn baby could ever use, she moved on to Harvey Nichols.

She'd forgotten to have breakfast, feeling sick with worry, and she'd had nothing to drink all morning either. She was too fixated on keeping going, moving, doing things, buying things.

So it was hardly surprising that her body finally demanded attention. She collapsed in a dead faint in the middle of the shoe department.

As she came round, she thought she must be hallucinating. For the first face she saw was Andrew's.

When Justine saw Steve's face, she struggled to contain her rising panic. He was red from the strain of containing his laughter.

'You've forgotten how to do it, haven't you?' he said. 'I thought you said it was like riding a bike, once you've learned, the skill stays with you for life.'

Justine would have thrown a lipstick at him but she didn't know which one to risk so she stuck her tongue out instead.

'I haven't forgotten,' she said crossly, 'I'm just trying something . . . different, I'm experimenting that's all.' But a glance at Steve's suppressed laugh made her crack as well.

She stared at the mirror and then down at the palettes of colour, willing them on to her face as effectively as they'd been applied the previous day. It wasn't helping. She was doing exactly what she'd been doing before, or so she thought, so why was she looking like Barbara Cartland?

The blusher was adhering to her cheekbones like industrial cement. It was not providing 'a subtle highlight to her bone structure, seamlessly uniting all the unique features of her face into a stunning whole'.

And the scarlet lipstick made her look pale and unwell. Or maybe she *was* pale and unwell. She had a hangover, something she hadn't gone through since her first child was born twelve years ago.

Her eyes no longer looked smoky and interesting, they looked as if she'd gone to bed in her make-up and rubbed her eyes during the night.

She could weep. She was meeting Max for lunch before

her afternoon shift, having told Steve that she was going out with a group of new mums who wanted to thank her for all her help.

She didn't feel guilty, or only a bit, because it was innocent, so far. Max might have been a little disappointed that the evening hadn't ended quite as he'd hoped but he'd been a perfect gentleman, or if not perfect, he hadn't dragged her down an alley, so that was promising.

Kate suspected worse, she knew. And she'd done nothing to correct the false assumption. It was part of the fun, the adventure, pretending that she was being naughtier than she really was.

And now she and Steve were laughing, something that hadn't been happening very much recently. So she was right. This was of benefit to them both, not just to her.

'What do you think?' she asked Steve pleadingly.

Oh oh, he thought. Dangerous territory. Say something vague.

'Lovely,' he said blandly.

Justine dropped her head into her hands. 'Is it *that* bad?' she asked in despair. The question was rhetorical. She knew how bad it was. Even her hair was misbehaving. She'd blow-dried it exactly how the hairdresser had shown her. But instead of spunky tufts making a rebellious statement, she had ended up with Little Orphan Annie ringlets that would make old ladies want to pat her on the head and give her sixpence.

Too late. There was nothing more she could do. He'll just have to take me as I am, she thought firmly.

As she left, Steve shook his head affectionately at her eccentric appearance. It's lucky for her it's just a girls' lunch, he thought.

*

Rebecca couldn't face another girls' lunch with with her secretary.

'Have you got any idea where Andrew's gone?' she asked Sally.

'All I know is he went out at the same time as Kate and they both said they'd be back at about two thirty.'

Rebecca's stomach churned up. So that was that. She'd been sitting at her desk all morning; they could have asked her if she wanted to join them for lunch. She'd conveniently forgotten her mini-tantrum in Kate's office.

The lines were drawn, then, Rebecca thought. Andrew's gone over to the Dark Side. Where does it leave me in this company and in Andrew's life?

At the beginning of the week, it had all been straightforward. She and Andrew were united in their plan to undermine Kate, to oust her quickly. And he'd seen what she was like. He couldn't have missed it. She was everything he always said he didn't like in a woman: hard, humourless, single-minded. And she was his boss, a woman boss. His biggest fear, almost a phobia. In fact, even if she'd been everything he loved in a woman, he would still have hated her because she was a woman and his boss. And Rebecca understood that. She felt the same.

And then, for no reason that she could fathom, he'd changed his attitude. He'd turned away from Rebecca towards Kate. She just didn't understand it.

Having lunch together. Without her. Then the thought occurred – had Ben gone as well? She didn't know if that was better or worse. If he had, then she would have been the only member of the team to be excluded, which would be terrible. If he hadn't, then Kate and Andrew had chosen to go out by themselves, which would be terrible.

At that moment, Ben walked by. Well, that answered

that question. She braced herself for the explosion. She'd said some awful things in her message last night, some of which she regretted because they made her look petty. Or potty. Or both. And he was the MD. It had not been a smart career move.

'Hi Rebecca. Have you seen Andrew or Kate?'

Rebecca narrowed her eyes suspiciously. What game is he playing now? Why isn't he screaming at me for saying all the things I said? Perhaps he's planning some kind of revenge. Or maybe he's acting as if nothing's happened, staying cool, because he knows that will annoy me even more. There's little worse than being ignored, she thought, especially when she had served him up one of the most creatively vitriolic speeches of her life. And she'd spared no detail.

His expression gave nothing away so she had no choice but to go along with him, feeling her way tentatively. 'Apparently they've gone out to lunch together,' she said.

And then he smiled. Rebecca couldn't stand it any longer. 'Do you mind telling me what the hell is going on here?' she asked. 'I thought we all hated her and suddenly Andrew is besotted with her and you're practically welcoming her into the family!'

Ben knew he couldn't bluff his way out. 'Look, let me put it like this. Nothing has changed. I still have every intention of having Kate Harris out of here within the month and Andrew in her place the same day. But I can't go into any details.'

Rebecca was only slightly mollified. 'I do live with Andrew. Do you not think I'm entitled to know what's going on?'

Ben had to tread carefully here. Andrew had told him all about the previous evening.

*

158

It had been a disaster. Andrew had forgotten to tell Rebecca that he was cooking her a special meal to cheer her up and, by the time she got home at eight forty-five, the food was burned along with a lot of her hopes.

Andrew was furious. He felt entitled to be angry when all his efforts had been wasted but, if he was being honest with himself, he was just releasing all the tension that had been mounting in him since he'd foolishly agreed to Ben's plan.

Since his rash resolution to trust his instincts and take wild forays into uncertainty, he had felt himself being sucked deeper and deeper into a quicksand of bad decisions.

He should never have agreed to try and seduce Kate. He wasn't clever enough or complex enough. And because his affairs with women had always been simple trans-actions with cleancut beginnings, smooth middles and swift painless ends, he'd never learned the language of relationship maintenance.

The general rule was that he'd smile at women, they'd respond and, with minimal effort, he'd have a new girl-friend. Now he was expected to win over a woman he didn't want, a woman who knew he was involved with someone else, and achieve this end in a matter of days. And for what?

The reasons which had made sense while Ben was selling them to him had all become blurry. He felt sure there must be a more reliable method of sabotaging a woman's first month of work, but he couldn't think of one. On top of this, Rebecca had been decidedly frosty recently. He didn't know why he should do something so taxing for her, if it was for her. And if it was for him, he wasn't sure it was worth it. He didn't know what was happening. He hated that feeling.

159

Rebecca didn't know what was going on either. Only a week earlier, she had began to think that it was time to get out of this relationship. Like all of Andrew's previous girlfriends, she had reached the stage where she was finding him incredibly annoying. The causes were countless: his obsession with tea towels which could only be used once, his weekly exploration of the fridge to check all the sell-by dates, his four chopping boards for different products, the way he ironed his jeans, the way he ironed *her* jeans.

But then, when she'd seen him behaving so strangely with Kate, so ingratiatingly, she'd felt less certain. The way he'd looked at her, almost adoringly, stabbed her. All she could think was that he was going to leave her for Kate. It was bad enough to be dumped by Ben; but at least she could console herself with the illusion that he had been forced into it by his married state. To be left for someone else, though, someone who would be working in the same office, purely because she was better or prettier or both than Rebecca, that would be unbearable.

She was reeling here, no longer focused. It wasn't just a question of getting rid of Kate and trying to recapture some of the possibilities that existed before she arrived. It was now a necessity for Rebecca that Andrew reject Kate and choose her. Rebecca simply couldn't handle another rejection right now. But unfortunately, she hadn't worked this out until about eight o'clock, after she'd left the fateful message on Ben's answerphone.

She had experienced a great sense of catharsis, and she'd felt light-headed afterwards, finally accepting that the link with Ben was severed, from her side. She could start looking ahead and, at this time, only Andrew was ahead. By the time she got home, ready to overwhelm

160

Andrew with renewed passion and an astonishing tolerance for his foibles, he was sullen with rage.

'Well, you could have told me that you were cooking,' she accused him.

Andrew glared at her. 'I always cook on a Thursday.'

Rebecca mentally added this to her growing list of Things That Annoy Me About Andrew: his bloody rotas. But she suppressed her frustration. She was late and that was wrong.

'I'm sorry,' she said humbly. 'Still, I'm here now, there's no need to spoil the evening.'

But Andrew's evening had been ruined the second the food was ready and Rebecca wasn't there. He couldn't stand lateness. (Rebecca added that to her list.) 'Could you not at least have phoned?' he said harshly. 'You know I hate a lack of communication.' (On the list already.)

'I was busy going through all the files that you and *she* dumped on me this afternoon.'

'It didn't have to be done tonight. You ought to be so on top of this account that you can handle the work in normal hours. If you're struggling, then you should have told me and I could have given you a hand.'

Now he was patronising her. (The list had gone off the page and was now too long to compute statistically.)

'I am quite capable of doing my job. In fact I am quite capable of doing *your* job and I am certainly capable of doing Kate's. In fact, maybe that's why you're so cosy with her all of a sudden. You've just realised that, if Kate goes, it might not be you who gets her job, it might be me. And you couldn't stand that. Better a stranger than your girlfriend. Am I right?'

Andrew was so angry, he did what he always did when confronted with emotional free-fall. He ran away.

He knew that Ben would be at the pub. When he'd heard from his mum that Jenny was stopping overnight, he had watched with amusement as Ben had trawled the building looking for company. In fact, Ben had been about to leave the pub when Andrew arrived. He sighed and took off his coat when he saw what a state Andrew was in.

'So what did you say to her?' Ben asked her, pleased to hear that things were going so badly with Rebecca.

'What could I say?' Andrew answered miserably. 'That I was going to be doing my utmost to make Kate fall in love with me but that you mustn't worry because it has nothing to do with the fact that our relationship is rocky?'

Ben brightened at this first mention of problems with Rebecca. 'She might have understood,' Ben suggested. 'It's a good plan.'

'It's a terrible plan!' Andrew shouted, knocking red wine over Ben's jacket. 'I don't understand it myself, so how could *she*? Whatever I feel for Rebecca, I don't want to hurt her, and it *will* hurt her if she feels betrayed. It's not fair. I'm not like that.'

Ben sighed. 'Then just say nothing and let her get on with things her way. She'll soon see that Kate is a tough cookie who won't let a little cold-shoulder treatment distract her from her mission. Then, in a few weeks, she'll understand why you did what you did. You'll be promoted, we'll give her some extra responsibility and everything will be back to the way it was.'

Andrew was still not happy, so Ben was forced to spend the entire evening with him, pacifying and reassuring his friend that everything would be fine.

Ben didn't get home until eleven thirty. He was exhausted. He'd only intended to have a couple of drinks then go home and have an early night. He was quietly dreading tomorrow's party and the stress was wearing him down.

I'd have been home and in bed by ten o'clock if Andrew hadn't turned up, he said to himself wearily as he unlocked the door.

And if he had been home by ten o'clock, then he would have been the one to hear Rebecca's devastating message instead of Jenny.

Chapter 10

'I suppose you know?' Jenny said to Andrew bitterly. They were in the restaurant and Jenny's face had a little more colour in it after being force-fed soup and bread by her brother.

She could tell by his face that he didn't have a clue what she was referring to so she shut up.

'No, go on, tell me,' he pressed. 'If something is wrong then I want you to tell me.'

Jenny was touched by his concern and angry with herself for even thinking that he might have been party to the deception. He probably had no idea that his girlfriend was on the rebound from Ben; she loved him too much to tell him. The ten-year age difference between them had not been as divisive as their parents might have imagined.

He had been protective and loving towards her from the day she was born. He always said that she was the first person he ever really loved, even more than his parents, with that painful love that can't bear to see the other person suffer in any way.

And when their father left, he took over the parental role, reading to her, helping her with homework while their mother was working. He attended most of her school functions, even though he was in his twenties and was enjoying a consuming career in marketing.

She knew that he was mocked for his controlling

tendencies and his compulsion for organisation. But she also knew that this stemmed from the time when he was leading two lives, looking after her as well as his career, and that only a stringent commitment to detail could enable him to succeed at both.

For the first time in their lives, she had responsibility for *his* happiness. They didn't see each other as often as she would have liked, and he knew that this was because he was engrossed in his new love. She had been thrilled to hear him talk about Rebecca with such hope. And she'd been so looking forward to meeting her.

So how could she tell him? Besides, it would destroy his faith in Ben. Their friendship was important to him, to them both. And if, just if, she managed to patch up this enormous rift in her marriage, then it would be so much easier to get on with normal life if Andrew was there, as he always was, cementing her and Ben together, liaising, uniting, listening to them both and mediating. He would never forgive Ben, she knew that.

Such control was astonishing for someone in her position and her condition. But this was the situation she had always feared most, even before she got married, and she had mentally rehearsed her actions and reactions a thousand times.

But she couldn't lie to him; he knew her too well. So she changed the subject. 'Oh ignore me, I'm just furious with Ben for insisting on this party tonight when I'm feeling so knackered. And I don't know what I'm saying half the time.'

Andrew wasn't totally convinced, but it was plausible and he was more concerned about her physical state than anything else. 'And you're sure you don't want me to call Ben?' he asked for the fifth time.

'I'm sure,' she said with strained patience.

'I think she's sure, Andrew,' Kate added before he had a chance to ask her again. Although she'd never met Jenny before, it hadn't taken her more than a couple of minutes to know that this was a profoundly unhappy pregnant woman and that her unhappiness was entirely due to her husband.

There had been an unpleasant moment when Jenny had mistaken her for Rebecca.

'You!' she'd spat at Kate while Andrew was helping her to her feet. Kate looked around her, wondering whether Jenny might have spotted one those irritating saleswomen in pharmacy coats trying to spray her with hideous expensive perfume.

No, Jenny was looking straight at her. Andrew looked puzzled.

'Do you know Kate?' he asked in surprise.

Jenny absorbed this information and rearranged her expression. 'Sorry, I thought you were someone else,' she apologised to Kate.

Andrew was too worried about Jenny to be bothered to follow this through. When she was finally standing, it was clear that she would be keeling over again within minutes if she didn't have something to eat and drink, so they made their way to the restaurant.

Great, Kate thought, just how I wanted to spend my lunch hour. Pretending to be someone I'm not with a man who can't make up his mind whether he hates me or can't get enough of me and his mad pregnant sister.

Great, Justine thought, just how I wanted to spend my lunch hour. Pretending to be someone I'm not with a man who wants to be with the woman I was pretending to be last night.

It took a second for Justine to read Max's mind and

166

discover just how bad she looked. He was wearing a mask of horror. She wanted to turn round and run away. But she couldn't. She was a grown-up.

What had she said to Kate? Imagine yourself as an actress playing a role. Think! Think! Think! She ran through the films she'd seen recently. *Billy Elliot*? Too northern. *Bridget Jones's Diary*? Too young. *Harry Potter*? Yeah, very funny. No more time, she screamed to herself as she approached the table. *Do* something. *Be* someone.

She went with the first character that came into her mind. When she looked back on the fiasco, she conceded that Mary Poppins was probably not the best choice.

Kate had to remind herself who she was. It was difficult to keep the act up out of the office.

'This is Kate Harris,' Andrew explained.

Jenny's face betrayed that she had worked out who this was and was not impressed. 'The one who got your job?' she pointed out bluntly.

Andrew closed his eyes. Don't go there, please, he pleaded silently with his sister. When he opened his eyes, Kate was looking at him curiously.

'What does she mean by that?' she asked him.

Andrew played with the cutlery and crockery on the table like a naughty child trying to find somewhere to hide his last Brussels sprout. Kate ignored his diversionary tactics and waited for him to answer. Eventually he weakened. Can't think why I never tried this tactic before, Kate thought, congratulating herself on another result.

'I applied for the job,' Andrew said simply.

Jenny wasn't going to let him off that easily. 'The only reason he applied in the first place was because Ben practically promised him that the job was his.'

167

Kate sat back. It was all making sense now; Ben's lack of interest in her during the interview, the hostility of the team towards her.

'What about Rebecca? Is she just angry on your behalf?' she asked Andrew, wanting to understand these people fully so that she could work out how to deal with them.

Jenny started breaking pieces of bread from her roll and placing them in her mouth with excessive care. She didn't want them to notice her reaction to Rebecca's name.

Andrew shook his head. 'No, she was turned down for a promotion herself a while ago. Ben told her, off the record, that it was because she was a woman, that the board were notoriously anti-women in senior positions. So when she heard you'd been hired, she was furious. She thought you must have inside influences or something.'

Kate interpreted this slightly differently. Maybe the appointment made Rebecca realise that the reason she didn't get the promotion herself was for other reasons, she thought.

She was about to apologise for something that was patently not her fault, when she stopped herself. It was the feel of her pink shoes pinching her toes that reminded her who she was supposed to be.

This was exactly the sort of moment when any display of weakness would be fatal. None of these people were her friends. On the contrary they all had reason to dislike and resent her. Everything inside her wanted to scream, 'Like me! I'm a nice girl! I'll resign and Andrew can have the job and Rebecca will be pacified and you'll all live happily ever after!'

But she'd come too far this week. If she backed down now, she might just as well resign her self to a life of being walked over.

She took a casual sip of her wine and looked coolly at Andrew. 'Then I'm going to have to prove to you that I won this job on merit, aren't I? Show you what I can do.'

Oh terrific, Andrew thought. Somehow I've managed to motivate her to work even harder, to achieve even more. This is hopeless. We're stuck with her. Ben will be thrilled.

Max was less than thrilled with his companion. How drunk was I last night? he asked himself. Perhaps it was the lighting. This is definitely not the same woman. He looked at her again.

Justine beamed a happy beam. She couldn't stop. She'd have to scream if she stopped concentrating.

'I know what you're thinking,' she said. And she really did.

Max strained to look amused. 'OK, I'll go along with it. What am I thinking?'

'That I look different in the daytime?'

Bingo. 'No, of course I wasn't,' Max said gallantly.

Justine ignored the comment, recognising it for what it was. 'Well, I don't know about you, but I think superficial appearances can be misleading.'

You've got that right, Max thought.

Justine ploughed on gamely, spooning syrup over every woefully inappropriate remark. 'So I think it can be fun to play with one's appearance, paint a sunny picture on a cloudy face, don't you agree? Life would be so boring if we all looked the same from day to day, wouldn't it?'

No it wouldn't, Max thought. It would be simple, not boring. We'd all know where we stand. But he had to say something. And it fell out before he could stop it.

'Is your hair supposed to look like that?' he asked.

169

Justine picked up the menu and held it in front of her face so that Max would not see her mouthing some surprisingly un-Mary-Poppins-like words.

Max picked up his menu and skimmed it, searching for the quickest way out of this place.

'I'm not over-hungry, think I overdid the vino last night. I'll just have the goat's cheese salad.' He called his order to a passing waiter, the note of urgency conveying his expectation of fast service.

'Same for me,' Justine called feebly, hoping the salad would arrive very, very quickly and be very, very small.

Max and Justine looked at each other across the table, then they both looked at their watches.

Kate looked at her watch. 'Sorry, I really have to be getting back to the office. Can't have Rebecca thinking I'm slacking, can I?'

Andrew forced a smile. 'I'll come with you.'

'Don't be silly, stay here, look after your sister.'

'No, I'll be fine. In fact I'm going to get in a taxi and go home for a nap. Honestly, I'll be fine,' insisted Jenny.

'Then let me at least put you in a taxi,' Andrew urged.

'It's not necessary. They can get me one on the door. Just go.'

She touched Andrew's hand affectionately. He stood up and kissed her reluctantly before leaving with Kate.

Jenny watched them go with interest. She knew her brother so well, that she sometimes suspected she could guess his feelings before he did. Like now. She'd felt the tension between them at the start of the lunch. This was hardly surprising under the circumstances. But Andrew's face had changed during the meal.

Whereas he had been looking at Kate with caution

in the beginning, he began slowly displaying signs of admiration as she kept her cool under attack. And by the end, she was certain that she'd seen something else, something personal and revealing. Andrew was starting to like Kate.

Jenny only had one priority in her mind right now, to get Rebecca out of Andrew's and, consequently, Ben's life. She couldn't approach the challenge of fixing her marriage – or ending it – until that loose end was tied up.

Yes, she thought, Kate would serve that purpose very well.

'Wait!' Andrew said, grabbing Kate's arm, then releasing it quickly. 'You still haven't bought anything for tonight.'

'It doesn't matter. I'll come as I am.' Kate was now anxious to recapture her professional image and get out of this shop as quickly as possible.

'It's still only ten past two. If we're quick, we can get something and still be back by two thirty.'

Kate shuddered at the prospect of buying an outfit in ten minutes. Even when she was buying her shapeless cardigans and skirts, it took longer than that. They had to fit her, after all. And this was a more contentious area altogether, completely unexplored territory.

But Andrew had subtly altered their direction back up to Fashion and now she was standing in front of a rail of small black skirts, leather skirts. She gravitated towards them because she'd seen a woman who was dressed like her choosing garments from the same rail. She must know what she's doing, Kate thought.

She picked out a skirt, clueless as to its appropriateness or if it would even suit her.

'That's fantastic!' Andrew exclaimed, making her jump. 'Why don't you try it on?'

This was too much. He was acting like a boyfriend. Surely businesswomen don't go and try on clothes while their subordinates wait outside, watching the handbags?

She was rescued from further tortuous analysis by a reassuringly pushy sales assistant.

'That will look great on you,' she said with a tad too much enthusiasm. 'And if I can suggest this top to go with it?' She flicked along a different rail until she came to a black chiffon top, totally transparent with a tiny silk bodice underneath to protect her modesty.

Kate wanted to laugh hysterically. She wanted to run out of this shop and sink gratefully into the calm, re-assuring atmosphere of Country Casuals where they appreciated an Englishwoman's restraint, or neurotic prudishness as Justine preferred to call it.

But Kate hadn't rehearsed for this scene. And if Kate had been a doormat in her professional world, then in the world of shopping, she was a fully fitted Axminster.

She simply could not say no to salespeople. She had wardrobes full of unsuitable clothes that she'd mistakenly touched only to be coerced into buying by predatory assistants.

Even in supermarkets she found herself being accosted by demonstrators trying to force unwilling shoppers to try new and generally disgusting products. Not only did Kate always stop and sample the organic garlic crisps and broccoli juice and banana curry, she always took the money-off coupon that was handed to her and obediently bought packets of the vile stuff. She couldn't not, just in case the demonstrator was watching her and was hurt by Kate's rejection.

But this was a million times worse. She had an audience. Andrew would witness her prevarication and pass the news of this fallibility back to the hit squad in the office.

She didn't think the 'scumbag' approach would work in this situation. Saleswomen will cheerfully answer to any name if it means a sale. There was only one solution. She would try on the clothes and buy them, whatever they looked like. Andrew could not avoid being impressed by her no-nonsense approach to shopping, her single-mindedness, her iron resolve. Hell, she'd be impressed herself if she saw a woman do that.

Oh my God, she thought when she saw herself in the mirror. I look like an expensive call girl, one of those women you see in hotel bars with dead eyes and drop-dead gorgeous bodies.

She was momentarily impressed by the sight of how good the reflection looked in revealing clothes, before she remembered that this was her. She flushed from her face to her legs.

'Come and show us!' the assistant called firmly.

Kate took a deep breath before emerging from her cubicle, head held rigidly high, scary smile superglued on her face.

'Yes, this will do fine. Thank you,' she said tightly before going straight back behind the curtain and tugging off the offending garments as if they were on fire.

Andrew and the assistant looked at each other.

'Is she always like this?' the assistant asked in surprise. 'Most women like to take ages choosing clothes.'

Andrew shrugged. 'I don't know. She's my boss. I've only known her a few days.'

Bizarre, the assistant thought. They make a right pair.

Within seconds Kate was back out, in her original

clothes and poised again. She handed the new clothes over to the assistant along with her credit card and a nod of acknowledgement.

Her assertiveness reaped appropriate rewards and the assistant scurried to the till to complete the transaction.

'Wow,' Andrew said. 'You don't mess about, do you?'

Kate raised her eyebrows. 'I have too many more important things to do to waste time on things like shopping,' she said with a calm she didn't feel.

'Well, I have to say, you looked great!' And he meant it. He really meant it. Although he'd only seen her for a fraction of a second, he'd been stunned by how unbusinesslike she'd appeared. He'd felt a pang of betrayal towards Rebecca as some new thoughts began coursing round his brain.

Only yesterday, he'd started to persuade himself that Rebecca might be the one for him. And now, the attraction that he was supposed to be feigning for Kate was feeling more real.

It was her determination that he was growing to appreciate, that and her single-mindedness. She was very like him in many ways. She would be surprised to know that he shopped in exactly the same way as she did. If a pair of trousers fitted him and looked acceptable, then he'd buy five pairs in different neutral shades and be out of the shop in ten minutes.

And, like her, he was difficult to derail. Before this business with Ben and his crazy plan, he was a steel girder, projecting unbending into the future. Other people had to fit in with him, that's how he operated, how he kept a grip on his world.

But he'd never met anyone like himself before. And the more he got to know Kate, the more he felt his initial resentment towards her drifting away, to be replaced with something more positive and more dangerous.

I hate this, he thought miserably. I like my life to be easy. One woman at a time, one goal at a time, everything pre-defined. This is getting messy and I'm not good at mess. I don't have much experience with it and I could make terrible mistakes. I *will* make terrible mistakes, I know I will.

The walk back to the office was uncomfortable. Andrew was asking himself questions for which he couldn't find any simple answers and Kate was wondering how she could possibly go to Ben's party looking like a Page Three girl.

Once they got back to the building, they made their way to Sally's desk to get any messages and any caustic comments she had saved up for Kate. She didn't look up from her typing.

'Rebecca was looking for you, Andrew,' she said with an accusing note in her voice.

Andrew felt as guilty as if he'd been rolling around on the grass with another woman. His red face betrayed him.

'Right, thanks. Do you know where she is?'

'Making coffee,' Sally said casually.

Kate stifled a smile at this.

'I'll go and talk to her in the coffee room,' Andrew said unhappily.

'Any messages for me, Sally?' Kate asked.

'Just one,' Sally said. 'Someone called Callum called you. I've left his number on your desk.'

'Hi, I hope you didn't mind me calling you at work,' Callum said.

'I was a bit surprised, that's all. I didn't think I

175

gave you my number,' Kate replied, knowing that she hadn't.

Callum sounded sheepish. 'I got your number from Justine, or rather, Max got it from Justine and passed it on to me. I know that's a bit of a cheek and I'll understand if you tell me to get lost and slam the phone down.'

At any other time, Kate would have done precisely that, but she was preoccupied with the reference to Justine. And Max. Callum was making them sound like a couple and they'd only met last night. It worried her.

'That's OK,' she said absently.

'Great!' Callum exclaimed in relief. 'So anyway, the reason I'm ringing is that I was wondering if you'd like to meet up. Just for a drink or something?'

As her pink shoes made their presence felt once more, Kate remembered that this was the man who liked women in cardigans and baggy skirts. She unconsciously kicked the shoes off, easing the transition back to her own self while talking to this man.

She didn't need this complication but couldn't think how to say 'no'. She squeezed her feet back into her pink shoes, which she had now come to see as possessing magic powers, hoping that she'd find the confidence to say what she wanted to say.

Nope. They weren't working. Her palms were becoming clammy again and she was diminishing in her own eyes as she weighed up her two options.

Option one: decline firmly and politely as any other normal woman would. No, can't do that, might hurt his feelings. And he'd thought she was so nice, so soft and sweet, wouldn't do to disillusion him. She couldn't forgive herself.

Option two: accept then find loads of excuses to cancel. Never mind that this was actually crueller to the poor man, it would be easier for Kate to manage. At least it would give him time to get used to the fact that he'd been wrong about her. She'd done this before. It gave her stress headaches but was usually effective after no more than two or three excuses.

Of course, there was always option three, to accept, go out with the man, enjoy herself and see where the relationship might lead but this was absolutely the wrong time for her to be going down that path.

'Sure,' she said with false brightness. 'That would be lovely.'

'How about this weekend?' Callum asked, encouraged by her cheerful acceptance.

'Sorry, I'm going to stay with my parents this weekend,' she lied smoothly. Well it was sort of true. She did need to see them, to talk through this New Zealand plan.

Callum wasn't deterred. 'Then how about Monday?'

He would doubtless go through all the days of the rest of their lives until she submitted, so she settled for Monday.

'If it can be lunch,' she said. Easier to cancel.

'That's fantastic!' Callum said, causing a well of guilt to spring inside Kate. 'I'll call you Monday morning and we'll arrange something.'

'I'll look forward to it,' Kate said, relieved that the conversation was about to end. She wouldn't have to think about this again until Monday. ''Bye'. She put the phone down with a sigh.

She picked up the receiver straightaway to call Justine, who was engaged. There was no time to try later. She had to raise her work output if she was going to win over these people. The lunch with Andrew had forced her mind back to the clause in her contract, the four-week condition.

She hadn't been too worried about it at the time. It seemed reasonable for them to have a safety net, a get-out should she turn out to be a blithering incompetent. And it was there for her benefit too, just in case things didn't work out for her.

But her main concern now was that Andrew and Rebecca and even Ben were banking on her falling on her face and being gone after the first month. And she could not let this happen. Even though she was not enjoying the job at the moment, mainly because of her so-called colleagues, she could not fail. She'd invested too much of herself in it. She would never go back to being a doormat. The only way for her was forward, a route she was taking the only way she knew how.

She was going to put everything into the next few weeks, both professionally and personally, to make this team respect her. And she would start at the party. She hoped it would be small and quiet; she would need to concentrate.

This is like a rugby club on a Saturday night, Kate thought grimly, looking about.

'I didn't know you knew each other,' Ben said curiously when Jenny kissed Kate warmly on both cheeks.

'We met today in Harvey Nicks,' Jenny said. 'I bumped into Andrew and Kate and we all had lunch together.' Her warning glance at Kate warned her not to mention the circumstances of their meeting.

Perhaps she doesn't want him to worry about her, Kate convinced herself. Ben beamed with pleasure at the notion of Jenny and Kate and Andrew all lunching together without Rebecca. He always had confidence in Andrew's abilities with women.

He felt a twinge of discomfort at the thought of the

three of them getting too cosy. Kate was never intended to be a permanent fixture in the future he was envisaging. One of the many last things he wanted at the moment was for Jenny and Kate to become buddies. Jenny had declared her determination not to like Kate before she met her. This was the woman who'd stolen her precious brother's job. It would be horribly ironic if Jenny came to like Kate so much that Ben would be pilloried for taking the job away from her and giving it back to Andrew.

This had the makings of a no-win situation but he had no time to address that tonight. Not when the doorbell had rung and Andrew and Rebecca had walked through the door.

Even the guests who didn't know them could tell that this was a couple who'd just had a row. Their body language screamed of tension. Neither touched or looked at the other. Their movements were still jerky from all the rage they'd been unleashing.

It had started in the coffee room and not finished until they'd rung Ben's doorbell. They had the same argument over and over again, a simple one, recognisable to us all and generally a reliable sign that a relationship was coming to a close. But neither was totally ready for this.

'Nice lunch?' Rebecca had asked coldly.

'You could have come, you know, if you hadn't been such an idiot earlier. Kate's all right really, once you get to know her.' Wrong thing to say, number one. 'I'm starting to understand why they took her on.' Wrong thing to say, number two. 'She's an amazing woman, not like any woman I've ever worked for before.' Wrong things to say, numbers three and onwards.

'I thought you said you'd rather sweep roads than

work for a woman, any woman, even me?' Rebecca said, prodding her finger towards him aggressively.

Andrew took a step backwards. 'But this is nothing to do with you and me. You were never even in the picture for this job. I'm the one who's missed out with Kate's appointment, so if I can accept her surely you can.'

Rebecca could almost hear her pulse thumping round her body, much too fast. He was saying things she didn't want to hear. And there were things he wasn't saying but that she knew were there, lurking in the subtext.

Andrew, meanwhile, was torturing himself silently for his rash decision to go along with Ben's original plan and for the idiotic misjudgement that stopped him from telling Rebecca what he was doing from the beginning. It was too late now. He'd started something that excluded Rebecca, a chain of events with unexpected emotional implications for him, ones he hadn't yet managed to absorb.

Rebecca couldn't stop herself from asking the wrong questions, women's questions. 'So how amazing is she?' She felt foolish, like a jealous woman. She *was* a jealous woman.

Andrew hoped that willpower alone would be able to prevent his face from betraying his true feelings. 'I'm talking about her professionally, nothing else.' But he was lying and Rebecca knew it. That was that then: she was losing him.

No, she would not lose him. Her sense of self was being eroded by the day and she needed some of it to be left intact before she moved on.

She deliberately relaxed her muscles and softened her face. She approached Andrew and leaned gently into him, waiting for him to envelop her. But he didn't. He was trying to sort out his feelings, to take control of them before they took control of him.

Right now, he felt little for Rebecca. He supposed he'd already begun the process of letting her go when she started showing the signs of irritation that always preceded a girlfriend's departure. It was hard to turn back. He was a man of habit and ritual and Rebecca was trying to break the symmetrical pattern that defined all his relationships.

All he wanted was for her to continue down the path she'd started on. He knew where he was with that. She was turning back and that wasn't allowed.

Rebecca felt humiliated by his lack of response. She pulled away roughly. Andrew was mortified at hurting her. Damn, he thought.

He pulled her back into his arms and stroked her hair absently. If Rebecca had settled for this, the difficult moment might temporarily have passed. But she couldn't leave things as they were.

'I've been thinking,' she said, too cheerfully. 'Maybe we could go shopping tomorrow for some new curtains?'

Andrew tensed and Rebecca felt his response immediately. 'I see. You were all in favour a couple of weeks ago. Is this to do with Kate?'

And then they went back to the beginning and had the same argument all over again.

By the time they reached Ben's house, they'd got back to the bit about the curtains, which were now 'bloody curtains', when the door opened.

The first thing Rebecca saw was Kate. She averted her glance immediately, not able to look at her right now, and turned her head slightly to look at the woman standing next to Kate.

The plate of canapés in her hand singled her out as

the hostess. Jenny. Rebecca looked at her more closely. It didn't take her long to notice Jenny's dominating feature.

The realisation of Jenny's advanced pregnancy swept through Rebecca's head along with some hasty calculations. Ben was watching her closely, watching her lips counting carefully and eyes narrowing dangerously as they absorbed the implications of the sums.

Then he saw that she'd worked it out.

Chapter 11

Stan had pulled all his favourite plays from the bookshelf.

'I think George Bernard Shaw goes down well anywhere and with any generation,' he said. 'Him and Oscar Wilde. New Zealand is no different to here in that respect. The audiences are the same, people looking for answers to the questions that they can't find in the newspapers.'

'Mmm,' Edie murmured.

'Or we could just put on a topless version of *Macbeth* with go-go dancers and rappers,' Stan added, checking to see if Edie was still on this planet.

'Mmm,' she said again.

'Edie!'

Edie jumped. She'd been going through her photo albums, half-listening to Stan. She felt confident tuning out since they'd been having this conversation since the day they were married. How one day they'd follow their big dream, or rather, Stan's big dream.

It had been a wonderful dream. But now it had shifted from dream to potential reality and Edie was having second thoughts.

'Sorry,' she said, 'I was just thinking about Kate. Did she seem stressed to you?'

'Of course she's stressed, she's got a new job and she's little Shirley Temple trying to play Margaret Thatcher. But she'll be fine. They'll all be fine.'

'Of course they will,' Edie agreed doubtfully.

'Now come here and tell me what you think for our opening production: *Lady Windermere's Fan* or *Oh! Calcutta?*'

Edie smacked him affectionately before giving all her attention to the plays. Or rather, most of her attention.

Rebecca turned slowly round to look for Ben, to confront him. He'd escaped to the kitchen, hoping to buy some time. This was too much for Rebecca. One slap in the ego too many, a lie too many. She couldn't restrain herself any longer. She was going to have to say or do something.

She dragged Andrew over to one side of the room by his sleeve. 'Why didn't you tell me your sister was pregnant?'

Andrew didn't answer immediately. He didn't understand why that should bother her; although he had long ago come to terms with the fact that he annoyed women for reasons he found strange, this was a new one. He formulated his reply carefully, not wanting to cause a scene here.

'I don't think there ever came a point in our conversations where it seemed relevant,' he said slowly, gauging her reaction to every word.

'Your only sister is going to have a baby and you didn't think it relevant to tell your girlfriend?' she said incredulously. 'One of the biggest milestones in your life and you kept it to yourself? On our second date, you told me the registration numbers of every car you'd ever owned and you didn't think to mention that you were going to be an uncle.'

Andrew swallowed awkwardly. He was trying to find a tactful way to avoid telling her the truth, that he hadn't

184

said anything because it was too important, too special, to share with her. That Jenny was probably closer to a daughter than a sister to him. That by telling a girlfriend, he would somehow be devaluing the news. This hadn't been a deliberate decision; he had only now recognised the motives behind his omission.

'Sorry,' he said.

Rebecca waited for him to say 'but' and add a plausible excuse she could cling to or an implausible one she could ridicule. Anything.

Nothing came. Andrew watched as Rebecca simmered up to a rising boil. He could only imagine that she was worked up from their arguing all afternoon; he was feeling pretty drained by it himself. But this seemed a bit petty. He risked saying so, hoping naively that he might be able to calm her down before she did something with serious repercussions.

'If you think about it, Rebecca,' he said, 'you never tell me anything about your family, nothing at all. At least you knew I had a sister.'

Rebecca pushed past him in search of a drink. There was no way she would allow him to break her down so easily. She didn't talk to anyone about her family. At least Andrew could console himself that it was nothing personal.

Rebecca was eighteen when her father was sent to prison for fraud. It was like finding out she'd been adopted, that her entire life had been built on a lie.

Her dad had been defrauding the bank where he'd worked for over ten years. There were never massive amounts involved, no Caribbean holidays or new cars every year. She and her brother hadn't even gone to private school. But their lives were comfortable and it seemed obvious, in retrospect, that his salary could not possibly have sustained their lifestyle without major excursions into debt.

Rebecca had never been refused new clothes and shoes – they were nothing extravagant but she never heard the word 'no'. Her brother Will had shown great potential as a show jumper and although their parents had drawn the line at buying him a horse, he was always kitted out in the best riding clothes.

As kids, they had no concept of price and its relationship to income. In that respect they were typical children. But, unlike their peers, when they asked for things, they would receive them.

'My dad works in a bank,' Rebecca would say with a shrug when her friends gasped at yet another pair of jeans. At that age, it appeared logical to equate working in a bank with lots of money.

When Rebecca turned sixteen, things changed. Her mum and dad became very quiet, always whispering and changing the subject when she or Will came into the room. And the refusals began. The words 'can't afford' started to be thrown at them. Rebecca was told she couldn't go on the school skiing trip, Will had to get a Saturday job to pay for his riding lessons.

Rebecca reacted by yelling at her parents, accusing them of meanness and selfishness. Will neglected his studies to work longer and longer hours to finance his riding.

The next two years were horrible. Rebecca was inflamed with adolescent paranoia, convinced that her parents had deliberately withdrawn all her privileges to make her miserable.

And then Will brought home the letter from his riding club. There was to be a competition in Portugal and his instructor thought that this could be Will's first step towards establishing himself as a potential professional.

But the trip would cost £750. Rebecca waited for her parents to break the news to him that he couldn't go, that they could no longer afford such luxuries. But five days later their father gave him a cheque for the full amount.

Rebecca could barely contain her indignation at the injustice. 'How come the money is magically there when Will wants it but not when I do?' she yelled at her parents, who were looking particularly pale.

'This is about his future,' they tried to say. But Rebecca wasn't listening. She stormed about the house, hurting her parents as often as she could.

A week later, her father was arrested. It was the size of the amount that had given him away. All his previous deceptions would have gone unnoticed, since he had kept them small, but this one set off alarm bells. With a little backtracking, the authorities discovered the full extent of his crime.

When he was sentenced, something of Rebecca died. All her memories had to be reexamined, the false ones excised and her life redefined. What shamed her most, the one fact that had driven her away from her home town in Suffolk, was her overwhelming resentment that her father should have taken that final risk for Will and not for her.

There, she'd admitted it. Part of her, a dishonourably big part, wished that he had taken such a chance for her, for the ski trip that she had wanted to go on so desperately. Because the only conclusion she could draw from his last venture into crime was that he loved Will more than he loved her.

She never visited her father in prison. She didn't know him any more. He had merely been a projection of her father, retouched and flashed on to a screen in lifelike colours. It took her two years to accept her rewritten history. By then, her father was out of prison. He was broken by the experience. He neither sought nor expected his children's forgiveness.

Will forgave him. Of course he did, Rebecca thought. His father had done it for him. And their mother had known for a long time. She hadn't condoned the last folly but she'd forgiven him.

Rebecca forgave none of them: not her father for ruining all her memories; not her mother for being complicit in the crime and not stopping it (although as she grew older, she recognised that her mother probably had little choice in this); and not Will, for being the one they loved most.

Rebecca's contact with her family dwindled. Her phone calls became less frequent, her visits almost non-existent, but always with good excuses. She took a degree that necessitated her spending a year in San Francisco and it was during that stay that she ceased contact altogether.

That's why she never spoke about them. Because it would mean thinking about them, which was too painful. After her father's betrayal she felt like a non-person, so she made it her life's goal to become a success as the new person she was creating. Professionally she would get to the top and personally she would find someone who loved her the most, more than anyone else.

She'd got so close to both. She was sure that this company would allow her to go all the way. Until Ben or Kate scuppered that idea, she couldn't decide who to blame. And although Andrew was not the man of her dreams, she had begun to believe that he might fall in love with her, to love her most. That's all she wanted, just to know the feeling for an instant.

But she couldn't say any of this to Andrew, because

then he would see her as she really was and would never want her. Nobody would.

She was about to say something noncommittal to Andrew when she saw he had gone and was talking to Kate. That's marvellous, she thought. In that case, I may as well deal with Ben. She marched resolutely towards the kitchen where she'd seen him sneaking earlier.

As she opened the kitchen door, she saw that Ben was chatting to one of his fellow directors from the office. Sighing, she went to find Sally. At least you knew where you were with her.

None of these people have a clue about me, Sally thought. She was fending off an almost infinite number of men who were queuing up to talk to the limited number of women here.

'So what do you do to have earned one of the few girls' tickets here tonight?' one such optimist tried.

'I work with Ben,' she said, refusing to say 'for'. Well, he's the one always going on about how I'm a full member of the team, she thought grumpily.

'So how come you're here by yourself?' the contender went on.

Sally graced him with a toxic stare. 'None of your business,' she snapped.

The man skulked away, defeated. He shook his head slightly at the other men who had been waiting their turn. They all took the hint and moved away.

Sally was in a foul mood. All this for Kate, she thought. Nobody threw a party for me when I joined. Or for Andrew or Rebecca, for that matter. And Andrew was Ben's friend. So don't tell me that women don't matter in this company.

She was waiting for Kate to slip away from Andrew

so that she could move in and pin her down. She needed to talk to the woman and this could be her only chance. Before Kate left in three weeks, she reminded herself optimistically. But Kate and Andrew did not look as if they would be separating in the near future.

Sally could not take her eyes off Kate's outfit. What does she think she looks like? she gasped to herself. Actually Sally knew how Kate looked: fabulous. And Sally was weak with envy. She would never have the confidence or the sheer nerve to wear such clothes. That was dressing beyond her status, something Sally never did.

Technically, in Sally's opinion, Kate had no right to look like that. As a senior executive, she ought to be wearing something very expensive but which commanded respect rather than announcing her sexuality. It might not be office hours, but she was still in professional mode.

Rebecca was watching Kate too, with equal doses of envy. But the difference between Sally and Rebecca was that Rebecca learned while Sally seethed. Rebecca had noticed that Kate was not as confident as she might like everyone to believe.

There were subtle signals, the constant tugging at the hem of the short skirt, as if she could make it longer; the folded arms to cover up the bodice on the revealing top; the nervous twiddling with her hair. No, Kate was not comfortable at all, which made Rebecca wonder why she'd chosen such an outfit in the first place.

'What do you think?' Sally asked Rebecca, nodding towards Kate.

Rebecca shrugged. 'Expensive and cheap at the same time – a remarkable achievement,' she said.

Sally giggled. 'Not quite the thing for the boss's party, I would have said.'

190

Rebecca quickly appraised Sally's clothes with some surprise. She was wearing the same clothes she'd had on at the office.

'Haven't you had a chance to go home and get changed?' she asked in surprise.

Sally blushed. 'No, I had things to do.' Her tone made it clear that she had no intention of elaborating on this.

Rebecca was curious. 'You really like being a woman of mystery, don't you? What's the big secret?'

'There's no big secret,' Sally said coldly.

But Rebecca wouldn't be fobbed off. 'Come on, Sally. That's not fair.' She dropped her voice to a whisper. 'You know about me and Ben. Your secret can't be bigger than that.' Rebecca silently corrected herself as she thought about her father's prison sentence. No that's too big a secret. That will always stay buried deep where it is.

Afterwards, Sally couldn't say exactly why she told Rebecca. Perhaps the time was right to tell someone. Perhaps it was the wine.

'I've got a daughter,' she said flatly. 'She's twelve.' She looked straight ahead, frightened to look into Rebecca's eyes and see the reaction that she'd always dreaded.

Rebecca looked stunned. 'You're kidding! But you can't have. You're only twenty-six.'

'Congratulations on working that out,' Sally said sarcastically. 'I hadn't realised.'

Rebecca softened her tone. 'So, how . . . I mean where is . . . ?' She couldn't think of appropriate questions, never having been put in this position before.

Sally helped her out. 'Don't worry no one ever knows what to say, that's why I don't tell anyone, any more.' She inhaled, trying to find courage in the air and suck it in. 'I was fourteen. It was the first time I did it and I didn't know I was pregnant until six months down the line.'

'What did your parents say?' Rebecca asked, appalled but fascinated.

'What do you think? They went crazy. Threatened to throw me out. When they calmed down, they sent me to my auntie's where I had the baby and stayed up there for two years, going to the local comprehensive while my auntie took care of her. After that, I came home. Mum and Dad had got used to the idea by then and loved their granddaughter, so they said they'd look after her while I got a job.'

'So is that why you never go out in the evenings?' Rebecca asked, as unconnected incidents now fell into place.

Sally nodded. 'It's easier now. She goes out a lot herself, gym club, piano lessons, that sort of thing. But I like to be be there when she's doing her homework.'

Rebecca looked at Sally and discovered that she wasn't the same person any more. The face was the same, the body was the same, but she now wore a sign over her head, in flashing neon lights, that screamed 'MOTHER!'.

'I knew this would happen,' Sally said sadly.

'What?'

'That you would think of me differently if you knew.'

Rebecca tried to change whatever it was in her expression that was giving her feelings away. 'No, that's not true. Well, I mean, obviously it's a lot to take in. But that's just because you're so young. And you don't seem . . .' She didn't go on, unsure if the comment was offensive.

She didn't need to. Sally knew what she'd wanted to say. 'I don't seem the mothering type?'

Rebecca didn't bother denying it. 'I didn't mean any-thing critical by that.'

In fact it was a compliment on how Sally had been

able to get on with her life without letting one really bad mistake scar her permanently. She told her so.

Sally was dubious. 'It's not easy. I've always felt I had to try harder. The only way you can really make it in a career, any career, is to be selfish, at least in the early days. You have to put in the hours, show commitment, do whatever is necessary, socialise, network and the rest . . .'

'Which is a bit difficult with a child at home,' Rebecca completed the sentence.

Sally nodded. 'But the real tragedy is that I need this career more than all the other girls. Not so I can have great holidays in Ibiza and go clubbing in the latest gear and drink Bacardi Breezers all night down the pub with a crowd of blokes. But for my daughter.'

'Children are expensive,' Rebecca suggested.

'Don't patronise me!' Sally snapped.

Rebecca recoiled.

'Sorry,' Sally said quickly. 'It's just you have no idea. How could you? I bet when you were growing up, you had everything you wanted, didn't you? All the latest stuff. And you went on holiday every summer, somewhere nice? And you just took it for granted that you could ask for anything and it would be yours.'

Rebecca said nothing but her lips had narrowed and her eyes were shining. Sally was horrified.

'What have I said? Oh God, I'm really sorry if I've upset you.'

Rebecca patted her arm to reassure her, as she brought her feelings under control.

Sally was still upset. 'Don't tell me, you grew up in terrible poverty. I'm such an idiot, always thinking that nobody could have had it as bad as me!'

Rebecca didn't know why she told Sally that night.

Perhaps it was the emotional fallout of a difficult week. Perhaps it was seeing Andrew with Kate, watching a good man drift visibly away from her. But for the first time in her adult life she told someone the whole story, and felt much better for it.

Now it was Sally's turn to be stunned. 'That's the most terrible thing I've ever heard. Poor you! And your poor parents!'

Rebecca screwed up her forehead. 'Poor parents? How do you make that out?' she asked, amazed that Sally could find any sympathy for them after the story she'd just heard.

Sally was surprised by Rebecca's surprise. 'Just imagine how desperate they must have been. Your father must have felt a complete failure as a man. He couldn't even give his family the things they wanted so he stole, risking his whole future, his whole life for you all. And you said he was a decent man?'

Rebecca tried to remember him but the memories were blurred at the edges. The decency remained sharp in her mind, though. 'Yes, he was decent. And proud,' she recalled.

'Then just think what it cost him to set aside all his principles like that!'

Rebecca had never thought about what it cost him, only what it cost her.

Sally went on. 'I'll tell you something, Rebecca. I know how he feels. When Chrissie asks me for new trainers and I have to say no, the look of disappointment on her face haunts me for days. And maybe if I'd ever been in the position where it was possible for me to take a little money, from a corporation that wouldn't miss it, I can't say that I wouldn't have been tempted. Just wait until you're a parent. Then you'll find

194

out how hard it is, how you'd do almost anything for your child.'

Rebecca was trying to collate all these new ideas and slot them in with all the old familiar concepts of resentment and unforgiveness that had fortified her over the years. They didn't fit well together; there wasn't enough room for them all in her head. Something would have to go.

She stood with Sally, sipping wine companionably, each a little lighter for having released a burden, each blessed with the preoccupation of someone else's problems, someone else's life.

They each felt as if they'd edged forward into slightly improved versions of themselves.

'Great party, Ben, but what's with all the men? Is there something you're not telling us?' Phil Jones punched Ben on the arm blokily.

Phil was the chairman of the board and Ben had felt it was politic to invite him along tonight with the other board members, who all also happened to be male.

'No, there was a communications problem,' Ben explained weakly.

Phil pretended to look worried. 'Bit alarming that, a communications problem from a man whose business is communications!'

Ben laughed politely. He'd never had much time for the macho bonhomie so enjoyed by the other men on the board.

While he'd lied to Rebecca about the reason for her lack of promotion, there was no doubt that this company was and always would be predominantly male. Kate's appointment had surprised him because of that but when he'd brought this up later, Phil had simply said, 'She was by far the best candidate for the job. If there had been a man who came close, you can bet we'd have taken him. I'm not that keen on women in business and I know you feel the same way.'

Ben quickly glanced about to make sure that nobody had heard this heresy.

Phil was edging closer to Ben to speak in confidence even though the kitchen was empty. 'Have you had any more thoughts about the figures?' he asked.

Ben knew what he was referring to. The end of year figures made grim reading. Business was down, way down. Some of their main clients were spending less and some had stopped spending altogether.

'I know that we really need to win the Saltech account,' he said.

'That's an understatement,' Phil pointed out. 'It's bloody vital! If we don't get it, well then, we're going to have to take a good look at staffing.'

Ben's stomach turned over. 'Let's not be hasty about it.'

'I'm sorry Ben, but I think haste is essential. The way I see it, if that team doesn't win that business, then we can't keep them on. They'll be dead weight.'

'But I thought we'd use them to carry on pitching for other new business?' Ben objected. That's how the job had been sold to Kate at the interview.

Phil shook his head. 'We'll use other groups, the ones who have existing business. With all the cutbacks, they've got some spare time, we can spread the new business presentations around them.'

Ben sat down on a stool by the breakfast bar. 'So we're going to let go some first-rate staff, some of whom have been here for years,' he reminded Phil, 'because of some short-term budgetary glitches.'

'Don't pretend that you don't understand the logic, Ben. I know you're thinking of your chum Andrew. He's your wife's brother, isn't he?'

This was a dig. Ben tried to play down the occasional implied accusations of nepotism.

'That's got nothing to do with this,' he said tightly.

Phil tried to appease him. 'Look Ben, I don't like this any more that you do, but we've no choice.'

'You can't just make this sort of decision without me, Phil. I'm the MD!'

'I'm not saying that this is a final decision. I'm saying that it's the only decision. You've seen the numbers, tell me if there's something else we can do, please, I'd love to hear it.'

Ben said nothing. He'd been ignoring the finances, hoping that the problem would lie dormant until the Saltech presentation. Then, when they'd won it, everything would be fine again.

Phil knew what Ben was thinking. 'You've been working on the assumption that the Saltech pitch is won already?'

Ben couldn't deny it.

'Well, I'm sorry to disillusion you, but it's far from won. And from what I've seen of that team, your chances are fading rapidly.'

Ben had to face this truth. He'd never lost a new business pitch before. Being a natural winner, he assumed there was some kind of magnet in him that attracted success towards him. And while he'd been playing manipulative games with this team, he'd unwittingly been sabotaging their chances.

How could I have made such a fatal misjudgement? he asked himself. But he knew how. He'd been distracted, by Rebecca and her threat to his marriage. Ironically, that's

197

where he got the idea for distracting Kate from her work. He knew only too well how effective some emotional entanglements could be in throwing you off course.

And now he could have lost them all their jobs. He felt sick.

'Anyway, I do have an idea to throw onto the table,' Phil suggested.

Ben didn't really want to hear it. Phil's ideas so far had been very depressing. 'Go on,' he said grudgingly.

'A mate of mine called me today. He's just started up a motivational centre in Wales.'

Ben groaned. 'Oh God, no! Grown-ups playing Cowboys and Indians and releasing their inner child and dancing naked over hot coals, that sort of thing.'

'Don't be so cynical!' Phil warned. 'It's nothing like that. They're going to specialise in team-building. Anyway, he's offering us a great discount because we're mates and because the centre is new.'

'And your point is . . . ?' Ben was being deliberately obtuse. He was still shaking with the shock of the damage he could have inflicted, on his staff.

'Don't pretend you don't get it, Ben. I suggest we send the Saltech team for a weekend, get them really working together. I've been hearing a lot of talk. They are not a happy bunch of campers. We don't stand a chance of winning the business if we don't have a team who are pulling together.'

Ben tried to imagine them all abseiling down cliff faces. Right now, Rebecca would be cutting Kate's safety rope with a psycopathic glint in her eyes. Andrew would be at the bottom gazing into space waiting for instructions. Sally would be moaning that she wanted to be the leader and how she was never the leader.

Phil had a point, Ben conceded.

198

'They won't like it,' Ben pointed out.

Phil snorted. 'Oh I don't know. I think you'll find they're quite enthusiastic when they hear that they're going to be unemployed if they don't learn how to work together.'

'They'll kill each other,' Ben muttered, thinking of the atmosphere in the office this afternoon.

'Then you'd better make sure they don't,' Phil warned.

Ben stood up. 'Sorry? You don't think I'm going, do you? My wife is about to have a baby, if you hadn't noticed.'

'I've spoken to her already. She says it's not due for another four weeks so you should be fine.'

'When did you plan for this to happen?' Ben asked, shocked at this all taking place without his knowledge.

'You leave a week tomorrow,' Phil said. 'All of you.'

Chapter 12

Ben opened the kitchen door as if he were about to face a gunfight, or rather something much worse than a gunfight. Bullets could be removed. The words that were going to be fired at him would be much more dangerous.

Where do I begin? he wondered. Maybe the best thing is to leave this all to Monday. Especially while Andrew is getting on so well with Kate, he observed with pleasure.

Then he spotted Rebecca bearing down on him. Her fists were clenched and her mouth was tightly closed as if she could barely hold in the stream of abuse that she was about to pour over him.

Jenny was watching them closely. He had to act fast. Change of plan, he thought quickly. Instead of avoiding Rebecca, he moved towards her, grabbing her elbow and guiding her over to where Andrew and Kate were standing. Jenny followed, wanting to hear everything that was being said.

Ben looked for Sally and called her over too. 'Are you OK, Sally?' he asked her, with genuine concern when she got there.

'Fine,' she said, but without her trademark rancour.

Ben couldn't waste any time on that. It was probably a women's thing, he convinced himself.

He stood in front of them, pulling his thoughts together before making his speech. He would have preferred more time to rehearse what he was going to say, but the impending confrontation with Rebecca had forced his hand.

At least this should distract her for a while, he thought.

'Right, now then. I know that a party might not be the most suitable location for this sort of thing, but I've just heard it myself and I think it's only fair to let you know where you all stand as soon as possible.'

They all looked shocked. This sounded serious. As if a puppeteer was pulling strings attached to their arms, they all, including Jenny, took a long drink from their glasses.

Ben cleared his throat. 'Here's the deal. The Saltech business is more critical to the future of the company that we'd previously assessed. So critical, in fact, that if we don't win the business . . . then there will have to be redundancies.'

Silence greeted this announcement, broken first by Rebecca.

'It'll be "last in, first out", won't it?' she pointed out eagerly, glancing briefly at Kate. All of a sudden things were looking up.

Ben shook his head. 'I'm afraid it won't. This isn't like a factory, with everyone doing the same work, making the same contribution. The personnel here are not interchangeable. Basically the staff who are working on accounts that are still active will keep their jobs and share out the new business work between them.'

He watched them take this in and draw the only conclusion. It was Andrew who gave it voice.

'So we will all be out. All of us?'

'I'm afraid so,' Ben said.

Sally had become white. Rebecca seemed to be in the initial throes of hyperventilation. Andrew appeared confused. Only Kate was calm, on the surface.

'But all this only happens if we don't win the business?' she said, wanting everyone to understand all the
facts here.

'Exactly!' Ben said enthusiastically, now understanding why Kate had been given the job in the first place.

They all turned to Kate without thinking, for the first
time acknowledging her leadership.

She seized the opportunity. 'Then we'd better make
sure we win it,' she stated matter-of-factly.

'I can help there,' Ben interrupted before they all
became too confident in their own abilities to pull this
off.

They all looked at him again, suspicion now fore-
shadowing his every announcement.

He felt exposed and vulnerable, more so because Jenny
was not supporting him as she would normally have done
in a situation like this. She wasn't even looking at him.
She was playing with her glass and her hair and her fingers
and looking strangely at everyone. Am I imagining it or
does she keep staring at Rebecca when she thinks no one
is looking? he asked himself.

He'd think about that later. This was more pressing.
He told them about the motivational centre in Wales.
Their reaction was much the same as his had been. But
in the minutes since Phil had brought the idea up, he'd
come to see it a potentially useful tool.

Everything was going to have change between these
people from now onwards. The people themselves were
going to have to change. And there was so little time
that they needed some drastic action; they couldn't hang
about waiting for each other to mellow.

'So we leave a week tomorrow,' he added swiftly,
hoping they wouldn't take in what he'd said until he'd
made a quick getaway.

202

Another failed ploy. 'Next week!' Sally said. 'But I can't. It's impossible. I've got a long weekend off booked.'

'But you said you weren't doing anything or going anywhere, that you were just going to veg out at home,' Ben pointed out. 'You can reschedule your break.'

'No I can't,' Sally said. 'It's not fair!'

Ben sighed. 'We're all going to have to make an effort here. I'm making the biggest sacrifice of all.'

'Surely you're not coming, Ben, not with the baby almost due?' Andrew shifted position so that he could stand protectively next to his sister.

Jenny patted his hand fondly. 'It won't be a problem, Andrew. I'm coming with you.'

'Are you mad?' Ben said to her in the bedroom a few minutes later. 'Of course you can't come.'

'I've already discussed it with Phil. The centre isn't just for groups of idiots playing games.'

Ben winced as she echoed his own initial feelings on the concept.

'Individuals can book to stay there as well,' Jenny continued. 'They can either be placed in a team with other individuals who want to join in the activities or they can just relax, enjoy the fresh air and the facilities. They've got a swimming pool and they're right on the edge of Snowdonia.'

Ben rubbed his temples; his stress levels were getting way out of control.

'But the baby?' he said.

Jenny tutted crossly. 'I'm not an invalid, you know. These are not Victorian times where the woman hides away and lies on chaises longues all day until the baby arrives.'

'No, I know that,' Ben protested without much con-
viction. He would have been much happier if Jenny
did stay in bed until the baby came. They were both
so precious to him, he couldn't bear the possibility of
something going wrong.

'It was only because of all your nagging that I took
maternity leave when I did,' she reminded him. 'If I'd
had my way, I'd be in court until my waters broke.'

Ben shuddered at the thought of his baby being born
in the Old Bailey. 'But you were glad you stopped, you
told me so, you were so tired.'

Yes, Jenny thought, I was glad. But I'm not going
to give you the satisfaction of knowing you were right.
About anything.

She decided to reason with him. She couldn't face the
prospect of his nagging her for the next week. 'Think
about it this way. You'll be away for a whole weekend.
And you know what the midwife said, the baby could
come any time now.'

She watched the panic rise in his eyes with satisfaction.
'So what would make you happier: to think of me all
alone, without you or Andrew, maybe going into labour
in the middle of the night, or knowing that you're right
there with me, that if anything happens, you'll be able
to deal with it?'

This was clever, Ben conceded. He'd been wondering
how he would be able to leave her by herself. His only
option had been to get her mother to come and stay, but
he recognised that the ordeal of a weekend with her mum
could induce an early birth.

'I suppose if you promise that you'll do *absolutely*
nothing all the time you're there,' he said, slowly accepting that he had no other choice.

He waited for her to hug him, which was what she

always did when she'd scored a victory over him. It made defeat acceptable. No hug came.

Rebecca steered Sally over to a corner, seeing that she was very distressed and now understanding why.

'I can't go!' she kept repeating. 'It's the start of half-term. I can't leave Chrissie. I have to be there. My mum and dad are going abroad on holiday.'

Rebecca stroked her back consolingly, scrambling around for a solution. 'Well, Jenny said that's she's going and she's about to give birth,' she hoped that she wasn't spitting this last bit. 'Maybe your daughter can come as well.'

'Of course she can't,' Sally said, shaking, 'then Ben will know, everyone will know, and I'll never get anywhere. I've worked so hard to keep the two elements of my life separate. I can't lose that division, everything will fall apart.'

She began to cry. Kate came over, looking concerned. Although Sally had been loathsome towards her, she didn't like to see her in tears. It made her think of herself.

'Sally, what's wrong?' she asked.

Rebecca placed her arm across Sally's shoulders defensively. 'I'm dealing with it,' she said coldly.

Kate raised her eyes to the ceiling. 'Rebecca, did you hear what Ben said? We're all going to lose our jobs if we don't stop all this nonsense and start working together. Now it's not the end of the world for me. This won't even make a dent in my career record. But don't you care about your own future?'

Rebecca had thought of little else since Ben had made the dramatic announcement. She knew she was going to have to accept this and ally herself to Kate. But she didn't have to be happy about it.

She made a supreme effort to rise above her hostility. 'You're right,' she said reluctantly.

Kate relaxed, appreciating how much that had cost Rebecca. She didn't want the momentum to disappear so she built on the development.

'Sally, you're going to have to tell us what the problem is, if we're going to be able to do anything about it.'

'She's already told *me*,' Rebecca said, unable to conceal the note of oneupmanship from Kate.

'I can't tell you,' Sally said, sobbing openly now. She looked to Rebecca for advice.

This was a lot of decision-making for Rebecca. She began to doubt her own suitability for leadership as she dithered over what to say.

But she knew what she had to do. It was making Sally see it. 'I think you're going to have to tell her,' she said.

Sally bent her head in defeat. She told Kate the story of her child and how this made it impossible for her to go on the course. Kate wanted to hug her but she had just managed to get a handle on her own current character and she felt that a hug would not be convincing.

Right conclusion for the wrong reasons. Sally would have stiffened if Kate had hugged her. She could not bear pity. All of her work would have been for nothing if she was to end up being thought of as a victim.

Kate knew that the kindest thing she could do for Sally would be to find an answer to her problem. With this in mind, she went to look for Phil.

'I believe this Motivation Centre is your idea?' she said.

Phil was taken aback. He hadn't yet got used to the transformation in the woman he remembered from the interview.

He would never admit it to anyone but the reason he employed her, the first time he had ever approved the appointment of a woman to a senior position, was that she was not like any of the female executives he'd seen and hated. She was so inappropriately dressed, as if she didn't want to be taken seriously. He found her endearing, sweet, self-effacing. Not hard and pushy with something to prove – at his expense.

But her business credentials were impeccable. He'd set her a few hypothetical challenges that had baffled him in the past and was impressed by her original, creative solutions. And she would definitely have a flair for presentation. She spoke confidently and intelligently, responding quickly to tricky questions from all sides.

She was better than all the other male candidates. The fact that she was a woman was, in her case, irrelevant.

And then she turned up on Monday like a 1950s film star who'd been reincarnated in a twenty-first-century corporation. He'd made personnel check that they'd sent the letter of appointment to the right person, because this woman bore no resemblance to the Kate Harris of a month ago. And office gossip had been filtering through to him. Kate's behaviour was frequently bizarre. He asked himself if she could be taking drugs or be a drinker.

He dismissed this idea and put the inconsistencies down to something female and incomprehensible. Thus, Kate's occasional lapses out of character were covered up by the pervading sexism that had kept women out of management in this company for so long.

But he began watching her very carefully. What he witnessed confirmed all his suspicions about aggressive women in business – they cause more division than a man.

Everyone resented her, the men and the women, not

that he understood the women's point of view. He'd been instrumental in appointing her to the most critical role that the company had established in years and team spirit had turned into battle fatigue.

It was precisely this fear that had made him amenable to his friend's timely offer. Frankly, the place sounded like Amateur Towers, but it was available and it was cheap.

He was gratified to note that within minutes of Ben's announcement, the team members were making efforts to get on for the first time that week.

When Kate walked over to him, he was doing all he could not to look at her legs. Those clothes! She couldn't be the same person, surely. He gave up. He'd have to start reading women's magazines, he decided. They probably had articles about how to succeed in interviews. Dress down, they must say, be all girly and sweet, then when you get the job, you can revert to your true self.

Seemed a dangerous strategy to him, but then he'd been fooled.

He smiled warmly at Kate. 'Yes. How have your team all taken it?' He believed in the old business rule – never ask a question unless you know the answer.

'Well, we were all a bit shocked by the news about our jobs being on the line but, on the whole, we think a team-building exercise is a good thing right now.'

Phil puffed up with this confirmation that he'd made a great decision. Unilaterally.

Kate was still talking so he had to put his pride on hold for a few minutes.

'I was wondering about this place. If Jenny is going, can I assume that it has facilities for guests who are not taking part in any courses?'

Phil repeated his friend's sales patter. 'That's what sets this apart from other such centres. It allows people to bring partners, even children, along, and they can either follow their own programme or enjoy the facilities. They're hoping they'll get more business from people who can't or don't want to be away from home for any length of time.'

'So someone could bring a partner along. Or a child?' she repeated.

'Absolutely!' Phil said. 'Why, is there something you forgot to tell us?' he added with a knowing wink.

'No, no,' Kate insisted, ignoring the wink with her now automatic cool disdain. 'But have you by any chance got the details of the place to hand?'

'It just so happens . . .' Phil said, pulling out a handful of leaflets from his pocket. 'I brought them along just in case Ben mentioned it tonight instead of waiting for Monday.'

'Thanks,' Kate said, snatching the whole handful as she turned to go back to her huddled group in the corner.

'She's keen,' he admitted to himself.

'Right, well I think I have the answer,' she announced to Sally and Rebecca.

Sally's eyes widened in hope. Kate ached for her. The awareness of Sally's personal situation gave her a new and open window into her character. She understood the tremendous pressure she must experience daily.

She made a mental note to herself to take Sally in hand while they were away and teach her some techniques for making herself more likeable. She was certain that Sally's life would improve immeasurably when she started to allow people to support her. But she'd have to make them want to support her first.

If ever I had a specialist subject, it would have to be the Art of Making People Like You, Kate thought wryly. But now is not the right time. She handed Sally a leaflet.

'You can bring your daughter along. Look. It should be really good fun. Then the evenings are free, so you'll still be able to spend some time together.'

Sally held the leaflet as if it were a lifebuoy. 'But what would I tell Ben?'

Kate inclined her head to acknowledge that this was a tricky one.

'You'll have to decide that for yourself,' she said.

Sally's voice was different when she spoke, slightly softer, but it might have just been the effect of the crying. 'Thanks,' she said.

Kate held her arms down, pretending she was being held in an armlock by a rampaging gunman. Any movement on her part and he could shoot her. This was the only way she could prevent herself from throwing her arms round Sally.

'But I don't understand,' her mum said the next day. 'Now you're all friends, surely you don't have to keep up this silly charade any more?'

Kate explained for the third time. 'We're not friends, mum, we're just not enemies any more. And I never treated them as enemies in the first place.'

'You called them "scumbag",' her dad pointed out reasonably.

'I didn't *call* them "scumbag", I just imagined calling them "scumbag" to maintain an edge to my voice,' she said, in exasperation.

'Well, it still doesn't sound very nice to me,' Stan grumbled. He was not in a good mood. Edie had been quiet and that always worried him.

'I know that this is a big move, Edie, but it's what we always planned,' he'd said to her last night, after she'd spent two hours on the phone to all the boys. Since their sons were spread out around the country, they hadn't been able to give them the news in person.

'I'm just saying that the boys haven't taken it very well. It makes me wonder if there's something that they're not telling us because they don't want to worry us.'

Stan put his pen down very carefully. He seldom lost his temper. He and Edie got on too well for that to happen very often. But he was worried about her diminishing enthusiasm for their planned emigration.

'It's a shock for them, that's all. They'll come round to it and realise that it's useful having parents overseas. Think of the holidays they'll be able to have with us.'

'But . . .'

'No buts, Edie. Leave them for a while to get used to the idea. They'll be fine. Kate was all right about it, wasn't she, and she was the one who worried you the most.'

When she looked at Kate, she had to agree that her daughter did seem to be all right. She was animated and cheerful. It was difficult to believe that she was the same Kate who had been in such a state on Monday.

Kate was explaining why the change in resolve didn't allow her to lower her guard. 'It makes it all the more important that I continue to appear strong,' she said. 'Our jobs depend on us working as a team and winning this piece of business. I'm supposed to lead this group and there's absolutely nothing to hold the group together, except me. There's a whole load of personal animosity that will be hard to ignore, and there are some complicated relationships going on that could cause the whole thing to fall apart.'

Edie sniffed. 'I still don't see why you can't be the leader and be nice,' she said.

But Kate knew that this was an impossibility. By the

end of the party, they were all looking at her to glue them together. Her coolness was a reassurance as they all floundered in uncertainty. The reason they accepted that they might be able to work under Kate effectively was precisely because she wouldn't expect them to become her friends. They wouldn't have to like her. That would be asking too much and would distract them from the more pressing task.

More importantly, she was to provide them with stability. It was a leader's job. But if they discovered that she was a fraud, that she was really a doormat, no more capable of remaining tough under pressure than they were, that she had been pretending all along, then the foundations would crumble.

'You'll just have to take it from me, Mum, I can't back down now.'

Stan saw that it was time to change the subject. 'So where is this place you're going then?' he asked.

She pulled out one of the leaflets and gave it to her mum.

'Ooh, look at this, Stan. It looks lovely,' she commented. 'Do you remember our honeymoon?'

'What sort of daft question is that?' Stan said, affectionately. 'How could I forget?'

'It was in Llandudno,' she told Kate, who already knew. They then spent an hour looking for their wedding photos and a further hour looking through them.

'Why did we never go back to Llandudno?' she asked Stan.

Stan thought about this. 'I don't know. The children came along and it was a long journey with little ones. It was easier to go down to the south coast.'

'But when they left home, why didn't we go back?' Edie really wanted an answer. But Stan didn't have one.

Edie was reminiscing. 'We were so happy, weren't we?'

'We still are, love,' Stan added anxiously.

Edie fingered her photo album with tender care. Then she looked up. 'Then let's go there,' she said finally.

'What do you mean?' Stan asked.

'What do you think? Let's go back to Llandudno. We can go next week. Kate can give us a lift.'

Kate looked alarmed at this suggestion. There were implications. She'd assumed that she would be travelling up with the others. 'Er, Mum, if I can, then of course I'll give you a lift. But I don't yet know how we're all getting up there.'

She really wanted to keep her work life and her family life totally separate. She'd constructed walls in her mind, dividing herself into different people. Keeping the divisions clear was essential if she wasn't to start making serious mistakes.

She was going to have spend two whole days, day and night, pretending to be the other person. It was a daunting challenge, one that she wasn't sure she could live up to. She'd hoped she could spend the journey preparing herself. It would be her last spell of solitude before the forty-eight-hour ordeal.

'Stan, you haven't said anything. You do think it's a good idea, don't you?' Edie asked, concerned.

Stan was more than concerned. He could only hope that this was to be a last farewell for Edie, that she needed to say goodbye to such an important place from their shared history before she could face their shared future in a new country.

But he had another worry. If she was taken back to the time and place when she was, they were, happiest, she'd never want to leave. She'd remember all the plans they'd made on that honeymoon, all the dreams they'd shared, the love that they vowed would never change. Then she'd want to spend the rest of their lives trying to recapture their past promise.

But he looked at her face. The expectation had given her a glow that had been missing for ages, years in fact. What choice did he have?

'I think it's a great idea,' he said warmly.

Kate forgot her own worries long enough to notice the tension between her parents.

'It was awful, Kate,' Justine whispered. Steve was in the living room playing Monopoly with the kids while Justine helped Kate prepare dinner in the kitchen.

'But nothing happened?' Kate asked again, wanting to be completely certain that Justine hadn't jeopardised her marriage.

Justine stopped stirring the gravy and stared wide-eyed at her friend. 'Nothing happened,' she said. 'How could it? I looked like Coco the Clown!' She continued stirring.

'But you look fine now,' Kate observed.

Justine groaned. 'That's because I'm wearing my old make-up.'

'You always looked great! I don't know why you had to go for such a dramatic change.'

Justine's stirring sped up to a whisking action. 'Because I don't want to look the same as I always looked. Which is why I'm going back to see the beauty consultant on Monday.'

Kate groaned. 'Oh no! I thought you'd got this out of your system.'

'What on earth made you think that?' Justine asked in surprise.

'From what you told me, your experience with Max was a disaster.'

Justine closed her eyes, hoping to blank out the vision of that awful lunch.

The goat's cheese salad had taken thirty-five minutes to arrive by which time Justine had jaw-ache from smiling so brightly and Max had eaten all the breadsticks from their table and the surrounding four tables as well, just to avoid having to talk to this woman who was obviously deranged.

'I'm sorry,' he said kindly, having devoured his salad in four and a half minutes, including ten cherry tomatoes which he swallowed without chewing. 'We had a lovely evening yesterday, but I think it was a bit like a holiday romance, a piece of magic that can never be recreated.'

'What you are trying to say,' Justine corrected him, 'is that yesterday you thought I was attractive and today I'm not?'

Max was gesticulating wildly for the bill, any bill; he'd pay anything to get away from this place, this situation. But he was going to have to answer this one. There was not another breadstick within a mile that he could use as a distraction. The manager had removed them from the remaining tables when he realised that this gluttonous man was stuffing his way through the restaurant's profits.

'It's not that,' Max protested. 'It's difficult for men. We never know where we are with women. You present yourself to us with your face in a mask. Then, when you take the mask off, or in your case put a scary carnival mask on instead, you act surprised when we don't respond the same way.'

'But all women wear make-up,' Justine said. 'It goes with the territory.'

Max's expression conveyed his firm belief that Justine's

215

make-up of the previous day went beyond the defined boundaries of facial enhancement and smack bang into the realms of Hammer Horror.

'I'm sorry, Justine. It must have been horrible. But didn't this teach you something?' Kate asked.

'Of course it did. It taught me that I need more practice.'

Kate was baffled. 'But I don't understand. Surely you don't want to go through that again? And it's bound to happen.'

Justine smiled mysteriously. 'Only if I ever take the mask off. Don't you see? That's exactly what I wanted. I don't want there to be any part of me on show. I'm not even trying to meet men.' Kate raised her eyebrows and pointed to her wedding-ring finger. Justine went red. 'Yes, I know, but I hadn't planned that. It was just a spur-of-the-moment decision. I wasn't going to sleep with him or anything. Just see where it led, what my options might have been in another life. It's just a role-playing game, like your one.'

Kate shook her head warningly. 'My situation is completely different. You have no idea how hard it is to sustain the act all day. You've just dabbled for an evening. It is exhausting having to suppress all your natural instincts and responses in favour of actions that feel wrong.'

'But you've found it easier as the week went on, you told me,' Justine said.

'The big difference between my "game", as you put it, and yours, is that I have nothing to lose except a job which is not going that brilliantly anyway. Take a look at what you've got to lose.'

'Who's lost something, Auntie Kate?' Justine's youngest son, Charlie, had walked into the kitchen with the Monopoly boot stuck in his ear. Although their dad was a doctor, the kids always came to Justine to sort them out. She was good at dealing with problems.

'Nothing,' Kate said absently, intrigued by the technique required to extract a foreign body from a wriggly boy's ear.

'We're going on holiday next week!' he said excitedly.

'Stand still!' Justine commanded.

'Yeah. It's half term.'

'I know,' Kate said.

'How do you know, out of curiosity?' Justine asked.

Kate waved her hand dismissively. 'Long story. Very complicated. So where are you going?'

Steve breezed into the kitchen, followed by two young banshees screaming about the injustice of life, fathers in particular. 'Haven't decided. We're just planning to load up the caravan and off we go. We borrowed it from one of the nurses at the hospital.'

'It'll be a bit cramped, won't it?' Kate offered, peeking through the curtains at the tiny caravan on the drive.

'Nonsense!' Steve countered. 'It'll be fun!'

Justine's face told Kate that this was not her idea of fun. Before she could open her mouth to make that very point, Kate hastily intervened.

'I'm going away next week as well,' she said.

'You didn't say,' Justine said accusingly.

'I'll bet you haven't give her a chance!' Steve pointed out. He was right, but Justine looked ready to have an argument with him on the subject. She appeared sensitive to all the criticisms that she'd accepted with equanimity in the past.

Fortunately, the object flew out of Charlie's ear at that point. 'There!' Justine pronounced triumphantly. 'So, let's eat!'

217

Over dinner, Kate told them about the course in Wales.

'Maybe you ought to do something like that,' Steve said to Justine.

Justine slammed her knife and fork down on to her plate. 'What's that supposed to mean?'

Steve was unbothered by her temper. She'd always been volatile. He barely noticed any more.

He swallowed his mouthful before going on, calmly. 'Just that these courses are also very good for individuals wanting to develop themselves, push themselves, find out what they're made of, that sort of thing.'

'Why would I need or want to do that?' Justine asked, her irritation growing.

'Isn't that what all this is about?' he said, pointing vaguely in the direction of her hair and face with his fork. 'Finding yourself, or whatever the current buzzwords are?'

'No,' Justine said, 'it's nothing to do with that. I found myself years ago. What I'm trying to do is lose myself.'

'Whatever.' Steve shrugged and carried on eating.

The children were passing round the leaflet that Kate had showed them.

'This looks fantastic, Mum, can we go here?'

'No!' Kate shouted with a touch too much emphasis. They all jumped and five forkfuls of peas cascaded to the floor. 'Sorry,' she said. 'I didn't mean to shout. But no, it's fully booked.'

Steve picked up the leaflet. 'That doesn't matter. There are loads of places with swimming pools and games rooms like this. Take a look at the scenery. I haven't been to Wales since I was in the Boys' Brigade. How about it, Jus?'

'Whatever,' Justine replied, without interest. She was still fuming from Steve's last comment.

'Wales it is then, kids!' Steve said. 'Hopefully by then your mum will have finished her moody.' He winked at the children, which enraged Justine even further.

With that, she shoved her chair back and stormed into the kitchen, banging the door behind her.

The kids watched this all with mild interest. Then they looked at Steve and began singing in perfect four-part harmony: 'Mum's having a moody! Mum's having a moody!'

Kate laughed at their enthusiasm, then stopped laughing when she thought of her parents and now her friends all descending on North Wales at the same time as her.

She shook off her discomfort by reminding herself that they might just as well be in Scotland. There should be no reason for them to bump into one another.

Chapter 13

It was Monday morning and Kate felt exhilarated. She'd bought some new shoes at the weekend to celebrate the transition of their relationships. She'd spent a week in the pink shoes and the looks she'd attracted had finally convinced her that the shoes had no right to life outside a wedding.

The shoes she'd bought were just as high as the pink ones, but black with a faint pattern. She'd felt very grown-up buying them. On the way to work, she'd held her head high and strutted down the street, rapping to herself, 'I'm a cool mother, oh yeah . . . I'm a babe, a cool funky chick . . .' And she didn't feel a bit silly, although she looked it.

'Nice shoes,' Rebecca said, casually as Kate walked into the office.

Kate suppressed her astonishment. 'Thank you,' she said warmly, quickly adding 'scumbag' to bring her grateful expression back in line. Whoops, I'm slipping, she warned herself. The triumph of the shoes was making her complacent.

'Shall we all meet in my office at ten?' she asked abruptly but not rudely. She'd been practising the addition of nuances to her tone over the weekend.

Rebecca didn't appear offended by this, Kate observed with relief. Perhaps this is going to work.

Rebecca was impossible to offend this morning. Life

was looking good after the weekend, despite the bad start of Friday night.

Ben had taken Andrew aside towards the end of the evening.

'Sorry I couldn't let you know in advance. Phil sprang it on me. It was a complete shock.'

Andrew looked puzzled. 'But you're the managing director, how could it have been a surprise? Aren't you supposed to know everything that's going on?'

Ben cursed himself for his bad luck in having his only affair with the woman who was to go on to become the girlfriend of his best friend who just happened to be his wife's brother. None of this was his fault, he'd convinced himself happily. At this precise moment, the worst part of all was that he couldn't talk to Andrew. He longed to explain why he had been so distracted recently, how he hadn't been able to focus on his work when his family life was so precarious.

But Andrew was the last person he could talk to about his problems. 'I've been distracted lately, the baby, you know,' he added vaguely.

Andrew looked sympathetic which made Ben feel bad, really bad. 'I'm sure Phil understands,' Andrew said.

Ben wanted to get away from this treacherous area quickly. 'Anyway, this is all good news for you,' he said with forced enthusiasm.

'How can this possibly be good news?' Andrew asked mournfully.

'Well, we can scrap that ridiculous plan. It would never have worked, I see that now.'

It took Andrew a few seconds to work out that Ben was referring to his campaign to make Kate fall in love with him. He was shocked to realise that he'd forgotten that this was a plot, a Machiavellian strategy. Since lunch earlier, their relationship had shifted to a new footing, one unfamiliar to Andrew.

He couldn't call it romantic, since Kate's manner discouraged any romantic notions. He couldn't call it friendship, since she'd erected a wall between the two of them, or more accurately, between herself and everybody else. Even more inexplicable was his memory that he had so hated the *idea* of Kate, the female manager.

If he were now asked how he felt about women in senior positions, he would still express horror. He couldn't shake the picture he had created of the cold, domineering woman, committed to emasculating men and undermining all other women. He'd built this prejudice on his one experience of a female boss, but had been reassured to find his view shared by men and women alike, wherever he went.

Maybe if he'd ever worked for a doormat, his opinions might have see-sawed dramatically in the other direction.

Maybe if he'd worked for a strong, decent woman who compromised neither her humanity nor her femininity, he might have chucked all his prejudices away and reached the more sensible conclusion that there were as many good and bad female managers as there were male.

Certainly Kate was having a strange effect on him, not only forcing him to reevaluate his opinions of women in management but also of the women with whom he'd formed most of his relationships.

He didn't think he had a 'type' as such. But looking back, he noted that most of his girlfriends had possessed a degree of fragility, of vulnerability. Even Rebecca had only taken an interest in him when she was damaged by her previous partner, whoever that bastard was, Andrew thought angrily.

They'd always praised his niceness, a word that didn't upset Andrew the way it seemed to annoy others. He'd never tried to be nice, or to be anything other than he was. And although all the women had left him, he didn't blame his even temperament, being fully aware that it was the other aspects of his personality, the annoying ones, that drove them away.

Being forced to pursue a woman who didn't attract him had opened a door to a side of him that had never been acknowledged. Like many good men, his qualities derived from his strength, the strength of character that allowed him to flaunt a decency regularly scorned in modern culture.

That strength had been there all the time, but only when he saw it in Kate did he recognise it as a reflection of his own self.

Kate was nothing like the other women of his life. She was assertive, forceful, powerful, commanding, separate. He even wondered if his emerging feelings for her represented the onset of an attraction of a whole new sort, and he'd been looking forward to exploring that possibility.

Now he wasn't going to get the chance. The game was over. They were all going to be one happy family. He would have no reason to be particularly friendly. Everyone would be friendly now.

He felt oddly lost.

'Andrew, are we going soon?' He hadn't known that Rebecca was there until she'd touched him gently on the arm.

'Yes, two minutes,' he'd replied, implying that he had to finish things off with Ben.

She'd left them hesitantly, sensing that something of

223

import was being discussed and feeling uneasy at being excluded.

'I'll have to go,' Andrew said to Ben.

'You don't look too happy about it,' Ben commented, hoping his pleasure didn't show.

'Of course I'm happy,' Andrew protested. Certainly life would be easier now, if they could ignore the threat of redundancy hanging over them.

Kate came over to say goodbye. She maintained her poise right up until the end. 'Thank you for the evening, Ben. I'll see you all on Monday.'

She left after nodding and smiling coolly at each of them. Rebecca thought she detected a hint, a tiny hint, of warmth in her farewell to Sally, but she knew that she must be mistaken.

Rebecca and Andrew got through the rest of the night without arguing, which was a blessed relief to them both. Rebecca had immediately grasped the necessity of getting over the bad feeling of the last week for the sake of all their jobs.

Everything was different now. They all wanted Kate to keep her job, because that would be proof that she, and the rest of the team, were on top of the Saltech pitch. They would have a good chance of winning the business and keeping their jobs.

In truth, Rebecca accepted that they'd treated the presentation as an academic exercise, a school project, with little of earth-shattering significance riding on it. It certainly hadn't occurred to any of them that their own jobs depended on the successful outcome.

None of them could say how they'd expected to succeed if they'd wasted the first four weeks on tripping Kate up and then had to get used to Andrew in charge for the last two.

Rebecca and Andrew had discussed it calmly over the weekend. Andrew was surprised that Rebecca didn't comment on Ben's lack of foresight in the matter. Perhaps she'd worked out the reasons for herself. He was willing to admit to a lack of insight into the human condition, never having spent that much energy analysing his own.

Both welcomed the relative normality of the two days. They did a supermarket shop on Saturday and, when Rebecca suggested shyly that they go and look for curtains, Andrew acquiesced.

On Sunday Rebecca got up early and went to buy all the Sunday papers, not making a single snide comment about Andrew's strange taste for the tabloids. She even got out the milk frother that was his most prized possession and made cappuccinos for them both with frothy milk, a challenge involving most of the jugs in the house and a pile of cloths to mop up the considerable spillage.

Andrew was touched by her efforts. Touched but nervous. He wasn't used to this reversal in impetus. Generally, once a woman started moving away from him, she kept moving, at ever-increasing velocity but always in the same direction.

Only a week ago, Rebecca had shown the early signs. By his reckoning, that meant that she'd be gone within a fortnight, a month tops. The events of the week had confirmed his assessment.

And now she was wooing him, that was the only word for it. And while it was sweet and loving, it made him very uncomfortable. He'd readied himself for her departure, even mentally laid the foundations for life afterwards. Now she was backpedalling.

But he couldn't. He'd never done it before and Andrew only tended to do things that he'd done a thousand times before with predictable outcomes. This was even making him lie, pretending to have a stomach upset to avoid making love. He had the dreadful suspicion that he would have to say something to her. He'd never done that before and the prospect made him feel sick.

There was no point in thinking about that at the moment. He had to keep things as they were for the next few weeks, for all their sakes. Never mind the spurious goals that he and Ben and Rebecca had formulated over the last week. This was simple. Keeping their jobs was the sole priority now.

Once their future was secure, he could break it to her gently. She'd have so much work on her hands that she wouldn't have time to miss him too badly. Or she could leave the company, with the triumph of the big win bolstering her CV and move on to the senior position she craved.

But it was a long, long weekend.

'I thought we should go through what we've done and set our major strategy by the end of the week. We won't all agree so we'll lay down our points of difference. Then, next weekend while we're away, we can try and work through them during one of the evening sessions. Agreed?'

Andrew and Rebecca nodded. They didn't dare argue with her. She looked fierce today. Must be the shoes, they both concluded separately.

Kate was about to continue when her phone rang. 'Excuse me,' she said. 'Hello?'

'Hi! It's me. Callum. You hadn't forgotten I was going to call, had you?'

Completely forgotten. 'Of course I hadn't.'

'You sound strained. Is everything OK?' he asked.

Kate didn't understand his point. Then she twigged.

226

He knew the soft and cuddly Kate, not the ruthless professional one. She flicked her shoes off surreptitiously behind her desk, hoping it would ease her subtly into her other role. Except she couldn't allow herself to go all the way because Andrew and Kate were there. All she could do was say as little as possible.

'Look, I'm sorry, I'm in the middle of a meeting,' she said, lowering her voice to mask its clipped tones, hoping to fool Andrew and Rebecca as well as Callum.

'Oh, of course,' Callum said. 'So what time shall we meet? You pick the time and place.'

Oh God. I want to cancel. How can I do that without appearing a total fool in front of my staff? I'd get all flustered, I always do. Think! Think!

Rebecca noticed that she was holding the receiver so tightly that her knuckles were white.

'Hello? Are you still there?' Callum was sounding anxious.

Kate knew she had to end this conversation now before she collapsed in a dribbling heap. So she just said it. 'One o'clock, La Grenouille, Kensington High Street?' she suggested.

'I know it,' Callum replied. 'Great. See you then. 'Bye.'

'Goodbye,' Kate said and put the phone down.

'Is everything OK?' Andrew asked, noticing that her face was rather shiny and that her hands were clenching and unclenching.

'Fine,' Kate replied. She stopped herself from explaining the phone call. They don't need to know, she reminded herself. They answer to me, not the other way round.

'Off to lunch?' Rebecca asked.

Kate looked away. 'Computer graphics man I've worked with before. Might be someone we can use on this,' she

227

added. Why did I say that? she asked herself in frustration at her own lapse. It was none of Rebecca's business.

But there was no time for self-recrimination. She had a far, far bigger problem on her hands. It was when she squeezed her feet back into her shoes that it struck her. She couldn't possibly meet Callum dressed like this. He'd made it clear that he despised women who dressed like this. He would be expecting to see her, the real her, that is, not the pretend her.

There was only one answer. She'd have to pop out and get something to wear before lunchtime. Something in the cardigan and baggy skirt department. Forget Harvey Nichols. She'd have to try somewhere else.

It mattered because all of a sudden she wanted to see him. The pressure of maintaining a pretence was leaving a mark on her. She couldn't switch off at the weekend and had actually called Steve 'scumbag' at one point.

Callum was the first man, first person, in ages who'd liked her as she was, as she liked herself. She needed a dose of that kind of real contact without artifice, without pretence.

Her work would just have to take second place for a few hours. She'd make the time up. She'd feel refreshed, revitalised by the release of being herself and being appreciated as herself for a couple of hours.

So no more arguments. Andrew and Rebecca had watched her processing the data leading to this decision with bewilderment. Her lips had been moving slightly as if she was talking to herself and her expression had veered from acceptance to denial to worry and back again.

They had no idea what she was deliberating about, but it was obviously something major. And finally she'd come to an end. It had been a fascinating show and their first firm sign that something was definitely amiss with Kate.

'Right,' she announced briskly, startling them both. 'If you can make a start, we can meet back here at three thirty and see how far we've got. I have to pop out briefly. I'll check in on my return, see if there any questions I can answer at this stage.'

Then she smiled an alarmingly bright smile. It was one they hadn't seen on Kate before but which they interpreted correctly as a smile of dismissal.

Kate walked quickly along the street, teetering on her heels. Damn, she thought, I'm going to need new shoes as well. She limped into Laura Ashley, drawing on vague memories of floaty dresses constructed like parachutes. But it was all different. They had cardigans, but they were boxy and cropped. The skirts were tailored and there were hardly any flowers outside the children's section.

What's going on here? she asked herself. A quick backtrack through her memory reminded her that she hadn't set foot in Laura Ashley since 1982.

She looked at her watch. It was ten thirty. By eleven thirty, she'd trawled all the big stores and most of the small ones, even the boutiques which didn't have prices but did have frightening women standing by the door, judging you worthy or unworthy of entering the portals.

In desperation, she spoke to a woman with the most approachable face in the least intimidating shop to ask why she couldn't buy long cardigans and loose, pretty skirts any more. The woman politely refrained from laughing.

'It's a . . . specific look,' she said, 'one that flits in and out of fashion in a random cycle. Right now, I'm afraid it's out.'

'When was it last in?' Kate asked miserably.

But the woman couldn't remember. However, she took

pity on Kate, mainly because there were no other customers and she was bored.

She coaxed Kate into explaining her predicament. She
found it fascinating. 'Well, I can't magic the exact clothes
you're describing from thin air, but I think I can still
help you.'

Kate would have accepted fashion advice from a brick-
layer at this stage.

'Anything!' she said pleadingly.

Kate had two choices. She could wear the new clothes
into the office, which was out of the question. Or she
could change into them in a loo somewhere outside the
building before lunch then change back out of them after
lunch. That would have to do.

She went back to the office, aware that a woman in
her position did her image little good walking in at noon
with an armful of carrier bags, only to leave thirty minutes
later for lunch.

What else can I do? she asked herself.

Needless to say, Ben saw her, as did Andrew, Rebecca
and Sally. They were all puzzled by the sight. None of
them liked to say what they were all thinking and ask her
if she'd been shopping. It seemed implausible, especially
after the announcements of Friday.

They voted unanimously to ignore this anomaly. She
must have good reason to be doing this, although they
couldn't think of one.

Ben stuck his head round her office door. She was
standing in the middle of the floor wearing a pair of flat
shoes. 'Are you all right?' he asked, unable to think of
a more respectful question.

Kate turned and glared at him. 'Of course I am!' she
snapped. 'Sorry,' she apologised immediately. She looked

down at her shoes and knew that she had to explain them. These were an oddity too far.

'Erm, I have a chiropody problem, I need to wear . . . remedial shoes to relieve the pain.' She didn't say any more, wise enough to know that any further explanation would just highlight the absurdity of the story.

Ben made a sympathetic noise. Strangely, it sounded reasonable to him. Jenny had gone out and spent a fortune on flat shoes when her bump started putting strain on her back and legs.

He didn't feel any need to understand the physical quirks of his staff as long as it didn't interfere with their work. Especially in this case at this time.

'Right. Well, I was wondering if we could all go out to lunch today, talk about where we're going to move from here, now that we're all committed to the same cause. At last,' he added with an apologetic smile.

Kate kicked off her shoes and sat down behind her desk to reclaim a little dignity.

'I'm really sorry Ben. Any day but today. Something important came up. A contact who might be of value to us. He can only meet today. But let's do it tomorrow. Or we could go out tonight?' She was anxious to prove that she was as enthusiastic as the others.

She knew she was sounding too keen. But she couldn't go back. This lunch was a major error of judgement although she hadn't actually chosen to go out, she'd been nudged into it by circumstance.

If she lost their respect at this point, she might never win it back, certainly not within the timespan that was dictating their plans.

'I'll tell you what. You go ahead with your lunch today without me. I can't cancel my . . . meeting, I'm afraid. But I do want to prove my loyalty to you all. So why don't I organise a get-together on, say, Thursday night to prepare for Saturday. Let our hair down. Maybe at my house?'

Immediately those last words fell out she wanted to pick them up and put them straight back into her mouth. She was Trying Too Hard, again. Kate blamed it on the shoes.

Ben was taken aback by her enthusiasm. It was the first sign of eagerness that she'd shown since joining them. Her cool had ceased being an irritation and had become an oasis to him, to them all. But he put this inconsistency down to the added pressure of the ultimatum he'd delivered to them.

'I'll tell the others. Sounds a great idea. Good for morale!' He left the office feeling confused but quite cheerful.

He passed on the message about Thursday night at Kate's house. Andrew and Rebecca were surprised. Kate hadn't seemed the type to invite work colleagues into any aspect of her private life. But they accepted. They had no choice.

Andrew was secretly thrilled. He looked forward to taking up the communication with Kate at the point they'd left off. Her odd behaviour this morning had made her into something of an enigma. He was more fascinated with her than before.

Rebecca was interested in seeing Kate's house. She'd never owned property herself, being terrified of debt and seeing a mortgage as no more than a massive, life-long one. Her family home had been repossessed after her father had gone to prison. It was the worst moment of the whole debacle and one that Rebecca would never inflict on herself. But this refusal gave her a disproportionately keen interest in other women's homes.

232

Sally was laid-back about the invitation. Having told Rebecca and Kate about her daughter, she could afford to relax. She no longer felt she needed to compensate for her handicap, which was how she had perceived her motherhood. She was even being quite pleasant today which had an uplifting effect on everyone who came into contact with her.

Ben was still unable to think about anything except Rebecca and her potential for harming his future. He was alarmed at Rebecca's calm demeanour and the easy atmosphere between her and Andrew.

Oh no, he thought. I'm going to have to think of something else. And quickly.

At twelve forty, Ben, Andrew, Rebecca and Sally were just coming out of the lift to head off for lunch when they caught sight of Kate, who'd left just before them. She was carrying the same bags she'd brought back into the office after her mysterious outing.

None of them said anything but they all looked bewildered. Ben felt obliged to contribute the one piece of information he possessed that might help them understand Kate's mystifying behaviour.

He beckoned them to come closer, not wanting to shout this across the lobby.

'She has a chiropody problem,' he said confidentially.

Chapter 14

Kate squeezed her way into the toilet in McDonald's, which was the only public loo she could find. She had to balance the bags on top of the cistern. Then cursing her lack of foresight for not having taken up yoga years earlier, she contorted herself out of her clothes, struggling to fold them neatly. The clothes she had bought today were blissfully soft and crease-resistant and slipped on without too much effort. Just the change of shoes and she was ready.

She dragged the bags out of the cubicle into the tiny handwashing area where she managed to brush her hair and reapply her make-up, switching to more muted tones.

Leaving the claustrophobic confinement of the converted cupboard, she breathed more easily as she climbed the stairs to the exit. A sullen McDonald's worker glared at her, recognising yet another non-customer using the loos.

She upped her speed to get out of the place as quickly as she could to minimise the risk of the smell of burgers clinging to her new clothes.

It was a short walk to the restaurant and she had calmed down by the time she got there. It was only when she entered through the impressive glass doors that she caught her first glimpse of herself in a full-length mirror. Initially she didn't recognise what she saw. Obviously she'd tried the clothes on in the shop but she'd been too flustered to pay much attention. And her hair and make-up had clashed with the low-key outfit.

She looked fantastic and she knew it. It was miles away from the sloppy, baggy style that she had favoured throughout her adult life but it fulfilled all the same criteria.

The dress wasn't floral or black but it was soft and feminine. It wasn't baggy and concealing but it skimmed her figure, reassuring the onlooker that she wasn't eight months pregnant. And it fell to just below her knees, not over-exposing her chunky calves that the sales assistant had translated into 'well defined'.

She felt light and different, enjoying the thrill that new clothes guarantee. When she saw Callum sitting at a table near the back, she walked over with the hint of a bounce in her step.

'To the future! To success!' Ben raised his glass and the others followed. It was a long time since the company had forked out for champagne at lunch, but Ben felt that the situation demanded it. Morale was rising, but it needed a fork-lift truck to take it up to the level where they could walk into a presentation and look like stars.

'So where exactly has Kate gone?' Sally asked.

'Out with some contact or other,' Andrew answered vaguely.

'Seems a bit odd at this point. It's too late to start thinking of bringing other people on board, I would have thought,' Rebecca observed.

'I don't see why,' Andrew objected. 'We've got a few weeks, plenty of time to incorporate some changes. Anyway, I thought we weren't going to have a go at Kate any more.'

He was very touchy about all things concerning Kate and couldn't stand to hear Rebecca criticise her.

Rebecca was surprised. 'I wasn't having a go at her, I was just commenting on the fact that it was strange for her to make a lunch appointment today of all days. She must have known that we'd all want to go out together after Friday.'

Andrew didn't argue with her. It would get personal and nasty and he didn't want that either.

Ben stepped in to relieve the tension. 'Are you all looking forward to next weekend, now that you've got over the initial shock?'

He was faced with three unenthusiastic expressions. Rebecca forced herself to smile. 'Well, it'll be a couple of days away. That'll be nice,' she added hopefully. She looked to Andrew for support.

Andrew didn't want to think about the weekend away. All of them living and working on top of each other with so many unresolved tensions simmering below the surface. It had to be disastrous.

But he smiled for Ben's sake. He'd been quite worried about Ben since Friday. Ben's confession that he hadn't been on top of his work had bothered him.

'Is Jenny OK?' he asked, watching Ben's face closely. His biggest fear was that Jenny wasn't well and that they were protecting Andrew from the news, knowing how much he worried about his sister.

'Yeah, she's fine,' Ben replied, smiling with far too many teeth.

Now Andrew was really worried. 'I don't believe you. I know when you're hiding something from me and it makes things worse. Now I'm imagining all sorts of terrible things about her or the baby. You've got to tell me what's wrong.'

He didn't spot the dread emerging on Rebecca's face as she watched Ben wrestle with the decision as to whether he should say something or not. Since she was fairly certain that she was at the root of the problem, she could only pray that he'd bluff his way out of this corner.

'It's nothing,' Ben said again with less confidence, this time. Then he paused. 'Well, there is something,' he admitted.

Rebecca felt she had to say something. She knew, or at least hoped, that Sally would understand her fears and forgive her for shifting the attention on to her. Before Ben could say anything, she blurted out, 'So, Sally, how does your daughter feel about the trip?'

Then Ben and Andrew stopped looking at each other and looked at her.

Callum looked at Kate admiringly. 'You look great!' he said.

Kate searched his eyes to make sure he was being sincere. While she was happy with her appearance, she knew that this man had expressed how much he liked the old-fashioned look when they met. And while she hadn't suddenly turned into Madonna, all conical bra and silver hot pants, she did feel rather . . . modern. Yet she was surprised how comfortable she felt in this new look.

Callum was obviously impressed. She hadn't been on the receiving end of such appreciation for a very long time. Now I understand why Justine is enjoying this, she realised. Except that I'm being myself, well, a slightly evolved version of myself. I'm being honest.

She had forgotten that she had concealed her professional persona from Callum when he'd made his feelings about female executives plain. She was becoming increasingly adept at separating the two halves of her life.

237

'Have you looked at the menu yet?' she asked, intending to go for the full three courses to make this lunch last.

'No,' Callum replied. 'I was waiting for you. So tell me more about the job. When we met you'd only just started so you couldn't really tell how it was going, but it's been a week now, hasn't it?'

Kate would have preferred not to talk about work, terrified that she might accidentally call him 'scumbag' if she went into work mode. But it was an obvious subject so she kept it simple. 'It's going well,' she said. 'It was a rocky beginning, there was some resentment about a woman being given the appointment, but we ironed out our differences and the future is looking promising.'

Callum nodded. 'I can see where the resentment comes from. I mean, not that I agree, but some of the worst excesses of women bosses give the rest of you a bad name.'

Kate wanted to order badly. He seemed to be warming up to this, apparently his favourite subject. She caught the waiter's eye and he gestured that he would be a couple of minutes.

Callum was on a roll now. 'But you did brilliantly well to win them over in just a week. I've known women who are hated from the day they start to the day they leave. It just shows how it doesn't always pay to be tough. It was probably your personality that smoothed the way for you. It would be impossible for everyone NOT to like you.'

To Kate's relief the waiter finally arrived. She decided to skip the starter in case this lunch became any more discomfiting.

Justine walked out of the salon feeling wonderful. She'd paid for an extra hour so that the beautician could give her some more tips on how to replicate the effects at home.

238

'I'm such a klutz,' she explained apologetically. 'I've never put make-up on properly, just slapped on the same products the same way since I first began.'

'That would explain the green eyeshadow,' the beautician commented acidly.

Justine was a model student, keen and attentive, asking lots of questions, even taking notes. She'd already been to the hairdresser to get her hair blow-dried again. This time, she watched even more carefully. 'I don't suppose there's any way you could do something to the shape so that it looked OK even when I don't do anything to it?' she asked, not hopeful of a positive answer.

The hairdresser looked at her with disdain. 'This is *the* cut,' he hissed. 'Gwyneth, Jennifer, they're all having this done! And I explained to you when you had it done that it demanded commitment. You assured me that you had that commitment. Now if you want to be beautiful you have to accept that it is a full-time job!'

Justine tried not to think of the sweaty and gory scenes of childbirth that awaited her at the hospital. She would have to keep the make-up on, at least until she got home. She was planning to take a Polarioid of her face so that she had something to refer to when she tried to do it herself.

It was one fifteen when she walked out on to Oxford Street. She was aware that people were looking at her, and not in horror. This was a novelty for her and a welcome one. She had always mocked Kate for her determination to avoid attention. It was a sore point with Justine because she also never got attention but, in her case, it wasn't through choice.

She would have quite enjoyed some admiring glances, wolf-whistles from builders, the occasional hoot of a car horn. She knew she didn't look the type but that didn't mean that she didn't feel the type. Even when she'd made the effort to dress up on nights out with Steve or Kate, she still seemed invisible.

She had gone straight from gawky adolescent to frumpy mother in one seamless move. And it wasn't fair.

She walked a little taller, feeling eyes follow her. I like this, she thought. I am now a woman who has a commitment to be beautiful. Who could ignore me? She spotted a new coffee bar in Bond Street and decided to go in. She saw herself as Gina Lollobrigida, sipping an ebony coffee without smudging her lipstick. She went in and sat down at a table.

Kate was enjoying herself. Callum was telling her his life story. She was a good listener, she'd always enjoyed listening far more than talking.

'So that's me, a farm boy turned city slicker!' he joked.

'Don't you miss living in the country?' Kate asked, never having understood the appeal of the country herself.

'Oh, I have every intention of going back eventually. The trouble with farming and country life in general is that it's hard to make a living. There's nothing glamorous about farming. It's hard bone-breaking work, every day of the year, just to survive. My parents had to give up in the end. They both became ill, neither of them were strong enough for that sort of life. We lost the farm and had to move into a council house in the nearest town.'

'That must have been hard,' Kate said.

'The worst part was that we had a great view of the valley where we'd lived.'

'I would have thought that would be the best part,' Kate said.

Callum shook his head. 'No, Dad and Mum both got office jobs in town. Every morning when they left to go to work, they had to face the beauty they'd left behind. It was a daily slap in the face, a reminder of their failure. They're still there, retired now, just sitting in their living room watching the view.'

Kate shook her head. 'I can't believe you'd want to take that chance, yourself.'

'I'm not going to take any chances. I'm going to make enough money in the next few years to buy a farmhouse outright. I'll keep my outgoings low and only have to make a modest living to maintain a decent lifestyle. And I'll have my parents back with me, helping.'

Kate was struck by the glimmer of steel she caught flashing in his eyes. He was not as soft as she'd originally thought. In fact, if he was planning to buy a farm outright in the next few years, he'd have to be utterly single-minded and possibly ruthless.

She reined in her feelings a little as she considered the implication of this unexpected development in his character.

Jenny sat in front of the television with a peanut butter sandwich. She didn't know what she was watching, some game show with rules she couldn't follow. But it was noise and she was grateful for a respite from the silence. She tore off tiny pieces of the sandwich and rolled them into little balls which she popped into her mouth and swallowed without chewing, like pills.

She was making herself eat properly for the baby's sake. If she hadn't been pregnant, she could happily have lain on the sofa all day and eaten baked beans from a can. The self-disgust would reflect her own emotional state.

She felt fat and spotty. She hadn't washed her hair for

241

three days. Her husband had been having an affair while she was pregnant. She'd listened to the message from Rebecca three times and worked out the timing from the various references.

It must have been her pregnancy, she thought, he must have been repulsed by me even then. God knows how he can even look at me now! And he's over-compensating by pretending to be loving and solicitous. His duplicity makes me sick!

She tore off a chunk of the sandwich and stuffed it in her mouth. The doorbell rang and she mumbled a curse through her full mouth. She chewed as fast as she could, wishing she'd chosen a more easily digestible sandwich filling, as she pulled herself to her feet and waddled to the door where the doorbell was now being pressed continually.

'WHAT?' she yelled into the entryphone.

'It's your mother,' an anxious voice replied. 'Can I come in?'

No, Jenny longed to shout. Go away. Go and sit on a park bench and tell strangers about your tragic life. I don't want to hear it. Not now.

She pressed the buzzer to let her mother in.

Barbara scurried into the house, surrounded by an almost tangible air of neurosis. Oh God, Jenny thought. She's going through one of her worrying phases. These are even worse that the moaning phases which are moderately less annoying than the paranoid phases.

'I've been worried sick about you all week and I can see I was right to worry,' she said, without drawing breath.

She collapsed on to the sofa, briefly glancing at the television screen and trying to fathom the rules of the game show. She failed too.

She pulled her coat off and took a long, calm look at Jenny. 'You look terrible!' she said. 'Have you spoken to your midwife?'

Jenny sighed and sat down in an armchair opposite her mother. 'It's nothing to do with the baby. That's all fine. I'm just tired. Is that any surprise? I am about to give birth. You've told me a thousand times about how ill I made you when you were pregnant and how my birth ripped you to shreds.'

Barbara looked surprised. 'I'm sure I wasn't quite so melodramatic, dear.'

Jenny raised her eyebrows and her mother had the good grace to concede the point. She didn't do that often. Must be because I'm pregnant, Jenny thought. What a pity I'm never doing this again.

Barbara continued. 'Anyway, I know the difference between tired and something else. And you're definitely something else. It's Ben, isn't it?'

Jenny got up to fetch herself a glass of water.

Barbara got up and ordered her back into the chair irritably. 'Oh for goodness' sake, Jenny, do sit down. If I can't do a few simple things for you when you are clearly in a bad way, then what is the point in having a mother at all?'

Jenny let her mother fetch the water, hoping that she would have forgotten her original question. A naive hope.

'So, it's Ben, isn't it?' she repeated.

Jenny thought carefully. She had never once said a single critical thing about Ben to her mother. Knowing Barbara's inflammatory views on men and husbands, she didn't dare risk setting her off. It had taken Jenny years to reach the point when Barbara accepted that Jenny would probably never share her opinions. Although Jenny couldn't know it, this fact was a comfort to Barbara. She

243

didn't wish the same level of misery and dissatisfaction on her daughter as she'd experienced herself. And she didn't think she could bear hearing that her daughter was suffering like that.

But Jenny couldn't think of a plausible lie. This was her mother, after all, who else could she talk to? In reality the answer was Andrew. She had female friends, but no really close ones, having concentrated with all her being on her career. She'd never needed friends that much, not with Andrew around.

But Andrew was the one person she couldn't talk to. Not about this, not about Rebecca. Like Ben, she now had one major goal to achieve before she could move on: she needed Rebecca out of Andrew's life. Until that happened, Jenny couldn't think straight.

She'd noticed Andrew talking to Kate and had thought back to the lunch in Harvey Nicols. He didn't know it, but he was attracted to Kate. Jenny knew it and was now placing all her hopes on using Kate to get Andrew away from Rebecca. That was one of the reasons she was going to Wales. She had two days and two evenings to work with.

And the other reason was to keep an eye on Rebecca.

'Please tell me!' her mother pleaded.

So Jenny told her.

'I didn't know you had a daughter,' Ben said with surprise.

'Neither did I,' Andrew said, also surprised, in his case that Rebecca hadn't mentioned it. Actually, Rebecca hadn't told him because she thought it would be disloyal to Sally, although the truth was obviously going to come out when Sally introduced Chrissie to them all at the weekend. But that was up to Sally, not her.

244

'Sorry, Sally,' she said, 'it just slipped out.' She hoped her eyes were communicating that she had felt she had no choice. Sally didn't seem interested in Rebecca's circumstances. She was mentally trying to work out how she should play this with Ben. Kate was one thing. She had been amazingly sympathetic and even helpful. But Ben was the MD. He was the hirer and firer.

She concluded that it made no difference what she said now; the existence of her daughter was out in the open, she couldn't take that back. So she might as well be honest. She'd worked her way through most kinds of deceit, which had brought her tension and not made any noticeable difference to her career. Maybe honesty might be effective. I'll give it a go, she thought.

Andrew and Ben listened sympathetically to her story. They were both good men and neither judged her for her teenage pregnancy. And they both understood her reluctance to let the story become common knowledge.

Sally turned to Ben. 'Let's face it, if I'd told you I had a twelve year-old-daughter, would you have given me the job?'

Ben thought about it. 'Well, surprisingly, it wouldn't have made a great deal of difference. I'm speaking to you in confidence now, although everyone knows that people think like this, it's mothers with babies or very small children who can cause the most upheaval in an office.'

He felt an invisible ray of accusation beaming in on him from working women all over the world. He coughed nervously before continuing. 'But I would deny ever having said that if you ever repeated it!' he warned jokingly.

Nobody was laughing. He ploughed on. 'But older children seldom cause problems. There are school holiday issues, but parents normally have arrangements for those sorted out by the time their kids are at secondary school age.'

Sally was encouraged by this. 'So are you saying that, if I apply for promotion, you wouldn't be put off by my having lied on my original job application form?'

'I hadn't actually thought of that,' Ben said. 'But generally, when you go for promotion, you fill in a new form. The old one is normally left in the files. As far as I'm concerned, there would be no need to refer back.'

Sally sat up cheerfully at that. Ben felt it necessary to temper his good news with a warning. 'I have to tell you, though, that there are no promotions coming up in the immediate future. Even if we win the Saltech account, that will only secure your jobs. The other departments will still have to become more efficient. What I'm trying to say is that, as people leave, we won't necessarily be replacing them or even promoting the ones left behind.'

And this made Andrew and Rebecca as well as Sally look at their futures from a different angle.

'Do you mind if I smoke?' the man asked as he sat down next to Justine.

Justine did mind and considered Kate's life-changing strategy of challenging this rhetorical question.

But the man was attractive and was gazing very appreciatively at her. 'Of course not,' she said. The man took the packet from his pocket. He offered the packet to her.

For one ludicrous moment Justine considered taking one, seeing pictures in her memory of Gina Lollobrigida smoking elegantly with Rock Hudson or James Garner or someone suave like that. It was a nice picture. But common sense prevailed on this one issue.

'I don't,' she said. 'Thank you anyway,' she added.

She carried on reading the *Guardian*, which she'd taken to buying in anticipation of such an occasion. She thought it added an interesting dimension of earnestness to her somewhat superficial appearance.

She'd been grateful when the man asked if he could join her. She found the paper deadly dull and didn't understand the cartoons. Her feelings of inadequacy were creeping back as she wished she had a *Daily Mail* with her.

But it turned out to be a shrewd choice because her companion also had the *Guardian* with him.

'Snap!' he said, as it fell from his raincoat pocket.

Justine smiled coolly, not wanting to appear too wholesome by smiling too broadly. She carried on reading, hoping this man was experienced in this sort of ad hoc encounter because she certainly wasn't.

'Jerry,' he said, 'Jerry Fitzgerald,' extending his hand in a businesslike fashion.

Justine took his hand and shook it, thinking quickly. 'Kate,' she said, because this was the first name that popped into her head and she wasn't clever enough to make up an entire name at a second's notice. 'Kate Harris.'

'So maybe we could do this again?' Callum was asking as he signed the credit card slip. 'But let's make it dinner, perhaps?'

Kate liked the note of uncertainty in his voice. It reflected a refreshing absence of presumption. Lunch had gone so well that he could have been forgiven for assuming another date was a certainty.

'I'd like that,' Kate said emphatically. Dinner would be much easier. She could go home, get changed and not have to go near a McDonald's. This reminded her to check her watch. It was two fifty-five and she was supposed to be meeting the others at three thirty. Plus she had to get changed back into her work clothes. She felt a throbbing at her temples as she contemplated the contortions of that cubicle again.

'How about later in the week?' Callum suggested.

Kate thought of the week ahead and knew it was an impossibility. It had been remiss of her to sneak away for this lunch as it was. She laughed to herself when she thought about how she had only agreed to do so because she couldn't think of a cool way to say 'no' in front of her staff.

Deceit occasionally brings its rewards as well, she thought.

'This week is a dead loss,' she said apologetically. She'd explained about the pressure that was on her to deliver this new business within weeks.

'I understand,' he said. 'So what about the weekend?'

Kate was about to accept when she remembered the trip to Wales. When she explained this to Callum, she could see that he was trying to discern whether she was making a whole list of long-term excuses to get out of ever having to see him again, as she had planned to do before lunch.

So she overcompensated to reassure him.

'Look,' she said, with childlike eagerness. She pulled out one of the leaflets that she'd left in her handbag after Friday's party. 'This is where we're going. I'm not particularly keen but I can see how it might help us bond together more quickly. And we do need that, believe me.'

'This looks beautiful,' Callum said, referring to the scenery in the photographs. 'Can I keep this?' he asked. 'Perhaps I could phone you over the weekend?'

'Of course!' Kate said, delighted that he had regained

his enthusiasm. 'But let me give you my mobile number. Then if you can't reach me via the centre, you can try me on this.'

Callum took the number. 'Thanks.'

They got up to leave. Callum helped her on with the delicate angora bolero that she had hooked over the back of her chair.

'Have a great time away,' he said, stroking her shoulders. 'I'll look forward to seeing you when you get back.'

'Me too,' Kate said warmly. 'And thanks for lunch.'

They left together and exchanged a friendly kiss before Callum jumped into a taxi and Kate began running to McDonald's.

Don't say it, Barbara warned herself. Don't say I told you so. Don't say pig or bastard or anything like that. Like many mothers, she possessed remarkable wisdom for the problems of her children that she was utterly incapable of applying to her own life.

She wanted to hug Jenny because Jenny was in such terrible pain and because she, the world's worst mother, was so achingly grateful that her daughter had confided in her. Jenny had never done this before, always preferring to share things with her brother. Barbara had understood this but it had always hurt her.

Now she wanted to prove herself worthy of the trust. She wanted to help Jenny with this horrible problem in a practical, positive way. No mention of castration, she reminded herself, that always annoys her.

'I don't really understand how you've been able to hide this from Ben.'

Jenny shrugged. 'I'm obviously a good actress. Besides, when you're pregnant, you're expected to behave strangely.'

249

'I suppose so,' Barbara said doubtfully. 'Just tell me one thing. What do you want?'

Jenny seemed surprised at the question. 'I don't understand.'

Barbara stroked her daughter's hair. 'That's the point I'm making, sweetheart. Here you are, you've spent four days thinking of nothing but this awful thing you've heard, trying to decide what to do about it, but you haven't decided what you want. I mean, do you want a divorce? To bring this baby up by yourself?'

'No!' Jenny exclaimed. 'No.' She was a little quieter. 'Of course I want this baby to have a father. But I'm not sure I want Ben as a husband. I don't know if I'll ever be able to trust him.'

'You'll need to talk to him before you reach that conclusion, if you're going to be fair. You don't know all the facts, yet, or the circumstances.'

Jenny began shredding tissues angrily. 'I know it wasn't a one-off. The message made it clear that it went on for a while.'

Barbara swallowed, feeling her daughter's pain. 'You still need to let him tell you why he did it. Even if the excuse isn't acceptable, even if you don't forgive him, you can't end your marriage on the word of a little slapper who might well have her own motives for causing trouble.'

Jenny's mouth hardened at the reference to Rebecca. 'We'll talk in Wales. She'll be there as well so I should be able to get all the facts. And Andrew will be there too. I'll do my best to protect him.'

Barbara hugged her daughter as closely as the enormous bump allowed. I'm going to protect him too. I'll deal with this Rebecca myself.

*

The atmosphere at the table had flagged noticeably since Ben's warning about promotions.

Rebecca made an effort to lift the conversation again, still worried that Andrew might return to his previous interrogation of Ben about Jenny. She tried to think of something neutral to say.

'Did you tell Ben we bought new curtains on Saturday, Andrew?' she said with alarming cheerfulness.

Andrew and Ben looked perplexed by this conversational non-starter.

'Why would I?' Andrew asked.

Rebecca giggled nervously. She didn't giggle as a rule and it didn't suit her.

Ben was bothered by this comment. He knew what she was saying. She was telling him that she and Andrew were settling down. She was tormenting him with the promise that she would be sticking around for a long time.

He sank even further into himself. Andrew noticed immediately.

'Right, that's it, Ben. I want you to tell me what's wrong with Jenny. Now!'

'They were purple with geometric shapes in different shades of grey,' Rebecca went on desperately.

'Shut up, Rebecca,' Andrew said, as kindly as he could, which wasn't very. 'Ben. Please!'

Ben blew out his breath, not knowing what to say and what to leave out.

'It started on Thursday night. She was absolutely fine when I spoke to her at your mum's. She was going to spend the night there. She said she was feeling a bit tired.'

Andrew nodded, encouraging him to go on. Rebecca was listening carefully, already alert to the reference to Thursday night.

'Well, that's about it,' Ben said. 'Since then, she's been behaving very strangely. I spoke to the midwife and she said that there was nothing wrong with Jenny physically. But something is up, I know it is.'

Andrew didn't understand it. 'You and Jenny normally talk about everything,' he said enviously. It was the sort of marriage he wanted for himself, but he didn't expect it.

'I know,' Ben agreed. 'And I've asked her a dozen times but she just acts all cross with me and says it's the pregnancy.'

'So she was fine on Thursday and not on Friday?' Andrew asked, wanting to get the facts clear.

Ben nodded.

'Then something must have happened in between then.' His face tightened. 'It has to be Mum. She'll have had one of her moods and taken it out on Jenny. Things can get really nasty between those two. I bet she's said something to upset her. Something about you, probably. You know how she feels about marriage.'

Ben shook his head. 'That was my first thought as well, but it's not that. Your mum was having one of her mad half-hours and Jenny wasn't standing for it. She got up and walked out. Your mum couldn't believe it!'

'I'd have liked to have seen that', Andrew said. 'So if it was nothing Mum said, it must have been something you said to her that night.'

Ben shook his head again. 'When I got home, I found her asleep on the sofa. I wasn't even expecting her. So I didn't disturb her and went straight to bed. Then, when we woke up in the morning, it started.'

Rebecca's breathing was becoming very shallow. 'What time did you get home that night?' she asked anxiously.

'Before eleven,' he said, wondering why Rebecca would be interested in that. 'Besides, Jenny's not one of those women who stands by the door with a rolling pin. She never cares what time I get in.'

'Then it's a mystery,' Andrew said. 'Maybe it's just the pregnancy. Some women go completely round the twist.'

'Maybe,' Ben said hopefully. 'I just wish I knew what was wrong.'

Rebecca kept her eyes pointed downwards. No you don't, she thought. Because I do know, and believe me, when you find out, you'll wish you'd never asked.

Stan sat on the living-room floor, packing his books away in crates. They weren't going for a few months but he enjoyed all the anticipation. He marvelled at the musty covers of his favourite books, wondering if they'd smell different after a few years in the New Zealand air.

Eventually he shifted, rubbing his aching back, and took a mouthful of his sandwich. Where's Edie? he thought. She knows I like us to have lunch together.

Edie was upstairs in Kate's old bedroom, which was now the guest room. She'd dragged down a fading shoebox from on top of the wardrobe and emptied the contents on to the floor. There must have been hundreds of photos there, possibly thousands, she thought as she skimmed through the muddle of sepia and black-and-white and colour snaps.

She opened the wardrobe and pulled out a large box that had been stuffed in there for years. In the bag were empty photo albums, all of which had been given to them as presents over the years. Every year she'd make the resolution on January 1st: this will be the year I sort all the photos out and put them in albums, But of course she never got round to it. Who does?

Then she lowered herself carefully to the floor and

253

started the epic task. She took a mouthful of her sandwich as she worked out a system.

Where's Stan? she wondered. He knows I like us to have lunch together. Then she forgot all about Stan and settled down to put her and her family's lives in order.

Chapter 15

By Wednesday, they were all in agreement that the week was going well as far as work was concerned. The group had fallen into a good rhythm, each cooperating with the others and keeping communications flowing.

There was not much time for lunches. Sally had been going and getting sandwiches for them all. She'd even volunteered for the job!

'Is it my imagination or is Sally a whole lot more easygoing since her big confession?' Ben asked Kate.

'Well, you knew her better than me before I arrived so I can't really comment,' Kate had said to avoid any sentimental outbursts. The subject of Sally made her feel warm and good, a feeling she had to suppress at work. Sally had gone into Kate's office earlier to thank Kate personally for organising her daughter's trip next week, even arranging for the company to pay for it.

This was a bit of a lie: Kate was actually paying for it herself. But she couldn't let Sally know this. Sally would probably be very offended and Kate would start getting the reputation for being a soft touch. That coffee maker would be moved one electric socket closer to Kate's office.

Kate had noticed Sally's change of temperament but she'd noticed changes in the others as well. Rebecca would never become a great buddy to Kate, but she'd been making an effort to be moderately friendly. Kate was grateful but tried not to appear over-grateful. Rushing out and buying cakes was probably over-grateful, she thought mournfully.

I can't believe I'm so thankful for so little, she told herself. Or maybe this is all I can hope for when I'm like this, Kate thought sadly.

When I was a doormat, everyone seemed to love me. I know it was a shallow sort of affection but I did like it. Perhaps real bosses never get anything more than passing courtesy, some social banter, but nothing approaching closeness.

Surely there's a middle way? Kate asked herself. Can't I make these people like me *and* respect me?

She was even more confused by Andrew. His attitude towards her seemed to vary from day to day. Kate was tempted to look up the movements of the moon to see if their pattern would explain his erratic behaviour. When they were working alone, he would begin by being frosty and strangely submissive, as if to emphasise her seniority. Then gradually he'd relax. She would take the chance of saying something unrelated to work and he'd respond without thinking. Then they'd be back to where they'd been on Friday night.

The more she thought about that party, the less sense it made. He'd been so charming, so pleasant. She was really starting to feel that he liked her. This was a tremendous achievement if it were true, because she'd won him over while sticking to her strong-woman act.

She'd had to keep a firm grip on herself to avoid relaxing entirely and letting her old self take over the conversation. She experimented by not thinking 'scumbag' at the end of her sentences. She slowly felt her old niceness creeping back. If only it was not inextricably linked to her passivity.

She liked him because he appeared to reflect her own standards of decency and kindness. He was nice in the same way she was nice. Well, not the 'she' she was at this moment, but the real 'she'.

What she really admired, and envied, was that he felt no need to cover up his character. She couldn't see him dressing in combats and striding into an office barking commands and practising kick-boxing moves in meetings to earn respect. But then again, she reminded herself, he didn't need to do anything to earn respect. He just had to ensure he didn't lose it by being a total buffoon. He didn't need to waste one valuable minute of his valuable time by agonising over who should make the coffee. He was a man.

He'd asked her about the films she liked and her favourite food and her favourite holidays.

'French to all three,' she'd answered.

'You don't believe in loosening up, do you?' he'd laughed.

'I can't afford to,' she'd replied, weakening under this onslaught from his charm.

'Why not?' Andrew asked, interested now that he had finally elicited a genuine response to one his questions.

Kate regretted the lapse and hoped to satisfy him with a vague wave and an 'Oh, you know, women at work, that sort of thing.'

He did know, in fact, feeling guilty for having pre-judged her himself before meeting her.

She tried to keep her sentences short after this but he was wearing her down. She'd been a cheese straw away from offering to top up his glass and hold his plate while he ate his chicken drumstick.

She'd understood that the announcement that their jobs were on the line must have profoundly shocked him, especially since he would have expected to hear it from Ben earlier than the others.

So she hadn't been too surprised that he was subdued on Monday. But his moods were up and down all over the place. Sometimes she thought she could feel him watching her but when she looked up, he'd be immersed in his work.

Rebecca had noticed the change in his moods as well. If it was her fault in some way, then she was doing all she could to win him over. But the more effort she made, the more it seemed to alienate him.

I have to leave her. I have to leave her. He couldn't get the thought out of his mind. The more effort he made to get back his previous feelings for her, to act as if he felt the same, the more dishonest he felt.

It was even harder when he looked at Kate. He averted his face and turned his chair so it was facing Rebecca, facing away from Kate's office. That's when it struck him.

He'd noticed that Rebecca had bought some new clothes. He hadn't shown much interest in them even though she'd seemed strangely interested in his opinion.

But now he saw the clothes on Rebecca, he realised what she'd done. She was dressing just like Kate.

'Kate, it's Steve.'

'Has something happened to Justine? Is it the kids?' she asked anxiously.

'They're all fine,' he said impatiently. 'Can't I phone you up when there's no major drama?'

Kate reminded him that the only times he'd called her before were to tell her about the births of the three children. He mumbled something inaudible.

'How did you get this number, Steve?' Kate asked.

'I found it in her drawer,' he said. 'And you mustn't tell her I phoned. She'll go mad!'

'Is everything OK?' she asked, noticing how down he sounded.

'No, it's not. Look, can I meet you for lunch? I need to talk to you.'

Kate groaned. 'I'm really sorry, but I can't. Did Justine tell you about the trouble here? I may be out of a job in a few weeks. No one else is taking lunches so I can't either. Sorry.'

Steve was getting desperate. 'Listen, I've just come out of High Street Kensington tube station. Can you at least pop downstairs, just for five minutes. I really need to talk to you.'

'Why can't you just tell me what it is on the phone?' she asked, wincing at the pile of papers on her desk that needed checking before the end of the day.

'This has to be in person. Trust me,' he said.

Kate sighed. 'OK. Ask the receptionist to phone me when you're here and I'll come down. But only five minutes, Steve.'

'Thank you, Kate. I'm really grateful. See you shortly.'

Kate put the phone down. She calculated that she had five minutes before Steve arrived. That would give her time to have a quick word with Justine.

'But why did you have to use my name?' Kate hissed down the phone.

'Don't get worked up!' Justine laughed, 'they'll never find out.'

'They?' Kate asked. 'How many men have you told that you're Kate Harris?'

'Just the three,' her friend replied. 'I told you it's a bit of fun. You should be pleased.'

259

Kate closed her eyes in disbelief. 'Tell me why I should be pleased that you are parading round London, looking odd, acting even more oddly and telling men that your name is Kate Harris?'

Justine tutted impatiently. It seemed obvious to her. 'I took what you were saying to heart. You were right. I shouldn't risk my marriage. So to prove that I have no interest in having affairs of any sort, I'm deliberately making a game of it. I'm just playacting, really playacting, with a made-up character and made-up name.'

'My name, not a made-up name,' Kate corrected.

'Whatever. I pretend to be someone else, I make up a whole life story, I reinvent myself each time. I change my make-up each time as well. I'm getting really good at that. And I note the reactions so that, the next time, I can adapt my character to see if that gets different reactions.'

Kate was horrified. Her otherwise sane friend was describing a sequence of insane events as if they were perfectly normal, as if she'd taken up t'ai chi.

'Where does Steve think you are when you're . . . doing whatever you call this?' she asked, hoping that her name didn't come into it anywhere.

'Out with the girls, something like that,' Justine said breezily. 'The truth is, I don't think he's bothered. We're getting on much better at the moment and, as I said, it's just a bit of fun. I'll probably stop when we get back from our holiday. I haven't got the energy to keep this up much longer!'

Kate exhaled in relief. That was what she had wanted to hear. A beep on her phone told her that a call was waiting for her.

'Sorry Justine, I've got to go. I'll call you tomorrow. 'Bye.'

*

Barbara sat in a coffee bar that faced the entrance to the building. She was there for one purpose: to catch a glimpse of Rebecca. All she wanted to do was find out what the woman looked like, so she could take her to one side when she got the chance and have some words. This was not as easy as it sounded. She lived and worked with Andrew and Barbara didn't want her son to know about this.

She was driven by her mission to make things right for her daughter and, indirectly, for Andrew as well.

She hadn't been a great mother but she would make up for all that now. She expected them to come out at lunchtime, although she couldn't tell what time that might be.

The waiter approached her again. 'Another coffee, madam?' he asked.

'I'm fine, thank you,' Barbara said, politely, not taking her eye off the window.

The waiter slunk back to the counter where the manager was waiting.

'Why didn't you tell her that she had to leave?' the manager hissed. 'She's been here nearly two hours already!'

'You tell her!' the waiter hissed back. 'She looks a bit funny to me.'

The manager looked over. She looked quite normal to him but then his mother had looked normal until that incident with the store detective in Sainsbury's . . . Maybe he'd leave her there after all.

Barbara was quite enjoying the sight of life coming and going before her. She'd led a full and busy life so this experience was a real luxury. She enjoyed imagining who all the people were and what their lives were like. Take that man, for instance, walking along with an *A to Z*, looking anxious. He's obviously one of those messengers who deliver important letters by hand. Looks like he's got the worries of the world on his shoulders – probably got a wife at home screaming at him to get a proper job. She chuckled to herself at the image of the harridan at home in her curlers with a cigarette dangling from the corner of his mouth.

The manager saw her laughing and congratulated himself on his decision to leave alone.

'Quite mad,' he muttered, smiling nervously at her when she caught his eye.

The man was not a messenger with a nagging wife. He was a surgical registrar with a wife going through a mid-life crisis, a rather early mid-life crisis. Steve jogged up the stairs and into reception, putting his *A to Z* away in relief. 'You're not easy to find, are you?' he said to the receptionist.

The receptionist stared at him blankly, waiting to find out who he was before she would decide just how much courtesy his position warranted. She had no intention of exhausting her muscles by smiling at someone who was only worthy of a curt nod. Steve stared back, noticing that her face looked much like Justine's this morning. It was that same uniform beige matt surface with colours sprinkled and daubed around until there was nothing left of the original person underneath.

'Sorry,' Steve said, apologising for his staring. He needn't have bothered. The girl liked being stared at. She had utter confidence in her looks and interpreted all attention as admiration which she accepted as her due.

'Erm, my name is Steve Woods and I'm here to see Kate Harris,' he said, reverting to his best doctor's voice. He'd clearly injected the correct note into his voice

262

because he was rewarded with the merest upturn of the vacuous girl's glossy, red mouth.

'Take a seat please,' she commanded with a nasal twang that made Steve want to laugh out loud at its incongruity to the girl's sophisticated appearance.

It took the girl a couple of attempts but she eventually got through to Kate and announced Steve's arrival. Kate was down in less than a minute.

At least, he assumed it was Kate. This terrifying apparition of power and efficiency looked nothing like the Kate he knew, with her woolly jumpers and unflattering skirts.

But as she approached, her Kate-ness began shining through. He stood up, transfixed by the illusion she'd managed to conjure up.

'Wow,' he said. 'I don't know what else to say!'

Kate steered him towards one of the small meeting rooms leading from the lobby. They kissed affectionately then sat down at the small low table in the centre of the room.

'It all makes sense now,' he said.

'What does?' Kate asked, fairly certain of what he was referring to but wanting to get the facts straight in case she said the wrong thing.

Steve lifted his hands in despair. 'Justine, of course. Have you seen her lately?' Before she could answer, he went on, 'Of course you have, you saw her last night.'

Kate sent up a silent curse. Thank you, Justine. You nearly landed me – and you – right in it.

'How did you think she looked? Honestly?' Steve asked, not bothering to hide his desperation.

Kate didn't want to answer this. She knew what he wanted her to say and she knew what Justine would want her to say. But her environment and her clothes and the effect she'd had on Steve when she approached him, gave her the confidence to say what *she* wanted.

Clothes are more powerful than I imagine, she told herself.

'It's just a phase she's going through. Like when you bought that motorbike?'

Steve stood up and began pacing round the room. 'It wasn't a motorbike, it was a scooter!'

Kate smiled at his discomfort. 'Yes, but you'd wanted a motorbike,' she reminded him. 'And you spent ages on the internet in bikers' chat rooms and started buying all the magazines.'

'I spent a couple of evenings on the internet, just to get some advice, and I bought a couple of magazines. It was hardly *Easy Rider*!'

'That's what I'm trying to tell you! That you were dabbling, dreaming a bit maybe, having fun fantasising about the possibilities.'

Steve was exasperated. 'Fantasising about motorbikes is not the same as fantasising about . . . whatever Justine is fantasising about and I think we can both guess what that is!'

'I think you're wrong,' Kate said. 'In fact I *know* you're wrong. She's making up for all the things she missed out when she was younger, messing about with make-up and her hair, that's all.'

'And going out all the time,' Steve added.

'Look, you're going away on Saturday. Why not see how the holiday goes. I think everything will settle down after that.'

'Do you think?' Steve asked, wanting to believe it.

'I do,' Kate said firmly. 'Now go back home or to work. Go and save lives and stop worrying about this.'

She stood up, wanting to get back to work. Then she

remembered something. 'It's lovely to see you, but why did you say you had to speak to me in person? We could easily have done this on the phone.'

Steve looked bashful. He began babbling. 'The thing is, with all the time and money Justine has been spending on her appearance, it started me thinking about how, maybe, she was getting dissatisfied with me. She made a few comments about me not caring about my appearance, letting myself go, that sort of thing. And I felt desperate, I had to do something, but it's harder for men, we can't just slap a new lipstick on and then wipe it off a day later. But I wanted to prove to her that . . .'

An ominous premonition crept over Kate. 'What have you done?' she interrupted, not wanting any more build-up.

He undid his shirt buttons and pulled the material down to reveal the top of his right arm, embellished with a large black tattoo.

'Are those the clothes you bought yesterday?' Andrew asked Rebecca.

Rebecca beamed. 'Yes. You said they looked nice, don't you remember?'

No, Andrew thought. But I probably did. It sounds like me. He was treading very carefully here.

'They are a bit different to your normal sort of thing, aren't they?' he asked casually.

Rebecca picked up on his tone. He should have expected that. He needed years of practice before he could deceive a woman with any real success.

'What do you mean by that?' she snapped. 'I thought you liked them.'

Oh dear, Andrew thought. I'm in trouble. Help.

Help didn't come so he blundered on. Helpless.

'I do like them. They're lovely. But normally you wear clothes that are . . .' he hadn't a clue how to describe her usual clothes. In desperation, he settled for, 'nice.'

Rebecca exploded. 'Are you saying that these clothes aren't nice? What's wrong with them in your expert opinion?'

Help. Help. Help.

Nope. Still no help.

'They are nice. But they are a bit . . . black.' There. He'd said it.

'And what's wrong with black?' She wasn't going to let go of this until Andrew was prostrate with repentance at her feet.

He ploughed on, knowing that nothing could save him except death. 'OK. I suppose what I'm trying to say is that you normally wear . . . colours and . . . longer skirts and . . . softer things.'

Rebecca mixed these words with the acid building inside her until it bubbled out of her in an eruption of accusation.

'Well, forgive me for trying to do something different. I had no idea that there was a rule that women had to wear the same clothes to work every day. Or that girlfriends weren't allowed to wear skirts of different length.' She was so angry, she'd run out of vitriol before she'd got to the good bits, the personal bits.

That made her furious. She stood up, slammed her chair back against the wall, leaving a hole in the plaster, and fumed off towards the door. Kate was walking through the door and narrowly avoided a collision.

'What's happened? Are you all right, Rebecca?' she asked. Rebecca ran past her. Kate glanced into the open-plan office to see Andrew standing up, looking bemused.

266

She went over to find out what had been happening. Morale was looking shaky to her at this point.

'What's going on?' she asked him.

He sat down at this desk. This needed careful thinking. He was way out of his depth. He didn't know what, and to whom, he should tell anything.

Kate became more forceful. 'Andrew,' she looked really distressed. 'I need to know if there's a serious problem.'

Andrew went cautiously. 'Have you noticed anything about Rebecca today?' he asked.

Kate tried to think back, but couldn't recall anything out of the ordinary.

Andrew, infuriated by his inability to make anyone understand where he was coming from, gave up on the subtle, tactful route altogether.

'For God's sake, am I the only one who's noticed? She's wearing your clothes!' he said loudly.

Barbara looked at her watch. It was one thirty. She couldn't drink any more coffee. She was buzzing with caffeine as it was, not having thought about ordering decaffeinated.

It looked as if Andrew and Rebecca were not coming out for lunch. And I'll bet that woman doesn't make him sandwiches, Barbara grumbled to herself. I'll have to speak to him, make sure he's eating properly, she thought. After I've dealt with *her*.

She thought back to the messenger and it gave her an idea. She stood up abruptly and walked over to the counter where the waiter and manager each took a step backwards. What's the matter with them? Barbara wondered.

'Can I pay, please?' she asked.

The two men exchanged glances. The manager spoke, nervously.

'That will be £8.50,' he said, with exaggerated patience.

Barbara shook her head in amazement. 'For a few cups of coffee!'

Yep. She was mad. The manager and waiter quickly gave her the change and ran to open the door to make sure she actually left.

Barbara didn't leave a tip. They were too shifty by far.

She walked over to the building and went up to the receptionist, who did not appreciate all these interruptions at lunchtime. She was trying to read her *Hair and Nail Monthly* magazine. The only time she hadn't minded the interruption was when that man had gone into the meeting room with Kate Harris and come out five minutes later, doing up his shirt. Incredibly, Kate had come out unruffled, not a hair or button out of place. Now *that* was cool. She would be rewarded by a 'Good morning' from the receptionist every morning after today.

Barbara cleared her throat and waited to be acknowledged. When that didn't happen, she put on her best barrister's voice and boomed, 'I'd like to see Rebecca Ramsden, please.'

The receptionist straightened on hearing the voice. It was a voice of authority. 'Can I say who's asking for her?' she asked with that twang again.

Barbara hadn't thought this through. Oh what the hell! 'Tell her it's Barbara Darlington.'

Kate closed her office door. She'd encouraged Andrew away from the open-plan arena where everyone had become silent after his outburst.

'What do you mean?' she asked

Andrew felt foolish. 'Perhaps it's my imagination, but when I tried to talk to Rebecca she went berserk.'

268

Kate tried to get him to talk sensibly. 'What about her clothes, my clothes?' she asked.

Andrew was curious. 'You must have seen what she was wearing?' he said.

Now Kate felt foolish. She hadn't paid the slightest attention to Rebecca's clothes, or anyone else's. They didn't interest her. She didn't notice subtle differences the way other women apparently did.

As far as she could recall, Rebecca had been wearing suits since she'd known her. But then most of the women wore suits; one suit was much like another to her untrained eye.

Andrew peered through the glass window that looked out on to the open office. Rebecca had returned to her desk and was on the phone. She looked flustered but was doing something with her make-up and a small mirror. As she stood up, Andrew beckoned Kate over.

Kate's gaze followed Rebecca as she walked over to the lift. She examined her clothes and suddenly understood Andrew's point.

She shrugged. 'I can see what you mean. It is much like my suit. But I don't see the problem. A black suit isn't a statement of individuality by any means. Your suit might be identical to Ben's. I wouldn't notice and, even if I did, I wouldn't read any significance into it.'

Andrew turned to look at her, puzzled. 'I thought women always noticed things like that.'

Kate reached for a safe exit from this minefield. 'You've been shopping with me. Remember?'

Andrew replayed the quickest purchase of an outfit he'd ever witnessed from a woman. 'I take your point. But I know Rebecca. I know her style. Her appearance, how she presents herself, is vital to her. Now

269

I'm no great fashion expert but Rebecca talks about her clothes, about why she chooses them, the *point* of them.'

'Lots of women are like that,' Kate commented.

'But for Rebecca, it's like a military exercise with an objective that has to be met at all costs. She has always stuck to the one style since she's worked here. It took her a while to work it out and she has great faith in her calculations.'

'I thought she got turned down for promotion.' Kate couldn't stop herself.

Andrew nodded grimly. 'She took that badly but Ben convinced her that even if she'd worn a suit of armour, she wouldn't have got that job. He told her that the company would never appoint a woman to a senior position.'

Kate felt little ragged pieces fall into perfect slots in her memory files. 'No wonder she was so resentful when I was hired. It was more than just you being overlooked.'

Andrew continued. 'So she carried on the way she always had. Until now.'

'So now she sees a woman getting promotion and decides that if she is to get ahead, like me, she has to take on some of my ways.'

'Exactly!' Andrew exclaimed. At last he'd made himself understood. He waited for Kate to rant at the nerve of Rebecca to steal her essence like that, to try and pretend to be Kate, that was the only way to put it.

Kate remained absolutely calm. 'That seems a perfectly good rationale. It's exactly what . . . many other women have done.'

Andrew was dumbfounded. 'You don't think it's weird?'

Kate shrugged. 'No,' she said simply.

Andrew bounced on the spot, wanting to say more but not daring to cross the line that Kate repeatedly drew between them.

I think it's more than that, he wanted to say. I think she's seen the way I look at you. I think she wants to be like you because of me, not because of the job.

But maybe Kate wouldn't think that was weird either. I am in a foreign country here and nobody around me speaks English.

He shook his head and left Kate's office. She watched him go with amusement.

'I'm a role model,' she said out loud. I'm a role model. It was the funniest joke she'd heard for years.

'Mrs Darlington?' Rebecca asked nervously.

Barbara stood up and appraised Rebecca with her barrister's eye. Imagining her in the dock at the Old Bailey, she skimmed the glossy veneer, recognising the quality of the work. She'd seen it a thousand times.

Any solicitor with a day's experience could put a client in good clothes and do her hair nicely. And the lawyer's seventeen-year-old secretary could take a hardened criminal and paint out the hardness in her face. Barbara had seen jurors smile sweetly at truly wicked women who'd been transformed by experts into wide-eyed nymphs you'd hire to look after your children.

Rebecca was good but Barbara knew what she was looking for. Wherever her eye landed, it found weakness and vulnerability. Rebecca was uncomfortable in those clothes, Barbara noticed. She clearly wasn't used to tightly fitting skirts or short jackets. The make-up was heavy but, ironically, she'd used it to conceal her softness and add suggestions of worldliness that she simply didn't have. And there was something else. The young woman had known pain and not quite survived it. It was throbbing just below her surface, waiting to be lanced when she was ready to let it go.

Oh no, Barbara concluded, she's just a nice girl. You silly, silly girl. What have you done? You want to be happy and you've gone and caused all this misery! That's not the way.

She wanted to take her in hand and set her on the right way. But she was not Rebecca's mother. She had her own children to consider and Rebecca was ruining both of their lives.

Edie stepped out of the salon, thrilled with the result. The hairdresser waved through the window at her. Lovely girl, Edie thought. Looks a bit like my Kate.

The girl had never had such an unusual request before. She had many women 'of a certain age' coming in with pictures of Catherine Zeta Jones and hopeless optimism. But this was the first time a customer wanted to look like herself – forty years ago.

It was quite a challenge. Edie's hair had been permed for her wedding day and was slicked into symmetrical waves across her head. She described the colour as 'chestnut with the sun setting on the tips'.

The stylist attacked this task with great enthusiasm. She had spent the morning doing cut and blow dries on sulky children accompanied by their difficult mothers supervising the removal of each individual hair, while their offspring cried, insisting that all the other girls had Victoria Beckhams.

And this woman was so sweet. Like her granny.

When it was finished, Edie cried. So did the stylist, and the junior who'd done her wash. Edie couldn't stop touching her hair all the way home. Her excitement was only tempered by uncertainty about how Stan would react when he saw her.

'Shall we go in here?' Rebecca said to her boyfriend's mother, pointing towards the small meeting room.

Barbara followed her without saying anything. The receptionist put her magazine down. She had worked it out. Barbara Darlington: must be related to Andrew, probably his mum. And Rebecca, that was his girlfriend. It looked as if they'd never met before.

It's all happening in that room, she thought wistfully. What a pity they don't have CCTV.

It was a brief meeting, much like Steve's and Kate's but without the tattoo finale.

Barbara stifled her instinctive sympathies but scrapped her original plans to vent on Rebecca all her feelings about the affair with her son-in-law. She couldn't be cruel. Well, no more than was necessary to achieve her aim.

She didn't waste any time. 'I know you had an affair with Ben and now my daughter knows.'

Rebecca sank into a chair. She'd convinced herself that it couldn't be true, that something would have been said by now if Ben's wife had known. Now, however, she had to face up to her actions.

'I'm so sorry,' she said sincerely.

'I'm sure you are,' Barbara said drily.

Rebecca heard the sarcasm. 'I didn't know she was pregnant.'

'You knew he was married,' Barbara shot straight back.

Rebecca nodded. 'What is Jenny going to do?' she asked nervously.

'She hasn't decided,' Barbara said.

273

Rebecca shuddered at the thousand possible outcomes that she would now have to consider. 'So why have you come to see me? I presume you don't want Andrew to know about this visit?'

Barbara faced her levelly. 'I don't mind if you tell him.'

Rebecca laughed at that. She knew when she was outsmarted. Of course she couldn't tell Andrew without explaining what his mother had wanted.

'Do you think this is funny?' Barbara asked incredulously.

Rebecca stopped laughing. That was when Barbara noticed that she'd been crying recently.

'No, I don't think it's funny. I'm laughing because this is a mess and I don't know what else to do. Sorry.'

Barbara wanted to get this out of the way before any more damage was done to anyone. 'So,' she said. 'Here's the thing. My daughter is expecting her first child in a few weeks. You have almost ruined her life. I say "almost" because she doesn't yet know if she can repair her marriage. She can't do anything while you're there, like a malicious genie.'

Rebecca swallowed, feeling each word like a pin through a fingernail. Barbara sped up.

'What makes it worse, if anything can make it any worse, is your relationship with Andrew. Her brother. Do you have any idea how close they are?'

Rebecca nodded slightly.

'While you are with him and a part of his life and, consequently, Jenny's life, she can't move forward. So I'd like you to end things with Andrew now.'

Barbara slowed her breathing down to restore her previous sense of calm.

'Just like that?' Rebecca asked. And what if I don't? was the unspoken question.

This was the question Barbara answered. 'If you don't, then I will tell Andrew what you have done.'

Chapter 16

Kate shut the front door behind her and slumped on the sofa, kicking her shoes off and stretching her toes.

It had been a strange day. She kept finding herself chuckling at intervals throughout it whenever she thought of Steve's tattoo. She had thought about phoning Justine and warning her. But this would not be fair on Steve. Whatever was going on in that marriage, she could not possibly know all the details and she therefore had no right to interfere.

'What exactly is it?' she'd asked Steve out of curiosity.

'Can't you tell?' he'd replied, dismayed. 'It's a J, an ornamental one. I was going to have the whole JUSTINE done but it was too painful, so I stopped at the J and I just asked Ricardo to decorate it a bit.'

Kate had fallen apart when she heard that the tattooist's name was Ricardo. Apparently, the pain had killed Steve's sense of humour so he hadn't seen anything funny in it.

'The man was a sadist,' he grumbled, still rubbing the design which looked red and sore.

'Do you think Justine will like it?' he'd asked hopefully. This was why he'd come to see Kate, to ask this one question. He needed reassurance, which seemed futile to Kate since unlike an excessive application of mascara this was an irreversible act of folly.

'Who can tell?' she'd answered vaguely, ushering him

276

out of the door with promises that everything would be fine.

The rest of the day had continued in bizarre mode. There had been the odd business with Andrew and Rebecca's clothes. She'd found that funny too. Well, Andrew's expression was comical, she reminded herself. Poor man, he hasn't got a clue about women, or possibly about people in general.

Rebecca, though, had taken it all really badly. When she came back to her desk, she was ashen. Andrew had spent the whole afternoon apologising but Rebecca had sat in front of her computer screen and hammered at the keys until everyone had gone home. She wouldn't talk to Andrew, who was distressed at upsetting her so badly, at all.

Kate wondered if she should intervene but figured that this was something personal between the two of them. Since she couldn't guess how a woman in her position would be expected to deal with this sort of issue, she did the sensible thing and ignored it.

Andrew had reluctantly left at six o'clock, saying he wanted to go and see Jenny. Rebecca had promised to see him at home later.

Kate looked at her home and drank in the surroundings. She'd bought this house five years earlier and spent all her time and money making it into a reflection of herself. Everything was neutral, the framework of the house being little more than a backdrop for the theatre of her possessions.

There was stuff everywhere you looked. She could sit in a chair and see her whole life represented. She'd taken all the tatty posters that had decorated her student digs and framed them, torn edges and all. They were hanging in symmetrical splendour, grouped around photos: school group shots, family snaps, studio portraits, too many baby pictures to count; she knew the names of every baby. Everyone of any significance in her life was on her wall.

She'd bought countless shelving units to display her memorabilia, or tat as other people preferred to call it. Every souvenir that she had ever bought or had been bought for her was there. Ornaments from all over the world, crumbling papier mâché models made by nieces and nephews, plastic toys from Christmas crackers, empty pots that had once held long-dead plants, Quality Street tins containing theatre ticket stubs. Even the notorious doormat lay in front of the door.

She'd drawn particular comfort from her house since starting the new job – and the new personality. There was no doubt that she was finding it easier to keep up the pretence since relations between her colleagues had improved. It hadn't been so necessary to prove herself and less conflict had arisen to resolve. But she was still on her guard.

Then, when she got home, she could familiarise herself with the original Kate once more. She could remind herself why she liked being the person she was. But she was occasionally experiencing the strangest feeling that this was the stage and her workplace was real life.

It was when she looked at her house that she made a big decision. I can't keep this up forever, she said to the cluttered room. The job isn't worth it. I'll have to leave.

She knew that she had to see this presentation through to the end. She had to lead this team to a win, for the sake of their jobs. But then she'd be off. Although she didn't know what she'd do, she certainly wouldn't go back to being a doormat. Whatever her decision was,

278

she would never expose herself to this kind of extreme pretence again.

Let's think about this logically, she said to herself. Clients like and respect me so I'll continue to work for clients. Colleagues either hate me or walk all over me, so I'll avoid having colleagues.

It's obvious, she realised. I'll work for myself. Just take freelance assignments. Do the things I'm good at, i.e. working, and completely eliminate the things I'm useless at, i.e. pretending to be someone I'm not.

She felt comfortable with this decision and surprised at the ease with which she reached it after years of struggling in large corporate environments.

She laughed to remember how much she had envied Rebecca when she'd first met her, with her obvious flair for dealing with junior and senior colleagues. She knew and accepted that she would simply never be like that.

But this led her to think of Andrew's comments. Kate had found nothing strange about Rebecca's attempts at self-improvement. She hadn't seen them as deceitful actions. They were just clothes.

Kate finally got it, that everyone acts, everyone pretends to be someone different at work, and some do it in their personal lives as well. If it was acceptable in Rebecca, then, Kate surmised, perhaps it was time for her to stop beating herself up about her own recent dramatic excursions.

Now what she needed to do was apply this essential truth to herself, build on who she was rather than invent a whole new Kate from scratch. It seemed so clear now.

But now was not the right time for yet another reinvention. She'd have plenty of time to think about that when she was out of work.

279

She felt all the muscles in her body begin to tense. Oh no! she thought. I'd completely forgotten. They're all coming round here tomorrow. Why did I have to open my big mouth? I suppose I'll have to tidy up.

She dragged herself to her feet and stood in the centre of the room. Where do I begin? she asked herself. Then it hit her like a friendly slap from an over-eager friend. Idiot! Why didn't I think of that? They *can't* come here.

'Why can't they come here?' her mother said as Kate dragged her into the house. 'You weren't making much sense on the phone.'

'Look at it, Mum. Just look.'

Edie obliged. 'It's a pigsty, sweetie, but you like living in a pigsty, you always have. It took me many years but I've finally accepted that this is how you choose to live. It would drive any normal person insane but—'

'Mum!' Kate cut her off before she could roll out every point she'd ever made about the hygiene issues, the sensory overload and many other objections to living in a state that bordered on squalor.

'Don't panic. We'll give it a good clean. It'll be fine. I've been dying to get a duster round those shelves.' Edie was rubbing her hands together in anticipation of a good clean.

Kate groaned. 'Mum, you're completely missing the point. Think about who these people are.'

Edie thought.

'Now think about who they think I am.'

Edie thought again.

'Now do you understand?' Kate asked at last.

Edie nodded. 'When your colleagues see this room, they'll get a fairly good idea that you're not quite the

280

single-minded, work-focused hard woman that you've presented to them.'

'That's right,' Kate said, sinking back into her chair.

'That's no problem,' Edie said, a few seconds later.

Kate looked doubtful. 'It's not?'

'No.' Edie looked around the room from a different perspective. 'We'll turn this room into that other woman's room.'

Kate stared at her mother. 'You're crazy! How can we do that tonight?'

Edie smiled. 'Just watch me,' she said. Then she took off her coat and, finally, her headscarf.

'Chrissie! I'm home!' Sally called from the hall. There was no reply. Sally looked puzzled. Her daughter should have been home by now.

She checked that she wasn't in the bedroom with headphones on. The house was empty. Sally's parents had left for Spain yesterday. Sally had been looking forward to being on her own with Chrissie for the first time.

She took off her coat and dumped her bag in the living room. She wasn't a worrier by nature. In many ways she and Chrissie had almost been children together. She made an effort to avoid nagging and tried to maintain a kind of friendship between them.

Recently, though, Chrissie had become secretive. This frightened Sally. Her biggest fear was that the daughter would repeat the mother's mistakes. She had made sure that Chrissie had known the facts of life since she was eight but that was no guarantee of anything. Sally herself had known everything there was to know except one crucial fact – that it could happen to her. She'd been a teenager, endowed with magical properties that protected her, like all adolescents, against getting old, getting caught, getting pregnant.

She'd spotted that false confidence emerging in her daughter and it was terrifying. All she could do was bombard her with facts, keep the dialogue open and trust her.

But there had been some hours unaccounted for in the last week, some unconvincing excuses, a lot more yawns at breakfast. Sally had spoken to Chrissie's form tutor and been reassured that her school work was as excellent as always.

It was unlikely that there was anything serious going on but that didn't help Sally. She decided that this was a communication problem. Chrissie might even have mentioned something this morning about being late. Sally knew that she was quite capable of forgetting something like that, and took comfort that this must be what had happened.

So it wasn't her fault when she found it. She didn't mean it, she really hadn't intended for it to happen. To keep calm, she'd busied herself with ironing, a chore she didn't mind. She saved a pile up until there was something long and mindless on television, then she worked her way through it.

She switched the TV on. It seemed odd to do that. Normally Chrissie was queen of the remote control. Like most houses which included a teenager, viewing revolved entirely around teenage preferences. Lots of *Buffy the Vampire Slayer*, *Hollyoaks* and anything with Ant and Dec.

Consequently, Sally had never had a chance to find her own favourites. It was soap time and she couldn't find a single programme which didn't require a two-year previous viewing history to follow the plot.

She switched the set off and put the radio on. She was still young enough to be able to relate to pop music so she stayed with the channel that Chrissie had preset. It enabled her to get through the ironing in twice her normal speed as she kept pace with the thumping rhythms of the current chart toppers.

I'll have to try that more often, Sally told herself with satisfaction. She folded up Chrissie's T-shirts and took them into her bedroom. It was a bit of a tight squeeze to fit them into the drawer, so she emptied it out to try and refold everything more efficiently.

That's when she found the envelope stuffed with ten-pound notes.

'What exactly is the plan of action?' Kate asked.

Edie had gone to her daughter's linen cupboard and brought through every sheet and duvet cover she could find. She was dropping them in piles on the floor.

'Well,' she said, exhausted already by her exertions. 'The most straightforward thing to do would have been to clear all the junk out of sight. But even you have to agree that the enormity of that task would require a whole team of shifters and an industrial-sized warehouse where you could dump all the stuff.'

Kate ignored the little barbs. She'd heard them all before.

'So it seems simpler to cover everything up.'

Kate looked doubtfully at all her bedlinen. 'With that?' she asked.

Edie sighed. 'Don't you watch the programmes? They take all the things that you have hanging around your house and garage and shed and use it to transform your decor.'

'I know what you're talking about,' Kate said. 'But

283

they tend to go to houses which just so happen to have shedloads of mahogany planks and chests full of cotton and velvet. I don't recall ever seeing them do a great deal with sheets and pillow cases.'

Edie looked cross. 'Do you want me to help you or don't you?'

Kate pacified her mother by fetching her a Babycham from the fridge. She always kept a stock of them for just such an emergency. When she returned, she couldn't see the carpet for outstretched material.

She went back into the kitchen and got herself a Babycham as well. I'm going to need this, she thought.

Jenny walked down the street, where the lights had just come on. It was busy with commuters returning from work. They're all walking so fast, she noticed. They must really want to get home. I remember when my house was my favourite place to be. Now I hate it there. I get out as often as I can. And knowing that Ben is going to be there makes it even worse. I can't stand being in the same room with him. I know how worried he is about me. Good!

She stopped in front of the dazzling lights of an estate agent. Everyone looks in estate agents' windows, even when they're not thinking of moving. They're compulsive. We like to look at homes in our price range and wonder if our lives would be different, better, in them. And we look at houses way beyond our pockets and dream.

That's all Jenny was doing, so she didn't know why she opened the door and went in.

'I'm just exploring some options,' she said to the excited salesman. As she said it, she convinced herself that this was the case.

The agent had expertly assessed Jenny and spotted a professional woman, probably wanting somewhere new to start family life with a new baby. He saw it with couples all the time. It was as if they wanted to draw a line under their life as a couple, put it behind them.

He'd noticed that the men were frequently less happy about this than the women. The men preferred that the step from marriage to parenthood not be so final and irreversible. They worried that the changes were going to be more profound that just an upset sleep pattern and some unfamiliar smells.

But the women welcomed the change. They'd changed physically as the baby grew inside them, so a different environment seemed appropriate. Most settled for a spot of redecoration but others, especially if they could afford it, went for a whole new house.

This woman was leaving it a bit late, the estate agent pondered. Still.

Jenny was too tired to resist his spiel. She ended up registering her interest in small houses with gardens. The agent was disappointed with the size of property she was considering. He'd expected her to be looking at four to five-bedroomed detached houses, at least.

He couldn't know, of course, that Jenny was mulling over a potential future as a single mother.

Edie and Kate were giggling as they struggled to drape the sheets over the shelving units. Kate was at the top of a ladder, unable to see anything with a double duvet over her head. She looked like a designer ghost.

'You'll have to direct me!' she shouted to her mum, her voice muffled by a double thickness of extremely expensive cotton.

'Reach your arms out slightly to the right!' Edie shouted back. 'Now lean forward and you should feel the top of the unit.'

Kate complied. With an athletic grunt, she thrust the edge of the duvet over the top and hooked the hem over the screws that were sticking out slightly from the wood.

Hah! Kate thought, I knew my sloppy workmanship would come in handy one day. She eased herself down the ladder carefully, then stood back with Edie to judge the success of their first placement.

'What do you think?' Edie asked, proud of her newly discovered flair for interior design.

'I think it looks as if I am a lunatic who has thrown a duvet cover over her shelves,' Kate concluded gloomily.

Edie smacked her on the arm. 'Don't be such a pessimist! It'll look fine once we have them all up. Let's pull the sheets out a bit so they drape more. It will look all romantic. Like a boudoir. Or a Turkish Delight advert.'

'Whatever you say, Mum.' Kate was too weary to do anything other than agree.

'Come on then!' Edie urged. 'Try that pink sheet next.'

Andrew had been rehearsing what he'd say to Rebecca all evening. He assumed that the reason for her silence was the 'discussion' about her clothes; he'd felt suitably chastised by Kate's reaction. Maybe he'd totally overreacted. Kate hadn't seemed remotely bothered by Rebecca's actions. He was even beginning to doubt his original assertion that she was copying Kate to try and win back his attentions.

Am I so arrogant, so self-centred, that I think that all her motivations must stem from me? He didn't like this possibility. And he didn't like to think he'd hurt her. Even though he now knew that he was going to leave her once the presentation was out of the way, he still wanted to avoid causing her unnecessary pain.

I wonder if I'm the only sexually active man in his late thirties who's never had to finish a relationship? he asked himself. I expect other men have got the hang of it before they turn eighteen. They probably make a total hash of it the first dozen times, ruin a few lives, before they find a system that works for them. Maybe there's a book I could buy. Or I could take Ben's advice.

He'd had a chat with Ben earlier at the house. Jenny wasn't there, which was a worry for them both although Ben was putting up a brave front by concealing his concern.

Andrew decided to help Ben take his mind off things by telling him his own problems with Rebecca. In fact he was surprised by the positive effects of his confession.

'So you're really going to end things with her?' Ben asked him emphatically.

'Yes,' Andrew said, 'but obviously not until after the presentation. I don't know how she'll react and I don't want to distract her from her work.'

Ben caught his eye and they both smiled at this reference to their aborted plan, ridiculous in retrospect, to 'distract' Kate and lead to her downfall.

'Of course,' Ben agreed. But frankly, he was so worried about Jenny that he would be prepared to jeopardise the presentation if it meant Rebecca disappearing from their lives immediately.

Andrew continued. 'My only problem is how to do it.'

Ben looked puzzled. 'How to do what?'

'To tell Rebecca. I've never done it before. Left someone, I mean.'

Ben shook his head in wonderment. He'd lost count of the speeches he'd delivered himself over the years. Unlike Andrew, Ben's girlfriends did not grow irritated by him and leave him after a predictable three-to four-month

287

cycle. His abstraction, the absence of any continuity in his life, made him compellingly attractive. His partners never had a chance to get bored.

But the price they paid for Ben's mercurial personality was that he inevitably drifted into the path of other women who were as drawn to him as they had been. And he seldom resisted. Why should he? Since his only sense of motion was forwards, it was a swift 'goodbye' to the existing chapter before starting a new book.

So, yes, Andrew had come to the right person for advice. Ben had methodically tried a number of lines that he'd picked up from books and films before settling on a line that he'd made his trademark sign-off.

Not for Ben the usual clichés. Ben had learned the hard way that these lines are used so often, everyone has cutting responses to them. He decided an original line was the only sensible approach.

'So what do you say?' Andrew asked, hoping for inspiration.

Ben cleared his throat. 'I start by saying something like: "I won't bore you with the old standard clichés of: 'It's not you, it's me' and 'I still love you but I'm not *in* love with you' or 'I don't deserve you.' No, you mean more to me than that. I'm going to be honest even though it doesn't make me look very good. I think we've drawn to a close. If I know it then, deep down, you probably know it too. So before things become nasty, while it's still good between us. I'm ending this." And then I kiss their hand, look at them lovingly and leave.'

'Left, you mean.' Andrew corrected him.

'What do you mean?' Ben asked.

'Left. In the past tense. This is what you said and did before you were married. You don't need to do it any more.'

'Of course,' Ben said, flustered. 'I was using the present tense for dramatic realism, to make you feel as if you were there.'

Andrew thought about the choice of words. He wasn't convinced. 'I suspect I've been dropped more times than you've done the dropping and nobody has ever said anything like that to me.'

'And don't you think you would have appreciated something individual, something sincere like that?'

Andrew tilted his head to consider this. 'Frankly, I don't think it would have made a difference what they said. All you hear is the message that it's finished. The other words tend to go over your head.'

'Then don't beat yourself about it. Just say whatever comes into your head.' Ben couldn't cover up his impatience at this wasted conversation. He was back to worrying about Jenny. Just then the phone rang. He picked it up.

'Hello?'

'Can I speak to Mrs Jenny Clarkson please?'

'No, I'm afraid Mrs Clarkson isn't here right now. I'm her husband, can I help?'

'Of course you can,' the agent said brightly. He always felt happier once he'd established contact with both sides of the couple. 'I'm James from Watson and Goldrigg.'

'Who?' Ben asked.

'Watson and Goldrigg, the estate agents.'

'Oh right,' Ben said. He was often called by estate agents asking if he was interested in putting his house on the market. He'd found the quickest way to get rid of them was to let them run through their patter, make all the points they'd been trained to make then say 'no thank you' and put the phone down. So he settled back to let James do his stuff for the next sixty or ninety seconds.

289

'It's a stroke of luck, really,' James said with pride.

Ben said nothing. He'd learned that making any response whatsoever added precious minutes to the conversation.

James acknowledged the tactic by carrying on. 'As soon as your wife left, we had a new property come on the market. And I think it could be exactly what you're looking for. Now obviously you're going to want to move fast, with the baby imminent. So I would suggest a viewing as early as possible.'

Now Ben was silent for other reasons. He had to work out what this man was talking about. He was forced to say something.

'Sorry. You say that my wife came in to see you?'

James sighed. Not again, he thought. This was always happening. The wife starts looking at houses without even telling the husband. It wasn't a major problem. In his experience, she would normally bring her husband round to her way of thinking. But they would have to have a big row first, though preferably not in his office.

'I can see that you'll need to speak to her first. Perhaps you or she could give me a call when you're both of one mind. But I would urge you to come back to me quickly. This really is a splendid opportunity to—'

'No thank you,' Ben said shakily, and he put the receiver down.

Andrew could hear the distress in Ben's voice. 'What is it?' he asked. 'What's happened? Is it Jenny?'

Ben turned to face him. 'She's gone looking for a new house.'

'I didn't know you were thinking of moving,' Andrew commented.

'Neither did I,' Ben replied ominously.

*

'Everything all right, love?' Sally asked Chrissie calmly when she came home.

'Course!' Chrissie said irritably. She was hypersensitive to any implied criticism from her mother, or the slightest hint that some personal questions were looming.

Sally concentrated all her energies on keeping her lips closed. The advantage of being a very young mother was that Sally still had vivid memories of all the mother/daughter quagmires that seem to dog every adolescence. If Sally wanted to tell her anything, she would do so. Any attempt at interrogation, however subtle Sally might think she was being, would send Chrissie scurrying defensively back into her teenage foxhole of paranoia and silence.

But she couldn't let this slip. While she was working out what to do or say next, Chrissie spoke.

'By the way, I'll be a bit late home tomorrow as well.'

Sally pretended to be engrossed in *Brookside*. 'Oh, OK,' she said casually. 'Doing anything nice?' she added nonchalantly.

'Nothing much,' Chrissie answered. 'Just a homework project with a boy from my class.'

Which boy? What sort of project? Will his parents be there? Are you on the pill? These were just some of the many questions that begged to be given voice. But Sally locked them up firmly. No, she told herself. You know what she'll say if you start on this line. Say nothing. So she said nothing.

But she was going to follow her daughter tomorrow.

Dear Mum and Dad,
Surprised? Not as much as I am. You'll probably faint when you get this letter. Did you wonder if I was still alive? I did send you a Change of Address

291

card but you didn't get in touch then so I wondered if you received it.

Or maybe you decided that there was no point in writing to me or calling me. I'd made it clear that I didn't want any communication from you. Not very nice of me, was it? You brought me up to be better than that.

I remember you always making me write thank-you letters the same day I got a present. I wasn't allowed to play with the toy until I'd done so. I always resented doing it; I thought you wanted to spoil my fun. But I see now that you just didn't want me to take anything for granted.

It got me thinking how the only people we don't send thank-you letters to are our parents. We really do take everything they do for us and give us for granted. We expect provision as a birthright. Which is fine when we're talking about the necessities of life but not when it's Christmas present lists that are a page long and love that is undeserved and not returned.

I've been doing some thinking today (better late than never, you'll be saying). I can now pinpoint when Dad first decided he had to do something drastic for his family. I went over the notes I made at the trial. I never threw them away. That's funny, isn't it?

It was when I'd asked for that doll's house in the toyshop window in the village. Do you remember? With the electric lights that worked and the sinks that let water come out of the taps when you filled them up? You said it was much too expensive. But I wouldn't listen. I said you were mean and cruel and didn't love me. I stopped eating. Or you thought I stopped eating. I was actually eating round at my friends' houses and just pretending to starve at home.

You must have been ill with worry. But I didn't care. And that's when Dad stole the first money.

Then I said I'd changed my mind and didn't want the doll's house any more. All I wanted was a Sindy doll like all my other friends. I wonder how Dad must have felt when I said that?

And do you know what else I've realised? That Dad could have said this at the trial. He could have said what a spoiled brat I was, what pressure I'd put on you and him. How I wasn't eating.

But he didn't.

And now I remember all those times when Dad was in prison and I screamed at you, saying you didn't love me and you'd ruined my life. And how you begged me to write to Dad if I wouldn't go and see him. But I didn't. And he never blamed me for that. He always understood.

So that's what I've been thinking. I suppose what got me started was wishing I had my mum and dad here with me right now. I could really do with my family.

But you've got every right to rip this up and chuck it in the bin. Selfish cow, you'll say. What a nerve, after all she's put us through.

I just wanted you to know anyway. That I'm sorry.

That's all really.

Love

Becky

Rebecca carried the letter to the postbox outside the office.

She'd needed to be alone when she wrote it and she felt a lot better for having done so.

When she got to the postbox, she hesitated. She stood there for – she had no idea how long. A post van pulled up and a postman jumped out and began emptying the box into his sack.

'Shall I take that for you, love?' he asked, holding the sack open.

Rebecca shook her head. 'No, that's OK,' she said, stuffing the letter into her handbag and going home to Andrew.

Chapter 17

Kate yawned all morning. She and Edie had been up until two o'clock in the morning, finishing the transformation. As Kate had expected, the room looked as if it had been covered in dustsheets ready for decorators.

'That's OK too,' Edie had said philosophically. 'They'll either think it's a sophisticated, modern new style or that you've got the decorators in. Either way, you've achieved your objective. Why should you care what they think? You've already decided that you're not staying in this job. In a few weeks' time, you'll say goodbye to these people and never see them again. They may buy you an expensive, comprehensive book on interior design but at least they won't buy you a doormat.'

Kate was too tired to argue. She had to admit that the room no longer bore any resemblance to its previous incarnation. She asked herself what she would deduce about the owner of such a room and decided that 'door-mat' would not be the first word that sprang to mind.

The words that *did* spring to mind included 'certifiable', 'pole-dancer' and 'anal retentive'. Well, that was all right then.

She tried to keep her eyes open as she went over the chart that Rebecca had finished last night. She'd done a good job, Kate observed, and finished it in amazing time. Both Rebecca and Andrew had been producing some top-quality work this past week.

She put down her pen and reflected on her previous jobs where she'd done most of the work herself rather than delegate. I was doing it to make myself popular but, in fact, it was a completely selfish act, she told herself, surprised at her own thoughts.

She finally saw the point of delegation. It wasn't just to spread the workload more efficiently; it was to allow everyone the opportunity to discover and develop their own skills. When all my past colleagues were wasting their days thinking up little tortures for me, they could have been furthering their careers. I held them back by doing their work for them. No wonder they were so cruel to me. They were just paying me back for my cruelty to them.

Kate had gone beyond being a doormat, if she was being scrupulously honest. While she withheld all the menial chores for fear of offending her secretaries, she kept the more significant tasks back as well, because she didn't think anyone could do them as well as she could.

She wasn't just an object of ridicule but of justifiable professional resentment.

Why did nobody tell me? she wondered, aghast at her lack of judgement.

'Why didn't you tell me?' Justine shouted angrily down the phone.

'How could I?' Kate said. 'I knew how you'd react. I couldn't believe it when Steve showed it to me. I mean, haven't you ever told him how you feel about tattoos?'

'No,' Justine admitted. 'It's never come up in conversation. I never thought it likely that my husband, a respected doctor, would one day go out and even consider getting a tattoo!'

'What have you been talking about for the past fifteen years, then?' Kate asked in astonishment. 'I mean, we

296

seem to end up talking about tattoos almost every time we go out.' There was always a waiter or a man on the next table or even just walking past the window who would attract the two women's attention and start them off.

'Conversation with a husband is different to conversation with a best friend, as you'll find out if you ever meet a man weird enough to marry you.'

Kate smiled at this typical reference to her single state. She wasn't bothered by it and suspected that Justine only insisted on dragging the subject up because she felt that Kate ought to be suffering as much as she was.

'So what did you say?' Kate asked, wishing she could have witnessed the big revelation.

Justine couldn't keep the chuckle out of her voice. 'I just stared at it. Told him that it was very funny and that he could go and wash it off now.'

'But surely you could see it was real?' Kate said. 'It was still red and scabby when I saw it.'

'I wasn't paying that much attention to it. He was standing behind me while I was doing my face.'

Kate sighed. 'Who were you yesterday?' she asked, dreading the answer.

'Oh, still Kate Harris. I always use that name, I'm getting good at saying it and it lends itself to lots of different accents.'

'I'll remember that,' Kate said. 'So what accent was it yesterday?'

'Slightest hint of mid-Atlantic. I was very slick, glossy lipstick but not a hint of shine anywhere else on my face. I'll show you how to achieve that look one day.'

'I can't wait,' Kate said dully.

'So I was very mysterious giving the impression that I could be anyone from an international banker or a film producer . . .'

'To an air stewardess?' Kate suggested. 'They are always immaculately groomed and made-up.'

'No, not an air stewardess!' Justine replied, crossly. 'Anyway, I met this man in the Harrods pet department – you meet the most interesting people there – and he said he'd buy me lunch in New York next time I'm there.'

The note of excitement in Justine's voice made Kate wonder if her friend had finally flipped.

'You do know that you won't be going to New York to have lunch with this man, don't you?' she asked, very carefully. 'That this is all a crazy fantasy?'

'Of course I do!' Justine answered miserably. 'I'm going to Wales on Saturday. With four other people in a two-berth caravan. Why would I want to even imagine I might be flying to New York with a man who buys everything, even his pets, in Harrods?'

'Why indeed?' Kate said with relief. 'Look, don't write this holiday off, just yet. It's not fair on the kids. Or Steve. Think of the effort Steve is making. To have a tattoo for you, I mean it's a compliment, if you think about it.'

'Do you remember when you told me that you'd read about a serial killer who had the names of his victims tattooed across his buttocks?' Justine reminded Kate.

'Point taken.'

'Thank you!' Justine said, happy with this. 'So anyway, if I don't speak to you beforehand, have a good trip! Oh, and good luck tonight. Have you got enough food in?'

Damn! Kate thought. Food. I knew I'd forgotten something. She grabbed her coat and dashed out of the door, bumping into Sally.

'Just a quick word,' Sally said.

'I'll be back in ten minutes. Minor emergency!' She didn't give Sally a chance to speak.

On the way out, she met both Rebecca and Ben. They

too tried to grab a word with her. She brushed them both off, wanting to get to Marks and Spencer before the lunchtime rush.

Why am I doing this? Jenny asked herself.

'And this is the second bedroom, or possibly the nursery?' the agent said with nauseating coyness.

Jenny looked at all the rooms dispassionately, finding it impossible to imagine herself living in this flat, or living anywhere with a baby. And without Ben. She'd let herself be talked into the viewing, mainly to annoy him.

'What's got into you?' he'd asked, as soon as he opened the door last night. Then he noticed how exhausted she was and pulled back his anger and frustration.

'I've been worried sick about you!' he said, more softly. 'You didn't leave me any note about where you were going and then I get a call from an estate agent and, well, what was I to think?'

Jenny rubbed her back, which was aching badly. The baby seemed to be pressing its feet against her spine, making it throb continuously. 'I don't know what you were to think. I'm sick of having to think about what you're thinking. Everything is not about you. I'm the one who weighs five hundred pounds and looks like a gorilla. I'm the one who is too tired to walk to the kitchen most mornings. I'm the one doing all the shopping still and looking after the house.'

Ben stopped himself from glancing round the house, which was in a state.

Jenny went on. 'I'm the one stuck here with no one to talk to and nothing to do except watch game shows that I don't understand. I'm the one who has empty hours to fill and thoughts jumbling around in my head that I can't make sense of. I'm the one carrying this baby,

Ben, not you. And if it makes me feel better, even a tiny bit better, to go and look at houses, then how dare you question me about that?'

Ben had been shocked by her rage, even more by her reddening face that gave him serious concern for her blood pressure. His only aim was to calm her down so he backed right off and spent the rest of the evening doing whatever she'd let him to make her comfortable.

This wasn't much, since every time he offered to make a cup of tea or rub her feet, she became riled again. I hope this baby comes soon, he thought.

The agent had quizzed Jenny cautiously about whether she'd discussed the move with her husband.

'I'm here, aren't I?' Jenny had snapped.

The agent had smiled nervously and carried on with the showing, making a mental note to himself to remember this deranged woman when his own wife brought up the subject of children.

Kate staggered back into the office with five carrier bags of food. She'd applied her usual multiples when calculating how much food to buy.

Let me see, she'd worked out. Me, Ben, Sally, Rebecca, and Andrew. That's five people. These packs never serve as many people as they claim to. So get enough food for ten people. Then double that, just in case someone else turns up. Then add a few packs of crisps, nuts, Twiglets, Bombay mix, cheesy biscuits, breadsticks. Then some bowls of salad. Then a gateau, a chocolate one, and a fruit gateau in case not everyone liked chocolate. And some after-dinner mints. And a cheese selection. And the biscuits to go with the cheese.

That should be enough, Kate thought, not absolutely convinced.

She sank into her chair and stretched her arms out to relax the muscles. Sally came in.

'Sorry about earlier,' Kate said. She was about to explain the urgency when she stopped herself. I'm the boss. I don't have to explain myself.

She looked forward to the day when she wouldn't have to watch what she said with such obsessive care, although her success in this job had taught her that some discernment was not a bad thing, that everybody indulged in a certain judicious censorship of their own excesses.

Sally hadn't expected her to explain herself and went on. 'All I wanted to say was that I'm really sorry but I'm not going to be able to make it tonight.'

'Has something happened, Sally?' she asked, concerned for Sally but not too worried about her non-appearance. There'd be more food to go round. You never knew if people were going to ask if they could bring someone at the last minute. It was always reassuring to know that one could be relaxed about surprise guests.

Sally looked at Kate, trying to reevaluate her boss in the light of her recent kindness. But she needed to tell someone. Her parents were away and Rebecca was in a world of her own this morning.

'I'm worried about Chrissie,' she said, going on to tell Kate about the money in the drawer.

Kate could understand her anxiety. It didn't sound good to her. Once more she had to restrain herself from applying a hug to the wound. And once more she was to learn that restraint was the most appropriate policy when dealing with Sally. Wow, she thought. What a lesson to learn. That you can be kind to someone without having to make them your lifelong friend.

Now all I have to do is retain this new knowledge and I could end up a well-rounded human being.

'What are you planning to do about it?' she asked simply.

Sally was infinitely grateful for Kate not telling her that she was imagining things, for suggesting a hundred innocent explanations for the money. She liked Kate more with each encounter. She wasn't touchy-feely like Rebecca, she'd never be much good at a girly lunch, but she was solid and strong. There were times when that sort of person was more use than any other.

'I'm going to follow her. See where she goes. Make sure that she's at least going where she says she's going.'

Kate nodded. 'That makes good sense.'

Sally could kiss her for this approval. 'Do you think so?'

'Yes, I do. It's what I'd do. I hope it turns out well.'

'Thanks Kate', Sally said brightly as she left.

'Oh Sally,' Kate called after her.

Sally turned round.

'Let me know how it goes.'

Sally nodded. 'I will. And thanks again.'

Sally left feeling better than when she'd gone in.

'How long are you going to keep this up?' Edie was following Stan round the house, then moving in front of him. Stan was refusing to look at her.

'Until you come to your senses,' he said shortly, turning abruptly and walking back into the kitchen.

Edie stood there, letting the exasperation wash over her, before following him into the kitchen. She was preparing to accuse him of being unreasonable again when she saw that he was sitting at the table, his head resting in his hands. She immediately forgot her anger.

'Oh Stan, whatever is the matter?'

Stan just sat there, stroking his head for a while before speaking.

'Can't you see? I mean, look at yourself. Since we first started talking about New Zealand, I've been looking forward, making plans, and while I've been doing that, you've been moving steadily in the opposite direction.'

'I don't understand,' Edie said.

'You've been going back in time, spending all those hours with the photos, wanting to relive the honeymoon and now . . .' He pointed at her hair, unable to find the word to describe how he felt about what she'd had done.

Self-consciously, Edie put her hand to her hair. 'But it wasn't supposed to mean anything. I just saw the photo and thought . . .'

Stan waited for her to tell him what she'd thought but Edie didn't finish the sentence.

'See!' he said. 'You don't even know you're doing it.'

'Doing what?' Edie asked, her voice shaking.

Stan swallowed emotionally. 'Moving away from me,' he said.

'What can I do for you, Ben?' Kate asked, noticing him lurking by the door like a naughty boy sent to the headmaster's office.

Ben came in looking apprehensive. 'I feel really bad about this.'

'About what?' Kate said, unnerved by his apprehension.

'I know I made a big speech about team spirit and how important it was that we all pulled together right now.'

Kate didn't like the sound of this. 'Go on,' she said.

303

'Well, the thing is, I'm afraid I'm not going to be able to make it your supper party tonight.'

Kate groaned out loud in her least professional voice. Ben was surprised at her reaction. 'I'm really sorry,' he repeated. 'But I know you'll understand when I tell you why. It's Jenny.'

'Is she OK? Is it the baby?' Kate asked quickly.

Ben was beginning to feel irrationally irritated by everyone's concern for Jenny and the baby. He couldn't recall the last time anyone asked how *he* was. He longed for this baby to be born and everything to get back to normal.

'She's fine,' he said, a little sharply. He caught himself losing control and calmed himself down. 'Well, physically she's fine. But she's behaving very strangely and I'm worried about her mental state.'

Now Kate was curious. 'Why? What's she doing?'

Ben looked a little sheepish. 'She's told all the local estate agents that we want to buy a smaller house.'

Kate burst out laughing. She couldn't help it.

Ben was offended. 'And she's gone to look at some of the properties!'

Kate coughed to mask the laughing. 'I'm sorry. I know I shouldn't laugh. But I thought you were going to say that she was shoplifting or exposing herself in the park.'

Ben was horrified. 'Don't even say such things!' Now he would worry that she could move on to even more embarrassing deeds before she finally gave birth.

'Sorry,' Kate said again. 'But it doesn't sound strange to me. I've got five sisters-in-law and they all went a bit crazy when they were pregnant. One of them took the cat for a walk instead of the dog one day. Put a lead on it as well! And one went everywhere in her slippers, including my brother's formal company dinner. They were *all* ratty.

304

My brothers were on the phone to me every day, they were as worried as you are now.'

'And how did it all turn out?' Ben asked, hoping to hear of the idyllic family life he craved, Mum baking cakes and Dad building tree houses.

Kate thought about her brothers and their families. Their lives were a jumble of noise and chaos, school runs, fights over the bathroom, never any hot water, snatched meals, snatched kisses, no money, steady hair loss in the dads, steady weight gain for the mums. She smiled.

'They are the happiest families alive,' she said truthfully.

Ben was comforted by this, if only slightly.

'Listen,' Kate said. 'Why don't you bring Jenny along? It might do both of you good to get out of the house. Sally can't come so there'll be plenty of food.' She congratulated herself on having the foresight to cater for the unexpected guest. Or ten.

Ben wasn't sure. 'She hasn't been too responsive to my suggestions recently,' he said, with admirable understatement. 'Maybe if you ask her yourself?'

Kate agreed to try. After he'd gone, she realised that she'd just got through an entire conversation with her boss without once having to check herself. I wonder if it's because I'm so comfortable with the new me, or if I slipped into the old me? The line was becoming blurred, but the outcome was positive so she didn't give it any more thought.

'Hello?' Jenny sounded as if she'd been disturbed in the middle of something critically important.

'Oh, I'm really sorry if I've disturbed you, Jenny. It's Kate. Kate Harris?'

It took Jenny a few seconds to remember who Kate

Harris was. She'd refused to accept the myth of pregnant women becoming forgetful and resented every reminder of its truth.

'Oh hi, Kate. No, you weren't disturbing me. I was sorting all my records and tapes into chronological order.'

Now *that* is worrying, Kate thought. 'The reason I'm ringing is to see if you can help me out.'

'In what way?' Jenny's voice brightened at the prospect of doing something practical. Anything at all.

'Well, you know this little supper party I've planned for tonight. Sally can't make it and Ben is refusing to come without you because he's so concerned about you. So I was hoping you'd agree to come as well.'

Jenny felt faint at the thought of a small gathering that included Ben, Rebecca and herself. 'Sorry, I'd love to come but I really can't. I'm shattered. All I want to do is have a long bath and an early night.'

Kate sighed. 'That's a shame but I do understand. I just thought it might make a change for you both to get out of the house.'

Jenny shuddered at the prospect of an entire evening at home with Ben. She'd been looking forward to his going out and not coming back till late. It hadn't even bothered her that Rebecca was going to be there. She'd entrusted that problem to her mum and knew that Rebecca wouldn't be in the picture much longer. All she cared about was not being alone with Ben.

She hated being forced into a corner but that was what was happening now. At least if they both went to Kate's, they'd be in company. Then she could plead exhaustion when she got home and not have to speak to him again until the morning. She was letting the days slip by, just waiting for a magic solution to present itself to her.

'All right then,' she said reluctantly.

Kate wasn't encouraged by this less than keen accept-ance. Still, she looked forward to a ravenous pregnant woman enjoying all the food.

'Great!' she said. 'Shall I tell Ben that you'll meet him there or do you want him to come and pick you up?'

'No!' Jenny was emphatic about this. 'I'll make my own way there.'

'Right,' Kate said. 'I'll look forward to seeing you then. About seven o'clock? 'Bye.'

She hoped that Jenny would cheer up when she got there. She didn't sound in much of a party mood just yet.

'Don't be so daft!' Edie said again. 'I've never heard so much nonsense! It's because you've been looking through your plays. You've started seeing drama and plots where there's just life and normal folk.'

Stan looked up. 'I don't know whether you're deceiving me or yourself when you say that.'

'There you go again! People don't talk like that. Not in the real world.' Edie was still touching her hair nervously as she spoke.

Stan snorted. 'Then maybe they should! Think about it. You haven't done one single thing to get ready for New Zealand. You haven't put one single thing in a box. Not so much as a saucepan.'

'That's because we've got ages before we go! And why make all this work for ourselves? We can afford to pay professionals to come in and pack up for us.'

'I thought it might be nice to do it ourselves. The preparation can be half the fun.' Stan was sounding petulant.

'But we should be enjoying our last months here. Making the most of them. What if we never come back, never see any of it again?' Edie's voice was trembling.

'Course we will!' Stan said. 'And the kids and grand-children have all said they'll come out to visit.'

Edie became stubborn. 'It's a big step. And you're forcing me to take it too quickly. Now you're the one who wanted to go to New Zealand and I've said I'll go. So I think the least you can do is let me decide what I do with the rest of my time here. *And* what I do with my hair.'

Stan recognised that tone. It was not to be argued with. It was time to back down. Besides, he'd heard the one thing he'd needed to hear. For the first time, she'd actually said she was coming with him.

Rebecca had found it hard to concentrate on her work until finally she had to go and speak to Kate. She kept turning Mrs Darlington's ultimatum over in her head. She'd managed to persuade her that she couldn't do anything until after the presentation. At least Barbara understood that. Both Andrew and Jenny had told her about it.

'And then you'll leave my son and leave the com-pany?'

Rebecca had nodded. She had no choice about leaving her job. The relationship with Andrew was now doomed and it would be unworkable for them to continue as close colleagues under such circumstances.

Maybe it was for the best. She couldn't realistically see herself getting any further in the company. She would learn from her professional errors, take a few tips from Kate Harris and try her chances elsewhere. She'd already been adopting some of Kate's style. Well, if it worked for her . . .

She went into the office to get Kate's address for this evening. She didn't dare ask Andrew if he had it. Even if she asked him the most simple question, it seemed to cause him anguish.

'Yes, Rebecca?' Kate said.

'I just came in about tonight.'

Kate's face sank. 'Tell me you're not cancelling. I've already had Sally drop out. Thank goodness I managed to persuade Jenny to come in her place, to make up the numbers. Ben thought she could do with a bit of cheering up!'

Rebecca processed this information efficiently. Jenny was going to be there and she knew about Rebecca. It was simple. Rebecca couldn't go. Apart from the horrible tension, there was the prospect of Jenny letting it all out. Or the stress might make Jenny ill or something. She didn't think Mrs Darlington would take that sort of news lightly.

'I'm really sorry,' she said suddenly, speaking quickly before she changed her mind.

'Oh no. Don't say it.'

Rebecca struggled to find an excuse that would pacify both Kate and Andrew.

'It's just I've had a disaster with the computer. I did something incredibly stupid and lost all yesterday's work.' The famous computer excuse.

Kate was suspicious. 'But didn't you have it backed up on disk?'

Rebecca thought fast. 'The computer crashed while the disk was still in the drive. When I got it back up and running, the computer erased everything on the disk.' It had happened to her once before so she was able to lie with confidence.

It had happened to Kate as well. Or rather it happened

to someone junior to her and Kate had ended up offering to redo all the work for the stunned girl.

Rebecca, seeing that her excuse had been plausible to Kate, carried on while she was doing well. 'Anyway, I've got to get it all down again so that it's ready for us to take away on Saturday.'

'I understand,' Kate said for what seemed like the tenth time today. 'Well, we'll miss you,' she added kindly.

I'll be eating chicken satay for a week, she thought gloomily. After Rebecca had left, she got up and shut her office door telling Sally that she was not to be disturbed for the rest of the afternoon unless there was a real emergency. She wanted to make quite certain Andrew had no opportunity to announce that he wasn't coming either.

She sat down to work, as the small room slowly filled with the pervading aroma of party food for 100 people.

Chapter 18

Jenny was the first to arrive. She forgot her foul mood as soon as she walked into Kate's house.

'What an incredible look!' she said.

Kate looked at her closely, trying to tell if she was being sarcastic. But Jenny was absolutely sincere. She walked around the room, fingering all the draping fabric. When she found a button in one of the pleats she called to Kate, who was putting Jenny's coat in the bedroom.

'Are these duvet covers?' she asked.

There was no point in denying it, Kate realised. 'Yes they are,' she said, waiting for mocking laughter.

Jenny was shaking her head admiringly. 'That's such a brilliant idea. I'd never have thought of it.'

Kate's instinctive honesty took her over. 'Me neither.'

Jenny understood. 'You used an interior designer?'

'It was my mum actually,' Kate said without thinking. She consoled herself with the fact that this was just her boss's wife not one of her colleagues. Her opinion was not that critical. This allowed her to relax a little, at least until one of the others arrived.

'Your mum?' Jenny repeated. 'That's incredible. My mum's idea of interior design is white emulsion and some tasteful Gainsborough reproductions.' She tried lifting the drapes to see what was underneath but Kate and Edie had tacked them down firmly.

'What's underneath these?' Jenny asked, trying to peek behind the joins.

'Oh nothing, just some plain units. They're just there to give the drapes some body and shape. Can I get you something to drink?' Kate was anxious to get Jenny away from the drapes. They were now looking dangerously flimsy and she was terrified that, with one carefully judged tug, they'd come tumbling down revealing the real Kate.

Jenny was still admiring the decor but accepted the offer of a drink gratefully. Kate poured her a long glass of fruit punch which Jenny downed in one. 'I'm so thirsty all the time,' she said apologetically as Kate poured her another.

'And hungry too, I'll bet,' Kate said.

'Well, that's the funny thing. I've completely lost my appetite,' Jenny said. Kate looked concerned so Jenny added hastily, 'But I'm not too worried, I drink a lot of milk so I should be getting enough nourishment. Even the thought or smell of food makes me feel nauseous at the moment.'

Kate wasn't remotely bothered about Jenny's levels of nourishment. She was thinking of the two tables completely covered in food in the kitchen. When she'd unpacked everything and laid it on to plates, she'd realised that she might have slightly over-catered.

Before she could sneak into the kitchen and sweep one of the table's contents into a bin liner, the doorbell rang. It was Andrew. He looked as if he had spent hours grooming himself with the aid of a butler hand-steaming creases into his trousers and polishing his shoes with a cashmere cloth.

But Kate was getting used to Andrew. He had probably not changed all day; once he was dressed as he wanted to be, he stayed that way.

'Jenny! I didn't know you were going to be here!' He

312

hugged his sister warmly. Kate liked the sight. It reminded her of herself with her brothers. She seldom saw such warmth between siblings in other families, which made her appreciate her own family all the more.

'Hi Kate,' he said, breaking away from the embrace. 'That was nice of you to invite Jenny.'

Kate didn't understand why Andrew hadn't heard about this earlier. 'Have you not been in the office today?' she asked.

Andrew shook his head. 'I was out with the researchers, remember?'

Kate had forgotten with the food crisis that had dominated her day. 'Sorry! How did it go?'

'Great. They insisted on taking me out to lunch. It was one of those American-style restaurants. I ordered a salad, thinking it would be a nice light meal, and they brought me a massive bowl with about half a pound of cheese, half a pound of ham, three hard-boiled eggs, drowning in blue-cheese dressing. Frankly I'd have been better off sticking to a burger and fries like the others! It took me an hour just to eat it. I don't think I'll be able to look at food for a week!'

Kate stopped herself from slapping him. Enforced restraint brought benefits.

Andrew was walking around the room, unable to hide his amazement. 'This is unbelievable!' he said. 'This is really you.'

Kate tried to see the room through his eyes and wondered what it meant that a room, cobbled together with sheets and pins by her mum after three Babychams, could be really her.

He, too, began trying to pull the material away to see what was underneath and he, too, was forced to have a drink to distract him.

'What is so great about this room,' he enthused, 'is that it's uncluttered and calming, but still expressive. If this had been my choice, I'd have just had empty walls but you've added substance to the empty walls to give them a feel of movement.'

Have I? Kate wondered if her mum had known all that. She suspected not. Although her mum had thrown herself into the job, Kate had noticed that she had her mind on something else. The hair was a dead giveaway.

'It looks lovely, Mum,' she had said, although, in truth, it didn't look right at all. The style was dated, but it was still a style that belonged on a young head, a young head forty years ago.

'What made you do it?' she asked, hoping she wasn't sounding critical. After all, her parents had been remarkably stoical about her own transformation. And it must have broken their hearts to see her with her lovely long hair cut short. They'd always loved her hair.

Edie touched her hair with pride. She loved it and was oblivious to any criticism. 'It was the only time in my life I felt beautiful,' she said wistfully. 'Everyone said so. I know all brides are beautiful but I really felt special.'

'But your hair looked lovely already, Mum,' Kate protested. 'What made you do something so . . . different?'

'Maybe it was thinking of Llandudno. It got me thinking of other things. How we used to be, your father and me. Then I was going through all the old photos. I don't know. I just thought it would be nice for your father to see me as I was.'

'Oh Mum!' Kate had said. 'Dad loves you as you are, you know that.'

'Yes, I do know,' Edie had said. Sadly.

Kate worried about it all night.

'So where are the others?' Andrew asked when Kate had poured him a glass of wine.

'Well, Sally can't come. She told me today.'

'Why not?' Andrew asked. 'I thought now all that stuff about her daughter is out in the open, she might have brought her with her. You wouldn't have minded, would you?'

No I wouldn't, thought Kate. But how can you tell that? Do you think you know me that well?

She couldn't betray Sally's confidence so she made a vague excuse about something coming up at Chrissie's school. Andrew accepted that without question. He and Jenny chatted while Kate stared at all the food. If this had happened at her previous firm, she would have parcelled up all the food and taken it into the office the next day. She'd have added some wine and thrown an impromptu party at lunchtime. And they would still have regarded her with scorn.

She smiled at her old naivety. She was daring to think, believe, that her new colleagues quite liked her. After less than a fortnight, they talked to her, said they liked her shoes, drank her wine, told her their deepest problems, their darkest secrets. She'd somehow managed to win their professional respect and even – or was she imagining it? – a degree of personal approval.

Now she had another question to ask herself. Could she maintain both while gradually dropping the tough act? Since making the decision that she would be leaving this company once the presentation was over, she realised that she could take some mild risks.

She intended to start during the weekend in Wales.

315

That still left her with the problem of what to do with the food, but she would have to think about that later. Right now she had two guests, both with no appetite, to entertain.

She went back into the living room to see Andrew and Jenny with their faces pressed right up to one of the white sheets pulled over a display cabinet.

'Kate, what have you got under here?' Jenny asked.

She was saved from having to find an answer by Andrew. He was looking at his watch. 'This isn't like Rebecca. She's normally good about time. I hope she hasn't got lost or something.'

'Sorry, Andrew, I should have said earlier. I assumed you'd have spoken to Rebecca in the day. She can't come.'

'Why not?' Andrew asked, not that sorry that she wasn't coming but surprised that she hadn't let him know.

Kate explained about the computer problem.

'Damn!' Ben said to the empty office. This was exactly the sort of occasion when he wished he was different. He'd taken a call from the New York office a few minutes ago. They needed a document updating and e-mailed to them tonight. He agreed to do this, thinking it would be a twenty-minute job. All the secretaries had left but he was capable of doing this himself. Not that he would ever dream of doing such a thing if there had been a secretary available – only an idiot would hire staff then do their work for them.

He had almost finished the work when the computer crashed; it was six o'clock. That meant that all the technical support staff would have gone home. He had never bothered getting to understand the workings of the computer, preferring to rely on specialist people to deal with specialist problems.

He wandered through the office hoping to find anyone at all with more knowledge than he had, but he found that he was the only one there. This was unusual, yet he'd been noticing that staff were treating Thursdays more and more like Fridays. He mooched back to his office, facing the fact that he was alone with this.

He'd skipped the introductory computer course that every other member of staff had attended. But he still had the manual. Somewhere. In the jungle on top of his desk or the drawers that hadn't been opened in months.

God, it was going to take forever. The document itself would only take a few more minutes, but first he had to get the computer working. That meant finding the manual, then the right section in the manual. Then following the instructions.

He picked up the phone.

'Justine?' Steve said.

'Mmm?'

'Can you just turn round for me?'

Justine sighed but obliged. Steve walked closer and looked her up and down as if she were a museum exhibit.

'Don't look at me like that! You'll make me self-conscious.' Justine squirmed.

Steve couldn't get a fix on it. She was wearing a dress that she'd worn before, on many occasions. It was her good dress, the one she wore to the hospital Christmas party and the school plays and when his mum came to Sunday lunch twice a year. But it didn't look the same. He was not a man who paid any attention to a woman's clothes, least of all his wife's clothes, but he

317

had been struck by Justine's appearance. Then it dawned on him.

'Justine. Have you put on weight since yesterday?' It was an insane question, he knew, even as he asked it. But there was no escaping the evidence. Since yesterday, when he'd watched her getting dressed for work, Justine had developed a backside.

He hadn't teased her about her flat rear end for years, since Kate had taken him to one side and warned him that Justine was prepared to humiliate him all through the hospital if he mocked her like that again.

He hadn't realised he was doing anything wrong. He loved her body. Justine had kept the same figure despite three children, a real achievement, he reminded her. He found that sameness reassuring, a rock, while his own body betrayed him.

He'd been one of those men who had never expected to age other than gracefully and athletically. He hadn't expected his hair to thin or his middle to thicken and they'd both let him down. He hadn't expected his chin to multiply or his chest hair to go grey and wispy but they'd gone ahead despite his protests.

He was forty-three and looked fifty-three. Justine was thirty-six and looked sixteen. But he didn't resent it. While she remained the same, he could pretend that he had too. That they were two halves of a whole. She stayed physically young on behalf of them both and he grew in maturity for them.

They worked well together as parents and a couple, balancing each other out. He would be fun, always playing crazy games with the children; she would be sensible, stopping them all from sticking their fingers in electrical sockets. She would be the first one to make him smile again after a tragedy at work; he would rub her shoulders soothingly after a day hunched over a woman in a difficult labour.

Her refusal to grow older gave him permission to age while still, through her, maintaining a foothold in his past.

After a series of bad experiences with some nurses in his early twenties, he'd been relieved to meet Justine. He'd found her beautiful. He still did. Not voluptuous, or glamorous in any obvious way, but absolutely right for her. He loved her angles, her concave stomach, her bony knees that woke him up at night. They all added to the continuity that was a foundation stone compared to the brutality of his professional life.

Now she was applying a chisel to that stone, recreating it in a new image. The hair, the make-up, he'd come to accept them as just a phase. He was keeping quiet about it. But he'd never expected this.

'Of course I haven't put on weight since yesterday! What are you talking about?'

Steve phrased the sentence as carefully as he could. 'It's just that, well, you seem to have grown a set of buttocks since yesterday.' There. He'd said it.

Justine tutted. 'Oh, that! They're just booster pants, reinforced with pads to lift what you've already got, give it all a bit of definition and add a little extra as well.'

'Oh. Booster pants. Of course they are.'

He'd never heard of such a device and couldn't imagine what this implied about his wife's state of mind.

He only had one question. 'Were you planning to take them to Wales?' he asked.

'Of course I'm not,' she said. 'If I took them, we'd have to leave one of the kids behind.'

Steve checked to make sure she was smiling. She was.

Thank God. But he was going to have to speak to Kate about this, soon.

Jenny heard her mobile phone ringing in her handbag. She took it out, apologising to Kate for the intrusion. It was Ben.

'Where are you?' she hissed. 'You should have been here ages ago.'

'Yes, I know. Listen, I'm sorry, I'm still at the office.'

'What are you doing there? You knew I was supposed to be meeting you here.'

Ben swore as he pressed a button on the computer and the screen went black. 'It can't be helped. The computer's broken down on me. I'm trying to get it working but I can't even find the manual.'

Jenny's hand tightened around the phone. 'Really?' she said, her voice becoming unaccountably high-pitched. 'That's a bit odd. In all the time you've been there, you've never so much as mentioned the computer, let alone had to fix it when it went wrong.'

Here she goes again! Ben thought. I must stay patient. She'll be fine once the baby is born.

'That's because I usually find someone to sort it out. But there's no one else here.'

'Really?'

He was running out of patience now. He was angry with himself for not being able to fix the computer quickly, something that almost everyone else in the building could probably do. 'Yes really, Jenny. I'm sorry I'm not there and I'll do my best to get there as soon as I can. But the longer I spend on the phone listening to you asking accusing questions, the longer I'll be stuck here.'

'Fine!'

'Can you just pass on my apologies to Kate and tell—'

'Fine!' Jenny repeated and switched the phone off. She didn't need to hear any more. She'd caught him in a blatant lie. She knew that Rebecca was in the building. Kate had said so and she seemed reliable; also she was too new to be involved in any of this mess.

And the excuse? Just happening to be the identical excuse Rebecca was using? That was so typical of Ben! Always taking short cuts. Not bothering to come up with an original excuse when a ready-made one was available. He didn't realise that she had already heard Rebecca's version.

So the two of them were together. After all the things Rebecca had said about him in that horrible message, she still took him back.

He'd made a big mistake tonight but she knew what she had to do. She was going straight to the office. She'd confront him, them and then . . . well, she didn't know what she'd do then.

She jumped up. Andrew and Kate had been watching her, waiting for her to explain what was going on. Her cheeks had become unusually red. 'That was Ben,' she said without emotion. 'He's still at the office with a computer problem, so I'm going to help him. I'm so sorry about this, Kate. But I'm sure Ben will explain.'

Kate was stunned. Andrew put his arm round his sister. 'Why don't you just go home and get some sleep? You look really tired. Ben will be fine. Rebecca can give him a hand. She's a whizz with computers.'

'I'm sure she is,' Jenny said drily. 'No, I'd like to help him myself. And then I'll go home. I really am sorry, Kate.'

Kate smiled bravely. 'That's OK, It's not your fault. It's just one of those things.'

Jenny kissed her affectionately before she left.

'I don't suppose you'd like to take some food with you, in case you get peckish in the car?' Kate asked hopefully.

Jenny went pale at the mention of food.

'No, of course you don't,' Kate said.

'Drive carefully, Jen,' Andrew said.

'I will,' she said, kissing her brother before she went.

Then Andrew and Kate were alone.

Rebecca sat alone in the flat listening to her old records and fingering the letter to her parents. While she felt better for having written it, she was nervous of how she'd feel if she actually sent it. Once you put a letter in a post box, you can't retrieve it. She'd tried it once when she was fifteen and had sent a love letter to a boy who lived down the road. Minutes later, she'd seen him with another girl. She'd waited by the post box for two hours for the postman to come and empty it. She'd begged him to give her the letter back but he refused. Said it was against the law.

The boy had never looked her in the face again and the family moved within the year. She'd often wondered if he'd put pressure on his parents after receiving her letter. It had been very *direct*.

Rebecca learned from this as she had done from all the negative experiences in her life. She learned to think carefully before consigning a letter to a post box.

But she was very tempted on this occasion. When she thought of that terrible encounter with Barbara Darlington, she didn't think of the words the woman had used to such powerful effect, the damage she'd wreaked on Rebecca. She just ached with envy for Andrew and Jenny, having a mother who loved them so much that she would fight for them. Rebecca wanted her mother in her corner, to fight for her, to defend her or simply shield her from the blows. She wanted her daddy to make her feel safe and beautiful.

But if she wanted the chance of finding those parents again, she had to take the chance of being rejected and she didn't know if she was strong enough.

'You must be able to eat something!' Kate said to Andrew, who'd gazed with horror at the tables in the kitchen.

Andrew tried to ignore the nagging nausea inching up his stomach. 'It's a wonderful spread. Of course I'll have something.'

He delicately picked up one of everything until his plate was full. He looked at it with dismay. Then he laughed. 'It's quite funny, this.'

'What is?' Kate asked, disappointed that he had filled a plate without making the slightest dent in the mass of food piled in front of her.

'I'd never have guessed that you were the sort of person who'd do this sort of thing,' he said, waving towards the tables.

Kate felt nervous, but curious at how much she'd given away of herself without meaning to. 'In what way?' she asked.

Andrew searched for suitable words. 'You and your living room, you are both . . . contained, controlled. Whereas this feast is sumptuous and . . .'

'Out of control?' Kate suggested.

That was exactly what Andrew had wanted to say. 'No, I didn't mean that at all! Well, yes I did. Sorry if that was offensive. It's just that my mum does this when she has people round. It always drove me and Jenny mad.'

'Thank you,' Kate said, amused by his lack of tact.

Andrew ignored the interruption, unaware that Kate

323

was being sarcastic. 'But the odd thing is, you're nothing like my mum in any other way. And that's strange because, in my experience, people are quite simple. They conform to a type and once they find the type that suits them they grow into it until they fit the mould perfectly.'

'That's a little simplistic,' Kate said. 'I think people are much more complicated than you make out.'

'Do you?' Andrew said. 'Everyone says that. But I disagree, I think they're very simple but they make their lives complicated when they start messing about with themselves, trying to be people they're not. If we all just stayed true to ourselves everything would be so much more manageable.'

He was thinking of Rebecca trying to be Kate. Kate was thinking of herself trying to be . . . somebody else.

Andrew suddenly noticed the silence. 'Oh God, I've gone too far, haven't I? I'm really sorry. This is your house. You've kindly invited us all round even though we were not very welcoming to you when you arrived and now it's just me and I'm criticising you for being over-generous with the food.'

Kate laughed. 'You haven't gone too far. You're right. I did go overboard with the food. I get that tendency from *my* mother.'

They swapped stories of their mothers. And a few bricks from the wall that Kate had erected around her began to crack.

Jenny parked outside the building now that parking restrictions had been lifted. She couldn't see Ben's car but that didn't mean anything. He could have parked it somewhere else so that nobody would know he was still in the building.

The night watchman smiled and waved her through to the lifts because she was pregnant. She filed this snippet away in her legal brain. Pregnant women are always presumed innocent of any intended or actual wrongdoing.

It was eerie in the building in the evening. Occasional lights punctuated the darkness, occasional computer blips accentuated the silence. She took the lift to the fifteenth floor and got out. There was complete silence and complete darkness. It took her a while to find some light switches.

Finally, she introduced some light back into the office. She still couldn't see any signs of life. But Ben and Rebecca would be keeping quiet if they didn't want to be discovered. She walked briskly to Ben's office, grateful that she'd been here enough times to be able to find it so efficiently.

The door was shut. She opened it dramatically, switched the light on. The office was empty. Jenny breathed out in disappointment. She took a quick look around. As usual it was a tip. She didn't know how he could even bear to stay in this room with all the junk around him.

On the table, she noticed that there was a computer manual propped open in front of the screen along with some tell-tale opened paper clips. So? she said to herself. Just because he was telling the truth about the computer doesn't mean that he's not with Rebecca. *She* must have stolen *his* excuse, not the other way round. She took stock of the evidence, wishing that her brain wouldn't keep fighting all her efforts to demand attention.

It took her ten times longer than it would have done if her faculties hadn't been hormonally impaired but she got there in the end. Of course! she thought. They both knew where Andrew was going to be for the whole evening.

325

Out. So the obvious place for them to go was Andrew and Rebecca's flat. Within forty-five seconds she had taken the lift downstairs and left the building.

Andrew and Kate sat companionably on her large sofa. Kate had kicked off her shoes but was still sitting stiffly, not finding it easy to bend her legs in the tight leather skirt. She was wearing the same clothes she'd worn to Ben's party. It had seemed simpler than going through the fiasco of buying yet another new outfit.

Kate had drunk more than she'd intended from the stress of watching the evening fall apart. She hadn't gone over the top but she could feel all her restraining muscles loosening.

Be careful! Watch what you say! She could hear the voices from somewhere inside her but she couldn't make out what they were saying. Even so she made an effort to keep the conversation at an appropriate level, staying on safe subjects.

'Do your clothes never crease?' she asked him, surprising even herself at how inappropriate a question she could ask when she really tried. 'I'm sorry,' she said immediately. 'That was a rude thing to say.'

Andrew wasn't bothered. 'I get asked that all the time,' he said. 'Other regular ones are: "Why do you have to tear out a page from a book when you've finished reading it and throw it away?", "Why do you have to hoover the garden shed?" and "Why do you have to remove all the plugs from the sockets before you leave the house?"'

Kate smiled. 'Fortunately I don't know you well enough to be aware of those little quirks, or I could well have gone down those roads too. I talk too much when I'm nervous.'

'You surprise me,' Andrew said. 'Again.'

'Why's that?'

'I'd never imagined that you could ever be nervous. You present yourself as very controlled, very sure of yourself. One of the things I first noticed about you was the way you used words so sparely. You never say more than you have to.' He looked embarrassed as he continued. 'If we're into confessions, then it's my turn. I found you a bit offhand in the beginning. You came across as a little rude. But I think that's because I had different expectations of a woman.'

'Have you never worked for a woman before?' Kate asked, steering back into safer waters.

Andrew closed his eyes to blot out the memory of his single experience. 'Yes, but that was not a success and I'd hoped that it was an exception.' He didn't believe this was a lie. 'What about you?' he asked Kate.

'Actually, I've never worked for a woman at all,' Kate admitted, surprised that she was only now recognising the fact.

Andrew suppressed a smile but Kate spotted it. 'What's so funny?' she asked.

Andrew shook his head. 'Nothing. Well, it's just that I could probably have guessed. You do have a rather . . . individual management style.'

Kate bristled at the implied criticism. 'You wouldn't say that if I were a man,' she retorted. 'Or if you did, it would be meant as a compliment.'

Andrew shrugged. 'Maybe. But if you'd had any experience of working for women, you'd understand that attitudes towards female bosses are different.'

Now it was Kate's turn to shrug. 'Maybe. I just resent the fact that "management style" should make a difference. I've spent over fifteen years delivering measurable successes in five different companies and still I get judged for my "style".'

Andrew nudged her in a gesture of conciliation and friendship. 'Don't let it get you down. I may have had the odd apprehension but you proved them misguided.' He paused. 'Eventually,' he added quietly.

'You must all have hated me,' Kate said, rather sad to think that she could have been a bit nicer after all.

'No!' Andrew said emphatically. 'Well, not exactly. But I can now see that it was difficult for you, coming into a new environment, none of us wanting you there. You were probably nervous. But you did come across as a bit . . . authoritarian.'

Kate vowed never to use the policewoman for inspiration if she were ever to play this sort of game again. Which she hoped she never would.

An awkward silence followed, the sort of silence where a relationship has taken an uneasy step up to another level but both parties are still giddy and considering stepping back down again.

Kate's next question came out without any intervention from her inner censors. 'You and Rebecca seem to have been tense this week. Is everything all right between you?' She wanted to put her hand over her mouth in horror. Even in her old jobs, she'd never have asked something so personal of a colleague she'd known for such a short time.

Andrew didn't seem to be offended. This intrigued Kate. Have I been getting it wrong all my life? she wondered. Instead of making coffee, could I have been talking like this to people? She'd always been terrified of being knocked back, of presuming friendship or intimacy where it wasn't reciprocated. So she'd bombarded individuals with visible signs of her desire to be their friend, waiting for them to interpret the signs and respond, one way or the other.

Now she had to accept that not everyone thought like that. Each overture might just be taken at face value. She'd been so careful of what she'd said in the past, anxious never to cause offence. Where had it got her? She had been considered so inoffensive as to be invisible, boring, characterless.

'No, everything isn't all right,' Andrew said finally. He'd been weighing up how he should answer this rather intrusive question, and hoped he'd managed to conceal his surprise at her interest.

There were reasons why he shouldn't answer. She was his boss and he could be jeopardising the way she related to him at work in the future. But there was another reason. He had finally accepted that he had feelings for Kate. He didn't know what they were because he hadn't dared explore them. In their situation there seemed little point. He felt now that he had to hold back from her until he could decide what he was going to do.

He was also bloated from the food he'd taken in today. It induced a kind of intoxication. He was reaching that maudlin stage where he could hear a lone piano playing 'One for my Baby and One More for the Road' in his head. The thought of Rebecca depressed him. And he told Kate so.

'I'm sorry,' Kate said, meaning it. She hadn't wanted the conversation to go like this. She was starting to feel quite depressed herself.

Andrew went on. 'Don't be. Rebecca and I are coming to the end but I was hoping she'd leave me before I had to leave her. I tend not to be hurt by endings whereas I know that she does.'

Kate was now finding this uncomfortable. She was

329

beginning to wish that she was sitting on that upright chair on the other side of the room. Their proximity on the sofa had evolved from companionable to suggestive of possibility.

They both seemed to sense this transition at precisely the same moment. They looked at each other in a way that had nothing to do with professional respect. The doorbell rang.

Who the hell could that be at this time of night? Rebecca wondered, dragging herself from bed and staggering to the door. She'd taken a sleeping pill that she had found left over from her holiday in Australia last year.

She opened the door and was pushed aside by an enormous crazed being who came screaming into the flat like a marauding Viking.

'Where is he?' she screamed. At this point, Rebecca began to emerge from her stupor and recognise her invader as Jenny.

'Where is who?' Rebecca replied, genuinely mysti-fied.

'Don't play games with me! Ben! My husband! Where is he?' Jenny was running through the flat, as well as a woman of her size could run, banging open doors.

Rebecca woke up fully at this point. 'He's not here, Jenny. I've no idea where he is. I assumed he was going to the party.'

Jenny marched up to Rebecca, standing in front of her, facing her down like a terrifying death mask. 'Don't lie to me! I've had enough lies! You said you were going to be at the office all evening sorting out the computer and, hey, guess what? So did Ben. Maybe in future you'll take the time to sort out more creative excuses.'

The random facts were starting to click into place

in Rebecca's foggy brain. She was filling in the gaps and coming up with a plausible explanation for Jenny's misunderstanding. 'I *did* lie about staying in the office. But I did it to avoid coming to the party when I found out you were going to be there. I don't know anything about Ben. I'm sorry.'

Jenny remembered the exercises she'd learned in antenatal classes and tried to calm down. Her baby was protesting wildly at this upheaval, kicking out at her, making her back almost seize up in pain.

She believed Rebecca. She didn't want to and, at the same time, she desperately did want to. Rebecca stood, not daring to move or speak while Jenny decided what she was going to do next. Don't have the baby here! Rebecca prayed silently. Anything but that.

She watched as a mask of calm acceptance descended miraculously on the previously explosive face before her. Jenny wished she were at home in bed and that it was two weeks ago and she knew none of this. She was so tired. She couldn't speak, her jaw muscles were too weak. She had to get home before she lost the energy to drive.

She walked past Rebecca slowly, saying nothing. Rebecca watched her go, stepping backwards nervously in case Jenny changed her mind and slugged her. But Jenny just kept her eye focused on the door and her mind focused on the only goal that mattered now – getting out of here.

After she'd left, Rebecca threw a coat over her pyjamas and ran out to the end of the street where, without any hesitation, she posted the letter to her parents.

'Ben! What are you doing here? Where's Jenny? Sorry, come in.'

Ben was taken aback by the welcome and by the

absence of people in Kate's house, apart from Andrew. But his main concern was for Jenny.

'What do you mean, where is Jenny? She was here when I phoned. I said I'd meet her here.'

Andrew stood up. 'But she drove over to the office to give you a hand with your computer problem. Didn't you see her?'

Ben became angry. 'Stupid woman! I found someone downstairs to sort it out. We had it finished in ten minutes. I drove straight here. What was she thinking of?'

He dialled her mobile phone number but she'd switched it off. When he tried the home number, the answer machine was on. So he left a message on both phones that he was on his way home.

'I'm sorry about this, Kate. Look, I'll see you tomorrow. OK?' He left without even having taken his coat off, or eaten a single mini-quiche.

She watched him leave then turned to find Andrew also putting his coat on. 'You're not going as well, are you?' she asked, not bothering to hide her despair.

'I'm sorry about this too. But I think I need to get home. I want to be close at hand in case there are any problems with Jenny.'

Kate nodded understandingly. 'Would you like to take some food to Rebecca?' she asked with a misjudged note of hope.

Andrew smiled. 'I don't think so, if you don't mind. She hasn't had much of an appetite recently.'

Thank you for telling me, Kate grumbled to herself.

Andrew kissed her goodbye. The kiss was on her cheek but she could have sworn it was more than just polite. It lasted half an emotion longer than formality dictated.

And she continued thinking of that as she sat in the kitchen eating quails' eggs and chocolate gateau.

After he'd left, Andrew sat in the car for a minute or two, getting his head in order. He'd come to a decision, well two decisions, in Kate's house and he needed to know that he was not being impetuous.

He wanted to get to know her, to find out where things might go with her. But he could never have a relationship with his boss. It was unthinkable. It was proving disastrous enough with Rebecca and they were just colleagues.

Besides, he couldn't stay at the company after he separated from Rebecca. There would be no chance of a transfer to another department, not with the current financial situation. His first decision was to end things with Rebecca straight away. She wouldn't be surprised, he was sure. And there seemed no point in waiting. Her work was already suffering with the tension between them. Then he could deal with his big decision.

If he wanted to move things on with Kate, it would have to be under very different circumstances. So, after the Saltech presentation, he would start looking for a new job.

Chapter 19

There was silence in the people carrier and it was a long way to Wales. It was February. It was grey. It was drizzling. It was freezing cold and the heating wasn't working properly.

Jenny was sitting next to Ben but both were looking out of the windows in opposite directions, straining their necks to avoid any chance of eye contact. Andrew was sitting next to Rebecca holding her hand out of duty. They both had dark circles under their eyes. Sally was sitting next to her daughter Chrissie who was in a permanent adolescent sulk and humming along aggressively to her Walkman. Sally was chewing her lips nervously. Stan and Edie were regretting not taking the train. Kate was driving and wondering what music would be most suitable for this funereal group.

Two whole days, she thought miserably. We'll all kill each other before afternoon tea. Or maybe we'll just die of apathy. She decided on some light classical music, hoping that it might exert a civilising influence on them all.

Her parents had brought a tape along. It was *The Best Classical Music Used In TV Advertising Ever! (Volume 4)*. Kate grimaced at the cover, wondering if Beethoven could ever have expected his music to be associated with tinned peaches.

But the choice had been good. The music had a

relaxing effect, everyone appreciating the comforting familiarity that saved them from having to meet the music on a higher plane.

Kate put her foot down, wanting to get this journey over with as soon as possible.

'Reach for the Stars!' Steve sang with the the kids for the twelfth time, while Justine asked whether it would be OK if she threw the SClub7 tape into the River Severn as soon as they entered Wales.

'Don't be so grumpy, Mum!' Steve shouted, while the children shrieked with laughter.

When Justine had embarked upon her quest for personal improvement, she had selected sophisticated images worthy of imitation. Steve had himself tattooed and transformed himself into the life and soul of *The Worst Party. Ever!*

Justine was not enjoying this holiday and they hadn't yet got on the motorway. It had taken her six hours to pack the caravan, constantly having to throw out all the little luxuries and many of the essentials that simply didn't fit in the tiny space.

'Where are all we going to sleep?' she'd asked Steve.

Steve had made the irritating hand gesture he always made to signify that he would work things out.

No,' Justine objected. 'I want to know now about the sleeping arrangement or I'm not going!'

Steve sighed. 'It was going to be a surprise but if you insist on spoiling the surprise . . .'

He went into the caravan and lifted one of the seats. From underneath he pulled out a large lumpy bag.

'Da dah!' he announced grandly.

Justine stared at the bag. 'What is that?' she asked flatly.

Steve looked hurt. 'It's a tent. Look! It's top of the range. Two-person. Very cosy!'

Justine turned her stare on to Steve. He winced at its ferocity. 'You expect me to sleep in a tent?'

Steve coughed nervously. 'Well, you see, we have to. The beds in the caravans, actually, they are not beds as such, more like thin mattresses, well they're all rather small. You and I won't fit on them.'

Justine couldn't believe what she was hearing. 'How can they be that small? You said the caravan belongs to someone at the hospital. Are they grown-up?' she asked sarcastically.

'Of course they are! But they are slightly, well, on the small side.'

Justine groaned. 'How small?'

'About five feet two,' he said quietly, hoping she'd mishear.

She didn't. 'I hate camping,' she said. 'More than anything. More even than tattoos!'

Steve's hand moved involuntarily to his shoulder. 'I thought we'd come to terms with that. I thought we'd decided that it would be a family joke, something that we could all look back on and smile at.'

Justine didn't smile. 'You decided that, not me.' But she had to confess that she didn't hate it as much as she'd expected. The thought of him undergoing all that pain for her had surprised her. Although it was the worst thing he had ever done, it was ironically the most romantic.

She was bathing it for him to keep it clean and help it to heal. The act was intimate and unusual. The discomfort served to subdue Steve's excesses and they'd found themselves talking, although not about the booster pants. Steve would never mention them again. Instead they talked about the past, their favourite subject. They

336

recalled the births of their children, the funny things the kids had said and done, their failed attempts at dinner parties, with the disastrous meals Justine had cooked and the disastrous jokes Steve had told.

They talked softly in the shorthand that they'd adopted through the marriage, each able to leave sentences unfinished, each able to say 'thingummy' confident that the other would know what it referred to.

They drew a veil over the long indeterminate periods where they'd had to pinch each other to remind themselves that they were alive.

They had almost regained their balance, and would have been able to start their holiday in a state of renewed marital harmony if it hadn't been for the rotten coincidence at the hospital.

Justine had finished work in the early afternoon and decided to surprise Steve by picking him up from work. When she got there, she found out he was dealing with a surgical emergency in A & E.

She watched him come out of the cubicle, talking seriously to another doctor. She loved watching him at work. He was a different person and yet she knew he had to be the same one. He held lives in his hands, hands that never shook, hands that had calmly lifted whoopie cushions from underneath him on sofas hours earlier. He told mothers that their child had died with a sensitivity and compassion that made Justine weep, then he would come home and tell jokes that would have the kids crying with laughter.

How does he do it? she'd always marvelled. And she appreciated the enormity of his achievement even more, now that she'd tried to divide herself up in the same way and failed so miserably.

Because Justine had always been one person, at work,

at home, anywhere. She hadn't planned it that way; maybe it was just that her choice of career had been so right for her that there had been no need to slip into a different identity.

This past week, she had come to learn that all her efforts to recreate herself were less to do with having fun pretending to be someone else and everything to do with finding alternative places to go, other people to be, when her own life became unbearable.

She longed to be able to call people 'scumbag' occasionally, or just think the word, as she'd advised Kate. She longed to be quiet and introspective without people asking if she was feeling all right. And if she couldn't be different in her work environment, then she thought she would have to find an outlet in her personal world.

But it hadn't worked.

'Kate! Kate Harris!'

Justine turned round to look for her friend and see who was calling her. But the man doing all the shouting was walking straight over to her.

And, walking towards her from the opposite direction, was her husband.

They were on the motorway and Kate had settled into the outside lane, driving steadily but itching to put her foot down. Kate never went faster than the speed limit. Even while she was keeping up the act of being a tough businesswoman, she couldn't speed.

Andrew noticed this but said nothing, filing it away in a drawer labelled 'Interesting Facts About Kate Harris'.

Sally watched her daughter sleeping, envying her that juvenile skill for sleeping anywhere for any length of time. She hadn't slept that well herself after the tension of the previous evening.

338

She hadn't thought the idea of following Chrissie through very well. It looked easy in films. You skulk in doorways, pretending to watch the multiple TV screens in electrical shops, sit in cafés smoking strong cigarettes and drinking dark brown tea in chipped, stained mugs. You find the conveniently derelict house and set up an observation post in the upstairs bedroom which has a working electrical socket into which you can plug your kettle.

But they never showed you how to follow a girl down a long suburban street with wide uncluttered pavements, no shops, no trees and every house bearing a NEIGHBOUR-HOOD WATCH! sticker in their living-room windows.

She'd had to stay way back and walk on tiptoe so that her heels didn't make a noise. And the result? She'd seen Chrissie enter a semi-detached house and the door shut behind her. That was it. Then Sally had been forced to go home, not wanting to wait for the police to arrest her for loitering suspiciously in a respectable street.

This never happened in *Beverly Hills Cop*, she thought, and for obvious reasons. What a waste of celluloid it would be. She would never watch thrillers with the same credulity again.

Chrissie arrived home an hour later.

'Did you get the project completed?' Sally asked her casually.

'The project? Oh yeah.'

Chrissie was eating something from the fridge. Sally shuddered to think exactly what.

She risked a controversial approach. 'I'd love to see it,' she said quietly.

'See what?' Chrissie asked.

'The project.'

Chrissie looked blank. 'Pete's got it. He's going to put

it on the computer and bring it into school tomorrow.'
The she grabbed a piece of cheese, smeared strawberry
jam on it and left the kitchen.

'Oh good,' Sally said. Oh God, Sally thought. I know
as much as I did before. What do I do now?

She tried to put this concern out of her mind for
the moment. She had a whole weekend with Chrissie
coming up when there would be plenty of time to talk.
She might even solicit Kate's help in getting Chrissie to
open up. She'd warmed to Kate in recent days. There
was still something oddly inconsistent about her, but
she liked the way Kate was kind in a brisk, efficient
way, not trying to become her best friend or engage
in emotional conversation that would embarrass them
both.

She was going to learn from Kate and make the most
of her positive influences, because she'd just come to a
big decision.

Her secret was in the open and initially she had been
thrilled to be told that it didn't change anything. This
would have been great if she hadn't wanted anything to
change, but she did.

So Sally had decided that, after the Saltech presentation, she would start looking around for a new
job.

Rebecca felt her hand resting in Andrew's and was aware
that he was just letting it sit there, not stroking it or
squeezing it. She knew he was being kind and loved
him for it. Yes, she thought she might really love him.
She could have laughed when she realised this, shortly
before she would have to leave him.

She loved him because he was staying with her even
while he didn't feel anything for her any more. He

340

hadn't said this but she'd known as soon as he got back from Kate's.

'You're early,' she'd said. She was sitting in the dark, thinking. The sleeping tablet was still in her system, fighting her attempts to stay awake. The chemical coupled with her bizarre alertness to make everything appear distorted, unreal.

Andrew told her the strange events of the evening, leaving out the innocent kiss he'd given Kate and the guilty feelings that it had awakened in him. Rebecca had listened with interest, understanding more than Andrew. She hadn't filled him in on the events at home, even though she was becoming more certain that he would soon find out.

Once a secret escapes it becomes a snowball, rolling down through people's lives, leaving icy scars, gathering momentum until it reaches the bottom and crashes into a tree, shattering on impact and causing devastating damage where it lands.

This secret had gone too far to stop.

'Have you been crying?' Andrew asked Rebecca. He'd never seen her cry before.

Rebecca kept her face down. 'I was just so tired. The computer glitch was the last straw. And it's all the pressure at work. I'll be fine once this presentation is over,' she said, favouring him with an optimistic smile which didn't convince him of anything.

This is my fault, Andrew thought. I've made her cry. He knelt beside her and hugged her. She relaxed into his body and hated him for being so decent and making her love him. She knew she should get out of this now, right now, before he left her, find some dignity by jumping before she was pushed.

But right now she wasn't strong enough. Even though

she knew that she had lost him already, she still needed his presence, just to be there, until she was stronger. She'd tell him in Wales, let him go. Surely a few more days couldn't make that much of a difference?

He'd held her all night, thinking of Kate, thinking of himself, but mostly thinking of Rebecca. He couldn't leave her. Not yet. He'd wait until they were in Wales. The unfamiliar surroundings might help.

Yes, he'd tell her in Wales, let her go. Surely a few more days couldn't make that much of a difference?

They sat in the traffic jam, Steve and the children still singing SClub bloody 7 songs. Justine simmered in the back of the car.

'This happens every time,' she muttered.

'What does?' Steve asked, while he rewound the tape to the beginning.

'You insist on taking us off the motorway and down all the side roads and we get stuck behind tractors or in roadworks.'

'But it's more fun than motorways, isn't it?' he said to the children.

'Yeah!' they screamed.

His cheerfulness was unbearable. She was still shaken by the events of yesterday, whereas he seemed to feel much better about everything. She couldn't understand why.

There had been a moment in the hospital where she'd thought she might be able to close her eyes really tightly and become invisible. She'd expected oppressive music to begin playing in the background, minor chords warning of a dreadful confrontation, where there could be only one winner.

One man was smiling, the other looking quizzical.

342

One, whose name she couldn't remember, she'd met in a bookshop coffee bar and told him she was a vet. The other was her husband.

'What are you doing here?' the man asked, laughing. 'Wrong sort of patients for you, aren't they?'

Justine stood still waiting for a resolution that didn't involve her or bloodshed. Steve reached her first. 'Why is that man calling you Kate?' he asked.

'Because that's her name,' the man said.

'No it's not,' Steve said. 'It's Justine and she's my wife.'

Justine was struck by how lacking in humour Steve had become. He didn't seem to spot the potential humour in this situation. She didn't either but she had been relying on Steve to supply some now he was Mr Tattoo the Happy Man.

Both men looked at her, waiting for answers. She quickly sorted out a clever speech in her head, cleared her throat, then she turned round and ran out of the hospital without saying a word.

The two men watched in shock as she left. One was thinking about the conversation that they would be having later. The other was wondering where her buttocks had gone.

As they crossed the Severn Bridge, Stan looked across at Edie, who was sleeping. He contemplated waking her but she'd looked so tired this morning he decided to let her sleep.

He remembered their excitement when they'd crossed into Wales on their honeymoon. They'd been on a coach since they didn't have a car in those days. It felt like going abroad. Everything had looked so green and different to them. Maybe it was their newly-wed eyes deceiving

343

them, enabling them to see beauty wherever they looked.

Stan had felt that nothing could compare to the beauty of his new wife. She'd fallen asleep on that first journey too, exhausted from the excitement of their wedding day. As he looked at her now, forty years later, he felt as if time had stood still. He knew it was the hair making his mind play tricks on him, but if he screwed his eyes up and didn't look too closely at the lines on her face and the dry wispiness of her hair, then she could pass as the same girl she'd been then.

He understood why she'd been looking back recently but he didn't want to do that himself. Not that he regretted any of their life, – they had been wonderful years – but he wanted to go forward now.

He hoped that this holiday would mark the end of Edie's relentless nostalgia. That she'd get it all out of her system, they'd get back home and she would start packing. Just one box, he prayed, let her pack just one box.

'There's no point in locking yourself in the bathroom,' Steve said patiently. 'You'll have to come out soon. The kids will be home and they'll all be bursting, you know what they're like.'

Justine knew and she reluctantly came out of the bathroom, but didn't look at Steve. She walked past him and went straight into the kitchen where she started peeling potatoes for chips.

'Just tell me,' he said simply. 'If you say it quickly, it will be over quickly.'

Justine turned round when she heard how his voice was shaking. His face was white and terrified.

She went right over to him and put her arms round him. He didn't respond.

'Are you leaving me?' he asked suddenly.

Justine stepped back and stared at him. 'Of course I'm not, don't be so silly!'

'Don't call me silly!' Steve said. 'After what I've seen and what that man told me after you'd run away, I don't know what to think.'

Justine put the potato peeler down. She sat at the kitchen table and told him what she'd been doing. Steve had worked most of it out from the one story he'd heard from the man at the hospital.

'Why?' he said. 'That's all I need to know.'

And Justine tried to make him understand. She knew she wasn't making much sense but she said it all regardless. It was a stream of consciousness, almost comic in its contradictions and eccentricities. 'I don't know why I did it, well I do, it was just a bit of fun, and I wanted to be different because I've always been the same and Kate had changed but she'd stayed the same underneath so I thought I could do the same and I used her name so that I would know it wasn't really me and it was just a game . . .'

Steve held up both his hands, begging her to stop.

'It's all right. It's all right. Really.'

Justine looked at him curiously. 'Really? Are you sure?'

'Yes I'm sure,' Steve said gently.

'So you understand?' Justine asked.

Steve shook his head. 'Not a word you've said, no. And if you gabbled for another hour, it wouldn't make a difference. You still wouldn't be making any sense. But I understand *you*. You think I don't but I do, I always have done. All I needed to know was that you and I hadn't changed and would never change. That this was your motorbike.'

345

The kids arrived back from school before they could get any further. But perhaps there was no need to go any further.

They were both cautious, tentative with each other for the rest of the day. It was only when Steve pulled the tent out that they could return to their comfortable sparring roles once more.

Steve seemed so relieved that this mad behaviour was really no more than a passing fantasy, as Kate had told him, that he was able to sweep it away in a box marked 'Over' and get back to normal.

Justine didn't find it that easy. Although it had been no more than a game, although she had been doing no more than playing roles, the whole experience had changed her slightly in a way she hadn't yet been able to define. While Steve thought that everything was the same, she felt different.

Jenny rested her hands on her bump. She was finding the journey intolerable. The only thing in its favour was that the physical discomfort distracted her from the turmoil in her mind.

By the time Ben had got home, she'd been home herself for about twenty minutes. She'd listened to the messages on the answering machine very warily, still reeling from the shock of that one awful message.

She heard six messages promising her that absolutely the right property for her had just come on to the market and that she absolutely must see it without delay before it was snapped up.

The she heard Ben's worried voice announcing that he was on his way home.

Good, she thought. Because it's finally time we talked.

*

Ben had his eyes closed but he was wide awake. He was pretending to be asleep so that he wouldn't have to talk to anyone and so that no one would notice that he and Jenny weren't speaking.

He felt sick from Thursday night's confrontation and only slightly comforted that she had still come to Wales with him.

'Jenny! Are you OK?' he'd called as soon as he'd unlocked the door.

He rushed into the house to see her sitting in the dark, thinking. He switched a light on but she yelled at him to switch it off again, which he did. He stood by the switch waiting for her to tell him what she wanted to do. He had heard determination, purpose in her voice and feared or hoped, he didn't know which to plump for, that she was about to tell him what was bothering her.

'I've been to see Rebecca,' she said softly.

Ben felt his legs become shaky as all the blood rushed to his head to deal with the dreams that were flying out of his consciousness. He felt shutters slamming down on images that had sustained him for so long. That formal portrait of him and Jenny and the baby under the Christmas tree that they would send out with their Christmas cards. Gone. That grainy snap of the three of them at the seaside building sandcastles. Gone. That camcorder film of the first nativity play while he and Jenny were embarrassed by their tears. Gone. His future. All gone.

'Haven't you got anything to say?' Jenny asked calmly.

'What exactly did she say?' Ben asked, clinging to the possibility that there was still hope while she was talking to him. And there were no suitcases in the hall.

Jenny laughed without humour. 'She didn't say anything. Tonight. She wasn't very talkative tonight. But last week, she couldn't get the words out quickly enough.'

She briefly recounted the circumstances and the content of Rebecca's message.

Ben was glad the lights were off because he couldn't bear for Jenny to witness his shame. Jenny was glad for the same reason. She was determined that she would not take pity on him. She preferred to imagine his face as it had been for this entire week when she'd known about his treachery. He'd looked exactly the same as he always looked. The betrayal hadn't changed him at all. That was the most disturbing element of this whole sordid episode.

She accepted that everyone had moments of weakness, everyone made mistakes, some of them terrible. But decent people, possessed of the requisite dose of humanity, would be scarred by their mistakes. And she'd scrutinised his face, his voice, all of him and had found nothing. That was his crime, not the affair, but the casual way he had incorporated it into his personal history where it evidently sat quite comfortably alongside his marriage and their future child.

'I'm so sorry,' he said feebly. 'What are you going to do?' He recognised that she was now in absolute control of his life.

'I haven't decided,' she'd said coldly.

She'd gone to bed, leaving him to spend the night on the sofa. A long, sleepless night. It was when the light began to peep through the curtains that he made his decision, one of many that he would be forced to make. He hoped he would convince Jenny that she was the most, no, the only, consideration in his life.

Rebecca would soon be out of their personal circle

when she and Andrew separated, an event that was imminent, thank God. But her presence would still be there at work, an unexploded bomb in Jenny's consciousness.

So he decided that, after the Saltech presentation, he would have to look around for a new job.

Kate had come off the motorway and was now driving towards Llandudno where, she'd explained to the others, she'd be dropping off her parents. They'd all been surprised. Frankly, she didn't seem the sort of person who drove her parents to Llandudno.

Kate had given her mum and dad strict instructions. 'You know where I stand with these people,' she'd warned them. 'You're not to say anything that will give me away.'

Stan and Edie had been quite intimidated by her tone. They could almost hear a whispered 'scumbag' at the end of each clipped sentence. But they were parents and used to being asked to modify their behaviour by their children. It had started when they asked not to be kissed at the school gates when they turned seven, but Stan and Edie had hoped they would be allowed to be themselves by now.

Kate had offered to drive because it gave her time to think. And she was thinking mainly about Andrew.

She had never had a relationship with a male colleague. This was hardly surprising considering the nature of her relationships with all her colleagues in the past. No post-Neanderthal man could have subjected himself to the twenty-four-hour-a-day servility that this would have entailed – not even for ironed socks.

But this situation with Andrew possessed the additional complication that she was senior to him. Of course that wouldn't be for much longer, but she couldn't tell him that she was planning to leave. It didn't speak highly of her commitment to the presentation that she would no longer be affected by its outcome.

She knew that he was attracted to her, she'd finally grasped that on Thursday night. But he was holding back. Partly because of Rebecca, she realised, but he, too, was probably put off by her position.

This is rich! she thought. If I'd been my normal weak self, this wouldn't have been a problem. He'd have had no respect for me but he wouldn't have felt intimidated. Although maybe the respect came before the attraction and was part of the attraction? There was a question to ponder, she pondered, as she steered the clumsy vehicle round twisting Welsh lanes.

It was all too confusing. She didn't know who she was supposed to be any more and she would be by herself in Wales without Justine to keep her grounded and provide a sounding board for her uncertainties.

She had one nagging concern about the situation with Andrew. If she hadn't made any progress with him before she left her job, while they were together nine hours a day, then how would they ever get anywhere after she'd gone?

Barbara looked out of the train window, oblivious to the spectacular views. She'd told Jenny that she was mad to go to Wales in her condition and in her current state of mind.

'Don't worry so much, Mum,' Jenny had said, 'Andrew will be there. I'll be fine.'

'But I don't understand why you have to go,' Barbara had pressed.

Jenny had shrugged. 'Neither do I, but I want to go. So that's that!'

Barbara had known when it was time to back down but she wasn't going to back out. When whatever was going to happen, happened in Wales, she would be there.

Chapter 20

'Hello, campers!'

Nobody laughed as the middle-aged man in a shell suit welcomed them with false bonhomie and a bad joke. He looked around at the blank faces and mentally scrapped his opening speech.

There were over 100 people gathered in the meeting room. None of them looked particularly keen to be there, particularly on a Saturday.

The sense of adventure evaporated for most of the guests when they arrived at the centre and found a rundown house covered in scaffolding surrounded by rows of prefabricated units.

'My name is Bernie.' Sniggers erupted in pockets around the room. He pretended to ignore them. 'First of all, I must apologise for the building works that are still going on. You are all businesspeople, you know what it is like to be at the mercy of merciless builders!'

He injected a pause at this spot, hoping for a laugh or a knowing smile. Or an acknowledging nod. Anything. Nothing. He tapped his microphone. 'Hello? Is this working?' he chuckled. Nobody chuckled back.

He cleared his throat and decided to talk very quickly then open the bar. 'You are our first guests, our guinea pigs, and we here at Venture Road want this to be a success for all our sakes. You've all been shown to your rooms. You've now got an hour to unpack and familiarise

352

yourselves with the house and the grounds. We'll all meet back here at five pm when you'll be given details of the weekend's activities.'

The large room echoed with the clatter of 100 chairs scraping backwards.

'One more thing!' Bernie bellowed into his microphone. Everyone stopped moving. 'The bar is now open!'

This announcement caused the first wave of enthusiasm of the day.

The Visions group had all been placed in one unit. They'd been perturbed to see the layout of the hut, because that's what it felt like, a hut. Rebecca, Kate, Sally and Chrissie were all in one room in two sets of bunk beds. Ben and Jenny had a double room which befitted their marital status.

'Am I missing something?' Andrew said. They went back to the front door and checked the layout again. This time they found a false door from which toppled a pull-down bed just inside the entrance.

'That's fantastic,' Andrew said miserably. 'I'm sleeping on a door in the corridor.'

Chrissie giggled. This was beginning to look like it might be fun. Sally glared at her.

They all huddled together in what was laughingly to be referred to as 'Andrew's bedroom' and surveyed their surroundings.

Andrew was still staring at his bed in disbelief. 'You do realise that, if anyone wants to go to the toilet in the night, they will have to climb over me.'

'I'll go first,' Chrissie said flirtatiously.

'Chrissie!' Sally warned.

But Chrissie's comment helped to lighten the gloomy mood that had descended on them in London and refused to lift.

353

'And if anyone snores, there's every chance that these walls will collapse,' Kate observed.

They all smiled. Not broadly, but it was the first smile for some hours. Then they went to their 'rooms' and unpacked, changing into the tracksuits that they'd been advised to wear throughout their stay.

Andrew had changed in the toilet since his 'room' had a large uncurtained window looking out on to a main path. He'd found himself waving to passers-by during his initial attempts at undressing without revealing any of his body. Once he got over the shock of the unusual sleeping arrangements, he'd been secretly pleased. A weekend away from Rebecca would be good for both of them. And there was no chance of a sneaky assignation in the middle of the night, not with the possibility of Sally's hormonally challenged daughter jumping on top of them en route to the toilet.

Ben and Jenny also welcomed the paper-thin walls. They learned in the first couple of minutes that the astonishing structure of the hut had an amplifying effect on even the softest whisper. They would not be able to say a thing in the confines of their bedroom that they were not prepared to share with all the the other occupants of the unit, if not the adjacent units as well.

Rebecca was grateful to have a bed to herself again. She would have to get used to it soon and this would be an easier transition back into single life than a direct move from Andrew's flat and bed.

Kate found the set-up claustrophobic. There were tensions going on here, some of which she understood and others she didn't. She'd assumed that there would be lot of arguing going on behind closed doors, a lot of crying and accusations, and ultimately, she hoped, a degree of resolution.

Since nothing at all was going to be said or resolved in here, in private, then she had to assume that it would all happen in public. She hoped that none of it would erupt when they were all tethered together on a sheer cliff-face.

Sally just welcomed anything that would make secrecy impossible and settled right in.

They all felt better after a couple of drinks. Changing into tracksuits had also liberated them from their previous selves, allowing them to relax and forget their professional status or job demarcations within company groups. It reminded Rebecca – and Kate – of how your personal appearance could affect your own behaviour and attitude as well as those of the people you met.

They were the ones who were happiest in tracksuits, relieved that they no longer had to think about clothes.

Kate had managed to stifle a chuckle when she saw Andrew in a sports suit (calling it a tracksuit would send the two-piece screaming back to its designer in tears) that, while it was undoubtedly practical, was the cleanest, sharpest, slickest leisure garment she'd ever seen.

'Don't say it,' Andrew warned, noticing her wrinkling eyes.

'But you said that you expect such comments,' Kate laughed. 'So go on, tell me, how did you get that up here in that tiny case without it being all creased like everyone else's clothes?'

'If I tell you, you'll mock me,' Andrew said calmly.

'I won't, I promise,' Kate replied, having no intention of keeping her promise.

Andrew leaned forward confidentially. 'The secret is to roll, not to fold,' he whispered, then sat back.

355

Kate beckoned him forward again. 'Will you have to shoot me now?' she asked.

Andrew glared at her. 'You said you wouldn't mock!' he accused.

'I didn't know it was going to be that funny,' Kate said.

Andrew slapped her leg affectionately, a gesture they both recognised was not something he would have done a few days earlier.

Rebecca recognised it too. She was watching them closely although Andrew and Kate were too wrapped up in each other to notice. She felt queasy, knowing that she'd lost him, and scared, knowing that she would be leaving her job soon. She wanted to go back to the shoebox they were staying in, pack her bag and go home to her mum and dad, never to see these people again.

But looking at Kate reminded her of what she could salvage from this tragedy. She would maintain her professionalism until the end, play a pivotal role in winning the new account, then leave in glory. In her next job, she would be a Kate, a leader. She'd learn from her carefully this weekend and work through the agony of loss that she was starting to suffer.

'Order, ladies and gentlemen, please!' Bernie had returned and was gratified to see some enthusiasm generating in the crowd. 'I hope you're all refreshed because this is where it all begins!'

'Oooooh!' a few dissidents murmured childishly. Bernie ignored them. His intensely irritating nature probably made selective hearing an essential survival technique to acquire.

'Each group will be competing against all the others over the course of the weekend. On top of that, my group leaders will be evaluating the individuals within each

356

group and the reports passed on to the senior executive in each company.'

Ben smiled encouragingly at all his group except Rebecca. He dared not look at her in case he found himself jumping up and slapping her.

Bernie was still talking. 'Now, I'm going to hand out copies of the weekend's schedules but I won't be going into too many details. We will be looking at how you deal with unforeseen challenges. But I will tell you where you need to be and what you need to bring for the first activity tomorrow – rafting.'

Everyone groaned. When they'd seen the thin layer of ice over the lake in the grounds, they'd all been cheered by the probability that there would be no water activities this week.

Falling fully clothed into a freezing Welsh lake in February – what a great contribution to management skills this offered, Ben thought, envying Jenny for half a second before remembering how unhappy she was.

Jenny and Chrissie were excused from the team talks. They really were guests and could do whatever they wanted.

An unlikely couple, they hit it off well in their first minutes alone.

'What shall we do now?' Chrissie had asked in the time-honoured fashion of adolescents everywhere.

Jenny had laughed and felt the baby kick her vigorously. I can't believe my baby will be like her one day, she thought. 'My legs are killing me after that journey,' she said. 'Do you mind if we go for a walk?'

'That'll be great!' Chrissie agreed.

Sally would have been staggered at her enthusiasm. Normally Chrissie moaned at being asked to walk 100 yards to the corner shop. But then Sally, despite her youth, hadn't yet understood the essential, timeless truth about children: *anything* a parent, particularly a mother, suggested was to be instantly resisted as a matter of principle.

Jenny was not Chrissie's mother, wasn't her enemy and would have no reason to want to make her do anything with wider implications for her long-term health and well-being. Going for a walk with her would be fine.

Without any discussion, Jenny linked her arm through the younger girl's and leaned on her slightly. Chrissie appreciated the responsibility and held herself high to support Jenny.

They walked through the grounds until the tatty house and prefabs were out of sight. Now they could see the beauty of the area.

'I need to sit down for a minute,' Jenny said, puffed from the exertion of the short walk.

'Of course,' Chrissie said solicitously, wiping a damp wooden bench with a dirty tissue she found in her pocket.

Jenny sat down gratefully.

'When are you having your baby?' Chrissie asked.

'Officially not for a couple of weeks,' Jenny said, 'but it could arrive at any time.'

'You're huge, aren't you?'

Jenny laughed at the girl's honesty. It was gloriously welcome after all the deceit and insincerity that had littered her life recently. 'Yes, I am,' she agreed.

'I'm never going to have children,' Chrissie announced emphatically.

'Why's that?' Jenny asked, wisely not arguing with the rashness of such a decision in one so young.

'They ruin your life,' Chrissie said sadly.

358

Jenny became more serious now. 'Who told you that?' she asked carefully. Kate had filled her in on Sally's story when they went to pick Sally and Chrissie up this morning.

Chrissie shrugged. 'Nobody. They didn't have to. You just have to look at my mum to work it out for yourself.'

Jenny was confused by this line of thinking. 'I don't understand what you mean. Your mum seems really happy with her life. She has a good job, she has a daughter she loves. And, from what I hear, she didn't need to keep you a secret from her employers. She's got to where she has on her own merits.'

She was exaggerating for Chrissie's sake. Ben had constantly talked about Sally's real attitude problem and how she hung on to her job by a constantly fraying thread. Kate however had told her that Sally's performance was transformed after her secret had been revealed. That's how deadly secrets can be, Jenny thought sadly, destructive, insidious, pervasive.

Chrissie was unmoved. 'Then how come she cries in bed at night when she thinks I'm asleep?'

Jenny couldn't give her an answer, but Chrissie wasn't looking for one. She already had it.

'I know why. It's because of all the things she couldn't do because of me when I was younger. And all the things she can't do now that I'm older. She hasn't had a boyfriend since I was born. And she never has any money, not for herself. It all goes on me. I try not to ask for too much but I still see her face when she has to refuse.'

Jenny swallowed. Everything made her tearful just now. She hadn't been able to switch the television on for days, finding herself weeping at soap operas she

359

didn't even follow. But Chrissie's pain was real and here.

'Actually Chrissie, I think a lot of your mum's problems are down to her age when she had you, not about you, as such. You know she loves you, don't you?'

Chrissie nodded silently.

Jenny went on. 'I know I can't deny that your mum must have made sacrifices, but I don't think she regrets any of them and, if you talk to her about it, you might find that she even has some plans to chase up some of those lost opportunities now you're older. So her life may have been put on hold but it's not ruined, not in any way.'

Chrissie looked encouraged by this. She understood what Jenny was saying. She'd seen the brochures for adult education courses that had come through the door this week.

'Besides,' Jenny said, cheered by Chrissie's elevating mood, 'you've got your own life to lead. Your mum wouldn't want you to be wasting your precious youth worrying about her.'

I'm not worrying about her, Chrissie thought, I'm doing something about it.

Stan and Edie walked along the promenade, clenching their teeth against the ferocious wind, hanging on to each other for warmth. They'd been hoping to find the little café they'd frequented during their honeymoon. When they found that it was now the Bingo section of a closed-up amusements arcade, they decided they'd settle for any café.

After ten more minutes fighting the blizzard, they were prepared to settle for anywhere that offered shelter.

Ten minutes after that, they were contemplating feigning heart attacks and being transferred in a warm, dry ambulance to a cosy, centrally heated hospital. At least you get tea in hospitals.

From Stan's point of view, the good part of all this was that Edie was now willing to be airlifted straight to New Zealand.

Just as they were about to give up and throw themselves into the sea for a quick death, they saw a welcoming fish and chip shop up a side street. They lifted their pace to a near-jog as the oasis beckoned them like a sultry temptress.

They flung the door open and collapsed into the grubby tiled interior. It took them a while to get their breath back and demist their glasses which had fogged over instantly in the wonderful blissful heat. Sighing with ecstasy, they draped their sodden coats over the chairs at the single table in the window.

At the counter they were heartened by the wide smile of the jolly ruddy-cheeked fish-fryer. He could see these people were tired, wet and emotional. They needed some freshly fried cod, a double portion of chunky chips and a massive pot of tea. And that's what he told them.

They would have expired in gratitude if they'd understood a word he said. Because he only spoke Welsh.

'What do you think about this?' Steve asked.

They all rubbed sight-holes in the steamed-up car windows. It was a futile exercise because all they could see was a sign reading HAPPY VALLEY! adorned with pictures of tents and caravans and barely clothed holiday-makers gambolling in the sunshine.

Justine giggled. She hadn't giggled for some time and the kids were delighted. Soon they were all giggling hysterically.

'That's it, then!' Steve said happily. 'Happy Valley

it is for us!' And they drove down a seemingly endless drive, still giggling, until they reached the reception, an impressive building with an equally impressive sign across the door reading CLOSED.

They all groaned.

'This is silly,' Justine said, gently. 'Every site we've stopped at is closed.'

'I should have realised we'd have problems in February,' Steve said sheepishly.

The children all turned and looked at their mum for an answer. That was what she did, sorted out the problems that Dad couldn't handle. And then Steve was hit miraculously by one of those inexplicable attacks of insight that some people only experience once or twice in their lives.

For Steve it was a first. He knew precisely what Justine was thinking and how she was feeling. While the actual moment of empathy passed in seconds, the effect was powerful enough to inspire him to say and do something dramatic.

'I think your mum is fed up of sorting things out, so guess what?'

'What?' the kids shouted obediently.

'Dad's going to make all the decisions this holiday and Mum's going to have all the fun!'

Justine laughed, really laughed. She hadn't realised it until Steve spoke, but this was exactly the kind of role-playing she'd craved for years: role reversal on the jobs that she felt had come to define her.

They couldn't swap careers, although Steve could probably deliver a baby as well as Justine. But they could exchange the chores, the tasks, for a short time. The ones that don't count so you daren't complain about and you never get round to reassessing. Her washing while

362

he dries, her navigating while he drives, her cooking while he sends out for pizza.

Now she could really let herself go. No more decisions. A comprehensive transformation which would cost nothing and wouldn't require that new push-up bra that she'd bought the day before and sneaked into her suitcase.

'Mum! What on earth are you doing here?'

Chrissie had felt Jenny wobble against her when she saw her mother sitting in the sun lounge. I thought mums only had this effect on kids when the kids were young, she thought. Don't tell me it lasts forever.

Barbara stood up, went to hug Jenny and helped her into a chair.

'Who's your new friend?' she asked, not recognising Chrissie.

'Mum, Chrissie. Chrissie, my mum. Chrissie's mum is Sally, Andrew's secretary. She's here on the course so Chrissie has come along for a holiday like me.'

Barbara extended her hand to Chrissie who shook it, always grateful to be treated like a grown-up.

'Pleased to meet you, Chrissie. And thank you for taking such good care of *my* little girl.'

Jenny looked at Chrissie and pulled a face which made the girl giggle.

'So, Mum. Now that we're all friends, will you tell me what you're doing here?'

'That leaflet you showed me made the place look so lovely and I haven't had a holiday for ages so I thought—'

Jenny interrupted her mum. 'Mum, you said that the place looked like Colditz and you went to the Caribbean a month ago.'

Her mum ignored this. 'Besides, there's a possibility

363

that my first grandchild could be born up here and I don't intend to be two hundred miles away when that happens.'

'Mum, if you've come to interfere, then you can turn round and go straight home. I appreciate your support but I'm handling this myself.'

Chrissie was fascinated by this exchange. She was learning that there were occasional advantages to being young. Barbara and Jenny were oblivious to her presence, perhaps thinking that she could not possibly understand what they were talking about.

But they didn't realise that she knew all about Rebecca and Ben. Her mum had told her.

Barbara was irritatingly appeasing. 'Of course you are,' she said placidly. 'But I'll be here if you need me.'

And to take some action if I think it's called for.

Stan and Edie sat with Geraint, chatting cheerfully over fish and chips. They had stood in horror when they realised the extent of their communications failure. Geraint had kept on trying different sentences, speeding up and slowing down, apparently getting more frustrated by his inability to make himself understood. Then, as the expression on their faces became genuinely distressed, his face lit up with the most wicked smile they had seen since their boys grew up.

'Aah! Caught you!' he said.

Stan and Edie looked apprehensive. They were not in the mood for tricks; they just wanted chips, tea and a sit-down.

Geraint extended his hand warmly. 'Geraint Wells,' he said. 'Sorry about that. I like to have a laugh and a joke with my customers.'

And I like to punch people like you, Stan thought, fuming after the stress this man had just put them through.

Edie caught her husband's expression and intervened quickly. 'Nice to meet you Geraint. I'm Edie and this is my husband, Stan.'

She shook hands with him and coerced Stan to do the same. He reluctantly obeyed. After forty years he was used to his wife making friends with every stranger who so much as smiled at them, but personally he would have drawn the line at the fish-fryer.

Nevertheless within minutes, they were as good as friends.

'Forty years,' he repeated, shaking his head in admiration. 'You're lucky, my Alice died fifteen years ago, so we didn't even make it to our silver wedding. We'd built this place up from scratch. We spent five years with a stall on the prom. We couldn't believe it when we got his shop. It was everything we'd dreamed about.'

Edie cooed sympathetically.

'Did you not think of selling up after she died?' Stan asked.

Edie glared at him.

Geraint wasn't offended. 'That would have been like Alice dying again. It was *our* dream, part of us both. So part of her lives on here with me. That's the wonderful thing about sharing a dream with someone and making it happen. You both become part of something bigger than the two of you, something that lasts as long as one of you is alive.'

Edie and Stan, moved by this, sat quietly for a few minutes.

Geraint noticed their reticence. 'What about you two? You must have a dream, surely? One that you share? What is it?'

And neither of them dared speak in case they didn't say exactly the same thing.

'. . . and I would recommend several layers of thin clothes rather than a few thick ones,' Bernie was droning.

'What about several layers of industrial insulating foam?' someone offered from the back of the room.

Sniggers rippled through the crowd. But Bernie was unstoppable.

'Now I'm not going to give you any clues about what you will have to do tomorrow, but I recommend that you spend this evening evaluating the strengths and weaknesses of your team members.'

Andrew and Kate were now sitting close to each other, whispering and giggling like the naughtiest children in the class. Ben watched them, approving of the speed with which Andrew was separating himself from Rebecca, but envious of the lack of complications they faced.

They could start a new relationship with no secrets and no lies to set down roots of decay. And they were both smart, they both possessed self-control. They wouldn't make stupid, irreversible mistakes.

For the first time in his life, he wished he could have been a different sort of person in the past. But this was foolish. There was only one sensible wish: that he could find a way to be different for the future and that Jenny would offer him a future worth changing for.

After the briefing session, it was time for supper. They piled out of the meeting room and headed towards the dining room at the other side of the house. Like schoolchildren, they found themselves dividing into pairs. Kate and Andrew fused together instinctively and chatted happily as they were jostled along, following the smell of institutional vegetables and something indeterminate but definitely containing cheese.

A mobile phone rang and 100 people stopped to check their pockets.

'It's mine,' Kate said incredulously. She checked the number on the display but it wasn't familiar. 'I won't be a second,' she mouthed to Andrew as she ducked out of the throng into an alcove. She had to place a finger in one ear to be able to hear the caller.

'Who?' she shouted, not sure she had heard correctly.

'It's Callum!' the voice shouted back.

Kate didn't know what to say or who to be. She could have said that she was really pleased to hear his voice. But she wasn't sure that would be true. She was enjoying herself with Andrew, relaxing, reverting slowly but firmly to her true character.

'Hello! Are you still there?' Callum yelled.

'Sorry! The reception went for a second. Listen, can I call you back when it's a bit quieter?'

'You won't need to,' Callum said.

Oh dear, I've offended him, Kate thought, perilously close to slipping back into full crowdpleaser mode. 'Why's that?' she asked.

'Because I'm standing right behind you.'

Kate spun round. And there he was.

Chapter 21

'What are you doing here?' Kate asked, taking in his expansive smile and his expensive tracksuit complete with corporate logo.

Callum looked down at his clothes. 'Guess?' he said wryly.

Kate smiled nervously, relaxing slightly in the knowledge that everyone was dressed roughly the same and she could not be judged on what she was wearing. But the change of clothes had upset her rhythm. She couldn't remember what they'd talked about at that lunch, what she'd told him, and she couldn't find her way back to the place where they'd left off so optimistically.

He'd crossed the line from her first life to her second. He didn't belong in this scene, in this play. He wouldn't know the plot, the characters, the lines, anything.

'You didn't say that you'd be coming—' she began, hoping she didn't sound accusatory.

Callum interrupted her. 'That's because I wanted it to be a surprise! I got the idea while you were talking about it. And besides, it sounded like a good idea for my own team. We're great believers in these team-building exercises, we take part in a number throughout the year.'

'So you booked up?' Kate said weakly.

'Yeah! I thought it would be fun. I was looking forward to seeing you again and I have to confess that

I was interested in getting a glimpse of you in action and seeing your professional style.'

Oh no, Kate thought.

Callum ignored the noticeable downturn on her mouth. 'And don't worry, I wouldn't do anything to embarrass you in this situation. I've brought my team here to work and learn. We intend to win the rafting race tomorrow!'

'I'm relieved to hear that,' Kate said. 'Because I need to make the most of this weekend.'

Callum brushed his hand over her arm. 'I remember you telling me about how important this was. I won't do anything to jeopardise your status with your staff. I respect you too much.'

Kate remembered why she'd liked Callum and she still did, but she didn't want him to be here. He was another factor to consider and she had plenty of factors already. One more might just topple the pile over.

Andrew had walked over to see who Kate was talking to. He was childishly peeved by the sight of Kate standing so close to that man.

Kate sensed his presence and turned round. 'Oh Andrew, let me introduce you to Callum . . . sorry, I don't know your surname?'

'Callum Steele,' he replied, extending his hand to Andrew.

'Andrew Darlington,' Andrew said, shaking hands.

They both waited for Kate to decide where they went from here. Kate was at a complete loss. She comforted herself with the thought that no one would be at ease in such a situation.

'Shall we go through?' she suggested brightly.

Then she turned and marched towards the dining room as Andrew and Callum hurried to keep up.

Fortunately the tables were labelled with company

369

names, so there was no need for Kate to negotiate a diplomatically acceptable seating plan. Callum looked disappointed. Andrew looked relieved.

'Well, we'll be seeing you tomorrow,' Kate said to Callum, with a tone that was halfway between apology and brusqueness.

'Right,' Callum said. He hesitated and Kate wondered for an awful moment if he was going to kiss her. He clearly thought better of the impulse and instead shook her hand, winking slyly as he turned to join his own group.

Thank God for that, Kate thought. She sat down at the table to find everybody looking at her.

Somewhere in Suffolk, two people sat in a kitchen, reading and rereading the letter their daughter had sent them.

'We have to talk about this, love,' Edward said.

'You know how I feel,' Ellen replied. But she couldn't stop touching the letter. 'She didn't care that we might be dead, that we might have been worried sick that *she* was dead. All these years.' She shook her head bitterly. 'I will never forgive her for how she treated you.'

She stopped speaking before the tremble that was affecting her whole body reached her voice.

Edward reached his hand out to cover his wife's. She'd aged dramatically in the years since Rebecca had left. He found it hard to forgive his daughter for that but he forgave her for feeling betrayed by him. He forgave her for never visiting him in prison. He forgave her for not listening to him or reading his letters. He wanted to see her and tell her all this.

But Becky needed to understand some things. Her parents couldn't know what she'd been doing with her life all this time, but they'd assumed she'd changed. In

370

fact, now they had proof. This letter was written by a completely different person to the selfish, shallow girl who had stormed out of their lives a lifetime ago. This Rebecca was an adult, a mature person, someone with judgement, with perspective, with the courage to say 'sorry' and to ask for forgiveness.

She couldn't know that they'd changed too. Children tend to believe that their parents stop evolving as people when they have children, that they become good, bad or indifferent parents but essentially non-persons in their own right.

Edward and Ellen had ceased existing as Rebecca's parents a long time ago, but had carried on growing since her departure. They had been stigmatised by Edward's crime, their friends had drifted away and Ellen had been forced to take low-paid clerical work to support them. Edward had never been able to find work again. Their son had emigrated to Canada as soon as he'd left university.

They had survived somehow but they'd paid a terrible price. Edward had a heart condition and Ellen was weak, bitter and prematurely old. Edward suspected that Rebecca wanted those other parents back, the mummy who'd prepared miniature birthday cakes for her doll's birthday parties, the daddy who'd read her *The Lion, The Witch and The Wardrobe* when she was six. She'd want Sunday lunch with crispy roast potatoes and vegetables yanked from the soil by her strong mother. She'd want everything as it was. And nothing was as it was.

Maybe Ellen was right about ignoring this contact but for the wrong reasons. Ellen didn't *want* to help Rebecca but Edward didn't think they *could* help her. They'd all changed too much.

*

371

Kate realised that she was expected to lead the conversation, that this was all part of the team-building exercise. She had attended lots of similar courses but never one where she'd been expected to actually build her team.

Her role had generally been to ensure that everyone had a wonderful time. In her opinion. She would sneak out in her car and buy chocolate and wine and candles and organise midnight feasts. Her idea of a good time came directly from Enid Blyton boarding-school books but her enthusiasm was infectious and her team was always the happiest group on any course. They usually flunked most of the exercises but they had the most fun.

And surely that was the point? she'd assumed.

But this seemed a more serious proposition. After all, they had a concrete aim, a goal that could represent job security for these people. They needed to become a team if they wanted to be in with a serious chance of winning a major account. A few nice meals and some games wouldn't do it.

She'd hoped that they'd be allocated someone who'd supervise them throughout the weekend, that her role would be no more than inspirational. She could do that, she was good at that. She could lead some community singing or get them all doing origami; that always drew people together.

But, no, she had to think of something with a touch more substance. OK, she thought, recalling one exercise from a previous course.

'Right,' she said formally. 'We all know why we're here this weekend. We're here to put our past differences behind us and find common ground, points of connection that can link us together, bind us into a cohesive group so that we form an unbeatable team in the competitive workplace.'

Phew! I'm motivated already, she congratulated herself. The others looked faintly amused but no one argued with the reasoning. Kate continued while there was no dissent.

'So, while we're waiting for our food to arrive, I thought we'd try something out. We all know each other to a greater or lesser extent. It might be interesting to see what impression we've made on our colleagues.'

Ben pressed his lips together. I'm not sure this is such a good idea, he thought. Some of us know exactly what impression we've made on certain colleagues and would prefer it to remain unsaid.

He'd spoken to Kate before dinner and explained to her that she would be leading the team this weekend despite his seniority.

'The object of the exercise is to bind the team together. I'm really just a peripheral member of the team so I'll take a back seat if it's OK with you.'

Kate had understood the logic and been grateful for his confidence. In fact, Ben's decision was motivated less by his professionalism and more by his overwhelming preoccupation with personal dramas.

They were the smallest group on the course, just the five of them. Jenny, Barbara and Chrissie were in a separate dining room choosing from an à la carte menu and enjoying a lovely relaxed meal. Lucky them, they all thought resentfully. With only five people playing this game, there was little scope for safe choices.

Kate could tell that her suggestion was not being very positively received but she could not back down without appearing to vacillate, a sin in a strong leader.

'So I will go first,' she said quickly. 'We will each say something positive and something negative about one person around the table. I'll start with Sally.' She chose her words very carefully indeed.

'I would say that Sally's most positive attributes are her loyalty and her recently demonstrated ability to adapt to altered circumstances. And on the negative side, I would only count a tendency to disregard the opinions of others, opinions which, if she gave them some consideration, could often surprise her with their encouragement and support.' Sally smiled gratefully, hoping that the spotlight could now be moved off her and not return.

Kate turned towards Andrew, hoping he would back her up in this. 'Andrew? Would you like to go next?'

No he wouldn't, but he knew that this question represented a gentle order.

He continued the theme that Kate had started, emphasising the positive and only choosing negative points with positive pay-offs.

'I'll choose Kate,' he said warmly. 'Her positive attributes include strength, resolve, single-mindedness and firm leadership. Among many others. On the negative side . . .' he hesitated before continuing. 'I would have to say that she doesn't relax enough. When she does, she allows softer, more empathetic qualities to come through that also have a place in management. I think if she brought more of herself into the office, the whole team would benefit from a more well-rounded leader.'

Kate had been astonished at the utter wrongness of his list of positive attributes and the utter rightness of her negatives. He'd attempted to fuse her two separate identities into one irreconcilable whole and failed totally. She smiled at his misguided kindness and moved on.

'Ben?' she said hopefully.

Ben was relieved to be next while he still had the option of commenting on Andrew.

'Andrew,' he said. 'Your most positive attributes are your self-discipline, your control, your absolute reliability, your attention to detail and your consistency. On the negative side, I can only think that all of the above might, on occasion, be taken to extremes which perhaps adds unnecessary stress to your life.'

He sat back, content with his tactful performance. Andrew was looking put out. 'Do you really think that, Ben?' he asked. 'But I could say exactly the same about you, except the other way round. I could say you *lack* self-discipline, control, any reliability or attention to detail and consistency and sometimes this lack has extreme consequences.'

Ben turned to Kate. 'Is this a free-for-all? Can we all just throw in our comments?'

Kate made a quick ruling. 'No! I think it is more sensible if you each just speak about one person.'

'But Andrew's had two goes. That's not fair. Why can't I have two goes?' Ben couldn't believe what he was saying. He was just spewing out words without any forethought. He assumed it was a delayed reaction to the shock he'd suffered when Jenny told him about Rebecca's message. He'd spent the last forty-eight hours watching every sound that came out of his mouth, not daring to utter the one random syllable that would set Jenny off again.

It had been almost unendurable. And now that Jenny wasn't here, he felt able to let go, say and do what he wanted.

Kate could feel her team-building exercise deteriorating into a primary school name-calling session. Ben had already gone back to playground sulks. She intervened again.

'I think the food will be arriving shortly,' (*Please!*) 'so why don't we hear from Rebecca?'

Rebecca seemed nervous. 'Who shall I describe? Every-one's been done.'

'Well, I haven't been done properly,' Ben said belligerently. 'Andrew's go didn't count, because he'd already had his.'

Kate wished she'd started the community singing after all.

'Besides,' Ben went on, 'I'm genuinely interested to know exactly what Rebecca thinks of me. Then I can say what I think of her.'

'No you can't,' Andrew objected, 'you said I wasn't allowed to have two turns.'

'But you already had when I said that,' Ben answered back.

'That's when I didn't know it was a rule. But you're the one that established the rule.'

'Yes but . . .'

'FOR GOD'S SAKE, SHUT UP, THE PAIR OF YOU!' Kate screamed at them.

Ben and Andrew were stunned into silence. So was the rest of the room.

Especially Callum, who had watched Kate's eruption in horror.

Justine sat in the tent listening to the rain thundering down above her head. She'd wedged a torch in the corner to provide some subtle light. Steve assured her that the tent was waterproof but, then again, he'd assured her that the caravan was big enough for all of them.

He'd stuck to his promise that he would take care of things and was currently preparing supper in the caravan. She'd insisted on taking her mobile phone into the tent in case he set fire to the caravan and she needed to call the fire brigade. And she hadn't been joking.

There wasn't much room in the tent even though it was supposed to be for two people. Justine thought that the packaging should be relabelled to say: 'For two people wearing thin/no clothes in the summer or one freezing cold woman padded up until she resembles a sumo wrestler.'

She heard Steve huffing and swearing as he ran from the caravan to the tent. She opened the flap door and let him in. Carefully holding two plates, he lowered himself into a crouch on the ground as he worked out where he was going to sit.

Justine relieved him of the plates and reorganised her legs so that there was room for him to sit, provided he perched on only one buttock.

'There!' he said, as he reached the ground and took his plate from Justine. 'I told you cooking wouldn't be a problem!'

Justine looked at the plate. 'I can make out the corned beef but what's the pinky stuff?'

'Well, I was going to do mash and beans but we only had one cooking ring so I cooked them together,' Steve said, proud of his improvisation skills.

'Lovely,' Justine said weakly. She ate every scrap of the food, including the lumps of instant mash powder that weren't dissolved. Steve hadn't cooked often in their marriage and she wanted to encourage him. But then again, she didn't want to encourage him too much. There was only so much uncooked potato powder that the human body can digest in a lifetime without recourse to colonic irrigation.

Steve had watched her anxiously. His desire to please almost made her weep. 'That was fantastic! It really was!' she said, enthusiastically.

'Pass me your plate,' he said, which she did. Steve

opened the flap and put the plates out on the grass in the rain. 'There. That's the washing-up taken care of!' He reached out his arm and brought in a can of Coke. 'Sorry it's not champagne,' he apologised, 'but I did find two plastic glasses.'

He opened the can, which sprayed over them both. 'Sorry,' he said again. He put the can and glasses down while he tried to wipe up the spillage with his trouser leg. He looked crestfallen.

Justine took his hand and kissed it. 'This is lovely,' she said, meaning it this time. 'You don't have to do any more for me. It's enough that you recognised what I needed and did all you could to provide it.'

'I didn't make a very good job of it, though, did I?' he said, not consoled by Justine's kindness.

'Oh, I don't know,' Justine said. 'I mean, the kids are in the caravan. It's pelting with rain so they'll probably be in there for some time. So we've got all this lovely damp, sticky, cold, cramped tent to ourselves!'

It took Steve a couple of seconds to realise that she was seducing him. They looked at each other and around them to consider the logistics of this adventure.

'We'll have to take turns at getting undressed. Only one person can move at a time in here,' she observed practically.

'That makes it all the more exciting!' Steve said, cheering up considerably. The two of them began giggling again. They'd been doing a lot of that today.

'Who said this wasn't a good idea?' Steve said scornfully as he almost collapsed the tent around them removing his shirt.

Justine conceded that he was right by blowing him a kiss from under the picnic rug that they were planning to use as a blanket.

'I'm freezing!' Steve said. 'Let me under that.'

He manoeuvred his way over to Justine's side, arms and legs kicking and nudging in multiple collisions.

'Ow!' Steve yelled suddenly.

Justine sat up in concern. 'What is it?' she asked.

Steve was rubbing his arm. 'It's nothing, just this tattoo giving me grief. Please don't say "I told you so". I've already acknowledged that my attempt at self-improvement was much more idiotic than yours.'

'Show me,' Justine insisted. She reached into her pocket for a second torch to see what was causing the problem.

'That's nasty,' she said, shining the torch on the red, weeping patch.

'It'll be fine,' Steve said. 'Ricardo said it might be sore for a few days.'

Justine shook her head. 'Look at it, Steve! You're a doctor and I'm a nurse! We both recognise an infected wound.'

Steve sighed. 'This isn't the sort of physical encounter I had in mind.'

Justine kissed him lovingly. 'There's a first-aid kit in the caravan. I'll see if there's something I can use to clean it. But if it gets worse tomorrow, we're going to have to get you to a doctor.'

'I *am* a doctor!'

Justine raised her eyebrows. 'You're a surgeon. Unless you're planning to amputate your own arm, I suggest we see someone a little less specialised!'

They spent the night as far away from each other as was possible in the cramped quarters to avoid knocking Steve's arm.

'This is romantic,' Steve thought ironically.

'This is romantic,' Justine thought sincerely.

*

Barbara was enjoying herself. Chrissie was good company and seemed to be having an uplifting effect on Jenny. Chrissie had been teaching her a Steps dance before supper and was now giving her a tutorial on current pop music.

'If you're going to have kids, you'll want to know all the right bands, or you'll look an idiot.'

Jenny laughed. 'I don't think this child will be into pop music for a few years. I'm envisaging a good few years of "Wheels on the Bus" first.'

Chrissie looked horrified. 'What good will that do her at school!' Chrissie had already decided that the baby would be a she. 'You'll be doing her far more favours if you give her a good musical education first.'

'By playing things like Steps?' Jenny asked, loving this girl.

Chrissie nodded. 'And all the rest. Westlife and Robbie Williams and Shaggy . . .'

Barbara had tuned out as soon as the word 'pop' had been uttered.

'Feeling old?' a man next to her said.

She realised that he was talking to her.

She grimaced. 'I did my share of pop music when I was a mother. Of course my children listened to any music that annoyed me.'

'Purely because you were the mother?' the man suggested.

'Exactly! But as a grandmother, I fully intend to teach this child to share my tastes. I shall take her to the opera, the ballet, to the Proms . . .'

'You already know that it's going to be a girl?'

Barbara stopped. 'Did I say "her"?' The man nodded.

'How amazing. I'm so sorry, I'm being terribly rude. My name is Barbara Darlington.' She extended her hand

'Matthew Jamison,' the man said, shaking hands warmly. 'And I'm fascinated to hear what has brought you here. This doesn't seem to be a natural habitat for you.'

Barbara talked him through the family tree. Matthew got lost at the son-in-law reference but nodded intelligently. He was an attractive man in his sixties. Whatever kind of life he'd led, his face conveyed that he had come to terms with his past and was accepting the present for as long as it was available to him.

Barbara liked him instantly. Her intuitive skills told her that he was honest and kind, the only two qualities she thought were worth anything.

'What about you?' she asked back.

'My son owns this place. I'm just here for moral support.'

They spent the rest of the meal sharing their views on how you should best support your children. During coffee, Barbara suddenly felt guilty for not introducing Jenny properly. But when she turned round, Jenny and Chrissie had gone. They'd left during dessert, Chrissie chuckling quietly at the sight of Barbara being chatted up, Jenny offering silent prayers of thanks that her mum had seemed to be enjoying it.

'So come on, Rebecca,' Ben said calmly, having retrieved his cool after Kate's outburst. They had endured a miserable supper despite Kate's best efforts to restore good humour to the table. 'Let's get this over with, then we can go back to our prefabricated hovel and put this day behind us.'

'Thank you, Ben,' Kate said coldly. 'But I am trying to raise morale, not club it to death with some blunt speech.'

Sally laughed, for which Kate was grateful. Ben had the grace to apologise.

Rebecca saw everyone looking at her, waiting for her to pass judgement on Ben. If only she had been able to have her turn before they ate, she could have carried off the act perfectly. But that was before she'd been forced to endure over an hour of Ben and Andrew poking at each other like children, scoring points in a game where there wasn't even a prize.

She blamed Ben for everything: for the affair, for her not being promoted, for not being at home to take her appalling message, for spoiling things for her and Andrew and, now, for dragging Andrew down into the dirt with him.

'What do I think of Ben?' she said very slowly.

Oh dear, Sally thought, understanding better than the others just what Rebecca might be planning to say. But she was helpless to prevent it.

Rebecca was cranking herself up. 'Well, let's start with the positive attributes.' She placed her finger on her chin and pretended to think deeply. 'Erm, hmm, ooh, no, sorry, can't think of any,' she said perkily.

Oh oh, Kate thought. What's going on here that I don't understand?

Rebecca was speaking more quickly now, more excitedly. 'So let's move right along to the negative points.' She rubbed her hands together.

'Where do we begin? Well, let me see: he has no respect for any other people apart from himself; actually I'm wrong, he doesn't have any respect for himself either, I mean look at how much care he takes in his appearance; his indiscipline causes endless problems for the loyal staff who work for him but he makes no effort to improve his appalling habits; he is disloyal, dishonest, insincere,

382

shallow and the least talented of any men in a senior position I have ever known—'

'THAT IS QUITE ENOUGH!' Kate yelled, once more silencing the entire room and attracting an increasingly disbelieving stare from Callum.

Rebecca shut up abruptly. She turned to Ben and smiled. 'Was that helpful?'

Andrew jumped up, almost knocking his chair over. He went round to Rebecca and grabbed her elbow roughly. 'I think we should discuss this. Let's go for a walk.'

Rebecca pushed him away but stood up and stormed out, leaving Andrew to trot after her. Kate watched them leave with dismay. She thought of all her policewomen role models who'd been helping her with her character and wondered if any of them had been in this position. It struck her as unlikely. She was going to have to handle this herself.

'So who knows anything about building rafts?' she asked Sally and Ben hopefully. They both considered the question for all of a second before standing up and heading to the bar. Kate followed them.

'So what was all that about?' Andrew asked Rebecca angrily.

The cold damp air had knocked most of the rage out of her. She just felt foolish now, foolish and scared. She grabbed hold of his hands.

'I don't know what came over me! I think it was the two of you bickering like that. You're better than that. You're better than *him* and he knows it. And look at the way he kept the details of the redundancies from you. You're supposed to be his best friend. You shouldn't trust him!'

Andrew snatched his hands back. 'Ben and I can argue

383

as much as we like! That's our business! We've been friends for years, you've known us for minutes.' He calmed down at the sight of Rebecca's face, which was beginning to crumple, and took her hands again.

'Look Rebecca, you've been unhappy for a while now. I don't know how much of this is my fault but I'll take my share of blame. But can't you just put your personal problems behind you for a few more weeks? Working together will be intolerable if you're going to be like this.'

'It won't happen again,' Rebecca said frantically. 'I know I was wrong but I've got it all out of my system now. And Ben should be a big enough man to be able to brush this off. So can we just forget about this? Please!'

He was surprised at himself, something that had seldom happened to him. He would have expected this final desperate plea to melt his resolve, to be unable to bear hurting her when she was already hurting so deeply.

It was her desperation that pushed him into action. Because he was terrified of what would follow the desperation if they carried on as they had been, the wound between them bleeding profusely over them both. He'd thought that they could just march on the spot for a while longer, hold tight, stop moving, until a more convenient time.

But this was it. Rebecca was getting damaged in the process, by the not-knowing, the pretence, the unspoken last words.

He took a deep breath, hoping his instincts would guide him through this new land. 'Rebecca, I'm so sorry. I don't know . . .'

She put her hands over her ears. 'Don't say it! Please! Not the old clichés. I've heard them all. Please don't!'

He didn't know what to do or say now. She must

384

know what was coming; she couldn't possibly think he might be able to find a way of doing it that wouldn't hurt. But that was asking too much of Andrew. Only someone very experienced in such matters could cope with such a request. Spontaneity comes hard for the terminally repressed.

Then he remembered. It came back to him. It wasn't a cop-out, surely. He was doing this for Rebecca's benefit. She was insisting. His retentive memory had retained the exact words.

'OK, I won't bore you with the old standard clichés of: "It's not you, it's me" and "I still love you but I'm not *in* love with you" or "I don't deserve you." No, you mean more to me than that. So I'm going to be honest even though it doesn't make me look very good. I think we've drawn to a close. If I know it then, deep down, you probably know it too. So before things become nasty, while it's still good between us, I'm ending this.'

He'd looked her in the eyes as he delivered the speech, watching as her despair turned to puzzlement, then horror, then homicidal fury.

She pulled herself back from him as if he were radioactive. 'How could you! How *dare* you! That's exactly what Ben said when *he* dumped me!'

Chapter 22

They stood in the rain, a grey sky casting appropriate gloom over the gloomy group.

'This is a great way to be spending a Sunday morning,' Sally grumbled.

'I suppose you'd normally be at church?' Ben suggested sarcastically. They all smiled at his little witticism.

'Yes, I would,' Sally replied simply, which silenced them instantly. They hadn't learned much of any practical use so far this weekend except how to respond with immediate silence to somebody's grossly mistimed or misjudged comments.

'Oh,' Ben said. 'Sorry.'

Sally smiled at his discomfort, at all their discomfort. They had all been quite at ease with her confession about her teenage pregnancy. But as soon as she mentioned church, they froze to the spot.

'Never mind,' she said to put them all out of their misery.

This odd exchange had the unexpected effect of releasing a lot of the tension that was overwhelming them. They each let go of their individual gripes and resentments and pondered the bizarre concept of someone they knew actually going to church in this day and age. Amazing, was the general consensus.

As they waited for their instructor to come and brief

them they stood separately around the red sheet covering all their materials. They had been ordered not to lift the sheet until they'd been given their instructions.

Kate had considered disobeying the order but after her screaming yesterday, she decided not to assert her authority too noticeably today. She was being treated with real deference and had immediately been offered the table's spare sausage at breakfast this morning, something that would go down in her personal history as the definitive symbol of respect.

Sally walked over to Kate. 'How did you sleep?' she asked amiably.

Kate grinned. 'I don't think any of us slept that well.'

She knew this to be a fact, having heard all the comings and goings of the night, just like the others.

The night had been punctuated almost hourly by Andrew's various groans of pain and irritation as he was trodden upon by every resident of Hotel Happy as they clambered over him to get to the bathroom.

The weirdness of the bustle was heightened by the absence of speech. They all knew that their every word could be overheard so anything that needed to be communicated had to be done with looks and gestures. Kate could only guess at some of the 'communications' by the vicious sighs and crisp thwacks of cotton sheets being yanked over ears that could take no more.

'What about you?' Kate asked, guessing what Sally wanted to be asked.

'I've been so worried about Chrissie,' she said straightaway, which told Kate that she'd been waiting to offload this for a couple of days.

'Why?' Kate asked simply, immensely flattered to be chosen as a confidante.

Sally told her about the unsuccessful attempt to follow

387

Chrissie and find out what she was doing. Then she got to the real reason for approaching Kate.

'I was wondering if you'd have a word with her. I mean, don't let on that I've told you to speak to her, but draw her out of herself, see if she tells you what she's up to without your having to ask her directly.'

Kate was amazed at the request. 'What on earth makes you think your daughter will talk to me?'

Sally was amazed at Kate's amazement. 'Because you have a way with people. They respect you. You give them confidence.'

Do I? Kate thought. Since when? But she could wonder about that later. Her own abilities were irrelevant right now.

'Thank you,' she said abruptly, trying to hide her emotion at such a direct declaration of admiration. She gathered herself before speaking further. 'But this is something you have to do and, frankly, you are better qualified than I am.'

Sally couldn't think of a single area in which she was better qualified than Kate and said so.

'How about motherhood?' Kate asked. 'And how about Chrissie? I know nothing about her. I don't know what has made her the person she is. But you do. She's made up of parts of you!'

'But she won't talk to me!' Sally exclaimed.

'Then talk to *her*,' Kate said. 'Tell her what's worrying you then leave it with her until she's had a chance to decide if she wants to to talk back. Don't corner her or threaten her or make her feel bad. Just talk to her.'

Sally nodded, not convinced by the advice because it hadn't been what she wanted to hear, but prepared to give it some consideration later.

Bernie arrived in a red tracksuit. 'Right, team, you

lucky folks have got me as your instructor today. Now don't cheer too loudly!'

Nobody cheered.

Bernie sauntered along. He didn't care what they thought. They were stuck with him whether they liked him or not; he got paid whether they liked him or not. This was just his job. He didn't take it personally: it was nothing to do with who he was.

'I'm going to uncover your boat now,' he announced and then, with a theatrical flourish, pulled off the red cover to reveal what looked like a rubbish tip.

There were metal drums, pipes, planks, old ropes, plastic sheets. Bernie let them rummage around for a minute or so.

'You have an hour to make a raft capable of carrying all of you across the lake to the other side. All the teams have the same materials. It will be a straight race. OK, your hour starts now.'

Everyone looked at Kate.

'Right,' Justine said, 'this has gone on long enough.'

She came out of the police station, her last port of call on an apparently futile search for a doctor who would agree to see a sick patient on a Sunday morning.

'What did they say?' Steve said, constantly aware of the throbbing agony in his arm.

'They found some phone numbers for me. So I called them all, every one of them.'

'And?' Steve was not in the mood for a long entertaining account of Justine's morning. He'd swallowed some paracetamol earlier which had barely taken the edge off his pain. Now that was wearing off as well.

'And they all said the same thing. That we should go back to our accommodation and wait there until they

389

could get out to us some time today. Almost certainly.'
Justine was livid.

'Did you tell him that we were camping? And that
I'm a doctor and know when I'm ill?'

Justine was annoyed by this interrogation. And tired
from a dreadful night's sleep. Even if she'd taken four
sleeping tablets and been offered a feather bed in a
soundproofed room, she couldn't have slept with Steve.
His temperature had soared and he'd emitted enough heat
to cause condensation to form on the inside of the tent.
This, in turn, dripped on to her face.

But although his temperature was high, his fever made
him shiver and he snuggled up close to Justine for warmth.
It was a form of torture, the only thing missing being
dazzling lights pointing into her eyes and a man in
a uniform with a sinister accent asking for her name
and rank.

Being a doctor, he was an appalling patient and, being
a nurse, she was appallingly intolerant when anyone in
her family was unwell.

But in the morning she saw the extent of his illness
and then became really worried. There was no reception
on her mobile phone in this valley so they'd had to load
up everything and everyone and drive around until she
found a signal. Then she'd pulled out her little booklet
laughably entitled *A Camper's Guide to Facilities in
North Wales*. She blamed herself for not noticing that
this title didn't include the key words: *That are Actually
Available to People in Months With an R in them*.

After wasting thirty minutes in the police station,
during which time the children had eaten all the food
in the caravan, Justine made a decision.

'We're getting you to hospital.'

*

390

'I was doing that!' Ben snapped at Andrew, who was trying to help him tighten a knot.

Andrew pushed Ben's hand out of the way. 'The objective is that the knot holds the wood to the can, so that the raft doesn't fall apart and drop us all in that freezing lake.'

Ben pushed Andrew away and snatched the rope back. 'Gee whiz! Thank you for the lecture on objectives. Oh and by the way, did you know that I was in the Sea Scouts when I was a boy? Surely you did? I thought you must know everything to elect yourself Knot King . . .'

'WILL YOU BOYS SHUT UP AND GET ON WITH THE JOBS I'VE GIVEN YOU!' Kate yelled.

Silence drifted across the lakeside. Kate's tantrums were becoming a major source of entertainment on this dull weekend. Some guests were wondering if Kate had been planted by the course organisers to provoke debate on management techniques.

Kate didn't bother looking around to see if Callum had once more witnessed this absolutely uncharacteristic display of her dictationship. She knew he had. Everyone else had – it was that kind of weekend.

But this seemed to be the only way to break through the aggression that was blinding and deafening her colleagues to any sound except the white noise of rage.

And it worked again.

It had now worked on the three occasions she'd used it in the last twelve hours. She hoped it wasn't going to become a habit, because it wouldn't get her very far in a Post Office queue.

She walked over to the men and pulled Andrew away, taking him to one side where they couldn't be heard.

'Right, that's it! This has been going on since breakfast. Now I know you're pals and maybe this is what you do,

391

have big fights then make up over ten pints of lager, but this is absolutely the worst time for it.'

Andrew glared at her. 'You can't know what he's done, so you have no right to judge me.'

Kate glared right back 'I don't care what he's done and I'm not judging you, I'm telling the pair of you that you have to put whatever it is behind you while we're here. When you get back home, when the Saltech presentation is over, you can take him down an alley and beat him senseless. We are here to undo the bad feeling of the past, not generate a whole bucketload more!'

Bernie jumped right between them, a game-show host's grin across his face. 'This is *good*!' he said. 'You are dealing with rifts promptly, asserting your authority, stamping your management style across the faces of your employees.'

'Go away!' she said irritably to him.

'Okey dokey!' he said cheerfully and tiptoed away, moving on to annoy Rebecca.

Andrew hated Kate. It only lasted a minute or so, but she was an ingredient in the soup blending inside him, a soup made up of all the conflicting events of the last two weeks that had brought him to this. He hated all of them. He felt betrayed, deceived, conned. He felt stupid and naive and trusting. He felt paranoid, suspecting that they'd all known about Ben and Rebecca, all except him.

But eventually a spoonful of reason returned and he had to accept that none of this had anything to do with Kate. She hadn't been around when this happened and she still had no idea what was going on. He was shouting at her, blaming her, when this was the woman who'd caused him to want to give up his job, who was disturbing his sleep. He was lashing out, an action

392

that always involved the risk of hurting an innocent bystander.

Kate watched with fascination as Andrew methodically brought himself back under control. He transformed himself back into the Andrew who'd forced down a plate of food to please her, who'd kissed her innocently and made her blush, who aligned the ruler and stapler on his desk.

'I'm sorry,' he said genuinely.

'I won't ask what has happened because you'd tell me if you wanted me to know,' Kate said, accepting his apology.

Andrew didn't stop to think. 'Ben had an affair with Rebecca before she went out with me,' he said emotionlessly. 'While Jenny was pregnant.'

Kate was struck dumb by this one simple fact that had caused so many complicated consequences. She had no time to go through the story with him now, although she wanted to. She felt like tying Bernie to a barrel, ditching him in the lake and running away from all this, preferably taking Andrew with her. But it was now doubly important that she keep him, and all of them, focused on their work.

Right now they had a warped perspective, believing that nothing mattered beyond the devastation of this single event. But if she left them to it now, then when they finally settled down and had pulled themselves together, they would all be jobless.

She would hold their heads above water, knocking them together if that's what it took, until they were ready for their synchronised swimming act once more.

Andrew stood there waiting for her to tell him where he should go now. Obviously he couldn't return to knots with Ben, nor could she send him to help Rebecca lash wood together. Kate cursed this turn of events that was scuppering all her plans, which had been pretty haphazard from the outset.

She'd have to swap everyone around. Andrew was currently the least stable of them all, so she'd have to keep him with her.

'Come on,' she said encouragingly. 'We're almost ready to get this raft together, let's do some trials with the barrels in the water.'

'Are you all right, Jenny?' Chrissie watched her new friend bending over and breathing heavily.

Jenny stood up again. 'Yeah, I'm fine. Just a twinge.'

'Do you want me to go and get your husband?' Chrissie said, still uneasy at Jenny's restlessness.

'He's the last person I want to see,' Jenny spat. Chrissie was shocked by her harshness.

'Sorry,' Jenny said. 'I didn't mean to disillusion you at such a young age!'

Chrissie's face hardened. 'I hate it when I'm talked down to.'

Jenny was mortified. 'I'm really sorry. I didn't mean to offend you.' She held out her hand to Chrissie.

Chrissie felt guilty for upsetting Jenny at a time like this. She took her hand. 'No, I'm the one who should be sorry. It's just the way you dismissed your husband. It made me . . .' She couldn't go on.

'What?' Jenny asked kindly.

'It made me think of my dad.'

Jenny screwed up her face. She didn't recall hearing about the father. 'What about him?'

Chrissie looked at her sadly. 'That's just it. I haven't got one. My mum made a decision twelve years ago that he wasn't going to have anything to do with me, *she* decided. And that was that. I'm the only girl in my class without a father. I mean, half of my friends have got two!'

Jenny drew Chrissie closer to her, not easy with her bump. 'I'm such an idiot, I didn't even think about that. I'm so sorry!'

Chrissie pulled back and looked at Jenny carefully. 'I'm just saying that you're doing exactly the same thing, deciding that your child isn't going to have a dad – without even thinking about what your child wants. And it's not fair. It's not fair!'

Edie felt Stan's forehead again. 'I don't care what you say, I'm calling for an ambulance.'

Stan moaned and fussed but Edie ignored him until she'd called the hotel reception and asked them to get an ambulance here as quickly as possible.

'Why do you always have to do that?' he snapped at her.

'What?' Edie said. 'You know you're ill. What else am I supposed to do?'

'I just wish you wouldn't do things when I specific-ally say I don't want you to. You're always doing this to me!'

Edie looked at him tolerantly. 'You're just in a state because you're so ill. You'll be fine when the doctors have sorted you out.'

Stan banged his head against the pillow in frustration. 'You're doing it again.'

Edie became alarmed. 'You mustn't get excited! Just lie still. You'll be fine.'

'Stop saying that!' Stan shouted, then fell back on his pillow.

Edie looked at him curiously. This was more than

being ill. It had taken a while to dawn on her. 'What is it, Stan? You've got me worried.'

Stan lay there gazing into space, weighing up the implications of telling her how he felt. Then he turned to her.

'Edie, I want you to think about the last forty years.'

Edie smiled. 'I think about it all the time.'

Stan wasn't smiling. 'Then think about the last time I decided what we were going to do. About anything.'

Edie didn't understand what he was getting at. She shook her head absently.

'Think about the last time I chose where we went on holiday, or when we moved, or when we bought a new car, or what names we gave to our children, or what schools they went to.'

'Stop it, stop it!' Edie cried. 'Why are you saying these things? We've always been partners. I've never done anything without your agreement.'

'Exactly!' Stan said, pulling himself up with difficulty. 'YOU! You made all the decisions. I was a docile rubber stamp, I went along with everything you wanted for a quiet life.'

Edie was shaking as all the certainties of her life became wobbly. She lowered herself on to the bed, unable to look her husband in the eye. She listened to the loud ticking of the cheap hotel clock as she searched her memory for any example of a decision that he'd made. Back she went. One year . . . two years . . . ten years . . .

There was a knock at the door and the paramedics came in.

'It won't float,' Ben stated bluntly.

'Yes, it will,' Andrew said, not sure of his facts but determined to argue with Ben on every issue.

'No, it won't.'

Then they both caught Kate's eye and stopped. She hadn't even needed to open her mouth.

Kate stood in front of the raft. 'Thank you, children! Now the raft is finished and I'm saying that it will float.' She'd had a quick word with Sally about prayer and asked her to put a word in for the buoyancy of this vessel.

Ben was swayed by her confidence. Maybe it will, he thought, maybe it will.

Kate went on. 'We have one more decision to make. There are five of us and all five of us have to reach the other side of the lake. It's a question of balance.'

She waited for them to catch up with her reasoning. Rebecca got there first. 'So one of us has to sit in the middle? What's the big deal?'

'Have you taken a good look at the raft, Rebecca?' Kate asked.

Of course she hadn't. Rebecca had been somewhere else mentally for the whole morning. She didn't know why she was here except she had nowhere else to go. This whole farce was like an out-of-body experience.

She walked over and immediately saw Kate's point. Whoever went in the middle wouldn't be sitting comfortably on a piece of wood but balanced precariously on two pipes held together with the last bit of rope in their pile. A small piece of rope. Tied by Andrew.

'Obviously the lightest person must go in the middle,' Ben said flatly.

'I disagree.' This came from Kate.

Ben snorted. 'How can you disagree? It's a basic rule of engineering.'

'But this isn't an engineering exercise, it's a team-building exercise.' Kate was speaking coldly to Ben and he shivered at her tone.

'No difference,' he said, equally coldly. 'If the bloody raft sinks, we all fall in that bottomless frozen lake and I think you'll find that team morale sinks with it.'

Kate's legs were shaking. She locked her knees to stop them from betraying her.

'The raft won't sink because of the seating arrangements. If it's good, it'll float regardless of the choice of middle person, if it's bad, it'll sink despite our crew obeying the laws of relativity or any other laws. Now we are going to draw lots. I have four long pieces of straw and one short one. We will each pick one and the owner of the short straw will take the central position.'

Ben had never been confronted like this. Except by Jenny of course, and that didn't count because he'd expected as much from marriage. But at work, he expected things to be different. That was why he had always loved his occupation.

Now he was being pushed out at home *and* in his workplace, his haven. He knew he had to fight but he couldn't. He'd never needed to before and he believed it was too late to learn, nor did he want to. He wanted the circumstances to change, not himself.

But the circumstances were in other people's hands, women's hands, and this was Kate's game. She'd won this one.

Not understanding what propelled him, he found himself thrust forward. Avoiding looking at Kate's face, he picked the first straw without saying another word.

The odds of one in five had been in his favour. But he still pulled the short straw.

It was when they were launching the raft into the lake that Callum could bear it no longer.

'Will you take a look at that!' one of his colleagues had said to him, as they watched Kate manoeuvring Ben into the centre of the raft. 'That goes beyond emasculation. The woman is a complete—'

'Yes, she is,' Callum said interrupting, not needing to hear any more. He'd filled in the blank himself.

But there was no more time for recriminations: the whistle had been blown. The race was on.

'Oh God! Chrissie! Go and get someone! Now!' Jenny was bent double in agony.

'But I don't want to leave you alone!' Chrissie cried.

'Just go! Get Ben, get my mum, get anyone!'

Chrissie didn't wait any longer. She ran back to the main house. When she got there, she found Jenny's mother having coffee with her new friend, Matthew.

'Mrs Darlington! The baby's coming! Jenny is screaming for you.'

Barbara panicked. 'But we don't even know where the nearest hospital is. I'll have to call an ambulance!'

'Can't your son-in-law drive you? I'm sure he'll want to,' Matthew suggested.

Barbara hadn't told Matthew about Jenny's marital difficulties.

'He's out playing with boats or some such nonsense!' she snapped. 'No, we'll call an ambulance.'

Matthew put his hand out to calm her. 'That could take ages out here. Listen, I've got a Land Rover out front and I know where the hospital is. Tell me where she is and I'll bring the car round. We should have her at the hospital in twenty minutes.'

'OK,' Barbara agreed gratefully. 'Thank you so much!'

Within five minutes, Jenny was loaded into the car and stretched on all fours across the back seat, braying like a donkey.

Chrissie watched them leave, still breathless and

emotional. They hadn't left her with any instructions but she felt responsible for Jenny and the baby. She'd been there when it started, she thought proudly. And when Jenny felt the baby make its first move, she had called out for her husband.

Chrissie had heard this with her own ears. She couldn't pretend she hadn't. This was the most important moment in the parents' lives as well as the child's first moment. If she could get the dad there for the arrival, well, at least the baby would know that her father loved her enough to be there. Chrissie couldn't do any more.

She started running towards the lake.

'Sit still!' Rebecca said crossly to Ben. 'I can't see where we're going!'

'Not only am I sitting still, I am hunched down so that nobody's vision is obscured. I am not moving my legs even though my feet are in the water and are completely numb. I am performing the role of human ballast like a true star!'

'Stop whingeing!' Sally said, struggling to hold on to the piece of wood serving as an oar. 'It's all right for you. You just have to sit there. We're the ones doing all the work.'

'And whose idea was that?' Ben snapped. 'If we'd done things my way, you would have been in the middle and I'd be rowing.'

Sally glared at Kate, forgetting their earlier rapport. She was cold, wet and exhausted. She didn't care about this team, she was leaving the company soon! Let them sink, then they'd all be rescued and could go and have a cup of tea and get changed into some warm, dry clothes.

Andrew was concentrating on the rowing, wanting to make it across to the other side and get off this thing.

Forget team-building, he couldn't bear being with these people. He hated Rebecca and Ben, was still slightly mistrustful of Sally and Kate was driving him mad with her contradictory moods and behaviour.

Rebecca was fairly mellow about the experience. It was over with Andrew. Ben hated her. Sally had moved on and didn't need her any more. Kate seemed to have turned into Russell Crowe in *Gladiator*, meeting all resistance head on and crushing it. Rebecca was going to be like that in her next job, maybe even in her next relationship.

Meanwhile she was rowing, in, out, in, out, a reassuring rhythm, lulling her, mindless but satisfying. They made visible progress and she didn't have to think about it. She wasn't ready for major thinking yet.

Kate had no space for thought. She was counting the seconds, the minutes until they left this godforsaken place, then the days until she left this godforsaken job and these godforsaken people. She allowed the numbers to fill her brain, hoping her ears would get blocked and she wouldn't have to listen to the whining.

Ben started up again. 'We may not be sinking,' he muttered, 'but we'd be going a lot faster if Sally was sitting here and I was sitting where Rebecca is.'

'Here we go again!' Andrew responded. 'Can't you just shut up? You're throwing us off our rhythm!'

'Andrew, you're going to drop your oar! Stop waving your arms about!' Rebecca yelled.

'Er, listen everyone, can you see that person over there?' Sally was pointing to a figure on the lakeside, waving frantically. She squinted. 'I think it might be Chrissie.'

They all turned to look, causing the raft to wobble violently.

'Careful!' Kate warned.

'She's trying to get our attention,' Sally said. 'She's shouting something.'

Ben sat upright, which almost tipped Rebecca overboard. He could only think of one emergency that would bring someone shouting and waving at them.

'Is it Jenny?' he asked anxiously.

This made Andrew jerk round. 'Is it?' he asked Sally.

'I don't know, I'm trying to hear.' But it was hopeless, they were too far away from her.

But Sally spotted that Chrissie had made contact with the people on the nearest raft, being steered in circles by eight aggressive men shouting at each other. They were passing the message to the next raft.

Kate was still trying to steady their platform. They were all getting soaked by the waves being slopped over them from the erratic movements of Ben and, now, Andrew.

Finally the message reached them. 'Someone's having a baby! They've gone to the hospital! Good luck!'

'Quickly!' Ben shouted. 'Turn this thing round. We've got to get back there now!'

'Ben, sit down or we're all going to fall in! Calm down!'

But it was too late. The raft had developed its own glorious rocking rhythm, an unstoppable to-and-fro, swaying in increasing arcs until, finally, inevitably, the raft turned over.

They were wearing buoyancy jackets which prevented them from drowning but they still had to float there in the water, waiting for rescue. They were too cold to swim, too tired, and the water had a powerful drag to it.

Bernie had called to them when he saw them capsize. 'Stay where you are! We'll come and get you!'

Ben and Andrew were making futile attempts to swim

or move in some way closer to the land where Chrissie was standing, waiting in shock.

But they gave in, feeling the numbness creep up their feet, legs, bodies, hands, arms. Their minds became numb as well, deadening the panic, the anxiety and all the reasons for their mutual animosity.

'Is everyone OK out there?' someone from a passing raft shouted.

'Yes thanks!' Kate called back. 'We're being picked up.'

The man turned to his fellow rafters and began whispering excitedly. Seconds later, they all heard it. Like football fans, the rafting team had prepared a chant that they performed with admirable harmony and timing considering the lack of rehearsal.

Clearing their throats dramatically, they sang:

> 'K-K-K-Katie! Wonderful Katie!
> You're the only d-d-d-doormat we adore!'

The words, the voices, penetrated Kate's frozen consciousness. With the tiniest twist of her head, she took a good look at the seven people waving and cheering at her.

'Hey! Katie! K-K-K-Katie!'

Of all the people to meet, on all the rafts, in all the lakes in Wales, she had to capsize next to the raft made by her old firm.

Chapter 23

Bernie wouldn't let them go to the hospital until they'd taken a shower and changed. Ben argued with him for five minutes.

'I'm not being difficult,' Bernie had said, 'but you have had a severe shock to your system. Any activity without warming yourself up could cause strain on the heart.'

Ben was stunned. 'We're going to the hospital, not hang-gliding! Don't you think that, if we are going to be experiencing any serious problems, the hospital might be the best place to be?'

Bernie was immovable. 'If you insist on disregarding my advice, then you will have to sign a disclaimer stating that you understand that your actions invalidate all insurance relevant to the accident and that . . .'

'Ben, let's just take the shower! We're wasting time here! And we'll be no use to Jenny like this.' Andrew dragged Ben away before he did something physical to Bernie with the disclaimer.

Ben and Andrew ran back to their hut where Kate had already showered and was dressed. 'Where have you been?' she said anxiously.

'Ask him!' Andrew said, angrily, gesturing towards Ben.

But Ben had run into the shower, tearing off his wet clothes on his way. Andrew began stripping himself, oblivious to Kate's presence.

She discreetly withdrew to her bedroom where she

404

began drying her hair with a towel. She listened with amazement to the noise outside. Andrew and Ben were tripping over each other but seemed for now to have put their differences behind them. They'd re-emerge, though, Kate was sure of that.

She was relieved that her own small drama had been temporarily sidelined. Chrissie's message and the capsizing of the raft had relegated the appearance of Kate's former colleagues to third place in everyone's list of concerns. Even so she suspected that they'd get round to it eventually. Especially Andrew if he had heard exactly what had been sung.

Her mobile phone rang. She checked the display, worried that it might be Callum, surprising her again. Although that seemed unlikely after her performance in front of him this weekend.

She didn't recognise the number.

'Hello?' she said.

'Kate, it's Mum.'

'What's up, Mum?' Kate said wearily.

'Now I don't want you to panic, but it's your dad.'

Kate was suddenly alert. 'What's the matter?'

Edie told her what had happened and where they were. 'I'm on my way,' Kate said briefly. 'Tell Dad I'm coming.'

She sat for a moment collecting herself. Neither her mum nor her dad had ever been in hospital during her life. All of Kate's brothers were born at home. They were famous in their neighbourhood for their health. Good genes, they'd agreed amongst themselves.

So Kate had naturally assumed that her parents were immortal. Now the thought that they might move to the other side of the world, that they might die there, took her breath away and wouldn't give it back.

405

She banged open the door to find Andrew half-dressed. They were both far too preoccupied to bother about modesty now.

'I need a lift to the hospital too,' she said.

Andrew took his eyes off his shirt buttons for a second to look at Kate. 'Has something happened?' he asked.

'It's my dad. He's ill,' she said. Then she started crying. For her father. For everything that was wrong and messy when it had once been right and simple.

Andrew put an arm round her, comforting her while finishing his dressing. 'Look,' he said, 'we'll be there in twenty minutes. Your dad will be fine.'

'How do you know?' Kate sniffed, aware that he was trying to make her feel better but wishing he wouldn't.

Andrew lifted her chin and smiled at her. 'Because I know his daughter. She is strong, the strongest woman I've ever known. She takes no prisoners, chops grown men down at the knees, builds boats, she is a modern Boadicea.'

Kate was shaking her head vigorously. 'I'm not any of those things . . .' she began.

Ben came out of his room with a formal shirt hanging over some creased trousers. He looked a recently released prisoner who had got out of the habit of wearing normal clothes. Kate was distracted by the sight. Then she understood. Jenny probably put his clothes out in the morning. And the rest. She probably supervises his haircuts, maybe cutting it herself, reads his reports and corrects his sloppy grammar.

She was not his other half, not even his better half: she was the greater, bigger part of him. No wonder he was distraught at the prospect of losing her. And that was looking a very real prospect.

406

'Tuck your shirt in,' she told him, sounding like his mother, unable to stop herself.

As if she were his mother, he complied.

She pitied him painfully. His vulnerability touched her. Hell, everybody's vulnerability touched her. Sally, Andrew, even Rebecca, she was worried about them all. And now Ben. She was supposed to be stopping this. Let them all worry about her now. But she found herself gently taking the keys from Ben and insisting on driving, even though she wanted to close her eyes and not wake up until everything was better.

Chrissie was still shaking when Sally went to find her in the sun room after she'd showered and changed. She was sitting in an alcove looking out on to the lake where the last rafts were reaching their goal and the last unfit executives were being fished out by Bernie, still proffering disclaimers like cigars to his disgruntled guests.

Sally picked up a jug of hot chocolate and carried it over to her daughter, possessed with love for her, wanting to hold her tight and kiss her a thousand times as she'd done when Chrissie was little.

'Are you OK, little one?' she asked tenderly. 'You must have been frightened.'

'She was in so much pain, Mum,' Chrissie said. 'Did it hurt like that when I was born?'

She'd never asked about her birth before and Sally hadn't given it much thought for many years.

'I suppose so but I can't remember. The wonderful thing about birth is that you get a beautiful child at the end and once a mother sees her child, she forgets all the pain that led up to the arrival.'

'Was Grandma with you?' Chrissie asked.

'No, she couldn't get there in time so I was alone. But it didn't matter, all I cared about was holding you.'

Chrissie breathed in and out three times before finding the courage to say what she wanted to say.

'Mum, do you promise not to shout at me if I ask you a question?'

'Go on then,' Sally replied, relieved that her daughter was still prepared to ask difficult questions, to talk to her.

'Why didn't you let my dad know about me?' she asked bluntly. 'He'd have wanted to be there, I know he would. And you might have been grateful. Jenny didn't want her husband to be there because they'd had a fight or something, but she called out his name when it was hurting.'

Sally ached for Chrissie. 'Oh, sweetheart, that's different. I was fourteen. And so was the boy! It seems silly calling him the father at that age!'

'But you were fourteen and you were my mother,' Chrissie said stubbornly.

Sally had always dreaded this conversation. She held Chrissie's hands and faced her firmly. 'Now you must listen to this carefully. I kept you because I wanted you. Your . . . father didn't want a child. I knew that. No fourteen-year-old boy wants to be a father. If he'd been there at the birth, it wouldn't have made any difference, he was too immature to grasp the reality of what was happening.'

'But what about later, when you were older? Perhaps you could have told him then? Or now?' Chrissie was getting worked up.

Sally shook her head. 'I know how badly you miss having a dad, but that isn't the answer. It would be far worse for you to become excited at the thought of having a father only for him to reject you.'

'I still want to see him,' Chrissie insisted.

Sally sipped her hot chocolate, praying for inspiration. Then she glanced at Chrissie, who was sticking her chin out, and understood that this decision was no longer hers to make. It was time to acknowledge that her daughter was growing up and had rights. The thought frightened her as it offered a foretaste of the time, not far in the future, when Sally would be alone again.

What excuses would she have then?

'OK,' she said suddenly.

'What?' Chrissie asked suspiciously.

'I'll start making some enquiries about . . . him. But I can't promise anything. And you're going to have to trust me to make the first approach. If he doesn't want to have anything to do with you, then you'll have to accept that.'

Chrissie jumped up, spilling her drink, and hugged Sally. 'Oh thanks, Mum. I've wanted this for so long. Thank you!' She sat down again, her eyes shining.

Sally enjoyed the moment before calculating that this might be the best time to take a big risk.

'Chrissie, now that I've proved I'm the world's greatest mother, do you promise not to shout at me if I ask *you* a question?'

'Go on then,' Chrissie agreed, amused at her mother's nervousness.

So Sally asked her about the money.

Andrew and Barbara sat in the waiting room, occasionally jumping up when a doctor or nurse passed.

'I can't believe she wanted him in there,' Barbara moaned for the tenth time.

Andrew was losing his patience with her. 'He's her husband, Mum!'

409

'Huh! After the way he treated her, I wouldn't call him a husband.' Barbara folded her arms, ready for a fight.

'That's funny. You still insist on calling Dad your husband though he left years ago, has a new wife and family and, according to you, was a dead loss as a husband in the first place.'

Barbara hated it when either of her children quoted her back. 'That's different. Anyway, I don't know how you can defend Ben. He's betrayed you as well.'

Andrew closed his eyes. He'd thought of little else since Rebecca's confession yesterday. 'I know, but I'm dealing with that. In fact I'm more angry with you right now.'

Barbara looked astonished. 'What have I done?'

'You knew about this and you chose not to tell me. What's more, you went to see *my* girlfriend to deliver an ultimatum, without telling me. Do you not think that, now I'm thirty-eight, you might accord me a little more respect? This is not school, I'm not being bullied by a fourth-former for my dinner money, I don't need my mum to go round to his mum and make threats on my behalf.'

Barbara switched on her most well-practised martyred expression. 'So that's what I get for trying to protect you and Jenny! All I want—'

Andrew wouldn't let her finish. 'Mum, we both know what you want. You want to live our lives for us, prevent our mistakes, interfere with our decisions. That was fine when we were five but not any more.'

Barbara's martyrdom was approaching Joan of Arc's in epic status. 'I can't help it if I love you.'

Andrew refused to be swayed by her tactic. 'Forget it, Mum. I've heard it a thousand times before. So we both know what you want for us. Now I'm going to tell you what Jenny and I want for you, what we've always

410

wanted. We want to be part of your life but not *all* of
your life. We want you to have other things, other people
to occupy your time. We want you to say that you can't
come to lunch at the drop of a hat because you have
other plans. We want you to say goodbye to the past,
to Dad. And start again.' He spoke more kindly now. 'I
think it's time, don't you?'

Before she could respond, a nurse popped her head
round the door. 'Would you like to come through now?'

Barbara and Andrew followed the nurse into the ward,
an arm's length distance apart from each other.

Justine made her way through to the ward where Steve
had finally been settled. He was attached to a drip and
was looking pale but less anxious.

They'd both been surprised that his condition had risen
to the status of an emergency by the time they'd reached
the hospital. 'How long has it been like this?' the junior
doctor had asked sternly.

Steve had completely forgotten that he was a far more
senior, experienced doctor than this boy and instantly
became the perfect patient, passive, compliant and apologetic.

'Sorry,' he and Justine had both said, unnecessarily.
Justine glared at Steve with the immediately recognisable
'I told you so' unspoken message that husbands every-
where could decipher.

'Couldn't you see the red of the infection spreading
towards your chest?' the junior asked.

'We were in a tent, the torchlight wasn't that strong,'
Justine replied, scowling at Steve while she was speaking
to the doctor.

Steve groaned inwardly. He would suffer for this for
years. It would become a regular anecdote, wheeled out

411

whenever they had friends over, embellished with each telling. And he couldn't believe he was thinking this, but he was looking forward to it.

He longed for all the blissfully dull normality of married life that had evaded them over the last two weeks. He longed for Justine to nag him because he rolled up his socks into balls before putting them in the washing. He longed for her to drive him mad by talking for half an hour on the phone to Kate in her loudest voice, all through *A Question of Sport*. He longed for them to talk about school runs in bed while she read a trashy romance and he cut his toenails.

He suddenly took her hand. The junior doctor noticed and felt obliged to reassure him. 'It's OK. I think we've caught it just in time. You're not going to die!'

Steve smiled at him. 'I never thought I was. I'm just looking forward to starting living again.'

Justine frowned, not understanding what he was talking about. Probably the infection, she told herself, must be making him delirious. But she squeezed his hand back. Look on the bright side, she thought. While he's in hospital, the kids and I can move into a hotel. No more instant mash. No more tent.

That made *her* smile.

Jenny sat up in bed, transfixed by her daughter, as she and Ben waited for the nurse to fetch Barbara and Andrew.

'She is the most beautiful thing I've seen in my life,' Ben whispered, hoarse with emotion as well as the beginnings of a bad chill.

Jenny either didn't hear him or chose not to respond. Ben couldn't leave it. He had to know before the others got here and any conversation apart from baby talk was impossible.

412

'We are going to be OK, aren't we?' he asked very quietly, part of him hoping Jenny wouldn't hear him and he could spend a few more seconds pretending everything was going to fine.

Jenny stopped cooing at the baby for a second, indicating that she'd heard his question. She was exhausted from the birth and sore from the stitches. She'd not thought of Ben and Rebecca for over four hours and was grateful to the pain for that.

But he was right. They needed this sorted out now. Chrissie had made her see how important it was that things were established for a baby from the first minute of life. This baby might not know or care who her parents were just now or even for the next six months or so. But she would grow up, as Chrissie had. When that happened, Jenny wanted to be able to answer her questions in the sure knowledge that all decisions had been taken with the baby's interest in mind, not Jenny's and certainly not Ben's.

She heard Barbara and Andrew approach and decided quickly. Without looking away from the baby, she said, 'You're her father, she needs you.'

Ben held his breath for a while longer, hoping she would go on to say that *she* needed him.

But she didn't say it. Now Ben had to decide if this was going to be enough for him.

Edie sat next to Stan's bed wanting to hold his hand but not daring to. She saw the tube going straight into his chest and another tube attached to his nose. He looked weak, ill and old. She loved him so much that it hurt. She wished she could be in that bed instead of him.

Have I ever told him that I felt like that? she wondered.

413

She couldn't even remember when she'd last said that she loved him at all. Or when he'd said it to her. They'd got out of the habit at some stage. Or did I get out of the habit first? she asked herself.

In the intervening hours while Stan was being tended by worried doctors and nurses, she'd had plenty of time to muse over his last unexpected words. Surely he'd been mistaken? It must have been the pneumonia taking hold, fogging his memory.

She promised herself that, when he woke, she would be able to present him with clear evidence that he was quite mistaken in his harsh judgement of her. They'd had the perfect marriage, everyone said so. They hardly ever argued. They were always laughing and singing, always attuned.

But she went back to his earlier accusation. He must have made some of their decisions. She mulled over the big family issues, like when they had children and how many. Well, obviously that had been down to her, it went without saying that this was the woman's decision. And moving house affected her more than Stan since she stayed at home, so of course she decided all the details to do with that.

Then she moved on to all the other matters. How could Stan possibly expect her to phone him up in the day and consult him on all the daily trivia that she had to deal with? He should be grateful that she took all this out of his hands.

And she liked to surprise him by arranging all the holidays. Besides, she had more time. She was with the children all day, so it made sense that she would know better than him what was best for them.

Stan had been gone for three hours. After three hours, she had run out of excuses and justifications. She hadn't

414

been able to come up with a single occasion where she had ever asked Stan his opinion, where he had given his opinion and where she had gone along with it.

Oh my God! she thought. What have I done?

Rebecca enjoyed the solitude of the hut. She lay on her bunk and fell unexpectedly asleep. It was liberating to know that it didn't matter if she snored or shouted obscenities in her sleep. Although the nap only lasted an hour, she woke up feeling revitalised. Knowing that Barbara, Ben, Jenny and Andrew were all elsewhere helped her feel upbeat about going over to the bar for a drink by herself. There was nobody she was afraid of meeting.

Being free of fear was a wonderful feeling. It had been a long time since she could enjoy such a blessing. She promised herself never to make choices that would place her in such a dire situation again.

She walked into the bar, bought herself a glass of wine, and found a seat by a window. The bar had been opened early for the benefit of all the rafting crews who had been transported back, wet, cold and very disgruntled.

Bernie had learned quickly during his first twenty-four hours in this job that there was no customer relations problem that could not be eased by opening the bar.

Rebecca felt surprisingly comfortable by herself. Maybe this was because the company she had been keeping in recent weeks had caused her such trouble. She looked out of the window, enjoying the view. She thought she could see Sally and Chrissie strolling through the grounds enjoying each other's presence.

She envied them both. She envied Sally for having Chrissie, for always having someone or something constantly there in her life, always the same, unchanging. And, maybe even more, she envied Chrissie for having Sally as her mother. She wanted to leap through the window, run after them and beg them to hold tight to each other, to never let each other go, no matter what the other might say or do.

'Can we join you?'

The voice made Rebecca jump. She saw that a group of six men and women were looking for somewhere to sit. They looked as tired as she'd felt when she'd climbed out of the water and she immediately invited them to sit down.

'Barry Dixon,' the first man said.

'Rebecca Ramsden,' she replied, shaking hands.

They went round the table giving their names, all of which Rebecca promptly forgot.

Barry noticed Rebecca's damp hair. 'Did you fall in too?' he asked, pointing to his own wet hair.

Rebecca nodded. 'Afraid so. What happened to you?'

The group began giggling, all talking at the same time. They'd obviously enjoyed the exercise more than we did, Rebecca observed wryly.

'It was Chris, he was going in when he should have been going out . . .'

'You can talk, I wasn't the one who suddenly stood up . . .'

'That's because I had water in my trousers!'

This went on until the story was told. Rebecca still had not the slightest idea what had happened.

Barry looked at Rebecca again. 'Didn't I see you in the water with Kate Harris?'

Rebecca looked surprised. 'How do you know Kate

Harris?' she asked, vaguely remembering the people on a raft all singing some kind of rugby song at Kate. But she hadn't paid much attention to the lyrics, being somewhat more concerned that she was developing hypothermia.

Again the noisy group all began talking at the same time. Rebecca listened to them in amusement.

'We used to work with her. She was great!'

'We *loved* Katie! She was such a fantastic sport.'

'She'd do anything for anyone! She was never too busy to help someone out.'

'And she was never one of those bossy cows you sometimes get who try to act like a man.'

'She was gorgeous! We really miss her.'

Rebecca took in all these eulogies, wondering if they were talking about the same person.

'I bet you couldn't believe your luck when she turned up!' Barry said. 'You never know what you're going to get when they tell you a woman's got a job.'

'Hey!' one of the two female group members said, in mock objection. 'Nothing wrong with women in power!'

'Unless you're working for one,' the other woman said, which made them all collapse laughing.

'I bet she's had a few tales to tell you about us!' another man chuckled.

Rebecca thought about this. 'Actually, she hasn't said anything.' Now she came to think about it, this was a bit odd. It was as if she'd been dropped into their office one day by a passing alien ship. She didn't speak about her past at all, not even in professional terms.

'She must have told you about the doormat!' Barry said finally.

'What doormat?' Rebecca asked.

*

Stan had woken up, groggy and sore, to find his wife babbling at him. He could grasp about every fourth word but he gradually got the message.

'I don't know how you've put up with me! Why didn't you tell me? Why didn't you argue with me? If I'd known what I was doing, I would have stopped. I would have changed . . .'

Stan lifted a weak finger to her lips to stop her. 'Sssh. Not now. I shouldn't have said what I did. It was the illness, not me.'

Edie covered up her face with her hands. 'That's not true! You said it because it was true. Even I know that now. I've been a terrible wife! I can't believe you didn't leave me!'

Stan let his finger drop to the bed. The action silenced Edie.

Stan wanted to be left alone to sleep, doze, be spoonfed soup, be dripfed narcotics. But Edie wouldn't stop until he'd laid the subject to rest. He gathered what little strength he had.

'Don't torture yourself. You were the best wife. Always. And you were the best mother. What difference does it make who chose what name for which child?'

Edie was momentarily pacified. 'But you were right. I was so pushy, so presumptuous.'

Stan shut his eyes. 'Please, Edie, not now.'

Edie backed down, sensing that he was not strong enough for this at the moment. She changed the subject, looking for something that might cheer him up.

'I was thinking about that lovely Geraint and what he said about our big dream. Do you remember?'

Stan remembered more than he dared say. It had opened a wound he'd hoped was long healed.

Edie continued. 'And then it came to me. When we

418

were on our honeymoon, there was that bus trip round the coast, do you remember?'

Stan nodded. Edie was encouraged.

'And we got out at that beach? And we saw that family all playing cricket on the beach?'

Stan could see them as if it had been yesterday.

Edie grabbed Stan. 'And that's when we decided. What our big dream was. You *must* remember. We looked at that family and said, "If God blesses us with a big healthy family like that our life together will be complete." That's what we said.'

'It's what *you* said,' Stan found himself replying.

Edie recoiled. 'Are you saying that you didn't want all of our children?'

Stan shook his head, tiring rapidly under this interrogation. 'Of course I'm not. I'm just saying that it wasn't *my* dream, it was *your* dream.'

Edie didn't know him any more. She now had to face the fact that their life had been built on the sand of a lie. She became angry.

'When you're married, Stan, you assume that your dreams are shared. I mean, all this stuff about going to New Zealand. When did I ever say I wanted to go there? That was *your* dream.'

Stan looked at her. 'Do you think I don't know that? But the difference is that I shared your dream. You don't want to share mine, do you?'

Edie didn't get a chance to answer. Kate arrived, marching into the ward, smiling bravely.

'Hi, Mum! Oh, Dad! I've spoken to the doctor and he says you should be fine.' She bent to kiss them both. 'You gave me such a scare. What were you thinking of going out in that sort of weather?' Her mum had explained about their outing yesterday. It seemed a probable cause for Stan's illness.

'Still,' she went on, more brightly now. 'At least you won't get weather like this in New Zealand!'

Edie and Stan both looked away from her and from each other.

Chapter 24

This was the worst part, just sitting around waiting.

They all felt that the presentation had gone well but it was so hard to tell. Everyone had played the match of their careers. Sally had put in a lot of unpaid overtime to produce some impressive graphics on the handouts. Andrew had worked like a trouper to check and double-check all the statistics that Rebecca had collated.

They'd become a seamless team, bonded by a shared experience that had affected all of their lives. They hadn't needed a team-building exercise to fix themselves back together on their return to London. There was nothing else to say. In fact, words were studiously avoided, each of them now appreciating the damage that could be inflicted by words, spoken harshly, casually or deliberately omitted.

Everything was out in the open. Instead of making them feel awkward, they felt purged. They truly did believe they were starting afresh, each assessing every other person from a new perspective

There was only one secret and that was being kept by Rebecca. She'd listened to the story of the doormat with astonishment. She'd immediately felt for Kate and couldn't imagine her humiliation at such a cruel gift. Possibly if any of the others had been told the story, they might have failed to spot the connection between the present and Kate's subsequent behaviour in her new job.

But Rebecca got it instantly, because she would have done exactly the same herself. She had been reinventing herself gradually since that first disappointment, when she had learned that she had been deceived by her parents for years and that, therefore, she wasn't who she thought she had been.

Nothing had compared to the dramatic sweep of that early example of enforced enlightenment. All her subsequent successes and failures had been relatively slim. Well, nobody had died or ended up in prison. But each result had led her to instigate modest changes in herself, to react positively or negatively, in her quest to become the person she was supposed to be.

'Is something wrong?' Kate had asked her when she'd returned from visiting her father in hospital.

She couldn't ignore the strange looks that Rebecca had been flicking towards her all evening.

Rebecca hadn't planned what to do with her new information. But Kate was looking tired and worried, and Rebecca knew now that this was a woman who had been given a doormat and survived it, even triumphed over it. She admired Kate for this and took hope from one woman's victory over unpromising circumstances.

'I'm just exhausted,' she said amiably, deciding that she would never tell anyone Kate's secret, not even Andrew. That was up to Kate.

But Andrew already knew. He'd had the same conversation with the same people a few hours after Rebecca. Once they'd realised that Kate was keeping it a secret, they felt honour-bound to share it with everybody. Even Bernie heard the full saga.

Andrew hadn't been as surprised as Rebecca. This unravelled the final knots in Kate that he hadn't been able to loosen. Finally Kate, the real Kate, came to life for him. She was flawed and she was vulnerable. And at last she made sense to him.

'I thought they said they'd be letting us know this morning?' Sally said anxiously.

'It *is* still the morning,' Kate said.

'It's five past twelve,' Ben argued, as nervous as them all.

'But that depends on whether your definition of "morning" is the period before noon or the period before lunch, which gives them up to one o'clock or thereabouts.' Andrew was calmly, reassuringly pedantic.

Ben didn't argue with Andrew. They'd stopped arguing. Their friendship was in crumbs and they didn't know if it could be rebuilt, but they'd formed a cautious truce since Flora's birth.

'Do it for me,' Jenny had begged.

Andrew had been holding his niece, a shrewd move by Jenny to stop him from overreacting. He hadn't been able to tense his muscles. This child was so fragile, so tiny. He was terrified of squeezing her too tightly, he loved her so much. All he wanted now was to ensure that nothing hurt Flora, ever.

He went to hand her back to Jenny, but his sister had plunged her hands into a bowl of washing up, determined that they would finish this conversation while he was physically restrained.

'I don't understand how you could have taken him back!'

'You don't have to,' Jenny replied calmly. 'It's nothing to do with you.' This sounded cool but was a bluff contrived to conceal the fact that she didn't have

423

a convincing rationale behind her decision.

If she had been forced to pick a single motivating factor, she would have pointed to Chrissie and her profound pain at having grown up without a father. Jenny was still a new mum, her faculties for judgement and discernment warped temporarily by her all-encompassing love for Flora.

She couldn't imagine there ever being a time when she would have desires for herself again. She was absolutely sure that she would want to spend every second of the rest of her life providing for her daughter, protecting her and generally smothering her with the sort of warm-clothes-in-summer attention that Barbara had lavished on her children throughout her life, driving them both to paralysing despair.

'Besides,' Jenny said, 'I am the wronged party here, not you.'

Andrew became indignant. 'I disagree. Both he and Rebecca lied to me.'

'Yes,' Jenny conceded. 'But they had their affair before you and Rebecca ever became involved. And you know that Ben would have confided in you if he hadn't been married to your sister.'

Andrew looked back to the years before Ben and Jenny's marriage. Ben had never hidden his sexual conquests from Andrew, never seeing anything wrong with them. Jenny was right, of course she was. But Andrew resented having his justifications for resentment taken away from him.

'Am I not allowed to feel hurt for how he treated you?' he asked.

Jenny looked at him fondly. 'Of course you are,' she said, 'but if I say I've forgiven him, then you are not doing me any favours by prolonging all this ill-feeling.

If you don't want to continue the friendship, then that's up to you, but I want you at least to be civil to him. I don't want Flora to grow up sensing tension between you. Because one day she'll want to know the reason.'

Again she thought of Chrissie, a tormented adolescent searching for every answer to every question that her short life had generated.

Andrew delicately pulled his niece more closely to him. 'OK,' he said, reluctantly. 'But we can never be friends again.'

He really missed having a friend, now. He wanted to talk to someone about Kate.

Kate sat nervously twirling a piece of material from her dress round her finger. She was wearing the dress that she'd bought for her lunch with Callum. On returning from Wales, she'd gone back to the same shop and allowed the woman there to guide her towards some more new ideas.

She felt much happier dressed like this, different to her doormat days, different to her scumbag days. And she'd noticed that her colleagues had instantly felt more relaxed around her in the new clothes. Incredible, she'd laughed to herself. I wished I'd known this ten years ago.

She looked at her watch again. 'Twelve twenty,' she said unnecessarily. She hoped her mum wouldn't ring again. She'd phoned every fifteen minutes since half past ten and Kate had yelled at her to stop calling, promising that she would let her know as soon as they had any news.

She realised that her mum was trying to keep busy, to keep her mind occupied.

Kate had been shocked when she'd gone to see her parents after their return from Wales. The house had

425

been so quiet. Packing cases sat in the middle of the living room floor, half-packed where Stan had left them before their holiday.

'Your dad's upstairs in bed,' Edie had said. 'Go up and see him. He's been looking forward to your visit. I'll make a cup of tea and bring it to you.'

Kate had climbed the stairs, ignoring a brooding sense of dread.

'Hi Dad!' she'd said. 'You're looking much better.' This was almost true. He looked better than he had in hospital but he seemed smaller somehow.

'Come and tell me what you've been up to, love!' he said affectionately.

Kate pulled a chair over beside the bed. 'Let me see. Starting in Wales. Well, we didn't win the "Team of the Weekend" trophy and we didn't win the rafting race and we didn't even bother entering the all-day challenge on Monday which would have involved us being tied together, blindfolded and abandoned, with no more than Twix bars, on a mountain from where you had to get back to base in five hours.'

'What did you do instead?' Stan asked, enjoying the light relief from Edie's tendency to burst into tears for no reason.

'We all signed disclaimers in quadruplicate and went down the pub where we stayed all day, apart from breaks for hospital visits.'

She left out a few things, such as Callum's company winning all the trophies and Callum smiling nervously at her before leaving Wales without saying another word to her. At the end she'd seen him exchanging phone numbers with another female guest, someone who hadn't taken part in the rafting challenge because she couldn't swim. And was sick on boats. And had long hair that took

426

ages to dry. And probably made coffee for everyone in her office.

'What have you done to that man?' Sally had asked. 'He seems petrified of you.'

'I think he's just scared of women,' Kate had observed, recognising the truth as soon as she'd said it.

'And what about that man you mentioned?' Stan asked, enjoying this rare time with Kate by himself.

Kate had told them of her confused feelings for Andrew and the part he'd played in her decision to give this job up. It had been something to say in hospital to fill the strained silences between her parents.

'The only thing I have to decide now is how much I tell him,' she said.

'About what?' Stan asked.

'About who I am. And how deceitful I've been,' Kate replied.

Stan shook his head. 'There's nothing to say, sweetie. You're not planning to work with him again are you?'

Kate shook her head emphatically. 'Definitely not! The one thing I've learned is the importance, the necessity, of separating the professional from the private with a big, unscalable wall. Anyway, I've already decided, I'm not going to work with anybody.'

She was clear on this. Her relationship with Andrew was going to be strictly personal. She smiled at the prospect.

Stan smiled back. 'Then there's no need to say anything. Do you think your mum has any idea of what I was like in work? Whether I was tyrannical? Or a doormat?'

Kate wagged her finger at him. 'Careful!' she said. 'Besides, I'd bet you were exactly the same at work as you are at home.'

427

'Then you'd lose your bet. Nobody is exactly the same in the workplace. We all adapt, we have to.'

'But now Andrew has seen what I can be like,' Kate countered.

Stan nodded. 'And is still interested in you. Which means it doesn't matter.'

'But the person he's interested in isn't the real me!' Kate was becoming argumentative. She was engaging in this debate with herself on a nightly basis.

'So what?' Stan said. 'Do you think your mother married the "real me" or even knows the "real me" after forty years?'

Kate was disturbed by the way his voice had dropped, as if he were telling her a secret that he hadn't shared with her mother.

'How can she not know you after all this time?' she asked.

Stan looked up to the ceiling. 'Because I loved your mother, because I still do, I let her believe I was different. That I wanted the same things she wanted, that I was happy if she was happy, that her dream was my dream.'

Now Kate understood. 'The New Zealand move. That's always been your dream, hasn't it?'

Stan nodded sadly. 'And staying here, building a life around our family, that's your mum's. But it's mine as well.'

Kate saw her father's aching sadness and wanted to weep for him. 'But Dad, you must have known that Mum would find it difficult to leave when the grandchildren were still coming.'

'My mistake, Kate, and one I want you to learn from, was to think that I was entitled to two dreams.' He held her hand tightly. 'So pick your dream very carefully, Kate. It might be your only one.'

428

Edie bounced into the bedroom singing, 'Tea for three and three for tea . . .' chirpily.

Stan sat up. 'Lovely, just what I wanted.'

'So what have you two been gossiping about?' Edie asked as she spooned sugar into her husband's tea, even though he'd been asking her not to for five years.

'This and that,' Stan said, winking at Kate.

'Did you tell her our news?' Edie said.

'You tell her, love.' Stan concentrated on his tea as if it were a cryptic crossword.

'Well, there are two pieces of news, actually. One is that Frank and Denise are expecting again.'

Kate spluttered, spitting tea over her lap. Her sister-in-law had said she would be having her tubes tied after the birth of her last child. In four years he hadn't ever slept for more than three consecutive hours. He never ate anything apart from frankfurters and cheese triangles. And he'd been barred from every playgroup in the Northeast by the age of three.

'She seemed a bit shocked,' Edie commented. 'I think it might have been a bit of an accident.'

Kate chuckled at the word 'accident'. She suspected that this was not the word being bandied around at Frank and Denise's house at the moment.

'And our other piece of news,' Edie announced, 'is the best. You're the first person we've told. And before you say anything, this was your dad's decision.' She put an odd emphasis on the word 'decision', waiting for Stan to confirm that this was true.

He smiled encouragingly and held out his hand for her to take.

Edie went on. 'Your father has decided – that we won't be moving to New Zealand after all!'

*

429

'How about Las Vegas? Or Ibiza? Or Club 18–30?'

Steve read out the destinations from the classified columns at the back of the paper.

Justine was laughing as Steve went on.

'Lapland to see Santa? Or Mardi Gras in New Orleans? Or a Cossack dancing course in Kiev?'

'OK! OK!' Justine cried. 'You win! We'll go on holiday. But *we'll* choose, not you.'

Steve pretended to look hurt. 'But I've just told you all my favourite choices.'

Justine put her hands on her hips. 'Steve, you would hate Las Vegas. And as for Club 18–30!'

Steve tucked his arms round her waist. 'But you would love it. So I think we should go.'

Justine moved his hands out of the way so that she could push him into a chair and plonk herself on his lap.

'And I don't,' she said firmly. 'This is our first holiday without the kids. We're going to choose somewhere we both want to go.'

He looked at her hair, which she had blow-dried straight so that the more extreme sticking-up tufts were under control. Like her more extreme impulses to change herself.

'That wasn't my most brilliant idea,' she'd concluded to Steve during his second day in hospital. 'I couldn't keep up with myself. The only thing that was constant in my life was my name.'

'And even that wasn't your own, it was Kate's,' Steve had pointed out reasonably, earning himself a sharp slap on the knee. 'But you must have felt something was missing in your life to want to change it?' Steve had gone on to ask.

Justine screwed up her nose. 'Do you know something? My mistake was not realising that *everybody* feels something is missing from their lives! I was distracted by

430

Kate and what she was doing to herself. It put an idea in my head. But if I hadn't been so crazy, I would have chucked it out the same way I close my ears when some daft old bat tries to read me my horoscope!'

Steve looked mystified. 'But I don't feel anything's missing from my life. Does that mean that I am the different one? Or that I may start feeling like this one day?'

Justine stroked his kind, unchanged face. 'Maybe, but you'd better promise that you tell me when that day comes. No sneaking out to shops to buy chest wigs and male corsets!'

Steve thought about this. 'The day you need to worry is when I start asking to borrow those booster pants of yours.'

Justine tried to punch him affectionately, accidentally catching him in the shoulder which was not fully healed.

'Aah!' he yelled. 'That hurt!'

'That's what happens when you try and change things that shouldn't be changed,' she said smugly.

Steve dropped to his knees suddenly, letting her collapse on the floor in a heap. As she rolled on the floor, giggling helplessly, he thought she looked sixteen. Again.

They heard the phone ring in Ben's office. Everyone jumped as Ben dashed off into the office to take the call.

'Hi Mum, it's me.'

'Hello, Jenny. Listen, I can't stop, I'm off out. Is everything OK?'

'Er, yes. I just called up for a chat and to see how you were. So where are you off to?'

431

'Matthew's coming down for a week. We're meeting in town for lunch then . . . who knows?'

Jenny could hear her mum's happiness and wished she could hug her.

'That's great! And maybe you could bring him over for dinner one night?'

Barbara hesitated.

'Mum!' Jenny warned.

'Sorry, love. Look, I've said I'll make an effort with Ben, that's all I can promise.'

'That's all I'm asking. Thank you,' Jenny said gratefully. 'And have a great time,' she added.

'I intend to,' Barbara replied with absolute determination.

Jenny put the phone down, glad that her mother had finally agreed to come to dinner. Having Matthew there would help keep them all civilised.

'Great!' Ben had said eagerly. Ben said everything eagerly to Jenny nowadays. He would willingly have had her name tattooed on his shoulder by the hygienically challenged Ricardo if it would have made her look at him the way she used to.

He let Jenny dictate every step in this process that he hoped would lead to a healing. She'd been frank with him in the hospital. Agonisingly frank.

'I stopped loving you the moment I heard about you and Rebecca,' she'd said coldly. 'And that hasn't changed. But I don't have the right to deprive our daughter of her father. You and I both know what it's like not to have a father at home. So I'm giving you the opportunity to try again. We'll be starting from scratch and I can't promise I'll ever get those old feelings back. I may never love you again. So it's up to you if you want to try.'

432

Ben hadn't needed any time to think about the offer. He'd accepted gratefully. It was more than he'd dared hope for. He would put up with her lack of affection, her occasional bitter remarks, the tormenting daily reminder of how they'd once been. This incredible stroke of luck was the second chance that so few people receive after a big mistake. And he intended to hold tight to it until the next stroke of luck came along. He knew it would. It always did. It had to.

They all looked at Ben, drinking in every line around his mouth and eyes, each wanting to be the first to guess the news by reading his face.

He allowed his eyes to wander over each of them. Then he sighed a big melodramatic sigh.

'We got it,' he said.

Sally had cried when Chrissie had told her what she'd been doing.

'Why couldn't you tell me?' she'd said. 'I've been so worried!'

Chrissie groaned. 'Have you never heard of the concept of surprise, Mum?'

'But whatever made you think I needed money?' Sally had asked, blowing her nose without dignity into a piece of toilet paper.

'I knew how unhappy you were at work, Mum. And you never spend any money on yourself. So I figured that you only did that job because of me, to buy me things. So I was going to prove to you that I could take care of myself. Then you could find a job you really liked, even if it paid less money.'

Sally thought back to that fourteen-year-old boy who had incidentally been the father of this remarkable child.

433

Had he been that special? Sally asked herself. Because she couldn't identify any part of herself that could have been responsible for Chrissie's unselfishness. Sally hadn't been like that when she twelve and she was certainly not like it now that she was twenty-six.

'I can't believe you've made so much money,' she said finally when she'd run out of tissue and was forced to use some self-control.

Chrissie laughed. 'Neither can I! But parents are happy to pay £15 an hour for extra tutoring. And you know how easy I find my school work. I was helping out my mates anyway. So when their parents told me they'd pay if I could make it a regular thing, well . . .' She shrugged.

Sally stared at her, proud and confused by this change-ling. 'Right,' she said. 'Thank you. Thank you so much for doing this for me. But it isn't necessary. I want you to use that money for yourself. To have fun. Because you've earned it. Then I'd like you to stop giving the extra lessons.'

Chrissie opened her mouth to protest but Sally stopped her.

'Just let me finish. I'd like you to stop so that you can concentrate on your own work. I know you find it easy and that's because you're clever. That means that you'll be able to do anything you want. Anything. And that makes you the luckiest person alive. Anywhere. So don't think about me. Think of yourself and just go. Don't look back.'

'What about you?' Chrissie asked worriedly.

Sally patted her on the hand. 'I'm going to do something no mother has ever done in the history of mother/daughter relationships.'

'What's that?' Chrissie said.

434

'I'm going to change and become more like my daughter.' Then Sally laughed loudly, much to her daughter's adolescent embarrassment.

After the hugs and the tears and the congratulations, Ben brought out the champagne which he opened with a satisfying pop.

'To you all!' he said, raising his glass. 'The winners!'

'The winners!' they all cheered, clinking glasses noisily.

Rebecca approached Ben quietly.

'Er, Ben. Can I have a really quick word please?'

Ben frowned. 'Can't it wait half an hour? Let's just enjoy this for a bit. You deserve it as much as the others.'

'It'll only take a minute,' she pleaded. She wanted to do this quickly while she still had the courage.

Ben was irritated by the interruption. 'All right,' he sighed, 'but I've got an announcement to make first.'

Rebecca stepped back, wondering what else there was for him to say.

Ben cleared his throat to attract everyone's attention. It took a couple of minutes but, eventually, there was quiet. His voice faltered as he spoke. 'As you know, I've made something of a pig's ear of my marriage recently. And behaved less than professionally in so doing. But amazingly, astonishingly and utterly undeservedly, Jenny has given me a second chance.'

Andrew looked down, biting back the bile.

Ben went on. 'So I need to demonstrate that I appreciate this chance by clearing away all the dead wood that's holding us both back. All the bad memories, bad associations, it all has to go.'

'Have you found a new job?' Kate asked.

'In a way,' Ben said. 'I've been asked to set up a new division in Manchester. It'll be a new start for Jenny and me.'

Kate was stunned by the news. She turned to Andrew, whose face was impassive.

'You knew, didn't you?' she asked him incredulously.

Andrew nodded slightly. 'I only found out yesterday. The chairman called me in . . .'

'And asked you if you'd be interested in Ben's job?' Kate enquired.

Andrew smiled. 'No, he asked me if I thought you'd be interested in Ben's job.'

Kate ached for Andrew. 'But that's terrible! You've worked here for years. Why would they favour me over you?'

'Because I'd already told him that I didn't want the job, that I was leaving.'

'But I'm leaving too,' Kate found herself shouting.

Rebecca looked over curiously at Kate and Andrew. She moved a little closer, feigning interest in the fire regulations and latest financial report on the notice-board.

Andrew and Kate stared at each other with mouths open.

'Why . . . ?' they both said. Then they both laughed nervously and said nothing, waiting for the other to speak first.

Kate remembered that she was the assertive one in this team and, for the last time as Andrew's boss, took the lead.

'I decided a while ago,' she said.

'Me too!' Andrew followed.

'When?' Kate asked, unable to believe what was happening.

Andrew looked awkward. 'After your party,' he said. 'But not just because of that,' he added.

'I decided before the party!' Kate said. 'For complicated reasons.'

'Like what, exactly?' Andrew asked.

Kate blushed and, for the first time in a month, didn't bother attempting to conceal it.

'Various things, but I knew it was time for a change. This last month brought it home to me how much I disliked corporate life. I'm going to go freelance. I think it will suit me.'

'I think you're right,' Andrew agreed.

'What about you?' Kate asked. 'Now that Ben's leaving, surely there's no need for you to go? And that's quite a promotion they're offering!'

Andrew shook his head. 'Like Ben, I think it's time for a new start. You can't just paint over the cracks formed by everything that's gone on in the last month or so.'

'So what will you do?' Kate asked.

'Oh I'm unashamedly corporate!' Andrew replied cheerfully. 'I get calls quite often from headhunters. I just thought it was time to take up one of the offers. I can fit in pretty much anywhere.'

'I think you're right,' Kate agreed.

Rebecca watched them move closer towards each other. She'd seen and heard enough.

'So what was it you wanted to say, Rebecca?'

Rebecca jumped at Ben's approach.

'Oh, er, it was, er . . .' She took a deep breath. 'Nothing,' she said finally. 'Nothing that can't wait.' She turned her back on him and walked over to Sally.

Ben walked away, happy to distance himself from Rebecca once more. He glanced wistfully at Andrew and Kate, wrapped up in each other. How ironic, he thought.

437

That was the only thing to turn out as Ben had planned and yet it had never truly been anything more than a frivolous ploy, a diversion from more serious concerns.

He shook his head sadly and slipped away from the little party where he was feeling like a gatecrasher.

'So what do you think?' Rebecca asked.

Sally was apprehensive. 'I don't know. I'd more or less decided that there was no future for me here. And I really need to make something of myself now, something that Chrissie can see and be proud of.'

'But that's just it!' Rebecca said. 'With Ben moved away and with Andrew and Kate leaving, there are some amazing opportunities here. For both of us!'

They stood together, thinking of the possibilities that were emerging in the light of these unexpected developments.

'We've always worked well together,' Rebecca continued. 'There's no reason why that can't continue, but at a senior level for both of us.'

She looked at Sally anxiously. All of a sudden, she didn't want to do this on her own. She wasn't strong enough to absorb all these changes without a safety net, a thread of continuity connecting her past to her future.

'Come on, Sally! We'll speak to the chairman on Monday, put ourselves forward. He'll be so frantic at everyone leaving, he'll be desperate to hold on to anything he can! We can keep this account ticking over nicely until we get a full team again, a team where we both play a role.'

And now Sally was wavering. 'I suppose we can give it a try,' she said tentatively.

'Great!' Rebecca exclaimed. 'I'll get us some more champagne.'

As she walked away, she pushed her letter of resignation to the bottom of her bag to tear up later.

OK, she thought, so this wasn't what she had planned, but surely this was what you were supposed to do? Respond to opportunity, adapt to new circumstances.

She smiled to herself. It would be the same place, but a different position, different dynamics. And that would allow her to become a different Rebecca.

'What do you think will happen now?' Andrew asked.

Kate shrugged. 'No idea. It's a bit of a mess. Do you care?'

Andrew considered it. 'Not much.'

They tapped glasses again.

'So,' Andrew said, 'I have two questions for you. Firstly, did you have any plans for tonight?'

Kate looked at him. 'Are you propositioning me? If so, the answer is yes. And the second question?'

Andrew organised his face into an innocent expression. 'Any chance of you making me a cup of coffee?'

They stood by the post box, deliberating over the final decision. In the end Ellen left it to Edward. 'You decide,' she said.

Edward fingered the letter. It was short.

It simply said:

Dear Becky, We would love you to come for Sunday lunch next week. Love, Mum and Dad.

Then Edward stopped thinking. Stopped analysing. Stopped regretting and dithering. He just posted it.